THE MAN IN THE IRON MASK

by

ALEXANDRE DUMAS

Abridged Edition

PRINTED IN DEAN & 41/43 Ludgate Hill SON Ltd. GREAT BRITAIN LONDON EC4

MADE AND PRINTED IN GREAT BRITAIN BY PURNELL AND SONS' LTD.
PAULTON (AVON) AND LONDON

SBN 603 03021 1

CONTENTS

Chapter		Page

CHAPTER I

TWO OLD FRIENDS

Whilst every one at court was busily engaged upon his own affairs, a man mysteriously entered a house situated behind the Place de Grève. This man walked along with a firm step, although he was no longer in his early prime. His dark cloak and long sword plainly revealed one who seemed in search of adventures; and, judging from his curly moustaches, his fine and smooth skin, beneath his sombrero, it would not have been difficult to pronounce that the gallantry of his adventures was unquestionable. In fact, hardly had the cavalier entered the house, when the clock struck eight; and ten minutes afterwards a lady, followed by a servant armed to the teeth, knocked at the same door, which an old woman immediately opened. The lady raised her veil as she entered; though no longer beautiful or young, she was still active and of an imposing carriage. Hardly had she reached the vestibule, than the cavalier, whose features we have only roughly sketched, advanced towards her, holding out his hand.

"Good-day, my dear Duchesse," he said.

"How do you do, my dear Aramis," replied the Duchesse.

He led her to a most elegantly furnished apartment. They sat down side by side.

"Chevalier," said the Duchesse, "you have never given me a single sign of life since our interview at Fontainebleau, and I confess that your presence there on the day of the Franciscan's death, and your initiation in certain secrets, caused me the liveliest astonishment."

"I can explain my presence there to you, as well as my initiation," said Aramis.

"But let us, first of all," said the Duchesse, "talk a little of ourselves, for our friendship is by no means of recent date."

"Yes, madame; and if Heaven wills it, we shall continue to be friends, I will not say for a long time, but for ever."

"That is quite certain, Chevalier, and my visit is a proof of it."

"You must have had some trouble to find me again," he said.

"Yes," she answered, "but I knew you were a friend of M. Fouquet's, and so I inquired in that direction."

"A friend! oh!" exclaimed the Chevalier. "I can hardly pretend to be that. A poor priest who has been favoured by so generous a protector is all that I pretend to be to M. Fouquet."

"He made you a bishop?"

"Yes, Duchesse."

"A very good retiring pension for so handsome a musketeer."

"Yes; in the same way that political intrigue is for yourself," thought Aramis. "And so," he added, "you inquire after me at M. Fouquet's?"

"Suffice it to know that I learnt you had returned from Vannes, and I sent to one of our friends, M. le Comte de la Fère, who is discretion itself, in order to ascertain it, but he answered that he was not aware of your address."

"So like Athos," thought the bishop; "that which is actually good never alters."

"Well, then, you know that I cannot venture to show myself here, and that the Queen-Mother has always some grievance or other against me."

"Yes, indeed, and I am surprised at it."

"Oh! there are various reasons for it. But, to continue, being obliged to conceal myself, I was fortunate enough to meet with M. d'Artagnan, who was formerly one of your old friends, I believe?"

"A friend of mine still, Duchesse."

"He sent me to M. Baisemeaux, the governor of the Bastille."

"And so Baisemeaux indicated to you——"

"Saint-Mandé, where I forwarded a letter to you."

"Which I have in my hand," said Aramis. The Duchesse, satisfied at having successfully alluded to the various difficulties of so delicate an explanation, began to breathe freely again, which Aramis, however, could not succeed in doing. "We had got as far as your visit to M. Baisemeaux, I believe?"

"Nay," she said, laughing, "further than that."

"In that case we must have been speaking about the grudge you have against the Queen-Mother."

"Further still," she returned; "we were talking of the connection——"

"Which existed between you and the Franciscan," said Aramis, interrupting her eagerly; "well, I am listening to you very attentively."

"It is easily explained," returned the Duchesse. "You know that I am living at Brussels with M. de Laicques?"

"I have heard so."

"Well, then, I have seen the King of Spain, who wished to do me a service, but was unable. He gave me recommendations, however, to Flanders, both for myself and for Laicques too; and conferred a pension on me out of the funds belonging to the order."

"Of Jesuits?"

"Yes. The general—I mean the Franciscan—was sent to me; and, for the purpose of conforming with the requisitions of the statutes of the order, and of entitling me to the pension, I was reputed to be in a position to render certain services."

"Good heavens! *You* obliged to receive a pension from the Jesuits?"

"No, Chevalier; from Spain."

"Except as a conscientious scruple, Duchesse, you will admit that it is pretty nearly the same thing."

"No, not at all."

"But surely, of your magnificent fortune there must remain——"

"Dampierre is all that remains."

"And that is handsome enough."

"Yes; but Dampierre is burdened, mortgaged, and almost fallen to ruin, like its owner."

"And can the Queen-Mother know and see all that, without shedding a tear?" said Aramis with a penetrating look.

"Yes, she has forgotten everything."

"You have, I believe, attempted to get restored to favour?"

"Yes; but, most singularly, the young King inherits the antipathy that his dear father had for me."

"Dear Duchesse, pray arrive soon at the circumstance which brought you here; for I think we can be of service to each other."

"Such has been my own thought. I need a sum of money to restore Dampierre."

"Ah!" replied Aramis coldly—"money? Well, Duchesse, how much would you require?"

"Oh! a tolerably round sum."

"So much the worse—you know I am not rich."

"In that case you have a friend very wealthy.—M. Fouquet."

"M. Fouquet! He is more than half ruined, madame."

"So it is said, but I would not believe it."

"Why, Duchesse?"

"Because Laicques has certain letters from Cardinal Mazarin which establish the existence of very strange accounts."

"What accounts?"

"Relative to various sums of money borrowed and disposed of. They establish the fact that the Surintendant, according to these letters, which are signed by Mazarin, had taken thirteen millions of francs from the coffers of the State. The case is a very serious one."

Aramis clenched his hands in anxiety and apprehension. "Is it possible," he said, "that you have such letters as you speak of, and have not communicated them to M. Fouquet?"

"Ah!" replied the Duchesse, "I keep such little matters as these in reserve. The day may come when they may be of service."

"You must be in sad want of money, my poor friend, to think of such things as these—you, too, who held M. de Mazarin's prose effusions in such indifferent esteem."

"The fact is, I am in want of money."

"And then," continued Aramis in cold accents, "it must have been very distressing to you to be obliged to have recourse to such a means."

"Oh! if I had wished to do harm instead of good," said Madame de Chevreuse, "instead of asking the general of the order, or M. Fouquet, for the five hundred thousand francs I require——"

"Five hundred thousand francs!"

"Yes; I require at least as much as that to restore Dampierre."

"Yes, madame."

"I say, therefore, that, instead of asking for this amount, I should have gone to see my old friend the Queen-Mother; the letters from her husband, the Signor Mazarini, would have served me as an introduction, and I should have begged this mere trifle of her, saying to her, 'I wish, madame, to have the honour of receiving you at Dampierre. Permit me to put Dampierre in a fit state for that purpose.'"

"It is a snare," thought the Bishop; "it is impossible that Anne of Austria could listen to such a woman as this."

"Well?" said the Duchesse.

"Well, madame, I should be very much astonished if M. Fouquet had five hundred thousand francs at his disposal at the present moment. And the Queen will certainly do for you what the Surintendant is unable to do."

"Oh! certainly."

"And so, you are now going to denounce M. Fouquet to the Queen," said Aramis.

"'Denounce!' Oh! what a disagreeable word. I shall not 'denounce,' my dear friend; I shall merely side against M. Fouquet, and nothing more. And once on friendly terms again with the Queen-Mother, I may be dangerous towards some persons."

"Stay a moment, Duchesse; would you like me to tell you why I will not buy your letters?"

"Pray tell me?"

"Because the letters you say are Mazarin's are false."

"What an absurdity."

"I have no doubt of it, for it would, to say the least, be very singular, that after you had quarrelled with the Queen through M. Mazarin's means, you should have kept up any intimate acquaintance with the latter."

But the Duchesse had said enough, and left the house where such tender friends had not been able to understand each other, only because they had understood each other too well.

CHAPTER II

WHEREIN MAY BE SEEN THAT A BARGAIN WHICH CANNOT BE MADE WITH ONE PERSON, CAN BE CARRIED OUT WITH ANOTHER

Aramis had been perfectly correct in his supposition; for hardly had she left the house in the Place Baudoyer, than Madame de Chevreuse proceeded homeward. She by this means thought she might succeed in throwing those who might be following her off their guard; but scarcely had she arrived within the door of the hotel, and hardly had assured herself that no one who could cause her any uneasiness was on her track, when she opened the door of the garden, and hurried towards the Rue Croix des Petits Champs, where M. Colbert resided.

A valet received the Duchesse with some indifference of manner. She ascended to the first floor of the beautiful new house very slowly, rested herself on the landing-place, in order not to enter the apartment out of breath, and appeared before M. Colbert, who, with his own hands, held both the folding-doors open. The Duchesse paused at the threshold, for the purpose of well studying him. At the first glance, the round, large, heavy head, thick brows, and ill-favoured features of Colbert, who wore, thrust low down on his head, a cap like a priest's, seemed to indicate that but little difficulty was likely to be met with in her negotiations with him, but also that she was to expect as little interest in the discussion of particulars; for there was scarcely any indication that the rough and uncouth nature of the man was susceptible to the impulses of a refined revenge, or of an exalted ambition. But when, on closer inspection, the Duchesse perceived the small piercing black eyes, the imperceptible twitching of the lips, on which were apparent traces of rough good humour, Madame de Chevreuse altered her opinion of him, and felt she could say to herself: "I have found the man I want."

"What is the subject, madame, which procures me the honour of a visit from you?" he inquired.

Madame de Chevreuse sat down in the arm-chair which M. Colbert advanced towards her. "Monsieur Colbert, you are the Intendant of Finances, and are ambitious of becoming the Surintendant?"

"M. Fouquet's fortune, madame, enables him to withstand all attempts. The Surintendant in this age plays the part of the Colossus of Rhodes; the vessels pass beneath him and do not overthrow him."

"Very good, Monsieur Colbert, since you persist in showing so much sensitiveness with me, as if you were ignorant that I am Madame de Chevreuse, and also that I am somewhat advanced in years; in other words, that you have to do with a woman who has had political dealings with the Cardinal de Richelieu, and who has no time to lose; as, I repeat, you do not hesitate to commit such an imprudence, I shall go and find others who are more intelligent and more desirous of making their fortunes."

"Nay, madame, show a little indulgence, I entreat you."

"Well, then, you do really consent to replace M. Fouquet."

"Certainly I do, if the King dismisses M. Fouquet."

"Again, a word too much; it is quite evident that if you have not yet succeeded in driving M. Fouquet from his post, it is because you have not been able to do so. Therefore, I should be the greatest simpleton possible, if, in coming to you, I did not bring you the very thing you require."

"I am distressed to be obliged to persist, madame," said Colbert, after a silence which enabled the Duchesse to sound the depth of his dissimulation, "but I must warn you that, for the last six years, denunciation after denunciation has been made against M. Fouquet, and he has remained unshaken and unaffected by them."

"There is a time for everything, Monsieur Colbert; those who are the authors of those denunciations were not called Madame de Chevreuse, and they had no proofs equal to the six letters from M. de Mazarin, which establish the offence in question."

"The offence!"

"I am delighted to see it makes an impression upon you."

"It is because the word, madame, embraces so many things."

"It embraces the post of Surintendant of Finance for yourself, and a letter of exile, or the Bastille, for M. Fouquet."

"Forgive me, Madame la Duchesse, but it is almost impossible that M. Fouquet can be exiled; to be imprisoned or disgraced, that is already a great deal."

"Oh, I am perfectly aware of what I am saying," returned Madame de Chevreuse coldly. "I do not live at such a distance from Paris as not to know what takes place there. The King does not like M. Fouquet, and he would willingly sacrifice M. Fouquet if an opportunity were only given him."

"It must be a good one, though."

"Good enough, and one I estimate to be worth five hundred thousand francs."

"Since you have fixed a price for the sale, let me now see the value of the articles to be sold."

"Oh, a mere trifle; six letters, as I have already told you, from M. de Mazarin; and the autographs will most assuredly not be regarded as too highly priced, if they establish, in an irrefutable manner, that M. Fouquet has embezzled large sums of money from the treasury."

"In an irrefutable manner, do you say?" observed Colbert.

"Perfectly so; would you like to read the letters?"

"With all my heart. Copies of course?"

"Of course, the copies," said the Duchesse, as she drew from her bosom a small packet of paper flattened by her velvet bodice. "Read," she said.

Colbert eagerly snatched the papers and devoured them.

"Excellent!" he said.

"It is clear enough, is it not?"

"Yes, madame, yes; M. Mazarin must have handed the money to M. Fouquet, who must have kept it for his own purposes; but the question is, what money?"

"Exactly,—what money? If we come to terms I will join to these six letters a seventh, which will supply you with the fullest particulars."

Colbert reflected. "And the originals of those letters?"

"A useless question to ask; exactly as if I were to ask you, Monsieur Colbert, whether the money-bags you will give me will be full or empty."

"Very good, madame."

"How much will you offer me?"

"Two hundred thousand francs," said Colbert.

The Duchesse laughed in his face, and then said suddenly, "Wait a moment, I have another arrangement to propose; will you give me three hundred thousand francs?"

"No, no."

"Oh, you can either accept or refuse my terms; besides, that is not all."

"More still! you are becoming too impracticable to deal with, madame."

"Less so than you think, perhaps, for it is not money I am going to ask you for."

"What is it, then?"

"A service. I am desirous of having an interview with Her Majesty."

"With the Queen?"

"Yes, Monsieur Colbert, with the Queen, who is, I admit, no longer my friend, and who has ceased to be so for a long time past, but who may again become so if the opportunity be only given her."

"Her Majesty has ceased to receive any one. She is a great sufferer; the paroxysms of her disease occur with greater frequency than ever."

"That is the very reason why I wish to have an interview with Her

Majesty; for in Flanders there is a great variety of these kinds of complaints."

"What, cancers—a fearful, incurable disorder?"

"Do not believe that, Monsieur Colbert. The Flemish peasant is somewhat a man of nature, and his companion for life is not alone a wife, but a female labourer also; it is she who draws the water from the well; she who loads the mule or the ass, and even bears herself a portion of the burden. Taking but little care of herself, she gets knocked about, first in one direction, and then in another, and very often is beaten by her husband, and cancers frequently arise from contusions."

"True, true," said Colbert. "You are undoubtedly, Madame la Duchesse, a woman of exceedingly great abilities; still I cannot but suppose that this charitable consideration towards the Queen in some measure covers a slight personal interest for yourself."

"I have not given myself the trouble to conceal it, that I am aware of, Monsieur Colbert. You said, I believe, that I had a slight personal interest? On the contrary, it is a very great interest, and I will prove it to you, by resuming what I was saying. If you procure me a personal interview with Her Majesty, I will be satisfied with the three hundred thousand francs I have claimed; if not, I shall keep my letters, unless, indeed, you give me five hundred thousand francs for them."

And rising from her seat with this decisive remark, the old Duchesse plunged M. Colbert into a disagreeable perplexity. To bargain any further was out of the question; and not to bargain was to pay a great deal too dearly for them. "Madame," he said, "I shall have the pleasure of handing you over a hundred thousand crowns; but how shall I get the actual letters themselves?"

"In the simplest manner in the world, my dear Monsieur Colbert— whom will you trust?"

The financier began to laugh silently, so that his large eyebrows went up and down like the wings of a bat upon the deep lines of his yellow forehead. "No one," he said.

"You surely will make an exception in your own favour, Monsieur Colbert?"

"In what way, madame?"

"I mean that if you would take the trouble to accompany me to the place where the letters are, they would be delivered into your own hands, and you would be able to verify and check them."

"I have reflected, madame, and I shall not accompany you."

"Really—and why not?"

"Because I have the most perfect confidence in you."

"You overpower me. But provided I receive the hundred thousand crowns?"

"Here they are, madame," said Colbert, scribbling a few lines on a piece of paper, which he handed to the Duchesse, adding, "You are paid."

"The trait is a fine one, Monsieur Colbert, and I will reward you for it," she said, beginning to laugh.

Madame de Chevreuse's laugh was a very sinister sound; every man who feels youth, faith, love, life itself throbbing in his heart, would prefer tears to such a lamentable laugh. The Duchesse opened the front of her dress and drew forth from her bosom, somewhat less white than it once had been, a small packet of papers, tied with a flame-coloured ribbon, and, still laughing, she said, "There, Monsieur Colbert, are the originals of Cardinal Mazarin's letters; they are now your own property," she added, refastening the body of her dress; "your fortune is secured, and now accompany me to the Queen."

"No, Madame; if you are again about to run the chance of Her Majesty's displeasure, and it were known at the Palais Royal that I had been the means of introducing you there, the Queen would never forgive me while she lived. No; there are certain persons at the palace who are devoted to me, who will procure you an admission without my being compromised."

"Just as you please, provided I enter."

"What do you term those religious women at Bruges who cure disorders?"

"Béguines."

"I am going to give directions to the head valet of the gentleman in waiting on Her Majesty to allow admission to a Béguine, who brings an effectual remedy for Her Majesty's sufferings. You are the bearer of my letter, you will undertake to be provided with the remedy, and will give every explanation on the subject. I admit a knowledge of a Béguine, but I deny all knowledge of Madame de Chevreuse. Here, madame, then, is your letter of introduction."

CHAPTER III

THE SKIN OF THE BEAR

Colbert handed the Duchesse the letter, and gently drew aside the chair behind which she was standing; Madame de Chevreuse, with a very slight bow, immediately left the room. Colbert, who had recognised Mazarin's handwriting, and had counted the letters, rang to summon his secretary, whom he enjoined to go in immediate search of M. Vanel, a counsellor of the Parliament. The secretary replied that, according to his usual practice, M. Vanel had just that moment entered the house, in order to render to the Intendant an account of the principal details of the business which had been transacted during the day in the sitting of the Parliament. Colbert approached one of the lamps, read the letters of the deceased Cardinal over again, smiled repeatedly as he recognised the great value of the papers Madame de Chevreuse had just delivered to him, and burying his head in his hands for a few minutes, reflected profoundly. In the meantime, a tall, large-made man entered the room; his spare thin face, steady look, and hooked nose, as he entered Colbert's cabinet, with a modest assurance of manner, revealed a character at once supple and decided,—supple towards the master who could throw him the prey, firm towards the dogs who might possibly be disposed to dispute it with him. M. Vanel carried a voluminous bundle of papers under his arm, and placed it on the desk on which Colbert was leaning both his elbows, as he supported his head.

"Good-day, M. Vanel," said the latter, rousing himself from his meditation.

"Good-day," said Vanel naturally.

Colbert coughed. "Vanel," he said suddenly to his protégé, "you are a hard-working man. I know. You must not grow rusty in your post of counsellor."

"What must I do to avoid it?"

"Purchase a high place. Mean and low ambitions are very difficult to satisfy."

"Small purses are the most difficult to fill, monseigneur."

"What post have you in view?" said Colbert.

"I see none—not one."

"There is one, certainly, but one need be almost the King himself to be able to buy it without inconvenience; and the King will not be inclined, I suppose, to purchase the post of Procureur-Général."

At these words, Vanel fixed his at once humble and dull look upon Colbert, who could hardly tell whether Vanel had comprehended him or not. "Why do you speak to me, monseigneur," said Vanel, "of the post of Procureur-Général to the Parliament; I know no other post than the one M. Fouquet fills."

"I believe, Monsieur Vanel, that it will be for sale before long."

"For sale! What, M. Fouquet's post of Procureur-Général?"

"So it is said. It is true that M. Fouquet's post might cost a good round sum. What would you bid for it, Monsieur Vanel?"

"Everything I am worth."

"Which means?"

"Three or four hundred thousand francs."

"And the post is worth——"

"A million and a half at the very lowest. I know persons who have offered one million seven hundred thousand francs, without being able to persuade M. Fouquet to sell. Besides, supposing it were to happen that M. Fouquet wished to sell, which I do not believe——"

"Ah! you have heard something about it, then; who told you?"

"M. de Gourville, M. Pélisson, and others."

"Very good; if, therefore, M. Fouquet did wish to sell——"

"I could not buy it just yet, since the Surintendant will only sell for ready money, and no one has a million and a half to throw down at once."

Colbert suddenly interrupted the consellor by an imperious gesture; he had begun to meditate. Vanel awaited the solution without venturing to precipitate it. "Explain fully to me the privileges which this post confers."

"The right of impeaching every French subject who is not a prince of the blood; the right of quashing all proceedings taken against any Frenchman, who is neither king nor prince. The Procureur-Général is the King's right hand to punish the guilty; he is the means whereby also he can evade the administration of justice. M. Fouquet, therefore, will be able, by stirring up the Parliaments, to maintain himself even against the King; and the King could as easily, by humouring M. Fouquet, get his edicts registered in spite of every opposition and objection. The Procureur-Généralship can be made a very useful or very dangerous instrument.''

''Vanel, would you like to be Procureur-Général?'' said Colbert suddenly, softening both his look and his voice.

''I!'' exclaimed the latter; ''I have already had the honour to represent to you that I want about eleven hundred thousand francs to make up the amount.''

''Borrow the sum from your friends, and if it should be needed, I will be your security.''

Vanel rose, quite bewildered by this offer which had been so suddenly and unexpectedly made to him. ''You are not trifling with me, monseigneur,'' he said.

''Stay; you say that M. Gourville has spoken to you about M. Fouquet's post.''

''Yes; and M. Pélisson also.''

''Well, Monsieur Vanel, you will go at once, and find out either M. Gourville or M. Pélisson. Do you know any other friend of M. Fouquet?''

''I know M. de la Fontaine very well.''

''Go to him, then, and try to procure an interview with the Surintendant.''

''Willingly—but the sum itself?''

''On the day and the hour you arrange to settle the matter, Monsieur Vanel, you shall be supplied with the money.''

''Monseigneur, such munificence! You eclipse kings even—you surpass M. Fouquet himself.''

''Stay a moment—do not let us mistake each other. I do not make you a present of fourteen hundred thousand francs, Monsieur Vanel; for I have children to provide for—but I will lend you that sum.''

''Ask whatever interest, whatever security you please, monseigneur: I am quite ready. And when all your requisitions are satisfied, I will still repeat, that you surpass kings and M. Fouquet in munificence. What conditions do you impose?''

''The repayment in eight years, and a mortgage upon the appointment itself.''

''Certainly. Is that all?''

''Wait a moment. I reserve to myself the right of repurchasing the post from you at one hundred and fifty thousand francs profit for yourself, if you do not follow out a line of conduct in conformity with the interests of the King and with my projects.''

''Ah! ah!'' said Vanel, in a slightly altered tone.

''Is there anything in that which can possibly be objectionable to you, Monsieur Vanel?'' said Colbert coldly.

''Oh! no, no,'' replied Vanel quickly.

''Very good. We will sign an agreement to that effect, whenever you like. And now, go as quickly as you can to M. Fouquet's friends, obtain an interview with the Surintendant; do not be too difficult in making whatever concessions may be required of you; and when once the arrangements are all made——''

''I will press him to sign.''

''Be most careful to do nothing of the kind; do not speak of signatures with M. Fouquet, nor of deeds, nor even ask him to pass his word. Understand this, otherwise you will lose everything. All you have to do is to get M. Fouquet to give you his hand on the matter. Go, go."

CHAPTER IV

AN INTERVIEW WITH THE QUEEN-MOTHER

The Queen-Mother was in her bedroom at the Palais-Royal with Madame de Motteville and the Senora Molena. A sharp, acute pain seized the Queen, who turned deadly pale, and threw herself back in the chair, with every symptom of a sudden fainting fit. Molena ran to a richly-gilded tortoiseshell cabinet, from which she took a large rock-crystal smelling-bottle, and immediately held it to the Queen's nostrils, who inhaled it wildly for a few minutes, and murmured:

"It will hasten my death—but Heaven's will be done!"

"We must put her to bed," said La Molena.

"Presently, Molena."

"Let us leave the Queen alone," added the Spanish attendant.

Madame de Motteville rose; large and glistening tears were fast rolling down the Queen's pallid face; and Molena, having observed this sign of weakness, fixed her black vigilant eyes upon her.

"Yes, yes," replied the Queen. "Leave us, Motteville; go."

Madame de Motteville bowed in submission, and was about to withdraw, when, suddenly, an old female attendant opened the doors. "The remedy!" she cried, delightedly, to the Queen.

"What remedy?" said Anne of Austria.

"For your Majesty's sufferings," the former replied.

"Who brings it?" asked Madame de Motteville eagerly; "Monsieur Vallot?"

"No; a lady from Flanders."

"Go, Molena; go and see!" cried the Queen.

"It is needless," suddenly replied a voice, at once firm and gentle in its tone, which proceeded from the other side of the tapestry hangings; a voice which made the attendants start, and the Queen tremble excessively. At the same moment, a masked female appeared through the hangings, and, before the Queen could speak a syllable, she added, "I am connected with the order of the Béguines of Bruges, and do, indeed, bring with me the remedy which is certain to effect a cure of your Majesty's complaint." No one uttered a sound, and the Béguine did not move a step.

"Speak," said the Queen.

"I will, when we are alone," was the answer.

Anne of Austria looked at her attendants, who immediately withdrew.

"The Queen of France must, indeed, be very ill," said Anne of Austria, "if it is known at the Béguinage of Bruges that she stands in need of being cured."

"Your Majesty is not irremediably ill."

Anne of Austria looked up, endeavouring to discover through the concealment of the mask, and through her mysterious language, the name of her companion, who expressed herself with such familiarity and freedom; then, suddenly, wearied by a curiosity which wounded every feeling of pride in her nature, she said, "You are ignorant, perhaps, that royal personages are never spoken to with the face masked."

"I have made a vow, madame, to attend and aid all afflicted or suffering persons without ever permitting them to behold my face. I might have been able to administer some relief to your body and to your mind, too; but, since your Majesty forbids me, I will take my leave. Adieu, madame, adieu."

These words were uttered with a harmony of tone and respect of manner that deprived the Queen of all her anger and suspicion, but did not remove her feeling of curiosity. "You are right," she said; "it ill becomes those who are suffering to reject the means of relief which Heaven sends them. Speak, then; and may you, indeed, be able, as you assert you can, to administer relief to my body — "

"Let us first speak a little of the mind, if you please," said the Béguine; "of the mind, which, I am sure, must also suffer."

"My mind?"

"There are cancers so insidious in their nature that their very pulsation is invisible."

"The evils to which you allude," she said, "are the conditions of the lives of the high in rank upon earth, to whom Heaven has imparted mind."

"You are as courageous, madame, I see, as ever, against your enemies. You do not acknowledge your confidence in your friends."

"Queens have no friends; if you have nothing further to say to me, — if you feel yourself inspired by Heaven as a prophetess — leave me, I pray you, for I dread the future."

"I should have supposed," said the Béguine resolutely, "that you would rather have dreaded the past."

Hardly had these words escaped her lips, than the Queen rose up proudly. "Speak," she cried, in a short, imperious tone of voice; "explain yourself briefly, quickly, entirely; or, if not — "

"Nay, do not threaten me, your Majesty," said the Béguine gently; "I came to you full of compassion and respect. I came here on the part of a friend."

"I do not understand you," replied the Queen; setting her teeth hard together in order to conceal her emotion.

"I will make myself understood, then. Your Majesty remembers that the King was born on the 5th of September, 1638, at a quarter past eleven o'clock."

"Yes," stammered out the Queen.

"At half-past twelve," continued the Béguine, "the Dauphin who had been baptized by Monseigneur de Meaux in the King's and in your own presence, was acknowledged as the heir of the crown of France."

"Quite true, quite true," murmured the Queen.

"Your Majesty's confinement took place in the presence of Monsieur,

His Majesty's late uncle, of the princes, and of the ladies attached to the court. The King's physician, Bouvard, and Honoré, the surgeon, were stationed in the antechamber; your Majesty slept from three o'clock until seven, I believe!"

"Yes, yes; but you tell me no more than every one else knows as well as you and myself."

"I am now, madame, approaching that which very few persons are acquainted with. Very few persons, did I say, alas! I might almost say two only, for formerly there were but five in all, and, for many years past, the secret has been well preserved by the deaths of the principal participators in it. The late King now sleeps with his ancestors. Péronne, the midwife, soon followed him, Laporte is already forgotten."

"It was eight o'clock," pursued the Béguine; "the King was seated at supper, full of joy and happiness; around him on all sides arose wild cries of delight and drinking of healths; the people cheered beneath the balconies; the Swiss guards, the musketeers, and the royal guards wandered through the city, borne about in triumph by the drunken students. Those boisterous sounds of the general joy disturbed the Dauphin, the future King of France, who was quietly lying in the arms of Madame de Hausac, his nurse, and whose eyes, as he opened them, and stared about, might have observed two crowns at the foot of his cradle. Suddenly, your Majesty uttered a piercing cry, and Dame Péronne immediately flew to your bedside. The doctors were dining in a room at some distance from your chamber; the palace was without either sentinels or guards. The midwife, having questioned and examined your Majesty, gave a sudden exclamation as if in wild astonishment, and taking you in her arms, bewildered almost out of her senses from sheer distress of mind, despatched Laporte to inform the King that Her Majesty the Queen wished to see him in her room. Laporte, you are aware, madame, was a man of the most admirable calmness and presence of mind. He did not approach the King as if he were the bearer of alarming intelligence. Therefore, Laporte appeared with a smile upon his lips, and approached the King's chair saying to him, — "Sire, the Queen is very happy, and would be still more so to see your Majesty." Animated, light-hearted, and full of gaiety, the King rose from the table, and said to those around him, — 'Gentlemen, I am going to see my wife.' He came to your bedside, madame, at the very moment Dame Péronne presented to him a second prince, as beautiful and healthy as the former, and said, — 'Sire, Heaven will not allow the kingdom of France to fall into the female line.' The King, yielding to a first impulse, clasped the child in his arms, and cried, 'Oh! Heaven, I thank thee!'"

At this part of her recital the Béguine paused, observing how intensely the Queen was suffering; she had thrown herself back in her chair, and with her head bent forward and her eyes fixed, listened without seeming to hear, and her lips moving convulsively, either breathing a prayer to Heaven or in imprecations against the woman standing before her.

"Ah! do not believe that, because there could be but one Dauphin in France," exclaimed the Béguine, "or that if the Queen allowed that child to vegetate, banished from his royal parents' presence, she was on that account an unfeeling mother. Oh! no, no; there are those alive who know the floods of bitter tears she shed; there are those who have known and witnessed the passionate kisses she imprinted on that innocent creature in exchange for a life of misery and gloom to which State policy condemned the twin brother of Louis XIV."

"Oh! Heaven!" murmured the Queen feebly.

"It is admitted," continued the Béguine, quickly, "that when the King perceived the effect which would result from the existence of two sons, both equal in age and pretensions, he trembled for the welfare of France, for the tranquillity of the State; and it is equally well known that the Cardinal de Richelieu, by the direction of Louis XIII, thought over the subject with deep attention, and after an hour's meditation in His Majesty's cabinet, he pronounced the following sentence: 'One prince is peace and safety for the state; two competitors are civil war and anarchy.'"

The Queen rose suddenly from her seat, pale as death, and her hands clenched together: — "You know too much," she said, in a hoarse, thick voice, "since you refer to secrets of State. Now, throw aside your mask, or I will have you arrested by my captain of the guards. Do not think that this secret terrifies me! Never shall it leave your bosom, for neither your secret nor your own life belongs to you from this moment."

Anne of Austria, joining gesture to the threat, advanced a couple of steps towards the Béguine. "Learn," said the latter, "to know and value the fidelity, the honour, and secrecy of the friends you have abandoned." And, then, suddenly threw aside her mask.

"Madame de Chevreuse!" exclaimed the Queen.

"With your Majesty, the sole living confidante of this secret."

"Ah!" murmured Anne of Austria; "come and embrace me, Duchesse."

And the Queen, leaning her head upon the shoulder of the old Duchesse, burst into a flood of bitter tears. "How young you are still!" said the latter, in a hollow voice, "you can weep!"

CHAPTER V

TWO FRIENDS

Madame de Chevreuse collected herself for a moment, and then murmured, "How far removed kings are from other people."

"What do you mean?"

"I mean that they are so far removed from the vulgar herd that they forget that others stand in need of the bare necessaries of life."

The Queen slightly coloured, for she now began to perceive the drift of her friend's remark. "It was very wrong," she said, "to have neglected you."

"Oh! madame, the King I know has inherited the hatred his father bore me."

"I cannot say that the King is very well disposed towards you,

Duchesse," replied the Queen; "but I could—secretly, you know——"

The Duchesse's disdainful smile produced a feeling of uneasiness in the Queen's mind. "Duchesse," she hastened to add, "you did perfectly right to come here, even were it only to give us the happiness of contradicting the report of your death."

"Has it been said, then, that I was dead?"

"Everywhere."

"Your Majesty will be sure to learn, in a particular manner, the day of my death."

"In what way?"

"Because your Majesty will receive the next day, under several coverings, everything connected with our mysterious correspondence of former times."

"Did you not burn them?" cried Anne in alarm.

"Traitors only," replied the Duchesse, "destroy a royal correspondence."

"Traitors, do you say?"

"Yes, certainly, or rather they pretend to destroy, instead of which they keep or sell it. Faithful friends, on the contrary, most carefully secrete such treasures, for it may happen that some day or other they would wish to seek out their Queen in order to say to her: 'Madame, I am getting old; my health is fast failing me; in the presence of the danger of death, for there is the danger for your Majesty that this secret may be revealed; take, therefore, this paper, so fraught with danger for yourself, and trust not to another to burn it for you."

"What paper do you refer to?"

"As far as I am concerned, I have but one, it is true, but that is indeed most dangerous in its nature."

"Oh! Duchesse, tell me what it is."

"A letter, dated Tuesday, the 2nd of August, 1644, in which you beg me to go to Noisy-le-Sec, to see that unhappy child. In your own handwriting, madame, there are those words, 'that unhappy child!'"

A profound silence ensued; the Queen's mind was wandering in the past; Madame de Chevreuse was watching the progress of her scheme.

"No one has ever loved or served me as you have done, Duchesse."

"Do not praise me too highly, madame," said the Duchesse, somewhat anxiously.

"I could never praise you as much as you deserve to be praised."

"Well, then, your Majesty can confer the greatest, the most ineffable pleasure upon me."

"What is it?" said the Queen, a little distant in her manner, from an uneasiness of feeling produced by this remark. "But do not forget, my good Chevreuse, that I am quite as much under my son's influence as I was formerly under my husband's."

"Will your Majesty do me the honour to pass a few days with me at Dampierre?"

"Is that all?" said the Queen stupefied. "Nothing more than that?"

"Good heavens! can you possibly imagine that in asking you that, I am not asking you the greatest conceivable favour. If that really be the case, you do not know me. Will you accept?"

"Yes, gladly. And I shall be happy," continued the Queen, with some suspicion, "if my presence can in any way be useful to you."

"Useful!" exclaimed the Duchesse, laughing; "oh, no, no, agreeable —delightful, if you like; and you promise me, then?"

"I swear it," said the Queen, whereupon the Duchesse seized her hand, and covered it with kisses. The Queen could not help murmuring to herself, "She is a good-hearted woman, and very generous too."

"Will your Majesty consent to wait a fortnight before you come?"

"Certainly; but why?"

"Because," said the Duchesse, "knowing me to be in disgrace, no one would lend me the hundred thousand francs which I require to put Dampierre into a state of repair. But when it is known that I require that sum for the purpose of receiving your Majesty at Dampierre properly, all the money in Paris will be at my disposal."

"Ah!" said the Queen, gently nodding her head in sign of intelligence, "you want a hundred thousand francs?"

"Quite as much as that."

"And no one will lend you them?"

"No one."

"I will lend them to you, if you like, Duchesse."

"Oh, I hardly dare to accept such a sum."

"You would be wrong if you did not. I know but too well that you never set a right value upon your silence and your secrecy. Push that table a little towards me, Duchesse, and I will write you an order on M. Colbert; no, on M. Fouquet, who is a far more courteous and obliging man."

The Queen wrote and handed the Duchesse the order, and afterwards dismissed her with a warm and cheerful embrace.

CHAPTER VI

LA FONTAINE IN THE CHARACTER OF A NEGOTIATOR

We now return to Saint-Mandé, where the Surintendant was in the habit of receiving his select society of epicureans. For some time past, the host had met with some terrible trials. Every one in the house was aware of and felt the minister's distress. No more magnificent or recklessly improvident *réunions*. Money had been the pretext assigned by Fouquet, and never *was* any pretext, as Gourville said, more fallacious, for there was not the slightest appearance of money.

Gourville and the Abbé Fouquet talked over money matters—that is to say, the Abbé borrowed a few pistoles from Gourville; Pélisson was engaged in finishing the peroration of a speech with which Fouquet was to open the Parliament. Presently Loret and La Fontaine would enter from the garden, engaged in a dispute upon the facility of making verses. The painters and musicians, in their turn, also, were hovering near the dining-room. As soon as eight o'clock struck the supper would be announced, for the Surintendant never kept any one waiting.

"Have you found a purchaser for my post of procureur-général?" exclaimed Fouquet.

"I have, monsieur," said La Fontaine.

"What is his name?"

"Vanel."

"Vanel!" exclaimed Fouquet, "Vanel, the husband of——"

"Precisely, her husband; yes, monsieur."

"Poor fellow!" said Fouquet, with an expression of great interest.

"He wishes to be everything that you have been, monsieur," said Gourville, "and to do everything that you have done."

"Why, you have not yet heard the *dénouement* of my story."

"If there is a *dénouement* why do you beat about the bush so much?"

"*Semper ad eventum.* Is that correct?" said Fouquet, with the air of a nobleman who condescends to barbarisms. To which the Latinists present answered with loud applause.

"My *dénouement*," cried La Fontaine, "is that Vanel, that determined blackbird, knowing that I was coming to Saint-Mandé, implored me to bring him with me, and if possible, to present him to M. Fouquet."

Within a quarter of an hour afterwards, M. Vanel was introduced into the Surintendant's cabinet. When Fouquet saw him enter, he called to Pélisson, and whispered a few words in his ear. "Do not lose a word of what I am going to say: let all the silver and gold plate, together with the jewels of every description, be packed up in the carriage. You will take the black horses: the jeweller will accompany you; and you will postpone the supper until Madame de Bellière's arrival."

Pélisson set off, not quite clear as to his friend's meaning or intention, but confident, like every true friend, in the judgment of the man he was blindly obeying. It is that which constitutes the strength of such men; distress only arises in the minds of inferior natures.

Vanel bowed low to the Surintendant, and was about to begin a speech.

"Do not trouble yourself, monsieur," said Fouquet; "I am told that you wish to purchase a post I hold. How much can you give me for it?"

"It is for you, monsieur, to fix the amount you require. I know that offers of purchase have already been made to you for it."

"Madame Vanel, I have been told, values it at fourteen hundred thousand livres."

"That is all we have."

"Can you give me the money immediately?"

"I have not the money with me," said Vanel, frightened almost by the unpretending simplicity, amounting to greatness, of the man, for he had expected disputes, and difficulties, and opposition of every kind.

"When will you be able to have it?"

"Whenever you please, monseigneur;" for he began to be afraid that Fouquet was trifling with him.

"If it were not for the trouble you would have in returning to Paris I would say at once; but we will arrange that the payment and the signature shall take place at six o'clock to-morrow morning."

CHAPTER VII

MADAME DE BELLIÈRE'S PLATE AND DIAMONDS

Hardly had Fouquet dismissed Vanel, than he began to reflect for a few moments:—"A man never can do too much for the woman he has once loved. Marguerite wishes to be the wife of a procureur-général—and why not confer this pleasure upon her? Let my thoughts be bestowed on her who has shown so much devotion for me. Madame de Bellière ought to be there by this time," he said, as he turned towards the secret door.

After he had locked himself in, he opened the subterranean passage, and rapidly hastened towards the means of communicating between the house at Vincennes and his own residence. The noise the Surintendant made aroused her; she ran to take from under the door the letter that he had thrust there, and which simply said, "Come, marquise; we are waiting supper for you." With her heart filled with happiness Madame de Bellière ran to her carriage in the Avenue de Vincennes, and in a few minutes she was holding out her hand to Gourville, who was standing at the entrance, where, in order the better to please his master, he had stationed himself to watch her arrival. She had not observed that Fouquet's black horses had arrived at the same time, smoking and covered with foam, having returned to Saint-Mandé with Pélisson and the very jeweller to whom Madame de Bellière had sold her plate and her jewels. Pélisson introduced the goldsmith into the cabinet, which Fouquet had not yet left. The Surintendant thanked him for having been good enough to regard as a simple deposit in his hands, the valuable property which he had had every right to sell; and he cast his eyes on the total of the account, which amounted to thirteen hundred thousand francs. Then, going for a few moments to his desk, he wrote an order for fourteen hundred thousand francs, payable at sight, at his treasury, before twelve o'clock the next day.

"A hundred thousand francs profit!" cried the goldsmith. "Oh, monseigneur, what generosity!"

"Nay, nay, not so, monsieur," said Fouquet, touching him on the shoulder; "there are certain kindnesses which can never be repaid."

"And you, monseigneur," cried the goldsmith, completely overcome, "are the noblest man that ever lived."

Fouquet let the worthy goldsmith pass out of the room by a secret door, and then went to receive Madame de Bellière, who was already surrounded by all the guests. The Marquise was always beautiful, but now her loveliness was more dazzling than ever.

"Well?" said Fouquet to Pélisson, in a low tone.

"Well, at last I have understood you," returned the latter; "and you have done excellently well."

"Supper is ready, monseigneur," said Vanel, with majestic air and tone.

The crowd of guests hurried less slowly than is usually the case with ministerial entertainments, towards the banqueting-room, where a magnificent spectacle presented itself. Upon the buffets, upon the side-tables, upon the supper-table itself, in the midst of the flowers and light, glittered most dazzlingly the richest and most costly gold and silver plate that could possibly be seen.

But the most remarkable object present was the cover which Fouquet had assigned to the Marquise. Near her was a pyramid of diamonds, sapphires, emeralds, antique cameos, sardonyx stones, carved by the old Greeks of Asia Minor, with mountings of Mysian gold; curious mosaics of ancient Alexandria, mounted in silver; massive Egyptian bracelets lay heaped up in a large plate of Palissy ware, supported by a tripod of gilt bronze which had been sculptured by Benvenuto. The Marquise turned pale, as she recognised what she had never expected to see again. A profound silence seemed to seize upon every one of the restless and excited guests. Fouquet did not even make a sign in dismissal of the richly-liveried servants who crowded like bees round the huge buffets and other tables in the room. "Gentlemen," he said, "all this plate which you behold once belonged to Madame de Bellière, who, having observed one of her friends in great distress, sent all this gold and silver, together with the heap of jewels now before her, to her goldsmith. This noble conduct of a devoted friend can well be understood by such friends as you. Happy indeed is that man who sees himself loved in such a manner. Let us drink to the health of Madame de Bellière."

The hours passed away so joyously, that, contrary to his usual custom, the Surintendant did not leave the table before the end of the dessert. He smiled upon his friends, delighted as a man is, whose heart becomes intoxicated before his head—and, for the first time, he had just looked at the clock. Suddenly, a carriage rolled into the courtyard, and, strange to say, it was heard high above the noise of the mirth which prevailed. Fouquet listened attentively, and then turned his eyes towards the antechamber. It seemed as if he could hear a step passing across it, and that this step, instead of pressing the ground, weighed heavily upon his heart. "M. d'Herblay, Bishop of Vannes," the usher announced. And Aramis's grave and thoughtful face appeared upon the threshold of the door.

CHAPTER VIII

M. DE MAZARIN'S RECEIPT

Fouquet would have uttered an exclamation of delight on seeing another friend arrive, if the cold air and averted aspect of Aramis had not restored all his reserve.

"Monseigneur," said Aramis respectfully, "I will begin by begging you to excuse me for having interrupted this merry meeting; and then, I will beg you to give me, as soon as pleasure shall have finished, a moment's audience on matters of business."

As the word "business" had aroused the attention of some of the epicureans present, Fouquet rose, saying: "Business first of all, Monsieur d'Herblay; we are too happy when matters of business arrive only at the end of a meal."

As he said this, he took the hand of Madame de Bellière, who looked at him with a kind of uneasiness, and then led her to an adjoining *salon*, after having recommended her to the most reasonable of his guests. And then, taking Aramis by the arm, he led him towards his cabinet. As soon as Aramis was there, throwing aside the respectful air he had assumed, he threw himself into a chair, saying: "Guess whom I have seen this evening?"

"Do not keep me in suspense," said Fouquet phlegmatically.

"Well, then, I have seen Madame de Chevreuse."

"The old Duchesse, do you mean?"

"Yes."

"Well! what harm can she meditate against me? I am no miser with women who are not prudes."

"Madame de Chevreuse knows very well that you are not avaricious, since she wishes to draw some money out of you."

"Indeed! under what pretext?"

"Oh! pretexts are never wanting with her. Let me tell you what hers is; it seems that the Duchesse has a good many letters of M. de Mazarin's in her possession."

"I am not surprised at that, for the prelate was gallant enough."

"Do you not suspect what I mean?"

"Not at all."

"Have you never heard speak of a prosecution being instituted for an embezzlement, or appropriation rather, of public funds?"

"Yes, a hundred, nay, a thousand times. Ever since I have been engaged in public matters I have hardly ever heard anything else but that."

"Very good; but take a particular instance, for the Duchesse asserts that M. de Mazarin alludes to certain particular instances."

"What are they?"

"Something like a sum of thirteen millions of francs, of which it would be very difficult for you to define the precise nature of the employment."

"Thirteen millions!" said the Surintendant. "I remember the story of those thirteen millions, now. Yes, yes, I remember them quite well."

"I am delighted to hear it; tell me about them."

"Well, then, one day Signor Mazarin, Heaven rest his soul! made a profit of thirteen millions upon a concession of lands in the Valtelline; he cancelled them in the registry of receipts, sent them to me, and then made me advance them to him for war expenses."

"Very good, then, there is no doubt of their proper destination."

"No; the Cardinal made me invest them in my own name, and gave me a receipt."

"You have the receipt?"

"Of course," said Fouquet, as he quietly rose from his chair, and went to his large ebony bureau inlaid with mother-of-pearl and gold. And with a confident hand he felt the bundle of papers which were piled up in the open drawer. "I remember the paper as if I saw it; it is thick, somewhat crumpled, with gilt edges; Mazarin had made a blot upon the figure of the date."

And as the Surintendant looked into the drawer, Aramis rose from his seat.

"This is very singular," said Fouquet.

"Your memory is treacherous, my dear monseigneur; look in another drawer."

Fouquet took out the bundle of papers, and turned them over once more; he then became very pale.

"Don't confine your search to that drawer," said Aramis; "look elsewhere."

"Quite useless; I have never made a mistake; no one but myself arranges any papers of mine of this nature."

"What do you conclude, then?" said Aramis, agitated.

"That Mazarin's receipt has been stolen from me; Madame de Chevreuse was right, Chevalier; I have appropriated the public funds; I have robbed the state coffers of thirteen millions of money; I am a thief, Monsieur d'Herblay."

"Oh!" said Aramis, smiling, "not so fast as that."

"And why not? why not so fast? What do you suppose Madame de Chevreuse will have done with those letters, for you refused them, I suppose?"

"Yes; at once. I suppose that she went and sold them to M. Colbert."

"Well?"

"I said I supposed so; I might have said I was sure of it, for I had her followed, and when she left me, she returned to her own house, went out by a back door, and proceeded straight to the Intendant's house."

"Legal proceedings will be instituted then, scandal and dishonour will follow."

"Those criminals who know how to find a safe asylum are never in danger."

"What! Make my escape! Fly!"

"No! I do not mean that; you forget that all such proceedings originate in the Parliament, that they are instituted by the Procureur-Général, and that you are Procureur-Général. You see that unless you wish to condemn yourself—"

"I am Procureur-Général no longer."

Aramis at this reply became as livid as death; he pressed his hands together convulsively, and with a wild, haggard look, which almost annihilated Fouquet, he said, laying a stress upon every distinct syllable, "You are Procureur-Général no longer, do you say?"

"No."

"Since when?"

"Since the last four or five hours."

"Take care," interrupted Aramis coldly; "I do not think you are in the full possession of your senses, my friend; collect yourself."

"I tell you," returned Fouquet, "that a little while ago some one came to me, brought by my friends, to offer me fourteen hundred thousand francs for the appointment, and that I sold the appointment."

Aramis looked as if he had been thunder-stricken. "You had need of money, then?" he said.

"Yes; to discharge a debt of honour." And in a few words, he gave Aramis an account of Madame de Bellière's generosity, and the manner in which he had thought it but right to discharge that act of generosity.

"Yes," said Aramis, "that is, indeed, a fine trait. What has it cost?"

"Exactly the fourteen hundred thousand francs—the price of my appointment."

"Which you received in that manner, without reflection. Oh! imprudent man."

"I have not yet received the amount, but I shall to-morrow."

"It is not yet completed, then?"

"It must be carried out, though; for I have given the goldsmith, for twelve o'clock to-morrow, an order upon my treasury, into which the purchaser's money will be paid at six or seven o'clock."

"Heaven be praised!" cried Aramis, clapping his hands together, "nothing is yet completed, since you have not been paid."

"But the goldsmith?"

"You shall receive the fourteen hundred thousand francs from me, at a quarter before twelve."

"Stay a moment; it is at six o'clock, this very morning, that I am to sign."

"Oh! I will answer that you do not sign."

"I have given my word, Chevalier."

"If you have given it, you will take it back again, that is all."

"Can I believe what I hear?" cried Fouquet, in a most expressive tone. "Fouquet recall his word, after it has been once pledged?"

"And so you are determined to sign the sale of the very appointment which can alone defend you against all your enemies."

"Yes, I shall sign."

"Whom are you in treaty with? What man is it?"

"A counsellor, of the name of Vanel."

Aramis became perfectly purple. "Vanel," he cried, rising abruptly from his seat; "Vanel! the husband of Marguerite Vanel."

"Exactly."

"Of your former mistress?"

"Yes; she is anxious to be the wife of the Procureur-Gènèral."

Aramis walked up straight to Fouquet, and took hold of his hand. "Do you know," he said very calmly, "the name of Madame Vanel's new lover?"

"Ah! she has a new lover, then: I was not aware of it; no, I have no idea what his name is."

"His name is M. Jean-Baptiste Colbert; he is Intendant of the Finances; he lives in the Rue Croix-des-Petits-Champs, where Madame de Chevreuse has been this evening, to take him Mazarin's letters, which she wishes to sell."

"Gracious Heaven!" murmured Fouquet.

"You now begin to understand, do you not."

"That I am utterly lost!—yes."

"Do you now think it worth while to be so scrupulous with regard to keeping your word?"

"Yes," said Fouquet.

"These obstinate people always contrive matters in such a way, that we cannot but admire them all the while," murmured Aramis.

Fouquet held out his hand to him, and at the very moment a richly-ornamented tortoise-shell clock struck six. The sound of a door being opened in the vestibule was heard, and Gourville came to the door of the cabinet to inquire if Fouquet would receive M. Vanel. Fouquet turned his eyes from the eyes of Aramis, and then desired that M. Vanel should be shown in to him.

CHAPTER IX

MONSIEUR COLBERT'S ROUGH DRAFT

Vanel, who entered at this stage of the conversation, was nothing less for Aramis and Fouquet than the full stop which completes a phrase. But, for Vanel, Aramis's presence in Fouquet's cabinet had quite another signification; and, therefore, at his first step into the room, he paused, and his look of astonishment soon became one of scrutinising attention. As for Fouquet, a perfect politician, that is to say, complete master of himself, he had already, by the energy of his own resolute will, contrived to remove from his face all traces of the emotion which Aramis's revelation had occasioned. He was no longer, therefore, a man overwhelmed by misfortune and reduced to resort to expedients; he held his head proudly erect, and indicated by a gesture that Vanel could enter. He was now the first minister of the State, and in his own palace. Aramis knew the Surintendant well; the delicacy of the feelings of his heart and the exalted nature of his mind could not any longer surprise him. Vanel was visibly overcome, and advanced into the middle of the cabinet, bowing to everything and everybody. "I am come," he said.

"You are exact, Monsieur Vanel," returned Fouquet.

"In matters of business, monseigneur," returned Vanel. "I look upon exactitude as a virtue."

"You would be wrong to exaggerate such notions as those, monsieur," said the Surintendant; "for a man's mind is variable, and a man may have wished for something yesterday of which he repents to-day."

Vanel felt a cold sweat trickle down his face. "Monseigneur!" he muttered.

"Yesterday I wished to sell."

"Monseigneur did more than wish to sell, for you actually sold."

"I know that, and that is the reason why now I entreat you; do you understand me? I entreat you to restore it to me."

"Alas! monseigneur, you see," he said, as he opened a large pocket-book, "I have brought the money with me,—the whole sum, I mean. And here, monseigneur, is the contract of sale which I have just effected of a property belonging to my wife. The order is authentic in every way, the necessary signatures have been attached to it, and it is made payable at sight; it is ready money, in fact, and, in one word, the whole affair is complete."

"Enough!" cried Fouquet. "Where is this deed?"

Vanel tremblingly searched in his pockets, and as he drew out his pocket-book a paper fell out of it, while Vanel offered the other to Fouquet. Aramis pounced upon the paper which had fallen out, as soon as he recognised the handwriting.

"I beg your pardon," said Vanel, "that is a rough draft of the deed."

"I see that very clearly," retorted Aramis, with a smile far more cutting than a lash of a whip would have been; "and what I admire most is, that this draft is in M. Colbert's handwriting. Look, monseigneur, look."

And he handed the draft to Fouquet, who recognised the truth of the fact; for, covered with erasures, with inserted words, the margins filled with additions, this deed—a living proof of Colbert's plot—had just revealed everything to its unhappy victim. "Well!" murmured Fouquet.

Vanel, completely humiliated, seemed as if he were looking for some deep hole where he could hide himself.

"Well!" said Aramis, "if your name were not Fouquet, and if your enemy's name were not Colbert—if you had not this mean thief before you I should say to you, 'Repudiate it'; such a proof of this absolves you from your word; but these fellows would think you were afraid; they would fear you less than they do; therefore sign the deed at once." And he held out a pen towards him.

Fouquet pressed Aramis's hand; but, instead of the deed which Vanel handed to him, he took the rough draft of it.

"No, not that paper," said Aramis hastily; "this is the one. The other is too precious a document for you to part with."

"No, no!" cried Fouquet; "I will sign under M. Colbert's own handwriting even; and I write, 'The handwriting is approved of.'" He then signed, and said, "Here it is, Monsieur Vanel." And the latter seized the paper, laid down his money, and made his escape.

As soon as Vanel had gone, the minister and the prelate, their eyes fixed on each other, remained silent for a few moments.

"Well," said Aramis, the first to break the silence; "first of all, let us talk about business. Did you not some time ago," he continued, as Fouquet looked at him with a bewildered air, "speak to me about an idea you had of giving a fête at Vaux?"

"Oh," said Fouquet, "that was when affairs were flourishing."

"A fête, I believe, to which the King invited himself of his own accord?"

"No, no, my dear prelate; a fête to which M. Colbert advised the King to invite himself."

"From to-morrow," interrupted Aramis quietly, "you will occupy yourself, without the slightest delay, with your fête at Vaux, which must hereafter be spoken of as one of the most magnificent productions of your most prosperous days."

"You are mad, Chevalier d'Herblay."

"I!—you do not think that."

"What do you mean, then? Do you not know that a fête at Vaux, of the very simplest possible character, would cost four or five millions?"

"I do not speak of a fête of the very simplest possible character, my dear Surintendant."

"But, since the fête is to be given to the King," replied Fouquet, who misunderstood Aramis's idea, "it cannot be simple."

"Just so; it ought to be on a scale of the most unbounded magnificence."

"In that case, I shall have to spend ten or twelve millions."

"You shall spend twenty if you require it," said Aramis, in a perfectly calm voice.

"Where shall I get them?" exclaimed Fouquet.

"That is my affair, Monsieur le Surintendant; and do not be uneasy for a moment about it. The money will be placed at once at your disposal, as soon as you shall have arranged the plans of your fête."

"Why did you not tell me that sooner, Aramis? There was a day when, with one million only, you could have saved me, whilst today——"

"Whilst to-day, I can give you twenty," said the prelate. "Such is the case, however—the reason is very simple. On the day you speak of, I had not the million which you had need of at my disposal; whilst now I can easily procure the twenty millions we require."

"I abandon myself to you unreservedly," Fouquet murmured.

"No, no; I do not understand it in that manner. I am unreservedly devoted to you. Therefore, as you have the clearest, the most delicate, and the most ingenious mind of the two, you shall have entire control over the fête, even to the very smallest details. Only——"

"Only?" said Fouquet, as a man accustomed to understand and appreciate the value of a parenthesis.

"Well, then, leaving the entire invention of the details to you, I shall reserve to myself a general superintendence over the execution."

"In what way?"

"I mean that you will make of me, on that day, a major-domo, a sort of inspector-general, or factotum—something between a captain of the guard and manager or steward. I will look after the people, and will keep the keys of the doors. You will give me your orders, of course; but will give them to no one but to me; they will pass through my lips, to reach those for whom they are intended—you understand?"

"No, I am very far from understanding."

"But you agree?"

"Of course, of course, my friend."

"That is all I care about, then, thanks, and now go and prepare your list of invitations."

"Whom shall I invite?"

"Everyone."

CHAPTER X

THE VICOMTE DE BRAGELONNE MAKES INQUIRIES

We wish our readers now to follow Raoul de Bragelonne's story.

He had arrived from London because he had been told of the existence of a danger; and almost on his arrival, this appearance of danger was manifest. His friend, de Guiche, had written and advised his return to France.

"I have hurried," said Raoul, as he seated himself beside his friend, "I have flown here; I came here in half the time the Government couriers usually take. Now, tell me, my dear friend, what did you want?"

"Nothing whatever, but to make you come."

"There must have been something else, I suppose?"

"No, indeed."

"De Guiche!"

"Upon my honour!"

"Your object in telling me to come was your hope that I should see with my own eyes, was it not? Nay, do not hesitate, for I have seen all."

"Well, then, I can only tell you what you can learn from every person you meet."

"From every one, do you say? It is talked about, then?"

"Before you say people talk about it, learn what it is that people can talk about. I assure you solemnly, that people only talk about what may, in truth, be very innocent; perhaps a walk——"

"Ah! a walk with the King?"

"Yes, certainly, a walk with the King; and I believe the King has already very frequently before taken walks with ladies, without, on that account——"

"You would not have written to me, shall I say again, if there had been nothing unusual in this promenade."

"I know that while the storm lasted, it would have been far better if the King had taken shelter somewhere else, than to have remained with his head uncovered before La Vallière; but the King is so very courteous and polite."

"This walk was followed by others, I suppose?"

"No—I mean yes; there was the adventure of the oak, I think. But I know nothing about the matter at all." Raoul rose. "Well, I will not add another word; I have said either too much or not enough. Let others give you further information if they will, or if they can; my duty was to warn you, and that I have done. Watch over your own affairs now, yourself."

"Question others! Alas! you are no true friend to speak to me in that manner," said the young man in utter distress.

"Is not d'Artagnan your friend?"

"Oh! true, true."

"Go to him, then. He will be able to throw some light on the subject."

The Captain was sitting buried in his leathern arm-chair, his spur fixed in the floor, his sword between his legs, and was occupied in reading a great number of letters, as he twisted his moustache. D'Artagnan uttered a welcome full of pleasure when he perceived his friend's son. "Raoul, my boy," he said, "by what lucky accident does it happen that the King has recalled you?"

These words did not sound over agreeably in the young man's ears, who, as he seated himself, replied, "Upon my word, I cannot tell you; all I know is that I have come back."

D'Artagnan increased the sharpness of his penetrating gaze which no secret was capable of resisting. "You are unhappy about something," he said.

"Dear Captain, I know very well that in all trials of *finesse*, as well as in all trials of strength, I shall be beaten by you. In two words, I am the most wretched of living beings."

"Oh! oh! why that?" inquired d'Artagnan, unbuckling his belt and softening the ruggedness of his smile.

"Because Mademoiselle de la Vallière is deceiving me."

"She is deceiving you," said d'Artagnan; not a muscle of his face had moved; "those are big words. Who makes use of them?"

"Every one."

"Ah! if every one says so, there must be some truth in it. I begin to believe there is fire when I see the smoke. It is ridiculous, perhaps, but so it is."

"Therefore you do believe me?" exclaimed Bragelonne, quickly.

"I never mix myself up in affairs of that kind; you know that very well."

Raoul buried his face in his hands, murmuring, "No, no; I have not a single friend in the world."

"Oh! bah!" said d'Artagnan.

"I meet with nothing but raillery or indifference."

"Idle fancies, monsieur. I do not laugh at you, although I am a Gascon. And, as for being indifferent, if I were so, I should have sent you about your business a quarter of an hour ago. How now, young man! do you wish me to disgust you with the girl you are attached to, and to teach you to execrate the whole sex who constitute the honour and happiness of human life."

"Oh! tell me, monsieur, and I will bless you."

"Do you think, my dear fellow, that I can have crammed into my brain all about the carpenter, and the painter, and the staircase, and a hundred other similar tales of the same kind?"

"A carpenter! what do you mean?"

"Upon my word I don't know; some one told me there was a carpenter who made an opening through a certain floor."

"In La Vallière's room?"

"I have told you for the last hour that I know nothing of the whole affair."

"But the painter, then? the portrait—"

"It seems that the King wished to have the portrait of one of the ladies belonging to the court."

"La Vallière's."

"Why, you seem to have only that name in your mouth. Who spoke to you of La Vallière?"

"If it be not her portrait, then, why do you suppose it would concern me?"

"I do not suppose it will concern you. But you ask me all sorts of questions and I answer you. You positively will learn all the scandal of the affair, and I tell you—make the best you can of it."

Suddenly the door opened, and one of the musketeers approaching d'Artagnan said, "Captain, Mademoiselle de Montalais is here, and wishes to speak to you."

MIM—B

"To me?" murmured d'Artagnan. "Ask her to come in; I shall soon see," he said to himself, "whether she wishes to speak to me or not."

The cunning Captain was right in his suspicions; for as soon as Montalais appeared, she exclaimed, "Oh, monsieur, monsieur, I beg your pardon, Monsieur d'Artagnan."

"Oh! I forgive you, mademoiselle," said d'Artagnan; "I know that at my age, those who are looking for me generally need me for something or another."

"I was looking for Monsieur de Bragelonne," replied Montalais.

"How very fortunate that is. Raoul, will you accompany Mademoiselle Montalais!"

"Oh, certainly."

"Go along, then," he said, as he gently pushed Raoul out of the cabinet; and then, taking hold of Montalais's hand, he said in a low voice: "Be kind towards him; spare him, and spare her too, if you can."

"It is Madame who has sent for him."

"Very good," cried d'Artagnan, "it is Madame, is it? — In an hour's time, then, the poor fellow will be cured."

"Or else dead," said Montalais, in a voice full of compassion. "Adieu, Monsieur d'Artagnan," she said; and she ran to join Raoul, who was waiting for her at a little distance from the door, very much puzzled and uneasy at the dialogue, which promised no good augury for him.

CHAPTER XI

TWO JEALOUSIES

Raoul was in Madame's presence. Henrietta, more charming than ever, was half lying, half reclining in her armchair, her little feet upon an embroidered velvet cushion; she was playing with a little kitten with long silky fur.

Madame seemed plunged in deep thought, so deep indeed, that it required both Montalais and Raoul's voice to disturb her from her reverie.

Every one at court of any perception at all, knew perfectly well the capricious fancy and absurd despotism of the Princess's singular character. Madame had been flattered beyond all bounds by the King's attentions; she had made herself talked about; she had inspired the Queen with mortal jealousy; Madame, in a word, in her attempts to cure a wounded pride, had found that her heart had become deeply and passionately attached. We know what Madame had done to recall Raoul, who had been sent out of the way by Louis XIV. Raoul did not know of her letter to Charles II, although d'Artagnan had guessed its contents. "Monsieur de Bragelonne," said the Princess, after a moment's pause, "have you returned satisfied?"

Bragelonne looked at Madame Henrietta, and seeing how pale she was, not alone from what she was keeping back, but also from what she was burning to say, said: "Satisfied! what is there for me to be satisfied or dissatisfied about, madame?"

Henrietta rose hurriedly and walked a few paces up and down her room. "What did M. de Guiche tell you?" she said suddenly.

"Nothing, madame."

"And that is what friends call friendship. But surely M. d'Artagnan, whom you have just left, must have told you."

"No more than Guiche, madame."

"Monsieur de Bragelonne," she said, "that which your friends have refused to do, I will do for you, whom I like and esteem very much. You hold your head high, as a man of honour should do; and I should regret that you should have to bow it down under ridicule."

"Ah!" exclaimed Raoul, perfectly livid. "It is as bad as that, then?"

"If you do not know," said the Princess, "I see that you guess; you were affianced, I believe, to Mademoiselle de la Vallière?"

"Yes, madame."

"By that right, then, you deserve to be warned about her, as some day or another I shall be obliged to dismiss Mademoiselle de la Vallière from my service——"

"Dismiss La Vallière!" cried Bragelonne.

Henrietta was for a moment struck with admiration at this sublime disbelief; and then, shrugging her shoulders, she said, "You do not believe me, I see. How deeply you must love her, and you doubt if she loves the King?"

"I do, until I have a proof of it. Forgive me, madame, but she has given me her word; and her mind and heart are too upright to tell a falsehood."

"You require a proof! Be it so. Come with me, then."

CHAPTER XII

A DOMICILIARY VISIT

The Princess, preceding Raoul, led him through the courtyard towards that part of the building which La Vallière inhabited, and, ascending the same staircase which Raoul had himself ascended that very morning, she paused at the door of the room in which the young man had been so strangely received by Montalais. The château was empty. The King, the courtiers, and the ladies of the court, had set off for Saint-Germain; Madame Henrietta was the only one who knew of Bragelonne's return, and, thinking over the advantages which might be drawn from this return, had feigned indisposition in order to remain behind. Madame was therefore confident of finding La Vallière's room and Saint-Aignan's apartment perfectly empty. She took a pass-key from her pocket and opened the door of her maid-of-honour's apartment. Bragelonne's gaze was immediately fixed upon the interior of the room, which he recognised at once; and the impression which the sight of it produced upon him, was one of the first tortures which awaited him. The Princess looked at him, and her practised eye could at once detect what was passing in the young man's heart.

"You asked me for proofs," she said, "do not be astonished, then, if I give you then. But if you do not think you have courage enough to confront them, there is still time to withdraw."

"I thank you, madame," said Bragelonne; "but I came here to be convinced. You promised to convince me, — do so."

"Enter then," said Madame, "and shut the door behind you."

Bragelonne obeyed.

"You know where you are, I suppose?" inquired Madame Henrietta.

"Everything leads me to believe I am in Mademoiselle de la la Vallière's room."

"You are."

"But I would observe to your Highness that this room is a room, and is not a proof."

"Wait," said the Princess, as she walked to the foot of the bed, folded up the screen into its several compartments, and stooped down towards the floor. "Look here," she continued; "stoop down, and lift up this trap-door yourself."

"A trap-door!" said Raoul, astonished; for d'Artagnan's words began to return to his memory, and he had an indistinct recollection that d'Artagnan had made use of the same word. He looked, but uselessly so, for some cleft or crevice which might indicate an opening or a ring to assist in lifting up some portion of the planking.

"Ah, I forgot," said Madame Henrietta, "I forgot the secret spring; the fourth plank of the flooring, — press on the spot where you will observe a knot in the wood."

Raoul, pale as death, pressed his finger on the spot which had been indicated to him; at the same moment the spring began to work, and the trap rose of its own accord.

"A staircase!" cried Raoul.

"Yes, and a very pretty one, too," said Madame Henrietta. "See, Vicomte, the staircase has a balustrade intended to prevent the falling of timid persons who might be tempted to descend the staircase; and I will risk myself on it accordingly. Come, Vicomte, follow me!"

"But before following you, madame, may I ask where this staircase leads to?"

"Ah, true; I forgot to tell you. You know, perhaps, that formerly M. de Saint-Aignan lived in the very next apartment to the King?"

"Yes, madame, I am aware of that."

"Well; he obtained the King's leave to change his former convenient and beautiful apartment for the two rooms to which this staircase will conduct us, and which together form a lodging for him, twice as small, and at ten times greater distance from the King, — a close proximity to whom is by no means disdained, in general, by the gentlemen belonging to the court."

"Very good, madame," returned Raoul; "but go on I beg, for I do not understand yet."

"Well, then, it accidentally happened," continued the Princess, "that M. de Saint-Aignan's apartment is situated underneath the apartments of my maids-of-honour, and particularly underneath the room of La Vallière."

"But what was the motive of this trap-door and this staircase?"

"That I cannot tell you. Would you like us to go down to Monsieur de Saint-Aignan's rooms? Perhaps we shall be able to find the solution of the enigma there."

And Madame set the example by going down herself, while Raoul, sighing deeply, followed her. At every step Bragelonne took, he advanced farther into that mysterious apartment which had been witness to La Vallière's sighs, and still retained the sweetest perfume of her presence. Had Raoul preserved a single doubt on the subject, it would have vanished at the secret harmony of tastes, and connection of the mind with the use of the ordinary objects of life. La Vallière, in Bragelonne's eyes, was present there in every article of furniture, in the colour of the hangings, in every thing that surrounded him. Dumb, and completely overwhelmed, there was nothing further for him now to learn, and he followed his pitiless conductress as blindly as the culprit follows the executioner; while Madame, as cruel as all women of delicate and nervous temperaments are, did not spare him the slightest detail. But it must be admitted that, notwithstanding the kind of apathy into which he had fallen, none of these details, even had he been left alone, would have escaped him. The happiness of the woman who loves, when that happiness is derived from a rival, is a living torture for a jealous man; but for a jealous man such as Raoul was, for one whose heart had for the first time been steeped in gall and bitterness, Louise's happiness was in reality an ignominious death, a death of body and soul.

One final pang was reserved for poor Raoul. Madame Henrietta lifted up a silk curtain, and behind the canvas he perceived La Vallière's portrait; Not only the portrait of La Vallière, but of La Vallière eloquent of youth, beauty, and happiness, inhaling life and enjoyment at every pore, because at eighteen years of age love itself is life.

"Louise!" murmured Bragelonne, — "Louise! is it true, then? Oh, you have never loved me, for never have you looked at me in that manner." And he felt as if his heart were crushed within his bosom.

Madame Henrietta looked at him, almost envious of his extreme grief, although she well knew that there was nothing to envy in it, and that she herself was as passionately loved by de Guiche as Louise by Bragelonne. Raoul interpreted Madame Henrietta's look.

"Oh, forgive me, forgive me, madame; in your presence I know I ought to have greater mastery over myself."

"Monsieur de Bragelonne," replied Henrietta, "a heart such as yours merits all the consideration and respect which a Queen's heart even can bestow. Regard me as your friend, monsieur. It was I, indeed, who, with more courage than any of your pretended friends — I except M. de Guiche — was the cause of your return from London; it is I, also, who have given you these melancholy proofs, necessary, however, for your cure, if you are a lover with courage in his heart, and not a weeping Amadis. Do not thank me, pity me even, and do not serve the King less faithfully than you have done."

Raoul smiled bitterly. "Ah! true, true; I was forgetting that; the King is my master."

"Your liberty, nay, your very life, is in danger."

A steady, penetrating look informed Madame Henrietta that she was mistaken, and that her last argument was not a likely one to affect the young man. "Take care, Monsieur de Bragelonne," she said, "for if you do not weigh well all your actions, you might throw into an extravagance of wrath; you must bend, you must submit, and must cure yourself."

"I thank you, madame; I appreciate the advice your Royal Highness is good enough to give me, and I will endeavour to follow it; but one final word, I beg."

"Name it."

"Should I be indiscreet in asking you the secret of this staircase, of this trap-door; a secret which, it seems, you have discovered?"

"Nothing is more simple. For the purpose of exercising a surveillance over the young girls who are attached to my service, I have duplicate keys of their doors. It seemed very strange to me that M. de Saint-Aignan should change his apartments. It seemed very strange, that the King should come to see M. de Saint-Aignan every day. I do not wish to be trifled with by the King, nor to serve as a cloak for his love affairs; for, after La Vallière, who weeps incessantly, he will take a fancy to Montalais, who is always laughing; and then to Tonnay-Charente, who does nothing but sing all day; to act such a part as that would be unworthy of me. I have thrust aside the scruples which my friendship for you suggested. I have discovered the secret. I have wounded your feelings, I know; and I again entreat you to excuse me; but I had a duty to fulfil. I have discharged it. You are now forewarned; the tempest will soon burst; protect yourself accordingly."

"You naturally expect, however, that a result of some kind must follow," replied Bragelonne, with firmness; "for you do not suppose I shall silently accept the shame which is thrust upon me, or the treachery which has been practised against me."

"You will take whatever steps in the matter you please, Monsieur Raoul, only do not betray the source whence you derived the truth. That is all I have to ask, that is the only price I require for the service I have rendered you."

"Fear nothing, madame," said Bragelonne, with a bitter smile.

CHAPTER XIII

KING AND NOBILITY

On his return from the promenade, the King found M. Fouquet waiting for an audience. M. Colbert had laid in wait for His Majesty in the corridor, and followed him like a jealous and watchful shadow. Fouquet, at the sight of his enemy, remained perfectly unmoved, and during the whole of the scene which followed scrupulously resolved to observe that line of conduct which is so difficult to be carried out by a man of superior mind, who does not even wish to show his contempt, from the fear of doing his adversary too much honour.

"Sire," he said, "I perceive by your Majesty's joyous air that you have been gratified with the promenade."

"Ah! M. Fouquet," cried the King, "there is nothing like the country. I should be very delighted to live in the country always, in the open air and under the trees."

"Your Majesty gratifies my utmost wishes in speaking in that manner, for I have a request to submit to you."

"On whose behalf, monsieur?"

"On behalf of the nymphs of Vaux, sire."

"Ah! ah!" said Louis XIV.

"Your Majesty, too, once deigned to make me a promise," said Fouquet.

"Yes, I remember it."

"Your Majesty is aware," said Fouquet, "that I destine my estate at Vaux to receive the most amiable of princes, the most powerful of monarchs."

"I have given you my promise, monsieur," said Louis XIV, smiling; "and a King never departs from his word."

"And I have come now, sire, to inform your Majesty that I am ready to obey your orders in every respect."

"Do you promise me many wonders, Monsieur le Surintendant?" said Louis, looking at Colbert.

"Yes, sire, if your Majesty will condescend so far as to accept my invitation."

"What day have you fixed?"

"Any day your Majesty may find most convenient."

"This is Tuesday; if I give you until next Sunday week, will that be sufficient?"

"The delay which your Majesty deigns to accord me will greatly aid the various works which my architects have in hand for the purpose of adding to the amusement of your Majesty and your friends."

Fouquet, therefore, took leave of Louis XIV, after a few words had been added with regard to the details of certain matters of business. He turned back again immediately, as soon indeed as he had reached the door, and addressing the King, said:

"Against every sense of propriety, sire, I forgot to inform your Majesty of a circumstance that has lately occurred of some little importance."

"What is it?"

"Sire," said Fouquet, with an easy unconcerned air, "since you have the kindness to forgive me, I am perfectly indifferent about my confession; this morning I sold one of the official appointments I hold."

"One of your appointments," said the King, "which?"

Colbert turned perfectly livid. "That which conferred upon me, sire, a grand gown and a stern air of gravity; the appointment of procureur-général."

The King involuntarily uttered a loud exclamation and looked at Colbert, who, with his face bedewed with perspiration, felt almost on the point of fainting. "To whom have you sold this appointment,

Monsieur Fouquet?" inquired the King.

Colbert was obliged to lean against the side of the fireplace. "To a councillor belonging to the Parliament, sire, whose name is Vanel."

"Vanel?"

"Yes, sire, a friend of Colbert," added Fouquet; letting every word fall from his lips with the most inimitable nonchalance, and with an admirably assumed expression of forgetfulness and ignorance. And having finished, and having overwhelmed Colbert beneath the weight of this superiority, the Surintendant again saluted the King and quitted the room, partially revenged by the stupefaction of the King and the humiliation of the favourite.

"Is it really possible," said the King, as soon as Fouquet had disappeared, "that he has sold that office?"

"Yes, sire," said Colbert meaningly.

"He must be mad," the King added.

Colbert this time did not reply; he had penetrated the King's thought, a thought which amply revenged him for the humiliation he had just been made to suffer; his hatred was augmented by a feeling of bitter jealousy of Fouquet; and a threat of disgrace was now added to the plan he had arranged for his ruin. Colbert was invited by the King to the fête of Vaux; he bowed like a man confident in himself, and accepted the invitation with the air of one who almost confers a favour and discreetly withdrew.

Then the usher appeared at the door of the cabinet. "What is the matter?" inquired the King, "and why do you presume to come when I have not summoned you?"

"Sire," said the usher, "your Majesty desired me to permit M. le Comte de la Fère to pass freely on any and every occasion, when he might wish to speak to your Majesty."

"Well, monsieur?"

"M. le Comte de la Fère is now waiting to see your Majesty."

A few minutes afterwards Athos, in full court dress, and with his breast covered with the orders that he alone had the right to wear at the court of France, presented himself with so grave and solemn an air that the King perceived, at the first glance, that he was not deceived in his anticipations. Louis advanced a step towards the Comte, and, with a smile, held out his hand to him over which Athos bowed with the air of the deepest respect.

"Monsieur le Comte de la Fère," said the King rapidly, "you are so seldom here, that it is a real piece of good fortune to see you."

"Your Majesty will remember that at the period of the Duke of Buckingham's departure, I had the honour of an interview with you."

"At or about that period, I think, I remember you did; only with regard to the subject of the conversation, I have quite forgotten it."

Athos started, as he replied, "I shall have the honour to remind your Majesty of it. It was with regard to a formal demand I had addressed to you respecting a marriage which M. de Bragelonne wished to contract with Mademoiselle de la Vallière."

"Ah!" thought the King, "we have come to it now. I remember," he said aloud.

"At that period," pursued Athos, "your Majesty was so kind and generous towards M. de Bragelonne and myself, that not a single word which then fell from your lips has escaped my memory; and, when I asked your Majesty to accord me Mademoiselle de la Vallière's hand for M. de Bragelonne, you refused."

"Quite true," said Louis dryly.

"M. de Bragelonne is now so exceedingly unhappy that he cannot any longer defer asking your Majesty for a solution of the matter."

The King turned pale; Athos looked at him with fixed attention.

"And what," said the King, with considerable hesitation, "does M. de Bragelonne request?"

"Precisely the very thing that I came to ask your Majesty for at my last audience, namely, your Majesty's consent to his marriage."

The King pressed his hands impatiently together. "Does your Majesty hesitate?" inquired the Comte, without losing a particle either of his firmness or his politeness.

"I do not hesitate — I refuse," replied the King.

"And may we, therefore, be permitted to ask your Majesty, with the greatest humility, for your reason for this refusal?"

"The reason! — a question to me!" exclaimed the King.

"A demand, sire!"

The King, leaning with both his hands upon the table, said in a deep tone of concentrated passion, "You have lost all recollection of what is usual at court. At court, please to remember, no one ventures to put a question to the King."

"Sire, I am obliged to seek elsewhere for what I thought I should find in your Majesty. Instead of obtaining a reply from you, I am compelled to make one for myself."

The King rose. "Monsieur le Comte," he said, "I have now given you all the time I had at my disposal." This was a dismissal.

"Sire," replied the Comte, "I have not yet had time to tell your Majesty what I came with the express object of saying, and I so rarely see your Majesty that I ought to avail myself of the opportunity."

"You are now becoming offensive, monsieur."

"Oh, sire! offend your Majesty! I? — Never! All my life through have I maintained that kings are above other men, not only from their rank and power, but from their nobleness of heart and their true dignity of mind. I never can bring myself to believe that my sovereign, he who passed his word to me, did so with a mental reservation."

"What do you mean? What mental reservation do you allude to?"

"I will explain my meaning," said Athos coldly. "If, in refusing Mademoiselle de la Vallière to M. de Bragelonne, your Majesty had some other object in view than the happiness of the Vicomte — "

"You perceive, monsieur, that you are offending me."

"If, in requiring the Vicomte to delay his marriage, your Majesty's only object was to remove the gentleman to whom Mademoiselle de la Vallière was engaged — "

"Monsieur! monsieur!"

"I have heard it said so in every direction, sire. Your Majesty's affection for Mademoiselle de la Vallière is spoken of on all sides."

The King tore his gloves, which he had been biting for some time. "Mademoiselle de la Vallière does not love M. de Bragelonne," said the King hoarsely.

"Does your Majesty know that to be the case?" remarked Athos with a searching look.

"I do know it."

"Since a very short time, then; for, doubtlessly, had your Majesty known it when I first preferred my request, you would have taken the trouble to inform me of it."

"Since a very short time, truly, monsieur."

Athos remained silent for a moment, and then resumed: "In that case, I do not understand why your Majesty should have sent M. de Bragelonne to London. That exile, and most properly, so, too, is a matter of astonishment to every one who regards your Majesty's honour with sincere affection."

The King, irritated beyond measure, especially because he felt that he was mastered, endeavoured to dismiss Athos by a gesture.

"Sire," replied the Comte, "I will tell you all; I will not leave your presence until I have been satisfied either by your Majesty or by myself; satisfied, if you prove to me that you are right,—satisfied, if I prove to you that you are wrong. Nay, sire, you cannot but listen to me. I am old now, and I am attached to everything that is really great and really powerful in your kingdom. I am a gentleman who shed my blood for your father and for yourself, without ever having asked a single favour either from yourself or from your father. I have never inflicted the slightest wrong or injury on any one in this world, and kings even are still my debtors. You cannot but listen to me, I repeat. I have come to ask you for an account of the honour of one of your servants whom you have deceived by a falsehood, or betrayed by a want of heart or judgment. I know that these words irritate your Majesty, but the facts themselves are killing us. I know you are endeavouring to find some means whereby to chastise me for my frankness; but I know also the chastisement I will implore God to inflict upon you when I relate to Him your perjury and my son's unhappiness."

The King during these remarks was walking hurriedly to and fro, his hands thrust into the breast of his coat, his head haughtily raised, his eyes blazing with wrath. "Monsieur," he cried suddenly, "if I acted towards you as the King, you would be already punished; but I am only a man, and I have the right to love in this world every one who loves me,—a happiness which is so rarely found."

"You cannot pretend to such a right as a man any more than as a king, sire; or, if you intended to exercise that right in a loyal manner, you should have told M. de Bragelonne so, and not have exiled him."

"You have forgotten you are speaking to the King, monsieur. It is a crime."

"You have forgotten you are destroying the lives of two men, sire. It is a mortal sin."

"Leave the room."

"Not until I have said this, 'Son of Louis XIII, you begin your reign badly, for you begin it by abduction and disloyalty! My race—myself too—are now freed from all that affection and respect towards you, which I made my son swear to observe in the vaults of Saint-Denis, in the presence of the relics of your noble forefathers. You are now become our enemy, sire, and henceforth we have nothing to do save with Heaven alone, our sole master. Be warned.'"

Thus saying, Athos broke his sword across his knee, slowly placed the two pieces upon the floor, and saluting the King, who was almost choking from rage and shame, he quitted the cabinet. Louis, who sat near the table, completely overwhelmed, was several minutes before he could collect himself; but he suddenly rose and rang the bell violently; "Tell M. d'Artagnan to come here," he said to the terrified ushers.

CHAPTER XIV

AFTER THE STORM

Our readers will doubtlessly have been asking themselves how it happened that Athos, of whom not a word has been said for some time past, arrived so very opportunely at court. We will, without delay, endeavour to satisfy their curiosity.

Bragelonne had left Madame and had proceeded at once straight to the apartments of Athos, who had been in Paris during the last two days, the Comte having been already informed of what had taken place, by a letter from d'Artagnan. Raoul arrived at his father's; Athos, after having held out his hand to him, and embraced him most affectionately, made a sign for him to sit down.

"I know you come to me as a man would go to a friend, Vicomte, whenever he is suffering; tell me, therefore, what brings you now."

The young man bowed, and began his recital; more than once in the course of it his tears almost choked his utterance, and a sob, checked in his throat, compelled him to suspend his narrative for a few minutes. However, he finished at last. Athos most probably already knew how matters stood; as we have just now said that d'Artagnan had already written to him; but, preserving until the conclusion that calm, unruffled composure of manner which constituted the almost superhuman side of his character, he replied, "Raoul, I do not believe there is a word of truth in the rumours; I do not believe in the existence of what you fear, although I do not deny that persons most entitled to the fullest credit have already conversed with me on the subject. In my heart and soul I think it utterly impossible that the King could be guilty of such an outrage upon a gentleman. I will answer for the King, therefore, and will soon bring you back the proof of what I say."

Athos dressed, and then left him, in order to wait upon the King; the result of that interview is already known to our readers.

When he returned to his lodgings, Raoul, pale and dejected, had not quitted his attitude of despair. At the sound, however, of the opening doors, and of his father's footsteps as he approached him, the young man raised his head. Athos's face was very pale, his head uncovered, and his manner full of seriousness; he gave his cloak and hat to the lackey, dismissed him with a gesture, and sat down near Raoul.

41

"Well, monsieur," inquired the young man, "are you quite convinced now?"

"I am, Raoul; the King loves Mademoiselle da la Vallière."

"He confesses it, then?" cried Raoul.

"Yes," replied Athos.

"And she?"

"I have not seen her."

"No; but the King spoke to you about her. What did he say?"

"He says that she loves him."

"Oh, you see — you see, monsieur!" said the young man with a gesture of despair.

"Raoul," resumed the Comte, "I told the King, believe me, all that you yourself could possibly have said; and I believe I did so in becoming language, though sufficiently firm."

"And what did you say to him, monsieur?"

"I told him, Raoul, that everything was now at an end between him and ourselves; that you would never serve him again. I told him that I, too, should remain aloof."

At this moment the servant announced M. d'Artagnan. This name sounded very differently to the ears of Athos and of Raoul. The musketeer entered the room with a vague smile upon his lips. Raoul paused. Athos walked towards his friend with an expression of face which did not escape Bragelonne. D'Artagnan answered Athos's look by an imperceptible movement of the eyelid; and then, advancing towards Raoul, whom he took by the hand, he said, addressing both father and son, "Well, you are trying to console this poor boy, it seems."

"And you, kind and good as usual, are come to help me in my difficult task."

As he said this, Athos pressed d'Artagnan's hand between both his own; Raoul fancied he observed in this pressure something beyond the sense his mere words conveyed.

"Yes," replied the musketeer, smoothing his moustache with the hand that Athos had left free, "yes, I have come also."

"You are most welcome, chevalier; not from the consolation you bring with you, but on your own account. I am already consoled," said Raoul; and he attempted to smile, but the effect was far more sad than any tears d'Artagnan had ever seen shed.

"That is well and good then," said d'Artagnan. "Do you know what I would advise you to do?"

"Tell me, monsieur, for the advice is sure to be good as it comes from you."

"Very good, then; I advise you, after your long journey from England, after your visit to M. de Guiche, after your visit to Madame, I advise you, I say, to take a few hours' rest; go and lie down, sleep for a dozen hours, and when you wake up, go and ride one of my horses until you have tired him to death."

And drawing Raoul towards him he embraced him as he would have done his own child. Athos did the like; only it was very visible that the kiss was more affectionate, and the pressure of his lips still warmer with the father than with the friend. The young man again looked at both his companions, endeavouring to penetrate their real meaning, or their real feelings, with the utmost strength of his intelligence; but his look was powerless upon the smiling countenance of the musketeer, or upon the calm and composed features of the Comte de la Fère. "Where are you going, Raoul?" inquired the latter, seeing that Bragelonne was preparing to go out.

"To my own apartments," replied the latter in his soft and sad voice.

Raoul, observing the perfect composure which marked every gesture of his two friends, quitted the Comte's room, carrying away with him nothing but the individual feeling of his own particular distress.

"Thank Heaven," he said, "since that is the case, I need only think of myself."

And wrapping himself in his cloak, in order to conceal from the passers-by in the streets his gloomy and sorrowful face, he quitted them, for the purpose of returning to his own rooms. The two friends watched the young man as he walked away with a feeling akin to pity, only each expressed it in a very difficult way.

"Poor Raoul!" said Athos sighing deeply.

"Poor Raoul!" said d'Artagnan shrugging his shoulders.

CHAPTER XV

WHAT RAOUL HAD GUESSED

As soon as Raoul had quitted Athos and d'Artagnan, and as soon as the two exclamations which had followed his departure had escaped their lips, they found themselves face to face alone. Athos immediately resumed the earnest air that he had assumed at d'Artagnan's arrival.

"Well," he said, "what have you come to announce to me, my friend?"

"I?" inquired d'Artagnan.

"Yes; I do not see you in this way without some reason for it," said Athos, smiling.

"The deuce!" said d'Artagnan.

"I will place you at your ease. The King is furious, I suppose?"

"Well, I must say he is not altogether pleased."

"And you have come to arrest me, then?"

"My dear friend, you have hit the very mark."

"Oh! I expected it. I am quite ready to go with you."

"Deuce take it!" said d'Artagnan, "what a hurry you are in."

"I am afraid of delaying you," said Athos, smiling.

"Very well, 'let us go,'" said d'Artagnan quietly.

"As I broke my sword in the King's presence, and threw the pieces at his feet, I presume that will dispense with the necessity of delivering it over to you."

"You are quite right; and, besides that, what the deuce do you suppose I could do with your sword?"

"Am I to walk behind or before you?" inquired Athos, laughing.

"You will walk arm-in-arm with me," replied d'Artagnan, as he took the Comte's arm to descend the staircase; and in this manner they arrived at the landing. Grimaud, whom they had met in the ante-room, looked at them as they went out together in this manner, with some little uneasiness; his experience of affairs was quite sufficient to give him good reason to suspect that there was something wrong.

"Ah! is that you, Grimaud?" said Athos kindly. "We are going——"

"To take a turn in my carriage," interrupted d'Artagnan, with a friendly nod of the head.

Grimaud thanked d'Artagnan by a grimace, which was evidently intended for a smile, and accompanied both the friends to the door. Athos entered first into the carriage, d'Artagnan following him, without saying a word to the coachman. The departure had taken place so quietly, that it excited no disturbance or attention even in the neighbourhood. When the carriage had reached the quays, "You are taking me to the Bastille, I perceive," said Athos.

"I?" said d'Artagnan. "I take you wherever you may choose to go; nowhere else, I can assure you."

"What do you mean?" said the Comte, surprised.

"Why, surely, my dear friend," said d'Artagnan, "you quite understand that I undertook the mission with no other object in view than that of carrying it out exactly as you liked. You surely did not expect that I was going to get you thrown into prison like that, brutally, and without any reflection. If I had not anticipated that, I should have let the captain of the guards undertake it."

"And so——?" said Athos.

"And so, I repeat again, we will go wherever you may choose."

"My dear friend," said Athos, embracing d'Artagnan, "how like you that is."

"Well, it seems simple enough to me. The coachman will take you to the barrier of the Cours-la-Reine; you will find a horse there which I have ordered to be kept ready for you; with that horse you will be able to do three posts without stopping; and I, on my side, will take care not to return to the King, to tell him that you have gone away, until the very moment it will be impossible to overtake you. In the meantime you will have reached Havre, and from Havre across to England, where you will find the charming residence of which M. Monk made me a present, without speaking of the hospitality which King Charles will not fail to show you. Well, what do you think of this project?"

Athos shook his head, and then said, smiling as he did so, "No, no; take me to the Bastille."

"You are an obstinate-headed fellow, dear Athos," returned d'Artagnan; "reflect for a few moments."

"My dear friend," replied Athos, with perfect calmness, "I should like to persuade you of one thing; namely, that I wish to be arrested; that I desire above all things that my arrest should take place."

D'Artagnan made a slight movement of his shoulders.

"Nay; I wish it, I repeat, more than anything; if you were to let me escape, it would only be to return of my own accord, and constitute myself a prisoner. I wish to prove to this young man, who is dazzled by the power and splendour of his crown, that he can be regarded as the first and chiefest among men only on the condition of his proving himself to be the most generous and the wisest among them. He may punish me, imprison or torture me, it matters not. He abuses his opportunities, and I wish him to learn the bitterness of remorse, while Heaven teaches him what a chastisement is."

"Well, well," replied d'Artagnan, "I know, only too well, that when you have once said 'no,' you mean 'no.' I do not insist any longer; you wish to go to the Bastille?"

"I do wish to go there."

"Let us go then! To the Bastille!" cried d'Artagnan to the coachman. And throwing himself back in the carriage, he gnawed the ends of his moustache with a fury which, for Athos, who knew him well, signified a resolution either already taken or in course of formation. A profound silence ensued in the carriage, which continued to roll on, but neither faster nor slower than before. Athos took the musketeer by the hand.

"You are not angry with me, d'Artagnan?" he said.

"I! – oh, no! certainly not; of course not. What you do from heroism, I should have done from sheer obstinacy."

"But you are quite of opinion, are you not, that Heaven will avenge me, d'Artagnan?"

"And I know some persons on earth who will lend a helping hand," said the captain.

CHAPTER XVI

THREE GUESTS ASTONISHED TO FIND THEMSELVES AT SUPPER TOGETHER

The carriage arrived at the outside gate of the Bastille. A soldier on guard stopped it, but d'Artagnan had only to utter a single word to procure admittance, and the carriage passed on without further difficulty. Whilst they were proceeding along the covered way which led to the courtyard of the governor's residence, d'Artagnan, whose lynx eye saw everything, even through the walls, suddenly cried out, "What is that out yonder?"

"Well, a carriage; very likely conveying a prisoner like myself."

At that very moment a second sentinel stopped d'Artagnan, and while the formalities were being gone through, Athos could see at a hundred paces from him the man whom his friend had pointed out to him. He was, in fact, getting out of the carriage at the door of the governor's house. "Well," inquired d'Artagnan, "do you see him?"

"Yes; he is a man in a grey suit."

"Athos, I will wager anything it is he."

"He – who?"

"Aramis."

"Aramis arrested? Impossible!"

"I do not say he is arrested, since we see him alone in his carriage."

"Well, then, what is he doing here?"

"Oh! he knows Baisemeaux, the governor," replied the musketeer slyly; "so we have arrived just in time."

"What for?"

"In order to see what we can see."

The carriage stopped where the one we have just now pointed out had stopped; namely, at the door of the governor's house. In a few minutes they were in the governor's dining-room, and the first face which attracted d'Artagnan's observation was that of Aramis, who was seated side by side with Baisemeaux, and awaited the announcement of a good meal, whose odour impregnated the whole apartment. If d'Artagnan pretended surprise, Aramis did not pretend at all; he started when he saw his two friends, and his emotion was very apparent. Athos and d'Artagnan however, complimented him as usual, and Baisemeaux, amazed, completely stupefied by the presence of his three guests, began to perform a few evolutions around them all. "By what lucky accident—"

"We were just going to ask you," retorted d'Artagnan.

"Are we going to give ourselves up as prisoners?" cried Aramis, with an affectation of hilarity.

"Ah! ah!" said d'Artagnan; "it is true the walls smell deucedly like a prison. Monsieur de Baisemeaux, you know you invited me to sup with you the other day."

"I!" cried Baisemeaux.

"Yes, of course you did, although you now seem so struck with amazement. Don't you remember it?"

Baisemeaux turned pale and then red, looked at Aramis, who looked at him, and finished by stammering out, "Certainly—I am delighted —but upon my honour—I have not the slightest—Ah! I have such a wretched memory. I beg you a thousand pardons. But now, once for all, my dear M. d'Artagnan, be sure that at this present time, as at any other, whether invited or not, you are perfectly at home here, you and M. d'Herblay, your friend," he said, turning towards Aramis; "and this gentleman too," he added, bowing to Athos.

"Well, I thought it would be sure to turn out so," replied d'Artagnan, "and that is the reason I came. Having nothing to do this evening at the Palais-Royal, I wish to judge for myself, what your ordinary style of living was like; and as I was coming along, I met the Comte de la Fère."

"The Comte is welcome, I am sure."

"And he will sup with you two, I suppose, whilst I, unfortunate dog that I am, must run off on a matter of duty. Oh! what happy beings you are, compared to myself," he added, sighing as loud as Porthos might have done.

"And so you are going away then?" said Aramis and Baisemeaux together, with the same expression of delighted surprise, the tone of which was immediately noticed by d'Artagnan.

"Most certainly," he said, pressing his friend's hand confidently; and he added in a low voice, "Wait for me, Athos; be cheerful and lively as possible, and above all, don't allude even to business affairs,

Baisemeaux led d'Artagnan to the gate. Aramis, with many friendly protestations of delight, sat down by Athos, determined to make him speak; but Athos possessed every virtue and quality to the very highest degree. If necessity had required it, he would have been the finest orator in the world, but on other occasions he would rather have died than have opened his lips.

CHAPTER XVII

WHAT TOOK PLACE AT THE LOUVRE DURING THE SUPPER AT THE BASTILLE

The King rose when the curtain before the door was raised. His first idea was that a letter from Louise had arrived; but, instead of a letter of love, he only saw his captain of musketeers standing upright and perfectly silent in the doorway. "M. d'Artagnan," he said, "ah! Well, monsieur? Is it done?"

"Yes, sire," replied the captain of the musketeers in a grave voice, "it is done."

"What did the Comte say?"

"Nothing at all, sire."

"Surely he did not allow himself to be arrested without saying something?"

"He said he expected to be arrested, sire."

The King raised his head haughtily. "I presume," he said, "that M. le Comte de la Fère has not continued to play his obstinate and rebellious part?"

"In the first place, sire, what do you term rebellious?" quietly asked the musketeer. "A rebel, in the eyes of the King, is a man who not only allows himself to be shut up in the Bastille, but still more, who opposes those who do not wish to take him there."

"Who do not wish to take him there!" exclaimed the King. "What do you say, captain! Are you mad?"

"I believe not, sire."

"Ah! Monsieur d'Artagnan, so you set your King at defiance."

"Sire! ——"

"Monsieur d'Artagnan! I warn you that you are abusing my patience."

"On the contrary, sire."

"What do you mean by 'on the contrary'?"

"I have come to get myself arrested too."

"To get yourself arrested, – you!"

"Of course. My friend will get wearied to death in the Bastille by himself; and I have come to propose to your Majesty to permit me to bear him company; if your Majesty will but give the word, I will arrest myself; I shall not need the captain of the guard for that, I assure you."

The King darted towards the table and seized hold of a pen to write the order for d'Artagnan's imprisonment. "Pay attention, monsieur, that this is for ever," cried the King in a tone of stern menace.

"I can quite believe that," returned the musketeer, "for when you have done such an act as that, you will never be able to look me in the

47

face again."

The King dashed down his pen violently. "Leave the room, monsieur!" he said.

"Not so, if it please your Majesty."

"How is that?"

"Sire, I came to speak gently and temperately to your Majesty; your Majesty got into a passion with me; that is a misfortune; but I shall not the less on that account say what I had to say to you."

"Your resignation, monsieur,—your resignation!" cried the King.

"No, sire; for there is no question of my resignation at the present moment. Your Majesty took up your pen just now to send me to the Bastille,—why should you change your intention?"

"D'Artagnan! Gascon that you are! who is the King, allow me to ask,—you or myself?"

"You, sire, unfortunately."

"What do you mean by 'unfortunately'?"

"Yes, sire; for if it were I——"

"If it were you, you would approve of M. d'Artagnan's rebellious conduct, I suppose?"

"Certainly."

"Really!" said the King, shrugging his shoulders.

"And I should tell my captain of the musketeers," continued d'Artagnan, "I should tell him, looking at him all the while with human eyes, and not with eyes like coals of fire, 'M. d'Artagnan, I had forgotten that I was the King, for I descended from my throne in order to insult a gentleman.'"

"Monsieur," said the King, "do you think you can excuse your friend by exceeding him in insolence?"

"Oh, sire! I should go much further than he did," said d'Artagnan, "and it would be your own fault. I should tell you what he, a man full of the finest sense of delicacy, did not tell you; I should say—'Sire, you have sacrificed his son, and he defended his son—you sacrificed himself; he addressed you in the name of honour, of religion, of virtue—you repulsed, drove him away, imprisoned him.' I should be harder than he was, for I should say to you—'Sire, it is for you to choose. Do you wish to have friends or lackeys—soldiers or slaves—great men or mere puppets? Do you wish men to serve you, or to bend and crouch before you? Do you wish men to love you, or to be afraid of you? If you prefer baseness, intrigue, cowardice, say so at once, sire, and we will leave you,—we who are the only individuals who are left, nay, I will say more, the only models of the valour of former times; we who have done our duty, and have exceeded, perhaps, in courage and in merit, the men already great for posterity. Choose, sire! and that too without delay. Whatever remains to you of great nobles, guard it with a jealous eye; you will never be deficient in courtiers. Delay not—and send me to the Bastille with my friend; for, if you have not known how to listen to the Comte de la Fère, whose voice is the sweetest and noblest when honour is his theme; if you do not know how to listen to d'Artagnan, the frankest and honestest voice of sincerity, you are a bad King, and to-morrow will be a poor King. And learn from me, sire, that bad kings are hated by their people, and poor kings are driven ignominiously away.' That is what I had to say to you, sire; you were wrong to have driven me to do it.''

The King threw himself back in his chair, cold as death, and livid as a corpse. Had a thunderbolt fallen at his feet, he could not have been more astonished; he seemed as if his respiration had utterly ceased, and that he was at the point of death. The honest voice of sincerity, as d'Artagnan had called it, had pierced through his heart like a sword-blade.

D'Artagnan had said all he had to say. Comprehending the King's anger, he drew his sword, and, approaching Louis XIV respectfully, he placed it on the table. But the King, with a furious gesture, thrust aside the sword, which fell to the ground and rolled to d'Artagnan's feet. Notwithstanding the perfect mastery which d'Artagnan exercised over himself, he, too, in his turn, became pale, and, trembling with indignation, said — "A king may disgrace a soldier, — he may exile him, and may even condemn him to death; but were he a hundred times a king he has no right to insult him by casting a dishonour upon his sword! Sire, a King of France has ever repulsed with contempt the sword of a man such as I am! Stained with disgrace as this sword now is, it has henceforth no other sheath than either your heart or my own! I choose my own, sire; and you have to thank Heaven and my own patience that I do so." Then snatching up his sword, he cried, "My blood be upon your head!" and with a rapid gesture, he placed the hilt upon the floor and directed the point of the blade towards his breast. The King, however, with a movement far more rapid than that of d'Artagnan, threw his right arm round the musketeer's neck, and with his left hand seized hold of the blade by the middle, and returned it silently to the scabbard. D'Artagnan, upright, pale, and still trembling, let the King do all to the very end. Louis, overcome, and softened by gentler feelings, returned to the table, took a pen in his hand, wrote a few lines, signed them, and then held it out to d'Artagnan.

"What is this paper, sire?" inquired the captain.

"An order for M. d'Artagnan to set the Comte de la Fère at liberty immediately."

D'Artagnan seized the King's hand, and imprinted a kiss upon it; he then folded the order, placed it in his belt, and quitted the room. Neither the King nor the captain had said a syllable.

"Oh, human heart! the guide and director of kings," murmured Louis, when alone, "when shall I learn to read in your inmost recesses, as in the leaves of a book! No, I am not a bad king — nor am I a poor king; but I am still a child, after all."

CHAPTER XVIII

POLITICAL RIVALS

D'Artagnan had promised M. de Baisemeaux to return in time for dessert, and he kept his word. They had just reached the finer and more delicate class of wines and liqueurs with which the governor's cellar had the reputation of being most admirably stocked, when the spurs of the captain resounded in the corridor, and he himself appeared at the threshold. Athos and Aramis had played a close game; neither of the two had been able to gain the slightest advantage over the other. They had supped, talked a good deal about the Bastille, of the last journey to Fontainebleau, of the intended fête that M. Fouquet was about to give at Vaux; they had generalised on every possible subject; and no one, excepting Baisemeaux, had, in the slightest degree, alluded to private matters. D'Artagnan arrived in the very midst of the conversation, still pale and much disturbed by his interview with the King. Baisemeaux hastened to give him a chair; d'Artagnan accepted a glass of wine, and set it down empty. Athos and Aramis both remarked his emotion; as for Baisemeaux, he saw nothing more than the captain of the King's musketeers, to whom he endeavoured to show every possible attention. But, although Aramis had remarked his emotion, he had not been able to guess the cause of it. Athos alone believed he had detected it. For him, d'Artagnan's return, and particularly the manner in which he, usually so impassible, seemed overcome, signified, "I have just asked the King something which the King has refused me." Thoroughly convinced that his conjecture was correct, Athos smiled, rose from the table, and made a sign to d'Artagnan, as if to remind him that they had something else to do than to sup together. D'Artagnan immediately understood him, and replied by another sign. Aramis and Baisemeaux watched this silent dialogue, and looked inquiringly at each other. Athos felt that he was called upon to give an explanation of what was passing.

"The truth is, my friends," said the Comte de la Fère, with a smile, "that you, Aramis, have been supping with a state criminal, and you, Monsieur de Baisemeaux, with your prisoner."

Baisemeaux uttered an exclamation of surprise, and almost of delight; for he was exceedingly proud and vain of his fortress; and for his own individual profit, the more prisoners he had, the happier he was; and the higher the prisoners were in rank, the prouder he felt. Aramis assumed an expression of countenance which he thought the position justified, and said, "Well, dear Athos, forgive me; but I almost suspected what has happened. Some prank of Raoul and La Vallière, I suppose?"

"Alas!" said Baisemeaux.

"And," continued Aramis, "you, a high and powerful nobleman as you are, forgetful that courtiers now exist—you have been to the King, I suppose, and told him what you thought of his conduct."

"Yes, you have guessed right."

"So that," said Baisemeaux, trembling at having supped so familiarly with a man who had fallen into disgrace with the King; "so that, Monsieur le Comte——"

"So that, my dear governor," said Athos, "my friend d'Artagnan will communicate to you the contents of the paper which I perceive just peeping out of his belt, and which assuredly can be nothing else than the order for my incarceration."

Baisemeaux held out his hand with his accustomed eagerness. D'Artagnan drew two papers from his belt, and presented one of them to the governor, who unfolded it, and then read, in a low tone of voice, looking at Athos over the paper, as he did so, and pausing from time to time: "'Order to detain in my château of the Bastille, Monsieur le Comte de la Fère.' Oh! monsieur! this is indeed a very melancholy honour for me."

"You will have a patient prisoner, monsieur," said Athos, in his calm, soft voice.

"A prisoner, too, who will not remain a month with you, my dear governor," said Aramis; while Baisemeaux, still holding the order in his hand, transcribed it upon the prison registry.

"Not a day, or rather not even a night," said d'Artagnan, displaying the second order of the King, "for now, dear M. de Baisemeaux, you will have the goodness to transcribe also this order for setting the Comte immediately at liberty."

"Ah!" said Aramis, "it is a labour that you have deprived me of, d'Artagnan;" and he pressed the musketeer's hand in a significant manner, at the same moment as that of Athos.

"What!" said the latter, in astonishment, "the King sets me at liberty!"

"Read, my dear friend," returned d'Artagnan.

Athos took the order and read it. "It is quite true," he said.

"Are you sorry for it?" asked d'Artagnan.

"Oh, no, on the contrary; I wish the King no harm; and the greatest evil or misfortune that any one can wish Kings, is that they should commit an act of injustice. But you have had a difficult and painful task, I know. Tell me, have you not, d'Artagnan?"

"I? not at all," said the musketeer, laughing; "the King does everything I wish him to do."

Aramis looked fixedly at d'Artagnan, and saw that he was not speaking the truth. But Baisemeaux had eyes for nothing but d'Artagnan, so great was his admiration for a man who seemed to make the King do all he wished. "And does the King exile Athos?" inquired Aramis.

"No, not precisely; the King did not explain himself upon that subject," replied d'Artagnan; "but I think the Comte could not well do better, unless, indeed, he wishes particularly to thank the King—"

"No, indeed," replied Athos, smiling.

"Well, then, I think," resumed d'Artagnan, "that the Comte cannot do better than return to his own château. However, my dear Athos, you have only to speak, to tell me what you want. If any particular place of residence is more agreeable to you than another, I am influential enough, perhaps, to obtain it for you."

"No, thank you," said Athos; "nothing can be more agreeable to me, my dear friend, than to return to my solitude beneath my noble trees, on the banks of the Loire." And then, turning to d'Artagnan, he said, "Let us go, my dear friend. Shall I have that greatest of all pleasures for me—that of having you as my companion?"

"To the city gate only," replied d'Artagnan, "after which I will

51

tell you what I told the King. I am on duty."

"And you, my dear Aramis," said Athos, smiling; "will you accompany me? La Fère is on the road to Vannes."

"Thank you, my dear friend," said Aramis, "but I have an appointment in Paris this evening, and I cannot leave without very serious interests suffering by my absence."

"In that case," said Athos, "I must say adieu, and take my leave of you. My dear Monsieur de Baisemeaux, I have to thank you exceedingly for your kind and friendly disposition towards me, and particularly for the specimen you have given me of the usual fare of the Bastille." And, having embraced Aramis, and shaken hands with M. de Baisemeaux, and having received their wishes for an agreeable journey from them both, Athos set off with d'Artagnan.

Whilst the *dénouement* of the scene of the Palais-Royal was taking place at the Bastille, let us relate what was going on at the lodgings of Athos and Bragelonne. Grimaud, as we have seen, had accompanied his master to Paris; and, as we have said, he was present when Athos went out; he had observed d'Artagnan gnaw the corners of his moustaches; he had seen his master get into the carriage; he had narrowly examined both their countenances, and he had known them both for a sufficiently long period to read and understand, through the mask of their impassibility, that something serious was the matter.

The first step he took was to search in his master's coat for M. d'Artagnan's letter; he found the letter still there, which contained the following:

> MY DEAR FRIEND,—Raoul has been to ask me for some particulars about the conduct of Mademoiselle de la Vallière, during our young friend's residence in London. I am a poor captain of musketeers, and am sickened to death every day by hearing all the scandal of the barracks and bedside conversations. If I had told Raoul all I believe I know, the poor fellow would have died from it; but I am in the King's service, and cannot relate all I hear about the King's affairs. If your heart tells you to do it, set off at once; the matter concerns you more than myself, and almost as much as Raoul.

Grimaud tore, not a handful, but a finger-and-thumbful of hair out of his head; he would have done more if his head of hair had been in more flourishing circumstances.

"Yes," he said, "that is the key of the whole enigma. The young girl has been playing her pranks; what people say about her and the King is true, then; our young master has been deceived; he ought to know it. Monsieur le Comte has been to see the King, and has told him a piece of his mind; and then the King sent M. d'Artagnan to arrange the affair. Ah! gracious goodness!" continued Grimaud, "Monsieur le Comte, I now remember, returned without his sword."

This discovery made the perspiration break out all over poor Grimaud's face. He did not waste any more time in useless conjecture, but clapped his hat on his head, and ran to Raoul's lodgings.

Raoul had mastered his grief, if not his affection; and, compelled to look forward on that perilous road on which madness and rebellion were hurrying him, he had seen, from the very first glance, his father exposed to the royal obstinacy; since Athos had himself been the first to oppose any resistance to the royal will. At this moment, from a very natural sympathy of feeling, the unhappy young man remembered the mysterious signs which Athos had made, and the unexpected visit of d'Artagnan; the result of the conflict between a sovereign and a subject revealed itself to his terrified vision. As d'Artagnan was on duty, that is, fixed to his post without possibility of leaving it, it was certainly not likely that he had come to pay Athos a visit merely for the pleasure of seeing him. He must have come to say something to him. This something, in such painful conjectures, was either a misfortune or a danger. Raoul trembled at having been so selfish as to have forgotten his father for his affection; at having, in a word, passed his time in idle dreams, or in an indulgence of despair, at a time when a necessity existed for repelling the imminent attack directed against Athos. The very idea nearly drove him wild; he buckled on his sword and ran towards his father's lodging. On his way there he encountered Grimaud, who, having set off from the opposite pole, was running with equal eagerness in search of the truth.

CHAPTER XIX

IN WHICH PORTHOS IS CONVINCED WITHOUT HAVING UNDERSTOOD ANYTHING

The numerous individuals we have introduced into this long story is the cause of each of them being obliged to appear only in his own turn, and according to the exigencies of the recital. The result is that our readers have had no opportunity of meeting our friend Porthos since his return from Fontainebleau. The honours which he had received from the King had not changed the easy, affectionate character of that excellent-hearted man; he may perhaps have held up his head a little higher than usual, and a majesty of demeanour as it were may have betrayed itself since the honour of dining at the King's table had been accorded him. After one of those dinners, during which Porthos attempted to recall to his recollection all the details of the royal banquet, half joyful, thanks to the excellence of the wines; half melancholy, thanks to his ambitious ideas, Porthos was gradually falling off into a gentle doze, when his servant entered to announce that M. de Bragelonne wished urgently to speak to him. Porthos passed into the vestibule where he found his young friend in the disposition of mind we are already aware of. He was escorted by Grimaud, and they had both ridden at full speed.

"Raoul," cried Porthos, surprised. "What is the matter?"

"The matter is that Monsieur le Comte de la Fère has by this time been arrested."

Porthos gave a start that would have thrown down a wall.

"Arrested," he cried out; "by whom?"

"By d'Artagnan."

"It is impossible," said Porthos.

"My dear friend; it is perfectly true."

Porthos turned towards Grimaud, as if he needed a second confirmation of the intelligence. Grimaud nodded his head. "And where have they taken him to?"

"Probably to the Bastille."

"What makes you think that?"

"As we came along we questioned some persons, who saw the carriage pass; and others who saw it enter the Bastille."

"Oh, oh!" muttered Porthos.

"What do you intend to do?" inquired Raoul.

"I? Nothing; only I will not have Athos remain at the Bastille."

"Do you know," said Raoul, advancing nearer to Porthos, "that the arrest was made by order of the King?"

Porthos looked at the young man, as if to say, "What does that matter to me?" This dumb language seemed so eloquent of meaning to Raoul, that he did not ask another question. He mounted his horse; and Porthos, assisted by Grimaud, had already done the same.

"Let us arrange our plan of action," said Raoul.

"Yes," returned Porthos, "that is the best thing we can do."

Raoul sighed deeply, and then paused suddenly.

"What is the matter?" asked Porthos; "are you faint?"

"No, only I feel how utterly helpless our position is. Can we three pretend to go and take the Bastille?"

"Well, if d'Artagnan were only here," replied Porthos, "I don't know about that."

Raoul could not resist a feeling of admiration at the sight of such a perfect confidence, heroic in its simplicity. These were truly the celebrated men who, by three or four, attacked armies, and assaulted castles! Those men who had terrified death itself, and who survived the wrecks of an age, and were still stronger than the most robust of the young.

"Monsieur," said he to Porthos, "you have just given me an idea; we absolutely must see M. d'Artagnan."

"Undoubtedly."

"He ought by this time to have returned home, after having taken my father to the Bastille. Let us go to his house."

"First inquire at the Bastille," said Grimaud, who was in the habit of speaking little, but that to the purpose.

Accordingly, they hastened towards the fortress, when one of those chances which Heaven bestows on men of strong will, caused Grimaud suddenly to perceive the carriage, which was entering by the great gate of the drawbridge. This was at the moment that d'Artagnan was, as we have seen, returning from his visit to the King. In vain was it that Raoul urged on his horse in order to join the carriage, and to see whom it contained. The horses had already gained the other side of the great gate, which again closed, while one of the sentries struck the nose of Raoul's horse with his musket; Raoul turned about, only too happy to find he had ascertained something respecting the carriage which had contained his father.

"We have him," said Grimaud.

"If we wait a little it is certain he will leave; don't you think so, my friend?"

"Unless, indeed, d'Artagnan also be a prisoner," replied Porthos, "in which case everything is lost."

Raoul returned no answer, for any hypothesis was admissible. He instructed Grimaud to lead the horses to the little street Jean-Beausire, so as to give rise to less suspicion, and himself, with his piercing gaze, watched for the exit either of d'Artagnan or the carriage. Nor had he decided wrongly; for twenty minutes had not elapsed before the gate reopened and the carriage reappeared. A dazzling of the eyes prevented Raoul from distinguishing what figures occupied the interior. Grimaud averred that he had seen two persons, and that one of them was his master. Porthos kept looking at Raoul and Grimaud, by turns, in the hope of understanding their idea.

"It is clear," said Grimaud, "that if the Comte is in the carriage, either he is set at liberty or they are taking him to another prison."

"We shall soon see that by the road he takes," answered Porthos.

"If he is set at liberty," said Grimaud, "they will conduct him home."

"True," rejoined Porthos.

"The carriage does not take that way," cried Raoul; and indeed the horses were just disappearing down the faubourg St. Antoine.

"Let us hasten," said Porthos; "we will attack the carriage on the road and tell Athos to flee."

"Rebellion," murmured Raoul.

Porthos darted a second glance at Raoul, quite worthy of the first. Raoul replied only by spurring the flanks of his steed. In a few moments the three cavaliers had overtaken the carriage, and followed it so closely that their horses' breath moistened the back of it. D'Artagnan, whose senses were ever on the alert, heard the trot of the horses, at the moment when Raoul was telling Porthos to pass the chariot so as to see who was the person accompanying Athos. Porthos complied, but could not see anything, for the blinds were lowered. Rage and impatience were gaining mastery over Raoul. He had just noticed the mystery preserved by Athos's companion, and determined on proceeding to extremities. On his part d'Artagnan had perfectly recognised Porthos, and Raoul also, from under the blinds, and had communicated to the Comte the result of his observation. They were desirous only of seeing whether Raoul and Porthos would push the affair to the uttermost. And this they speedily did, for Raoul presenting his pistol threw himself on the leader, commanding the coachman to stop. Porthos seized the coachman and dragged him from his seat. Grimaud already had hold of the carriage door. Raoul threw open his arms, exclaiming, "M. le Comte! M. le Comte!"

"Ah! is it you, Raoul," said Athos, intoxicated with joy.

"Not bad, indeed!" added d'Artagnan, with a burst of laughter, and they both embraced the young man and Porthos who had taken possession of them.

"My brave Porthos! best of friends," cried Athos, "it is still the same with you."

"He is still only twenty," said d'Artagnan, "brave Porthos!"

"Confound it," answered Porthos, slightly confused, "we thought that you were being arrested."

"While," rejoined Athos, "the matter in question was nothing but my taking a drive in M. d'Artagnan's carriage."

"But we followed you from the Bastille," returned Raoul, with a tone of suspicion and reproach.

"Where we had been to take supper with our good friend M. Baisemeaux. Do you recollect Baisemeaux, Porthos?"

"Very well, indeed."

"And there we saw Aramis."

"In the Bastille?"

"At supper."

"Ah!" said Porthos, again breathing freely.

"He gave us a thousand messages for you."

"And where is M. le Comte going?" asked Grimaud, already recompensed by a smile from his master.

"We were going home to Blois."

"How can that be?"

"At once?" said Raoul.

"Yes, right forward."

"Without any luggage?"

"Oh! Raoul would have been instructed to forward me mine, or to bring it with him on his return, *if* he returns."

"If nothing detains him longer in Paris," said d'Artagnan, with a glance firm and cutting as steel, and as painful (for it reopened the poor young fellow's wounds), "he will do well to follow you, Athos."

"There is nothing to keep me any longer in Paris," said Raoul.

"Then we will go immediately," replied Athos.

"And M. d'Artagnan?"

"Oh! as for me, I was only accompanying Athos as far as the barrier, and I return with Porthos."

"Very good," said the latter.

"Come, my son," added the Comte, gently passing his arm round Raoul's neck to draw him into the carriage, and again embracing him. "Grimaud," continued the Comte, "you will return quietly to Paris with your horse and M. de Vallon's, for Raoul and I will mount here and give up the carriage to these two gentlemen to return to Paris in; and then, as soon as you arrive, you will take my clothes and letters and forward the whole to me at home."

Athos descended from the carriage and mounted the horse which had brought Porthos, and which seemed no little pleased at the exchange. Then they embraced, clasped each other's hands, interchanged a thousand pledges of eternal friendship. Porthos promised to spend a month with Athos at the first opportunity. D'Artagnan engaged to take advantage of his first leave of absence; and then, having embraced Raoul for the last time: "To you, my boy," said he, "I will write." Coming from d'Artagnan, who he knew wrote but very seldom, these words expressed everything. Raoul was moved even to tears. He tore himself away from the musketeer and departed.

D'Artagnan rejoined Porthos in the carriage: "Well," said he, "my dear friend, what a day we have had!"

"Indeed we have," answered Porthos.

CHAPTER XX

M. DE BAISEMEAUX'S "SOCIETY"

The reader has not forgotten that, on quitting the Bastille, d'Artagnan and the Comte de la Fère had left Aramis in close confabulation with Baisemeaux.

"Tell me, my dear M. Baisemeaux," said he, "have you never any other diversions at the Bastille than those at which I assisted during the two or three visits I have had the honour to pay you?"

This address was so unexpected that the governor, like a vane which suddenly receives an impulsion opposed to that of the wind, was quite dumbfounded at it. "Diversions," said he, "but I take them continuously, monseigneur."

"Oh, to be sure! And these diversions?"

"Are of every kind."

"Visits, no doubt?"

"No, not visits. Visits are not frequent at the Bastille."

"What, are visits rare, then?"

"Very much so."

"Even on the part of your society?"

"What do you term by my society—the prisoners?"

"Oh, no!—your prisoners, indeed! I know well it is you who visit them, and not they you. By your society I mean, my dear de Baisemeaux, the society of which you are a member."

"Oh, Monsieur d'Herblay!"

"Consider now, don't deny it."

"But believe me."

"If, on the contrary, you are one of the members of this society, you will immediately answer me,—yes, or no."

"Begin your questions," answered Baisemeaux, trembling.

"Well," resumed Aramis, "there is in the society of which I speak, and of which, as it seems, you are not a member—"

"Allow me," said Baisemeaux, "I should not like to say absolutely."

"There is an engagement entered into by all the governors and captains of fortresses affiliated to the order." Baisemeaux grew pale.

"Now the engagement," continued Aramis firmly, "is of this nature."

Baisemeaux rose, manifesting unspeakable emotion. "Go on, dear M. d'Herblay; go on," said he.

Aramis then spoke, or rather recited the following paragraph in the same tone as if he had been reading it from a book. "The aforesaid captain or governor of a fortress shall allow to enter, when need shall arise, and on demand of the prisoner, a confessor affiliated to the order." He stopped, Baisemeaux was quite distressing to look at, being so wretchedly pale and trembling. "Is not that the text of the agreement?" quietly asked Aramis.

"What! you are——" cried Baisemeaux, looking at Aramis almost in terror.

"The confessor affiliated to the order," said Aramis, without changing his voice.

But, gentle as the words were, they had the same effect on the unhappy governor as a clap of thunder. Baisemeaux became livid, and it seemed to him as if Aramis's beaming eyes were two forks of flame, piercing to the very bottom of his soul. "The confessor!" murmured he; "you, monseigneur, the confessor to the order!"

"Yes, I; but we have nothing to unravel together, seeing that you are not one of the affiliated."

"Monseigneur, I do not say that I have nothing to do with the society."

"Ah, ah!"

"But," replied the unhappy man, "having no notice, I was far from expecting."

"Does not the Gospel say, 'Watch, for the moment is known only of God.' Do not the rules of the order say, 'Watch, for that which I will you ought always to will also.' And on what pretext is it that you did not expect the confessor, M. de Baisemeaux?"

"Because, monseigneur, there is at present in the Bastille, no prisoner ill."

Aramis shrugged his shoulders. "What do you know about that?" said he.

"But, nevertheless, it appears to me——"

"M. de Baisemeaux," said Aramis, turning round in his chair, "here is your servant, who wishes to speak with you;" and, at this moment, de Baisemeaux's servant appeared at the threshold of the door.

"What is it?" asked Baisemeaux sharply.

"Monsieur," said the man, "they are bringing you the doctor's return."

Aramis looked at Baisemeaux with a calm and confident eye.

"Well," said he, "let the messenger enter."

The messenger entered, saluted, and handed in the report. Baisemeaux ran his eye over it, and raising his head said, in surprise, "No. 12 is ill."

"How was it then," said Aramis carelessly, "that you told me everything was well in your hotel, M. de Baisemeaux?" And he emptied his glass without removing his eyes from Baisemeaux.

At that moment, a sergeant put his head in at the door.

"Monsieur," said the sergeant, "the sick man, No. 12, has commissioned the turnkey to request you to send him a confessor."

Baisemeaux very nearly sank on the floor; but Aramis disdained to reassure him, just as he had disdained to terrify him. "What must I answer?" inquired Baisemeaux.

"Just what you please," replied Aramis, compressing his lips; "that is your business. *I* am not governor of the Bastille."

"Tell the prisoner," cried Baisemeaux quickly—"tell the prisoner

"Well, then, try to understand me." The prisoner looked fixedly at Aramis. "Sometimes it seems to me," said the latter, "that I have before me the man whom I seek, and then——"

"And then your man disappears,—is it not so?" said the prisoner, smiling. "So much the better."

Aramis rose. "Certainly," said he; "I have nothing further to say to a man who mistrusts me as you do."

"And I, monsieur," said the prisoner, in the same tone, "have nothing to say to a man who will not understand that a prisoner ought to be mistrustful of everybody."

"Do you remember, fifteen or eighteen years ago, seeing at Noisy-le-Sec a cavalier accompanied by a lady in black silk, with flame-coloured ribands in her hair?"

"Yes," said the young man; "I once asked the name of this cavalier, and they told me he called himself the Abbé d'Herblay. I was astonished that the Abbé had so warlike an air, and they replied that there was nothing singular in that, seeing that he was one of Louis XIII's musketeers."

"Well," said Aramis, "that musketeer and abbé, afterwards Bishop of Vannes, is your confessor now."

"I know it; I recognised you."

"Then, monseigneur, if you know that, I must further add a fact of which you are ignorant—that if the King were to know this evening of the presence of this musketeer, this abbé, this bishop, this confessor, *here*—he, who has risked everything to visit you, would tomorrow see glitter the executioner's axe at the bottom of a dungeon more gloomy and more obscure than yours."

While hearing these words, delivered with emphasis, the young man had raised himself on his couch, and gazed more and more eagerly at Aramis.

The result of his scrutiny was that he appeared to derive some confidence from it. "Yes," he murmured, "I remember perfectly. The woman of whom you speak came once with you, and twice afterwards with another." He hesitated.

"With another woman, who came to see you every month,—is it not so, monseigneur?"

"Yes."

"Do you know who this lady was?"

The light seemed ready to flash from the prisoner's eyes. "I am aware that she was one of the ladies of the court," he said.

"You remember that lady well, do you not?"

"Oh, my recollection can hardly be very confused on this head," said the young prisoner. "I saw that lady once with a gentleman about forty-five years old. I saw her once with you, and with the lady dressed in black. I have seen her twice since with the same person. These four people, with my master, and old Perronnette, my jailer, and the governor of the prison, are the only persons with whom I have ever spoken, and, indeed, almost the only persons I have ever seen."

"Then you were in prison?"

"If I am a prisoner here, there I was comparatively free, although in a very narrow sense—a house which I never quitted, a garden surrounded with walls I could not clear, these constituted my residence; but you know it, as you have been there. In a word, being accustomed to live within these bounds, I never cared to leave them. And so you will understand, monsieur, that not having seen anything of the world, I have nothing left to care for; and therefore, if you relate anything, you will be obliged to explain everything to me."

"And I will do so," said Aramis bowing, "for it is my duty, monseigneur."

"Well, then, begin by telling me who was my tutor."

"A worthy and, above all, an honourable gentleman, monseigneur; fit guide both for body and soul. Had you ever any reason to complain of him?"

"Oh, no; quite the contrary. But this gentleman of yours often used to tell me that my father and mother were dead. Did he deceive me, or did he speak the truth?"

"He was compelled to comply with the orders given him."

"Then he lied?"

"In one respect. Your father is dead."

"And my mother?"

"She is dead for you."

"But then she lives for others, does she not?"

"Yes."

"And I—and I, then" (the young man looked sharply at Aramis) "am compelled to live in the obscurity of a prison?"

"Alas! I fear so."

"And that, because my presence in the world would lead to the revelation of a great secret?"

"Certainly, a very great secret."

"My enemy must indeed be powerful, to be able to shut up in the Bastille a child such as I then was."

"He is."

"More powerful than my mother, then?"

"And why do you ask that?"

"Because my mother would have taken my part."

Aramis hesitated. "Yes, monseigneur; more powerful than your mother."

"Seeing, then, that my nurse and preceptor were carried off, and that I, also, was separated from them—either they were, or I am, very dangerous to my enemy?"

"Yes; a peril from which he freed himself, by causing the nurse and preceptor to disappear," answered Aramis quietly.

"Disappear!" cried the prisoner—"but how did they disappear?"

"In the surest possible way," answered Aramis;—"they are dead."

The young man turned visibly pale, and passed his hand tremblingly over his face. "From poison?" he asked.

"From poison."

The prisoner reflected a moment. "My enemy must indeed have been very cruel, or hard beset by necessity, to assassinate these two innocent people, my sole support; for the worthy gentleman and the poor nurse had never harmed a living being."

"In your family, monseigneur, necessity is stern. And so it is necessity which compels me, to my great regret, to tell you that this gentleman and the unhappy lady have been assassinated."

"Oh, you tell me nothing I am not aware of," said the prisoner, knitting his brows.

"How?"

"I suspected it."

"Why?"

"I will tell you."

At this moment the young man, supporting himself on his two elbows, drew close to Aramis's face, with such an expression of dignity, of self-command, and of defiance even, that the Bishop felt the electricity of enthusiasm strike in devouring flashes from that seared heart of his, into his brain of adamant.

"Speak, monseigneur. I have already told you that by conversing with you, I endanger my life. Little value as it has, I implore you to accept it as a ransom of your own."

"Well," resumed the young man, "this is why I suspected that they had killed my nurse and my preceptor."

"Whom you used to call your father."

"Yes; whom I called my father, but whose son I well knew I was not."

"Who caused you to suppose so?"

"For the same reason that you, monsieur, are too respectful for a friend, he was also too respectful for a father."

"I, however," said Aramis, "have no intention to disguise myself."

The young man nodded assent, and continued: "Undoubtedly I was not destined to perpetual seclusion," said the prisoner; "and that which makes me believe so, above all, now, is the care that was taken to render me as accomplished a cavalier as possible. The gentleman attached to my person taught me everything he knew himself—mathematics, a little geometry, astronomy, fencing, and riding. Every morning I went through military exercises, and practised on horseback."

"But you have not said a word about history."

"My tutor sometimes related to me the principal deeds of the King, St. Louis, King Francis I, and King Henry IV."

"Is that all?"

"Very nearly."

"This also was done by design then; just as they deprived you of mirrors, which reflect the present, so they left you in ignorance of history, which reflects the past. Since your imprisonment, books have been forbidden you; so that you are unacquainted with a number of facts, by means of which you would be able to reconstruct the shattered edifice of your recollections and your hopes."

"It is true," said the young man.

"Listen, then; I will in a few words tell you what has passed in France during the last twenty-three or twenty-four years; that is, from the probable date of your birth; in a word, from the time that interests you."

"Say on." And the young man resumed his serious and attentive attitude.

"Do you know who was the son of Henry IV?"

"At least I know who his successor was."

"How?"

"By means of a coin dated 1610, which bears the effigy of Henry IV; and another of 1612, bearing that of Louis XIII. So I presumed that, there being only two years between the two dates, Louis was Henry's successor."

"Then," said Aramis, "you know that the last reigning monarch was Louis XIII?"

"I do," answered the youth, slightly reddening.

"Well, he was a prince full of noble ideas and great projects, always, alas! deferred by the troubles of the times and the struggles that his minister Richelieu had to maintain against the great nobles of France. The King himself was of a feeble character; and died young and unhappy."

"I know it."

"He had been long anxious about having an heir; a care which weighs heavily on princes, who desire to leave behind them more than one pledge that their thoughts and works will be continued."

"Did the King, then, die childless?" asked the prisoner, smiling.

"No, but he was long without one, and for a long while thought he should be the last of his race. This idea had reduced him to the depths of despair, when suddenly, his wife, Anne of Austria——"

The prisoner trembled.

"Did you know," said Aramis, "that Louis XIII's wife was called Anne of Austria?"

"Continue," said the young man, without replying to the question.

"When suddenly," resumed Aramis, "the Queen announced an interesting event. There was great joy at the intelligence, and all prayed for her happy delivery. On the 5th of September, 1638, she gave birth to a son."

Here Aramis looked at his companion, and thought he observed him turning pale. "You are about to hear," said Aramis, "an account which few could now give; for it refers to a secret which they think buried with the dead or entombed in the abyss of the confessional."

"And you will tell me this secret?" broke in the youth.

"Oh!" said Aramis with unmistakable emphasis, "I do not know that I ought to risk this secret by entrusting it to one who has no desire to quit the Bastille."

"I hear you, monsieur."

"The Queen, then, gave birth to a son. But while the court was rejoicing over the event, when the King had shown the new-born child to the nobility and people and was sitting gaily down to table to celebrate the event, the Queen, who was alone in her room, was again taken ill, and gave birth to a second son."

"Oh!" said the prisoner, betraying a better acquaintance with the affair than he had owned to, "I thought that Monsieur was only born a——"

Aramis raised his finger: "Let me continue," he said.

The prisoner sighed impatiently, and paused.

"Yes," said Aramis, "the Queen had a second son, whom dame Perronnette, the midwife, received in her arms."

"Dame Perronnette!" murmured the young man.

"They ran at once to the banqueting-room, and whispered to the King what had happened; he rose and quitted the table. But this time it was no longer happiness that his face expressed, but something akin to terror. The birth of twins changed into bitterness the joy to which that of an only son had given rise, seeing that in France (a fact you are assuredly ignorant of) it is the oldest of the King's sons who succeeds his father."

"I know it."

"And that the doctors and jurists assert that there is ground for doubting whether he who first makes his appearance is the elder by the law of Heaven and of nature."

The prisoner uttered a smothered cry, and became whiter than the coverlet under which he hid himself.

"Now you understand," pursued Aramis, "that the King, who, with so much pleasure, saw himself repeated in one, was in despair about two; fearing that the second might dispute the first's claim to seniority, which had been recognised only two hours before; and so this second son, relying on party interests and caprices, might one day sow discord and engender civil war in the kingdom; by these means destroying the very dynasty he should have strengthened."

"Oh, I understand!—I understand!" murmured the young man.

"Well," continued Aramis; "this is what they relate, what they declare; this is why one of the Queen's two sons, shamefully parted from his brother, shamefully sequestered, is buried in the profoundest obscurity; this is why that second son has disappeared, and so completely, that not a soul in France, save his mother, is aware of his existence."

"Yes! his mother who has cast him off!" cried the prisoner in a tone of despair.

"Except, also," Aramis went on, "the lady in the black dress; and finally, excepting——"

"Excepting yourself—Is it not? You, who come and relate all this; you, who arouse in my soul curiosity, hatred, ambition, and, perhaps, even the thirst of vengeance; except you, monsieur, who if you are the man whom I expect, whom the note I have received applies to; whom, in short, Heaven ought to send me, must possess about you——"

"What?" asked Aramis.

"A portrait of the King, Louis XIV, who at this moment reigns upon the throne of France."

"Here is the portrait," replied the Bishop, handing the prisoner a miniature in enamel, on which Louis was depicted, life-like, with a handsome lofty mien. The prisoner eagerly seized the portrait, and gazed at it with devouring eyes.

"And now, monseigneur," said Aramis, "here is a mirror." Aramis left the prisoner time to recover his ideas.

"So high!—so high!" murmured the young man, eagerly comparing the likeness of Louis with his own countenance reflected in the glass.

"What do you think of it?" at length said Aramis.

"I think that I am lost," replied the captive; "the King will never set me free."

"Monseigneur," answered Aramis, with a respect he had not yet manifested, "the King, mark me, will, if you desire it, be he who, quitting his dungeon, shall maintain himself upon the throne, on which his friends will place him."

"Tempt me not, monsieur," broke in the prisoner bitterly.

"But I, monseigneur, wish you to be a king for the good of humanity."

"Ah!" said the Prince, with fresh distrust inspired by the word; "ah! with what then has humanity to reproach my brother?"

"I forgot to say, monseigneur, that if you would allow me to guide you, and if you consent to become the most powerful monarch on earth, you will have promoted the interests of all the friends whom I devote to the success of your cause, and these friends are numerous."

"Numerous?"

"Less numerous than powerful, monseigneur."

"Explain yourself."

"It is impossible; I will explain, I swear before Heaven, on that day that I see you sitting on the throne of France."

"But my brother?"

"You shall decree his fate. Do you pity him?"

"Him, who leaves me to perish in a dungeon? No, I pity him not."

"So much the better."

"And now, are you aware of one thing, monsieur?"

"Tell me, my Prince."

"It is that I will hear nothing further from you till I am clear of the Bastille."

"I was going to say to your Highness that I should only have the pleasure of seeing you once again."

"And when?"

"The day when my Prince leaves these gloomy walls."

"Heavens! how will you give me notice of it?"

"By myself coming to fetch you."

"Yourself?"

"My Prince, do not leave this chamber save with me, or if in my absence you are compelled to do so, remember that I am not concerned in it."

"And so I am not to speak a word of this to any one whatever, save to you."

"Save only to me." The Prince offered his hand to Aramis, who sank upon his knee and kissed it. "It is the first act of homage paid to our future King," said he. "When I see you again, I shall say, 'Good-day, sire.'"

"Till then," said the young man, pressing his wan and wasted fingers over his heart,—"till then, no more dreams, no more strain upon my life—it would break! Oh, monsieur, how small is my prison—how low the window—how narrow are the doors! To think that so much pride, splendour, and happiness, should be able to enter in and remain here!"

"Your Royal Highness makes me proud," said Aramis, "since you infer it is I who brought all this." And he rapped immediately on the door. The jailer came to open it with Baisemeaux, who, devoured by fear and uneasiness, was beginning, in spite of himself, to listen at the door. Happily, neither of the speakers had forgotten to smother his voice, even in the most passionate outbreaks.

"What a confessor!" said the governor, forcing a laugh; "who would believe that a mere recluse, a man almost dead, could have committed crimes so numerous, and so long to tell of?"

Aramis made no reply. He was eager to leave the Bastille, where the secret which overwhelmed him seemed to double the weight of the walls. As soon as they reached Baisemeaux's quarters, "Let us proceed to business, my dear governor," said Aramis.

"Alas!" replied Baisemeaux.

"You have to ask me for my receipt for one hundred and fifty thousand livres," said the Bishop.

"And to pay over the first third of the sum," added the poor governor, with a sigh, taking three steps towards his iron strong-box.

"Here is the receipt," said Aramis.

"And here is the money," returned Baisemeaux, with a threefold sigh.

"The order instructed me only to give a receipt; it said nothing about receiving the money," rejoined Aramis.

"Adieu, Monsieur le Gouverneur!"

And he departed, leaving Baisemeaux almost more than stifled with joy and surprise at this regal present so liberally bestowed by the confessor extraordinary to the Bastille.

CHAPTER XXII

WHO MESSIRE JEAN PERCERIN WAS

Since the departure of Athos for Blois, Porthos and d'Artagnan were seldom together. D'Artagnan, ever faithful, one morning thought about Porthos, and being uneasy at not having heard anything of him for a fortnight, directed his steps towards his hotel, and pounced upon him just as he was getting up. The worthy Baron had a pensive —nay, more than pensive—a melancholy air.

"But you seem in the dumps here?" exclaimed d'Artagnan.

Porthos replied by a look expressive of dejection. "Well, then, tell me all about it, Porthos, my friend, unless it is a secret."

"The fact is, I have received an invitation for the fête at Vaux," said Porthos, with a lugubrious expression.

"Well! do you complain of that? The King has caused a hundred mortal heartburnings among the courtiers by refusing invitations. And so, my dear friend, you are really going to Vaux?"

"Indeed I am!"

"You will see a magnificent sight."

"Alas! I doubt it, though."

"But what is it then?"

"'Tis that I have no clothes!"

D'Artagnan stood petrified. "No clothes, Porthos, no clothes!" he cried, "when I see at least fifty suits on the floor."

"Fifty, truly; but not one which fits me!"

"I understand your difficulty. You have how many new suits? nine? thirty-six? and yet not one to wear. Well, you must have a thirty-seventh made, and give the thirty-six to Mouston."

"Ah, monsieur!" said Mouston, with a gratified air. "The truth is that monsieur has always been very generous to me."

"Do you mean to think that I hadn't that idea, or that I was deterred by the expense? But it wants only two days to the fête: I received the invitation yesterday; made Mouston post hither with my wardrobe, and only this morning discovered my misfortune; and from now till the day after to-morrow there isn't a single fashionable tailor who will undertake to make me a suit."

"That is to say, one covered all over with gold, isn't it?"

"I wish it so! all over!"

"Oh, we shall manage it. You won't leave for three days. The invitations are for Wednesday, and this is only Sunday morning."

"'Tis true; but Aramis has strongly advised me to be at Vaux twenty-four hours beforehand."

"How, Aramis?"

"Yes, it was Aramis who brought me the invitation."

"Ah! to be sure. I see. You are invited on the part of M. Fouquet."

"By no means! by the King, dear friend. The letter bears the following as large as life: 'M. de Baron du Vallon is informed that the King has condescended to place him on the invitation list—"

"Very good; but you leave with M. Fouquet?"

"And when I think," cried Porthos, stamping on the floor, "when I think I shall have no clothes, I am ready to burst with rage! I should like to strangle somebody or destroy something."

"Neither strangle anybody nor destroy anything, Porthos; I will manage it all; put on one of your thirty-six suits and come with me to a tailor."

"Pooh! my agent has seen them all this morning."

"Even M. Percerin?"

"Who is M. Percerin?"

"Only the King's tailor!"

"Oh, ah, yes," said Porthos, who wished to appear to know the King's tailor, but now heard his name mentioned for the first time;—"to M. Percerin's, by Jove! I thought he would be too much engaged."

"Doubtless he will be; but be at ease, Porthos; he will do for me what he won't do for another. Only you must allow yourself to be measured."

"Ah!" said Porthos, with a sigh, "'tis vexatious, but what would you have me do?"

"Do? as the others do; as the King does."

"What! do they measure the King too? does *he* put up with it?"

"The King is a beau, my good friend, and so are you, too, whatever you may say about it."

Porthos smiled triumphantly. "Let us go to the King's tailor," he said; "and since he measures the King, I think, by my faith, I may well allow him to measure me."

The King's tailor, Messire Jean Percerin, occupied a rather large house in the Rue St. Honoré, near the Rue de l'Arbre Sec.

It was to the house of this great lord of tailors that d'Artagnan took the despairing Porthos.

They both alighted and made their way on foot towards the establishment. D'Artagnan, pushing on Porthos, succeeded in gaining the counter, behind which the journeymen tailors were doing their best to answer queries. The line of discontented lords formed a very remarkable picture. Our captain of musketeers, a man of sure and rapid observation, took it all in at a glance; but having run over the groups, his eye rested on a man in front of him.

"Well, my dear Monsieur Molière, but you will go and tell M. Percerin I am here."

"I!" exclaimed Molière, in the tone of a courageous dog, from which you snatch the bone it has legitimately gained; "I disturb myself! Ah! Monsieur d'Artagnan, how hard you are upon me!"

CHAPTER XXIII

THE PATTERNS

In about ten minutes Molière reappeared, making another sign to d'Artagnan from under the hangings. The latter hurried after him, with Porthos in the rear, and after threading a labyrinth of corridors, introduced him to M. Percerin's room. The old man, with his sleeves turned up, was gathering up in folds a piece of gold-flowered brocade, so as the better to exhibit its lustre. Perceiving d'Artagnan, he put the silk aside, and came to meet him, by no means radiant with joy, and by no means courteous, but take it altogether, in a tolerably civil manner.

"The captain of the musketeers will excuse me, I am sure, for I am engaged."

"Eh! yes, on the King's costumes; I know that, my dear Monsieur Percerin."

"Once made, they will be the most beautiful in the world, but that they may be the most beautiful in the world, they must first be made; and to do this, captain, I am pressed for time."

"My dear Percerin," said d'Artagnan, "you will make a dress for the Baron. 'Tis I who ask you."

"To you I will not say nay, captain."

"But that is not all; you will make it for him at once."

"'Tis impossible before eight days."

"By no means, dear Monsieur Percerin, above all if *I* ask you," said a mild voice at the door, a silvery voice which made d'Artagnan prick up his ears. It was the voice of Aramis.

"Monsieur d'Herblay!" cried the tailor.

"Aramis," murmured d'Artagnan.

"Ah! our Bishop," said Porthos.

"Good morning, d'Artagnan; good morning, Porthos; good morning, my dear friends," said Aramis. "Come, come, M. Percerin, make

the Baron's dress; and I will answer for it you will gratify M. Fouquet."
And he accompanied the words with a sign, which seemed to say,
"Agree, and dismiss them."

It appeared that Aramis had over Master Percerin an influence
superior even to d'Artagnan's, for the tailor bowed in assent, and
turning round upon Porthos, "Go and get measured on the other
side," said he rudely.

Porthos coloured in a formidable manner. D'Artagnan saw the
storm coming, and, addressing Molière, said to him in an undertone,
"You see before you, my dear monsieur, a man who considers himself
disgraced if you measure the flesh and bones that Heaven has given
him; study this type for me, Master Aristophanes, and profit by it."

Molière had no need of encouragement, and his gaze dwelt upon
the Baron Porthos. "Monsieur," he said, "if you will come with me, I will
make them take your measure without the measurer touching you."

"But how in the world can it be done?" asked Porthos, delighted.

"Monsieur," said Molière, bowing, "if you will deign to follow me,
you will see."

Aramis observed this scene with all his eyes. Perhaps he fancied
from d'Artagnan's liveliness that he would leave with Porthos, so as
not to lose the conclusion of a scene so well begun. But, clear-sighted
as he was, Aramis deceived himself. Porthos and Molière left together
alone. D'Artagnan remained with Percerin. Why? From curiosity,
doubtless; probably to enjoy a little longer the society of his good
friend Aramis. As Molière and Porthos disappeared, d'Artagnan drew
near the Bishop of Vannes, a proceeding which appeared particularly
to disconcert him.

"A dress for you also, is it not, my friend?"

Aramis smiled. "No," said he.

"Ah! you had something particular to say to M. Percerin? Why did
you not tell me so at once?"

"Something particular, certainly," repeated Aramis, "but not for
you, d'Artagnan. But, at the same time, I hope you will believe that
I can never have anything so particular to say that a friend like you
may not hear it."

"Oh, no, no! I am going," said d'Artagnan, imparting to his voice
an evident tone of curiosity; for Aramis's annoyance, well dissembled
as it was, had not a whit escaped him; and he knew that, in that impenetrable mind, everything, even the most apparently trivial, was
designed to some end; an unknown one; but one which, from the
knowledge he had of his friend's character, the musketeer felt must
be important.

On his part, Aramis saw that d'Artagnan was not without suspicion,
and pressed him. "Stay, by all means," he said, "this is what it is."
Then turning towards the tailor, "My dear Percerin," said he, "I am
even very happy that you are here, d'Artagnan."

"Oh, indeed," exclaimed the Gascon, for the third time, even less
deceived this time than before.

Percerin never moved. Aramis roused him violently by snatching
from his hands the stuff upon which he was engaged. "My dear

69

Percerin," said he, "I have near at hand, M. Lebrun, one of M. Fouquet's painters."

"Come in, M. Lebrun, come in," said Aramis.

"I' faith, I am quite in the dark," quoth Percerin.

"My dear M. Percerin," Aramis continued, "you are making fine dresses for the King, are you not? One in brocade, one in hunting-cloth, one in velvet, one in satin, and one in Florentine stuffs?"

"Yes; but how do you know all that, monseigneur?" said Percerin, astounded.

"It is all very simple, my dear monsieur; there will be a hunt, a banquet, concert, promenade, and reception. These five kinds of dress are required by etiquette."

"You know everything, monseigneur!"

"And a great many more things, too," murmured d'Artagnan.

"But," cried the tailor, in triumph, "what you do not know, monseigneur, is the colour of the materials, and the nature of the ornaments, and the cut, the *ensemble,* the finish of it all!"

"Well," said Aramis, "that is precisely what I have come to ask you, dear Percerin."

"Ah, bah!" exclaimed the tailor, terrified, though Aramis had pronounced these words in his sweetest and most honeyed voice.

"At the outset I appear to be hazarding an absurd question, do I not?" said Aramis. "But d'Artagnan, who is incarnate wisdom itself, will tell you that I could not do otherwise than ask you this."

"Let us see," said the attentive musketeer, perceiving with his wonderful instinct that they had only been skirmishing till now, and that the hour of battle was approaching.

"Let us see," said Percerin incredulously.

"Why, now," continued Aramis, "does M. Fouquet give the King a fête?—Is it not to please him?"

"Assuredly," said Percerin. D'Artagnan nodded assent.

"Well, then; this is the surprise we intend. M. Lebrun here is a man who draws most exactly."

"Yes," said Percerin; "I have seen his pictures, and observed that the dresses were highly elaborated. That is why I at once agreed to make him a costume—whether to agree with those of the Epicureans, or an original one."

"My dear monsieur, we accept your offer, and shall presently avail ourselves of it; but just now M. Lebrun is not in want of the dresses you will make for himself, but of those you are making for the King."

Percerin made a bound backwards, which d'Artagnan,—calmest and more appreciative of men—did not consider overdone; so many strange and startling aspects wore the proposal which Aramis had just hazarded. "The King's dresses! Give the King's dresses to any mortal whatever! Oh! for once, monseigneur, your grace is mad!" cried the poor tailor in extremity.

"Help me now, d'Artagnan," said Aramis, more and more calm and smiling. "Help me now to persuade monsieur, for *you* understand, do you not?"

"Eh! eh!—not exactly, I declare."

"What! you do not understand that M. Fouquet wishes to afford the King the surprise of finding his portrait on his arrival at Vaux; and that the portrait, which will be a striking resemblance, ought to be dressed exactly as the King will be on the day it is shown?"

"Oh! yes, yes;" said the musketeer, nearly convinced, so plausible was this reasoning. "Yes, my dear Aramis, you are right; it is a happy idea. I will wager it is one of your own, Aramis."

"Well, I don't know," replied the Bishop; "either mine, or M. Fouquet's." Then scanning Percerin, after noticing d'Artagnan's hesitation, "Well, monsieur Percerin," he asked, "what do you say to this?"

"I say that——"

"That you are doubtless free to refuse. I know well—and I by no means count upon compelling you, my dear monsieur. I will say more; I even understand all the delicacy you feel in taking up with M. Fouquet's idea; you dread appearing to flatter the King. A noble spirit, M. Percerin, a noble spirit!" The tailor stammered. "It would, indeed, be a very pretty compliment to pay the young prince," continued Aramis; "but as the Surintendant told me, 'If Percerin refuse, tell him that it will not at all lower him in my opinion, and I shall always esteem him, only——'"

"Only?" repeated Percerin, rather troubled.

"Only," continued Aramis, "'I shall be compelled to say to the King,'—you understand my dear Monsieur Percerin, that these are M. Fouquet's words—'I shall be constrained to say to the King, "Sire, I had intended to present your Majesty with your portrait, but owing to a feeling of delicacy, slightly exaggerated perhaps, although creditable, M. Percerin opposed the project."'"

"Opposed!" cried the poor tailor, terrified at the responsibility which would weigh upon him; "I to oppose the desire, the will of M. Fouquet when he is seeking to please the King! Oh, what a hateful word you have uttered, monseigneur. Oppose! Oh, 'tis not I who said it. Heaven have mercy on me. I call the captain of the musketeers to witness it! Is it not true, Monsieur d'Artagnan, that I have opposed nothing?"

D'Artagnan made a sign indicating that he wished to remain neutral.

But already Percerin, goaded by the idea that the King should be told he had stood in the way of a pleasant surprise, had offered Lebrun a chair, and proceeded to bring from a wardrobe four magnificent dresses, the fifth being still in the workmen's hands. The painter set to work to draw and then to paint the dresses. But Aramis, who was closely watching all the phases of his toil, suddenly stopped him.

"I think you have not quite got it, my dear Lebrun," he said; "your colours will deceive you, and on canvas we shall lack that exact resemblance which is absolutely requisite. Time is necessary for attentively observing the final shades."

"Quite true," said Percerin, "but time is wanting, and on that head, you will agree with me, monseigneur, I can do nothing."

"Then the affair will fail," said Aramis quietly, "and that because of a want of precision in the colours."

Nevertheless Lebrun went on copying the materials and ornaments with the closest fidelity—a process which Aramis watched with ill-concealed impatience.

"What in the world, now, is the meaning of this imbroglio?" the musketeer kept saying to himself.

"That will certainly never do," said Aramis; "M. Lebrun, close your box and roll up your canvas."

"But, monsieur," cried the vexed painter, "the light is abominable here."

"An idea, M. Lebrun, an idea! If we had a pattern of the materials, for example, and with time, and a better light——"

"Oh, then," cried Lebrun, "I would answer for the effect."

"Good!" said d'Artagnan, "this ought to be the knotty point of the whole thing; they want a pattern of each of the materials. *Mordieux!* will this Percerin give it now?"

Percerin, beaten in his last retreat, and duped, moreover, by the feigned good-nature of Aramis, cut out five patterns and handed them to the Bishop of Vannes.

Lebrun packed up, Percerin put back the dresses into the closet, Aramis put his hand on his pocket to assure himself the patterns were secure,—and they all left the study.

CHAPTER XXIV

ANOTHER SUPPER AT THE BASTILLE

The Bishop of Vannes, much annoyed at having met d'Artagnan at M. Percerin's, returned at Saint Mandé in no very good humour.

He went to exchange a parting word with the Surintendant. "Oh, everyone is laughing!" said Fouquet with a sigh.

"And do not you laugh, monseigneur?"

"My dear M. d'Herblay," answered Fouquet, "if I fall——"

"Well; if you fall?"

"I shall, at least, fall from such a height, that I shall shatter myself in falling." Then giving himself a shake as though to escape from himself, "Whence come you," said he, "my friend?"

"From Paris—from Percerin."

"And what have you been doing at Percerin's, for I suppose you attach no such great importance to our poets' dresses."

"No.—I went to prepare a surprise."

"Surprise!"

"Yes; which you are to give the King."

"And will it cost much?"

"Oh! a hundred pistoles you will give Lebrun."

"A painting?—Ah! all the better!"

Fouquet grasped his hand. "And where are you going?" he said.

"I am off to Paris, when you shall have given me a certain letter."

"For whom?"

"M. de Lyonne."

"And what do you want with Lyonne?"

"I wish to make him sign a *lettre de cachet.*"

"*Lettre de cachet!* Do you desire to put somebody in the Bastille?"

"On the contrary—to let somebody out."

"And who?"

"A poor devil—a youth, a lad who has been bastilled these ten years, for two Latin verses he made against the Jesuits."

"'Two Latin verses!' and for 'two Latin verses,' the miserable being has been in prison for ten years!"

"Yes."

"And has committed no other crime?"

"Beyond this he is as innocent as you or I."

"On your word?"

"On my honour."

"And his name is——?"

"Seldon."

"Yes.—But it is too bad. You knew this, and never told me!"

"'Twas only yesterday his mother applied to me, monseigneur."

"And the woman is poor."

"In the deepest misery."

"Oh! Heaven!" said Fouquet, "you sometimes bear with such unjustice on earth, that I understand why there are wretches who doubt in your existence. Stay, M. d'Herblay." And Fouquet, taking a pen, wrote a few rapid lines to his colleague Lyonne. Aramis took the letter and made ready to go.

"Wait," said Fouquet. He opened his drawer, and took out ten government notes which were there, each for a thousand francs. "Stay," he said; "set the son at liberty, and give this to the mother; but, above all, tell her not——"

"What, monseigneur?"

"That she is ten thousand livres richer than I. She would say, I am but a poor surintendant! Go! and I hope that God will bless those who are mindful of His poor!"

"So also do I hope," replied Aramis, kissing Fouquet's hand.

And he went out quickly, carrying off the letter for Lyonne and the notes for Seldon's mother.

Seven o'clock sounded from the great clock of the Bastille. It was the supper hour of the unfortunate captives.

Baisemeaux, seated at table, was rubbing his hands and looking at the Bishop of Vannes, who, booted like a cavalier, dressed in grey, and sword at side, kept talking of his hunger and testifying the liveliest impatience. M. de Baisemeaux de Montlezun was not accustomed to the unbending movements of his greatness, my Lord of Vannes, and this evening Aramis volunteered confidence on confidence.

"Bravo!" said Baisemeaux, and he poured out a great glass of wine and drank it off at a draught, trembling with joy at the idea of being, by hook or by crook, in the secret of some high archiepiscopal misdemeanour. While he was drinking he did not see with what attention Aramis was noting the sounds in the great court. A courier came in about eight o'clock as François brought in the fifth bottle, and, although the courier made a great noise, Baisemeaux heard nothing.

"The devil take him," said Aramis.

"What! who?" asked Baisemeaux. "I hope 'tis neither the wine you drink nor he who is the cause of your drinking it."

"No; it is a horse, who is making noise enough in the court for a whole squadron."

"Pooh! some courier or other," replied the governor, redoubling his numerous bumpers.

"You forget me, Baisemeaux! my glass is empty," said Aramis, showing his dazzling goblet.

"Upon honour, you delight me. François, wine!"

François re-entered; Baisemeaux took from his hands the courier's order. He slowly undid it, and as slowly read it. Aramis pretended to be drinking, so as to be able to watch his host through the glass. Then, Baisemeaux having read it: "What was I just saying?" he exclaimed.

"What is it?" asked the Bishop.

"An order of release! There, now; excellent news indeed to disturb us!"

"Excellent news for him whom it concerns, you will at least agree, my dear governor!"

Baisemeaux leaned back to ring for François, and by a very natural motion turned round towards the door. The order had remained on the table; Aramis seized the opportunity when Baisemeaux was not looking to change the paper for another, folded in the same manner, and which he took from his pocket. "François," said the governor, "let the major come up here with the turnkeys of the Bertaudière." François bowed and quitted the room, leaving the two companions alone.

CHAPTER XXV

THE GENERAL OF THE ORDER

"François, tell the major to go and open the cell of M. Seldon, No. 3, Bertaudière.

"Seldon!" exclaimed Aramis, very naturally. "You said Seldon, I think?"

"I said Seldon, of course. 'Tis the name of the man they set free."

"Oh! you meant to say Marchiali?" said Aramis.

"Marchiali? Oh, yes, indeed. No, no, Seldon."

"I think you are making a mistake, Monsieur Baisemeaux."

"I saw 'Seldon' in letters as large as that," and Baisemeaux held up his finger.

"And I read 'Marchiali' in characters as large as this," said Aramis, also holding up two fingers.

"To the proof; let us throw a light on the matter," said Baisemeaux, confident he was right. "There is the paper, you have only to read it."

"I read 'Marchiali,'" returned Aramis, spreading out the paper. "Look."

Baisemeaux looked, and his arms dropped suddenly.

"Yes, yes," he said, quite overwhelmed; "yes, Marchiali. 'Tis plainly written Marchiali! Quite true!"

"Ah!"

" 'Tis a wonder! I still see this order and the name of Seldon, Irishman. I see it. Ah! I even recollect that under this name there was a blot of ink."

"No, there is no ink; no, there is no blot."

"Oh! but there was, though; I know it, because I rubbed the powder that was over the blot."

"In a word, be it how it may, dear M. Baisemeaux," said Aramis, "and whatever you may have seen, the order is signed to release Marchiali, blot or no blot."

"Monseigneur," he said, "this Marchiali is the very same prisoner whom the other day a priest, confessor of *our order*, came to visit in so imperious and no secret a manner."

"I don't know that, monsieur," replied the Bishop.

" 'Tis no such long time ago, dear Monsieur d'Herblay."

"It is true. But *with us*, monsieur, it is good that the man of to-day should no longer know what the man of yesterday did."

"In any case," said Baisemeaux, "the visit of this Jesuit confessor must have given happiness to this man."

Aramis made no reply, but recommenced eating and drinking.

"Are you going to release Marchiali?" he said. "What mellow and fragrant sherry this is, my dear governor."

"Monseigneur," replied Baisemeaux, "I shall release the prisoner Marchiali when I have summoned the courier who brought the order, and above all, when, by interrogating him, I have satisfied myself."

"The order is sealed, and the courier is ignorant of the contents. What do you want to satisfy yourself about?"

"Be it so, monseigneur; but I shall send to the ministry, and M. de Lyonne will either confirm or withdraw the order."

"What is the good of all that?" asked Aramis coldly.

"What good?"

"Yes; what is your object, I ask."

"The object of never deceiving oneself, monseigneur, nor being wanting in the respect which a subaltern owes to his superior officers, nor infringing the duties of that service which one has voluntarily accepted."

"Very good; you have just spoken so eloquently that I cannot but admire you. It is true that a subaltern owes respect to his superiors; he is guilty when he deceives himself, and he should be punished if he infringe either the duties or laws of his office." Baisemeaux looked at the Bishop with astonishment.

"It follows," pursued Aramis, "that you are going to ask advice, to put your conscience at ease in the matter?"

"Yes, monseigneur."

"And if a superior officer gives you orders, you will obey?"

"Never doubt it, monseigneur."

"Well, Monsieur de Baisemeaux," said Aramis, bending an eagle glance on the governor, "I adopt so frankly your doubts, and your mode of clearing them up, that I will take a pen, if you will give me one."

Baisemeaux gave him a pen.

"And a sheet of white paper," added Aramis.

Baisemeaux handed some paper.

"Now, I—I, also—I, here present—incontestably, I—am going to write an order to which I am certain you will give credence, incredulous as you are!"

Aramis took a pen and wrote. Baisemeaux, in terror read over his shoulder.

"A.M.D.G." wrote the Bishop; and he drew a cross under these four letters, which signify *ad majorem, Dei gloriam,* "to the greater glory of God"; and thus he continued, "It is our pleasure that the order brought to M. de Baisemeaux de Montlezun, governor, for the King, of the Castle of the Bastille, be held good and effectual, and be immediately carried into operation.

(Signed) D'Herblay,

"General of the Order, by the grace of God."

Baisemeaux was so profoundly astonished, that his features remained contracted, his lips parted, and his eyes fixed. He did not move an inch, nor articulate a sound.

"Come, come," said Aramis, after a long silence, during which the governor of the Bastille had slowly recovered his senses, "do not lead me to believe, dear Baisemeaux, that the presence of the General of the Order is as terrible as His, and that men die merely from having seen Him. Take courage; rouse yourself; give me your hand, and obey."

Baisemeaux, reassured, if not satisfied, obeyed, kissed Aramis's hand, and rose. "Immediately?" he murmured.

"Oh, there is no pressing haste, my host; take your place again and do the honours over this beautiful dessert."

"Monseigneur, I shall never recover such a shock as this; I who have laughed, who have jested with you! I who have dared to treat you on a footing of equality!"

"Say nothing about it, old comrade," replied the Bishop who perceived how strained the cord was, and how dangerous it would have been to break it.

Baisemeaux reflected; he perceived, at a glance, the consequences of this withdrawal of a prisoner by means of a forged order; and, putting in the scale the guarantee offered him by the official order of the General, did not consider it of any value.

Aramis divined this. "My dear Baisemeaux," said he, "you are a simpleton. Lose this habit of reflection when I give myself the trouble to think of you."

And at another gesture he made, Baisemeaux bowed again. "How shall I set about it?" he said.

"What is the process for releasing a prisoner?"

"I have the regulations."

"Well, then, follow the regulations, my friend."

Baisemeaux obeyed. He summoned his lieutenant, and gave him an order.

Half an hour afterwards they heard a gate shut in the court; it was the door to the dungeon, which had just rendered up its prey to the free air. Aramis blew out all the candles which lighted the room but one, which he left burning behind the door. Steps drew near.

"Go and meet your men," said Aramis to Baisemeaux.

The governor obeyed. The sergeant and turnkeys disappeared. Baisemeaux re-entered, followed by a prisoner. Aramis had placed himself in the shade; he saw without being seen. Baisemeaux, in an agitated tone of voice, made the young man acquainted with the order which set him at liberty. The prisoner listened without making a single gesture, or saying a word.

"You will swear ('tis the regulation that requires it)" added the governor, "never to reveal anything that you have seen or heard in the Bastille."

The prisoner perceived a crucifix; he stretched out his hands, and swore with his lips. "And now, monsieur, you are free; whither do you intend going?"

The prisoner turned his head, as if looking behind him for some protection, on which he ought to rely. Then was it that Aramis came out of the shade: "I am here," he said, "to render the gentleman whatever service he may please to ask."

The prisoner slightly reddened, and without hesitation passed his arm through that of Aramis. "God have you in his holy keeping," he said, in a voice of firmness of which made the governor tremble as much as the form of the blessing astonished him.

"Adieu, Baisemeaux," said Aramis.

The horses were in waiting, making the carriage shake again with their impatience. Baisemeaux accompanied the Bishop to the bottom of the steps. Aramis caused his companion to mount before him, then followed, and without giving the driver any further order, "Go on," said he. The carriage rattled over the pavement of the courtyard. An officer with a torch went before the horses, and gave orders at every post to let them pass. During the time taken in opening all the barriers, Aramis barely breathed, and you might have heard his "sealed heart knock against his ribs." The prisoner, buried in a corner of the carriage, made no more sign of life than his companion. At length a jolt more severe than the others announced to them that they had cleared the last watercourse. Behind the carriage closed the last gate, that in the Rue St. Antoine. No more walls either on the right or left; heaven everywhere, liberty everywhere, and life everywhere. The horses, kept in check by a vigorous hand, went quietly as far as the middle of the faubourg. There they began to trot. Little by little, whether they warmed over it, or whether they were urged, they gained in swiftness, and once past Bercy, the carriage seemed to fly, so great was the ardour of the coursers. These horses ran thus as far as Villeneuve St. Georges, where relays were waiting. Then four instead of two whirled the carriage away in the direction of Mélun, and pulled up for a moment in the middle of the forest of Senarl. No doubt, the order had been given the postilion beforehand, for Aramis had no occasion even to make a sign.

"What is the matter?" asked the prisoner, as if waking from a long dream.

"The matter is, monseigneur," said Aramis, "that before going further, it is necessary your Royal Highness and I should converse."

"I will wait an opportunity, monsieur," answered the young Prince.

"We could not have a better, monseigneur; we are in the middle of a forest, and no one can hear us."

"The postilion?"

"The postilion of this relay is deaf and dumb, monseigneur."

"I am at your service, M. d'Herblay."

"Is it your pleasure to remain in the carriage?"

"Yes, we are comfortably seated, and I like this carriage, for it has restored me to liberty."

"Wait, monseigneur; there is yet a precaution to be taken."

"What?"

"We are here on the highway; cavaliers or carriages travelling like ourselves might pass, and seeing us stopping deem us in some difficulty. Let us avoid offers of assistance which would embarrass us."

"Give the position orders to conceal the carriage in one of the side avenues."

"'Tis exactly what I wished to do, monseigneur."

Aramis made a sign to the deaf and dumb driver of the carriage, whom he touched on the arm. The latter dismounted, took the leaders by the bridle, and led them over the velvet sward and the mossy grass of a winding alley, at the bottom of which, on this moonless night the deep shades formed a curtain blacker than ink. This done, the man lay down on a slope near his horses, who, on either side, kept nibbling the young oak shoots.

"I am listening," said the young Prince to Aramis; "but what are you doing there?"

"I am disarming myself of my pistols, of which we have no further need, monseigneur."

CHAPTER XXVI

CROWN AND TIARA

Black was the darkness which fell wide and dense from the summits of the intertwining trees. The carriage, covered in by this vast roof, would not have received a particle of light, not even if a ray could have struggled through the wreaths of mist which were rising in the avenue of the wood.

"Monseigneur," resumed Aramis, "you know the history of the government which to-day controls France. The King issued from an infancy imprisoned like yours, obscure as yours, and confined as yours; only, instead of ending, like yourself, this slavery in a prison—this obscurity in solitude—these straitened circumstances in concealment, he was fain to bear all these miseries, humiliations, and distresses, in full daylight, under the pitiless sun of royalty; or an elevation so flooded with light, where every stain appears a miserable blemish and every glory a stain. The King has suffered; it rankles in his mind;

and he will avenge himself. He will be a bad king. I say not that he will pour out blood, like Louis XI or Charles IX, for he has no mortal injuries to avenge; but he will devour the means and substance of his people; for he has himself undergone wrongs in his own interest and money. In the first place, then, I quite acquit my conscience when I consider openly the merits and faults of this Prince; and if I condemn him, my conscience absolves me."

Aramis paused. It was not to listen if the silence of the forest remained undisturbed, but it was to gather up his thoughts from the very bottom of his soul—to leave the thoughts he had uttered sufficient time to eat deeply into the mind of his companion.

"You are the son of King Louis XIII, brother of Louis XIV, natural and legitimate heir to the throne of France. In keeping you near him, as Monsieur has been kept—Monsieur, your younger brother—the King reserved to himself the right of being legitimate sovereign. The doctors only could dispute his legitimacy. But the doctors always prefer the King who is to the king who is not. Providence has willed that you should be persecuted; and this persecution to-day consecrates you King of France. Now see, then, what this Providence, which you have so often accused of having in every way thwarted you, has done for you. It has given you the features, figure, age, and voice of your brother; and the very causes of your persecution are about to become those of your triumphant restoration. To-morrow, after to-morrow—from the very first, regal phantom, living shade of Louis XIV, you will sit upon his throne, whence the will of Heaven, confided in execution to the arm of man, will have hurled him, without hope of return."

"I understand," said the Prince, "my brother's blood will not be shed, then."

"You will be sole arbiter of his fate."

"The secret of which they made an evil use against me?"

"You will employ it against him. What did he do to conceal it? He concealed you. Living image of himself, you will defeat the conspiracy of Mazarin and Anne of Austria. You, my Prince, will have the same interest in concealing him, who will, as a prisoner, resemble you, as you will resemble him as king."

"I wish to discuss a point with you; the conditions you intend imposing upon me. It is your turn to speak, M. d'Herblay."

"The conditions, monseigneur?"

"Doubtless. You will not allow so mere a trifle to stop me, and you will not do me the injustice to suppose that I think you have no interest in this affair. Therefore, without subterfuge of hesitation, tell me the truth?"

"When I shall have asked your Highness a question."

"Do so."

"I sent to your Highness a man in my confidence, with instructions to deliver some closely-written notes carefully drawn up, which will thoroughly acquaint your Highness with the different persons who compose and will compose your court."

"I perused all the notes."

"Attentively?"

"Interrogate me, then, and I will be a scholar repeating his lesson to his master."

"We will begin with your family, monseigneur."

"My mother, Anne of Austria! all her sorrows, her painful malady. Oh! I know her — I know her."

"Your second brother?" asked Aramis, bowing.

"To these notes," replied the Prince, "you have added portraits so faithfully painted that I am able to recognise the persons, whose characters, manners, and history, you have so carefully portrayed. Monsieur, my brother is a fine, dark young man, with a pale face; he does not love his wife, Henrietta, whom I, Louis XIV, loved a little, and still flirt with, even although she made me weep on the day she wished to dismiss Mademoiselle de la Vallière from her service in disgrace."

"You will have to be careful with regard to watchfulness of the latter," said Aramis; "she is sincerely attached to the actual King. The eyes of a woman who loves are not easily deceived."

"She is fair, has blue eyes, whose affectionate gaze will reveal her identity. She halts slightly in her gait; she writes a letter every day, to which I shall have to send an answer by M. de Saint-Aignan."

"Do you know the latter?"

"As if I saw him, and I know the last verses he composed for me, as well as those I composed in answer to his."

"Very good. Do you know your ministers?"

"Colbert, an ugly, dark-browed man, but intelligent enough; his hair covering his forehead; a large, heavy, full head; the mortal enemy of M. Fouquet."

"As for the latter, we need not disturb ourselves about him."

"No; because necessarily you will require me to exile him, I suppose?"

Aramis, struck with admiration at the remark, said, "You will become very great, monseigneur."

"You see," sdded the Prince, "that I know my lesson by heart, and with Heaven's assistance, and yours afterwards, I shall seldom go wrong. Well, then, now for M. Fouquet. What do you wish me to do for him?"

"To continue him as Surintendant, as he has hitherto acted, I entreat you."

"Be it so; but he is the first minister at present."

"Not quite so."

"A King, ignorant and embarrassed as I shall be, will, as a matter of course, require a first minister of state."

"Your Majesty will require a friend."

"I have only one, and that is yourself."

"You will have many others by-and-by, but none so devoted, none so zealous for your glory."

"You will be my first minister of state."

"Not immediately, monseigneur; for that would give rise to too much suspicion and astonishment."

"You shall be nominated before two months are past, Monsieur d'Herblay. But that is a matter of very trifling moment; you would not offend me if you were to ask more than that, and you would cause me serious regret if you were to limit yourself to that."

"In that case I have something still further to hope for, monseigneur."

"Speak! speak!"

"You will not be a King such as your father was; delicate in health, slow in judgment, whom all things wearied; you will be a king governing by your brain and by your sword; you will have in the government of the state no more than you could manage unaided; I should only interfere with you. Besides, our friendship ought never to be, I do not say impaired, but in any way affected, by a secret thought. I shall have given you the throne of France, you will confer on me the throne of St. Peter. Whenever your loyal, firm, and mailed hand shall have joined in ties of intimate association the hand of a pope such as I shall be, neither Charles the Fifth, who owned two-thirds of the habitable globe, nor Charlemagne, who possessed it entirely, will be able to reach to half your stature. I have no alliances, I have no predilections; I will not throw you into persecutions of heretics, nor will I cast you into the troubled waters of family dissension. I will simply say to you: The whole universe is our own; for me the minds of men, for you their bodies. And as I shall be the first to die, you will have my inheritance. What do you say of my plan, monseigneur?"

"I say that you render me happy and proud, for no other reason than that of having comprehended you thoroughly. Monsieur d'Herblay, you shall be Cardinal, and when Cardinal, my Prime Minister; and then you shall point out to me the necessary steps to be taken to secure your election as Pope, and I will take them. You can ask what guarantees from me you please."

"It is useless. I shall never act except in such a manner that you are the gainer; I shall never ascend the ladder of fortune, fame, or position, until I shall have first seen you placed upon the round of the ladder immediately above me; I shall always hold myself sufficiently aloof from you to escape incurring your jealousy, sufficiently near to sustain your personal advantage and to watch over your friendship."

"I believe it. There is my hand on it, Monsieur d'Herblay."

"Allow me to kneel before you, sire, most respectfully. We will embrace each other on the day we shall both have on our temples, you the crown, and I the tiara."

"Still embrace me this very day also, and be, for and towards me, more than great, more than skilful, more than sublime in genius; be kind and indulgent—be my father."

Aramis was almost overcome as he listened to his voice; he fancied he detected in his own heart an emotion hitherto unknown to him; but this impression was speedily removed. "His father!" he thought; "yes, his Holy Father."

And they resumed their places in the carriage, which sped rapidly along the road leading to Vaux-le-Vicomte.

CHAPTER XXVII

CHÂTEAU DE VAUX-LE-VICOMTE

The château of Vaux-le-Vicomte, situated about a league from Mélun, had been built by Fouquet in 1655, at a time when there was a scarcity of money in France; Mazarin had taken all that there was, and Fouquet expended the remainder. If the Château de Vaux possessed a single fault with which it could be reproached, it was its grand, portentous character.

With a perfect reliance that Aramis had made arrangements fairly to distribute the vast number of guests throughout the palace, and that he had not omitted to attend to any of the internal regulations for their comfort, Fouquet devoted his entire attention to the *ensemble* alone; in one direction Gourville showed him the preparations which had been made for the fireworks; in another, Molière led him over the theatre; at last, after he had visited the chapel, the *salons*, and the galleries, and was again going downstairs, exhausted with fatigue, Fouquet saw Aramis on the staircase. The prelate beckoned to him. The Surintendant joined his friend, and, with him, paused before a large picture scarcely finished. Applying himself heart and soul to his work, the painter, Lebrun, covered with perspiration, stained with paints, pale from fatigue and inspiration of genius, was putting the last finishing touches with his rapid brush. It was the portrait of the King, whom they were expecting, dressed in the court-suit which Percerin had condescended to show beforehand to the Bishop of Vannes.

In the direction of Mélun, in the still empty, open plain, the sentinels of Vaux had perceived the advancing procession of the King and the Queens. Her Majesty was entering into Mélun, with her long train of carriages and cavaliers.

"In an hour — " said Aramis to Fouquet.

"In an hour!" replied the latter, sighing.

"And the people who ask one another what is the good of these royal fêtes!" continued the Bishop of Vannes, laughing, with his false smile.

"Where are you going?" returned Fouquet, with a gloomy look.

"To my own apartment, in order to change my costume, monseigneur."

"Whereabouts are you lodging, d'Herblay?"

"In the blue room on the second story."

"The room immediately over the King's room?"

"Precisely."

"You will be subject to very great restraint there. What an idea to condemn yourself to a room where you cannot stir or move about."

"During the night, monseigneur, I sleep or read in my bed."

"And your servants?"

"I have only one person with me. I find my reader quite sufficient. Adieu, monseigneur; do not over-fatigue yourself; keep yourself fresh for the arrival of the King."

CHAPTER XXVIII

NECTAR AND AMBROSIA

M. Fouquet held the stirrup of the King, who, having dismounted, bowed most graciously, and more graciously still held out his hand to him, which Fouquet, in spite of a slight resistance on the King's part, carried respectfully to his lips. The King wished to wait in the first courtyard for the arrival of the carriages, nor had he long to wait, for the roads had been put into excellent order by the Surintendant, and a stone would hardly have been found of the size of an egg the whole way from Mélun to Vaux; so that the carriages, rolling along as though on a carpet, brought the ladies to Vaux, without jolting or fatigue, by eight o'clock. They were received by Madame Fouquet, and at the moment they made their appearance, a light as bright as day burst forth from all the trees, and vases, and marble statues. This species of enchantment lasted until their Majesties had retired into the palace.

As for the King, his eyes filled with tears; he dared not look at the Queen. Anne of Austria, whose pride, as it ever had been, was superior to that of any creature breathing, overwhelmed her host by the contempt with which she treated everything handed to her. The young Queen, kind-hearted by nature and curious by disposition, praised Fouquet, ate with an exceedingly good appetite, and asked the names of the different fruits which were placed upon the table.

The King had expressly declared that so long as he remained under M. Fouquet's roof he did not wish his own different repasts to be served in accordance with the usual etiquette, and that he would, consequently, dine with the rest of the society; but, by the thoughtful attention of the Surintendant, the King's dinner was served up separately, if one may so express it, in the middle of the general table; the dinner, wonderful in every respect, from the dishes of which it was composed, comprised everything the King liked, and which he generally preferred to anything else.

When the supper was finished, the King expressed a wish not to lose the promenade. The park was illuminated; the moon, too, as if she had placed herself at the orders of the lord of Vaux, silvered the trees and lakes with her bright phosphoric light. The air was soft and balmy; the gravelled walks through the thickly set avenues yielded luxuriously to the feet. The fête was complete in every respect, for the King, having met La Vallière in one of the winding paths of the wood, was able to press her by the hand and say, "I love you," without anyone overhearing him, except d'Artagnan, who followed him, and M. Fouquet who preceded him.

The night of magical enchantments stole on. The King having requested to be shown his room, there was immediately a movement in every direction. The Queens passed to their own apartments, accompanied by the music of theorbos and lutes; the King found his musketeers awaiting him on the grand flight of steps, for M. Fouquet had brought them on from Mélun, and had invited them to supper. D'Artagnan's suspicions at once disappeared. He was weary, he had supped well, and wished, for once in his life, thoroughly to enjoy a fête given by a man who was in every sense of the word a king. "M. Fouquet," he said, "is the man for me."

The King was conducted with the greatest ceremony to the chamber of Morpheus, of which we owe some slight description to our readers. It was the handsomest and the largest in the palace. Lebrun had painted on the vaulted ceiling the happy, as well as disagreeable dreams with which Morpheus affects kings as well as other men. Everything that sleep gives birth to that is lovely, its perfumes, its flowers, and nectar, the wild voluptuousness or deep repose of the senses, had the painter enriched with his frescoes. It was a composition as soft and pleasing in one part as dark and gloomy and terrible in another. The poisoned chalice, the glittering dagger suspended over the head of the sleeper; wizards and phantoms with hideous masks, those half-dim shadows more terrific than the brightness of flame or the blackness of night; these, and such as these, he had made the companions of his more pleasing pictures. No sooner had the King entered the room than a cold shiver seemed to pass through him, and on Fouquet asking him the cause of it, the King replied, as pale as death,—

"I am sleepy, that is all."

"Does your Majesty wish for your attendants at once?"

"No; I have to talk with a few persons first," said the King. "Will you have the goodness to tell M. Colbert I wish to see him." Fouquet bowed and left the room.

CHAPTER XXIX

A GASCON, AND A GASCON AND A HALF

D'Artagnan had determined to lose no time, and in fact he never was in the habit of doing so. After having inquired for Aramis, he had looked for him in every direction until he had succeeded in finding him. Besides, no sooner had the King entered into Vaux, than Aramis had retired to his own room, meditating doubtlessly some new piece of gallant attention for His Majesty's amusement. D'Artagnan desired the servants to announce him, and found on the second story (in a beautiful room called the Blue Room, on account of the colour of its hangings) the Bishop of Vannes in company with Porthos and several of the modern epicureans. Aramis came forward to embrace his friend, and offered him the best seat. As it was after awhile generally remarked among those present that the musketeer was reserved, and wished for an opportunity for conversing secretly with Aramis, the epicureans took their leave. Porthos, however, did not stir; for true it is that having dined exceedingly well, he was fast asleep in his arm-chair; and the freedom of conversation therefore was not interrupted by a third person. Porthos had a deep, harmonious snore, and people might talk in the midst of its loud bass without fear of disturbing him. D'Artagnan felt that he was called upon to open the conversation.

"Well, and so we have come to Vaux," he said.

"I am told that the King began by showing a great distance in his manner towards M. Fouquet, but that His Majesty became much more cordial afterwards."

"You did not notice it, then, since you say you have been told so?"

"No; I was engaged with those gentlemen who have just left the room about the theatrical performances and the tournament which are to take place to-morrow."

"Ah, indeed! you are the comptroller-general of the fêtes here, then?"

"You know I am a friend of all kinds of amusement where the exercise of the imagination is required; I have always been a poet in one way or another."

"Do you know what idea occurred to me this evening, Aramis?"

"No; tell me what it was, for I should never be able to guess it."

"Well, the idea occurred to me that the true King of France is not Louis XIV."

"What!" said Aramis involuntarily, looking the musketeer full in the eyes.

"No, it is Monsieur Fouquet."

Aramis breathed again, and smiled. "Ah! you are like all the rest, jealous," he said. "I would wager that it was M. Colbert who turned that pretty phrase. He comes of a mean race, does Colbert."

"Quite true."

"When I think, too," added the Bishop, "that that fellow will be your minister within four months, and that you will serve him as blindly as you did Richelieu or Mazarin——"

"And as you serve M. Fouquet," said d'Artagnan.

"With this difference, though, that M. Fouquet is not M. Colbert."

"True, true," said d'Artagnan, as he pretended to become sad and full of reflection; and then, a moment after, he added, "Why do you tell me that M. Colbert will be minister in four months?"

"Because M. Fouquet will have ceased to be so," replied Aramis.

"He will be ruined, you mean?" said d'Artagnan.

"Completely so."

"Why does he give these fêtes, then?" said the musketeer, in a tone so full of thoughtful consideration, and so well assumed, that the Bishop was for a moment deceived by it. "Why did you not dissuade him from it?"

The latter part of the phrase was just a little too much, and Aramis's former suspicions were again aroused. "It is done with the object of humouring the King."

"By ruining himself?"

"Yes, by ruining himself for the King."

"A singular calculation that."

"Necessity."

"I don't see that, dear Aramis."

"Do you not? Have you not remarked M. Colbert's daily increasing antagonism, and that he is doing his utmost to drive the King to get rid of the Surintendant?"

"One must be blind not to see it."

"And that a cabal is formed against M. Fouquet?"

"That is well known."

"What likelihood is there that the King would join a party formed against a man who will have spent everything he had to please him?"

"True, true," said d'Artagnan slowly, hardly convinced, yet curious to broach another phase of the conversation. "There are follies and follies," he resumed, "and I do not like those you are committing."

"What do you allude to?"

D'Artagnan went up to his friend, took hold of both his hands, and looking him full in the eyes, said, "Aramis, do you still care for me a very little?"

"What a question to ask!"

"Very good. One favour then. Why did you take some patterns of the King's costumes at Percerin's?"

"Come with me and ask poor Lebrun, who has been working upon them for the last two days and two nights."

"Aramis, that may be the truth for anybody else, but for me——"

"Upon my word, d'Artagnan, you astonish me!"

"Be a little considerate for me. Tell me the exact truth; you would not like anything disagreeable to happen to me, would you?"

"My dear friend, you are becoming quite incomprehensible. What suspicion can you possibly have got hold of?"

"Do you believe in my instinctive feelings? Formerly, you used to have faith in them. Well then, an instinct tells me that you have some concealed project on foot."

"I—a project!"

"I am convinced of it."

"I am undertaking nothing," said Aramis.

"Aramis, a voice speaks within me, and seems to enlighten my darkness, it is a voice which has never yet deceived me. It is the King you are conspiring against."

"The King?" exclaimed the Bishop, pretending to be annoyed.

"Your face will not convince me; the King, I repeat."

"You to suspect me of wishing to assassinate the King!"

"Who spoke of that at all?" said the musketeer.

"Well, let us understand each other. I do not see what any one can do to a legitimate King as ours is, if he does not assassinate him." D'Artagnan did not say a word. "Besides, you have your guards and your musketeers here," said the Bishop.

"True."

"You are not in M. Fouquet's house, but in your own."

"True; but in spite of that, Aramis, grant me, for pity's sake, but one single word of a true friend."

"A friend's word is the truth itself. If I think of touching, even with my finger, the son of Anne of Austria, the true King of this realm of France—if I have not the firm intention of prostrating myself before his throne—if in every idea I may entertain to-morrow here at Vaux will not be the most glorious day my King enjoyed—may Heaven's lightning blast me where I stand!" The earnestness of his words, the studied slowness with which he pronounced them, the solemnity of his oath, gave the musketeer the most complete satisfaction. He took hold of both Aramis's hands, and shook them cordially. Aramis had endured reproaches without turning pale, and had blushed as he listened to words of praise. D'Artagnan, deceived, did him honour; but d'Artagnan, trustful and reliant, made him feel ashamed. "Are you going away?" he said as he embraced him, in order to conceal the flush on his face.

"Yes; my duty summons me. I have to get the watchword. It seems I am to be lodged in the King's ante-room. Where does Porthos sleep?"

"Take him away with you, if you like, for he snores like a park of artillery."

"Ah! he does not stay with you, then?" said d'Artagnan.

"Not the least in the world. He has his room to himself, but I don't know where!"

"Very good!" said the musketeer, from whom this separation of the two associates removed his last suspicion, and he touched Porthos lightly on the shoulder. The latter replied by a terrible yawn. "Come," said d'Artagnan.

"What, d'Artagnan, my dear fellow, is that you? What a lucky chance! Oh, yes—true; I had forgotten; I am at the fêtes at Vaux."

"Hush!" said Aramis. "You are walking so heavily, you will make the flooring give way."

"True," said the musketeer; "this room is above the dome, I think."

"And I did not choose it for a fencing-room, I assure you," added the Bishop. "The ceiling of the King's room has all the sweetness and calm delights of sleep. Do not forget, therefore, that my flooring is merely the covering of his ceiling. Good-night, my friends, and in ten minutes I shall be fast asleep." And Aramis accompanied them to the door, laughing quietly all the while. As soon as they were outside, he bolted the door hurriedly; closed up the chinks of the windows, and then called out, "Monseigneur!—monseigneur!" Philippe made his appearance from the alcove, as he pushed aside a sliding panel placed behind the bed.

"What are we to do, now?"

"You will go and take up your post at our place of observation, and watch the moment of the King's retiring to rest, so as to learn how that ceremony is performed."

"Very good. Where shall I place myself?"

"Sit down on this folding-chair. I am going to push aside a portion of the flooring; you will look through the opening, which answers to one of the false windows made in the dome of the King's apartment. Can you see?"

"Yes," said Philippe, starting as at the sight of an enemy, "I see the King!"

"What is he doing?"

"He seems to wish some man to sit down close to him."

"M. Fouquet?"

"No, no; wait a moment——"

"Look at the notes and portraits, my Prince."

"The man whom the King wishes to sit down in his presence is M. Colbert."

We have seen that Louis XIV had sent for Colbert and that Colbert had arrived. The conversation began between them by the King according to him one of the highest favours that he had ever done; it was true the King was alone with his subject. "Colbert," said he, "sit down."

The intendant, overcome with delight, for he feared he should be dismissed, refused the unprecedented honour.

"Does he accept?" said Aramis.

"No, he remains standing."

"Let us listen then." And the future King and the future Pope listened eagerly to the simple mortals whom they held under their feet, ready to crush them if they had liked.

"Colbert," said the King, "you have annoyed me exceedingly to-day."

"I know it, sire."

"Very good; I like that answer. Yes, you knew it, and there was courage in having done it."

"I ran the risk of displeasing your Majesty, but I risked also concealing what were your true interests from you."

"What! you were afraid of something on my account?"

"I was, sire, even if it were of nothing more than an indigestion," said Colbert; "for people do not give their sovereigns such banquets as the one of to-day, except it be to stifle them under the weight of good living." Colbert waited the effect which this coarse jest would produce upon the King; and Louis XIV, who was the vainest and most fastidiously delicate man in his kingdom, forgave Colbert the joke.

"The truth is," he said, "that M. Fouquet has given me too good a meal. Tell me, Colbert, where does he get all the money required for this enormous expenditure,—can you tell?"

"Yes, I do know, sire."

"M. Fouquet, therefore, is rich—very rich, and I suppose every man knows he is so."

"Every one, sire—the living as well as the dead."

"What does that mean, Monsieur Colbert?"

"The living are witnesses of M. Fouquet's wealth,—they admire and applaud the result produced; but the dead, wiser and better informed than we are, know how that wealth was obtained—and they rise up in accusation."

"If the dead therefore were to speak——"

"They do speak sometimes, sire—read."

"Ah!" murmured Aramis, in the Prince's ear, who, close beside him, listened without losing a syllable, "since you are placed here, monseigneur, in order to learn your vocation of a king, listen to a piece of infamy of a nature truly royal. You are about to be a witness of one of those scenes which the foul fiend alone can conceive and execute. Listen attentively; you will find your advantage in it."

The Prince redoubled his attention, and saw Louis XIV take from Colbert's hand a letter which the latter held out to him.

"The late Cardinal's handwriting," said the King.

"Your Majesty has an excellent memory," replied Colbert, bowing; "it is an immense advantage for a King who is destined for hard work to recognise handwritings at the first glance."

The King read Mazarin's letter, and, as its contents are already known to the reader, in consequence of the misunderstanding between Madame de Chevreuse and Aramis, nothing further would be learned if we stated them here again.

"I do not quite understand," said the King, greatly interested.

"Your Majesty has not yet acquired the habit of going through the public accounts."

"I see that it refers to money which had been given to M. Fouquet."

"Thirteen millions. A tolerably good sum."

"You say that these thirteen millions are found to be wanting in the accounts?"

"I do not say so, but the registry does."

"And this letter of M. Mazarin indicates the employment of the sum, and the name of the person with whom it was deposited?"

"As your Majesty can judge for yourself."

"Yes; and the result is, then, that M. Fouquet has not yet restored the thirteen millions."

"That results from the accounts, certainly, sire."

"Well, and consequently —— "

"Well, sire, in that case, inasmuch as M. Fouquet has not yet given back the thirteen millions, he must have appropriated them to his own purposes; and with those thirteen millions one could incur four times and a little more as much expense, and make four times as great a display, as your Majesty was able to do at Fontainebleau, where we only spent three millions altogether, if you remember."

"Are you aware what is the natural consequence of all this, Monsieur Colbert?" said the King, after a few minutes' reflection.

"No, sire, I do not know."

"Well, then, the fact of the appropriation of the thirteen millions, if it can be proved —— "

"But it is so already."

"I mean, if it were to be declared and certified, Monsieur Colbert."

"I think it will be to-morrow, if your Majesty —— "

"Were we not under M. Fouquet's roof, you were going to say, perhaps," replied the King, with something of nobleness in his manner.

"The King is in his own palace wherever he may be, and especially in houses which his own money has paid for."

Louis XIV at last raised his eyes, and finding Colbert attentively waiting for his next remark, said, hastily changing the conversation, "Monsieur Colbert, I perceive it is getting very late, and I shall now retire to bed. By to-morrow morning I shall have made up my mind."

"Very good sire," returned Colbert, greatly incensed, although he restrained himself in the presence of the King.

The King made a gesture of adieu, and Colbert withdrew with a respectful bow. "My attendants," cried the King; and, as they entered the apartment, Philippe was about to quit his post of observation.

"A moment longer," said Aramis to him, with his accustomed

gentleness of manner; "what has just now taken place is only a detail, and to-morrow we shall have no occasion to think anything more about it; but the ceremony of the King's retiring to rest, the etiquette observed in addressing the King, that indeed is of the greatest importance. Learn, sire, and study well how you ought to go to bed of a night. Look! look!"

CHAPTER XXX

COLBERT

History will tell us, or rather history has told us, of the various events of the following day, of the splendid fêtes given by the Surintendant to his sovereign. There was nothing but amusement and delight allowed to prevail throughout the whole of the following day; there was a promenade, a banquet, a comedy to be acted.

The evening came. The King had expressed a wish not to walk in the park until after cards in the evening. In the interval between supper and the promenade, cards and dice were introduced. The King won a thousand pistoles, and, having won them, put them in his pocket, and then rose, saying, "And now, gentlemen, to the park." He found the ladies of the court already there. Colbert was waiting for or upon him at the corner of one of the avenues; he was most probably waiting there in consequence of a rendezvous which had been given him by the King, as Louis XIV, who had avoided him, or who had seemed to avoid him, suddenly made him a sign, and they then struck into the depths of the park together. But La Vallière, too, had observed the King's gloomy aspect and kindling glances; she had remarked this; and, as nothing which lay hidden or smouldering in his heart was impenetrable to her affection, she understood that this repressed wrath menaced some one; she prepared to withstand the current of his vengeance and intercede like an angel of mercy. Overcome by sadness, nervously agitated, deeply distressed at having been so long separated from her lover, disturbed at the sight of that emotion which she had divined, she accordingly presented herself to the King with an embarrassed aspect, which, in his then disposition of mind, the King interpreted unfavourably. Then, as they were alone, or nearly alone, inasmuch as Colbert, as soon as he perceived the young girl approaching, had stopped and drawn back a dozen paces—the King advanced towards La Vallière and took her by the hand: "Mademoiselle," he said to her, "should I be guilty of an indiscretion if I were to inquire if you are indisposed? for you seem to breathe as if you were oppressed by some secret cause of uneasiness, and your eyes are filled with tears."

"Oh! sire, if I be indeed so, and if my eyes are indeed full of tears, I am sorrowful only at the sadness which seems to oppress your Majesty."

"My sadness? You are mistaken, mademoiselle; no, it is not sadness I experience."

"What is it then, sire?"

"Humiliation."

"Humiliation? oh! sire, what a word for you to use."

"I mean, mademoiselle, that whatever I may happen to be, no one else ought to be the master. Well, then, look around you on every side, and judge whether I am not eclipsed—I, the King of France—before the king of these wide domains. Oh!" he continued, clenching his hands and teeth, "when I think that this king——"

"Well, sire?" said Louise terrified.

"—That this king is a faithless, unworthy servant, who becomes proud and self-sufficient with property which belongs to me, and which he has stolen. And, therefore, am I about to change this impudent minister's fête into a sorrow and mourning, of which the nymph of Vaux, as the poets say, shall not soon lose the resemblance."

"Oh! your Majesty——"

"Well, mademoiselle, are you about to take M. Fouquet's part?" said Louis impatiently.

"No, sire; I will only ask whether you are well informed. Your Majesty has more than once learned the value of accusations made at the court."

Louis XIV made a sign for Colbert to approach. "Speak, Monsieur Colbert," said the young Prince, "for I almost believe that Mademoiselle de la Vallière has need of your assurance before she can put any faith in the King's word. Tell mademoiselle what M. Fouquet has done; and you, mademoiselle, will perhaps have the kindness to listen. It will not be long."

"Speak, monsieur," said La Vallière to Colbert, who had advanced; "speak, since the King wishes me to listen to you. Tell me, what is the crime with which M. Fouquet is charged?"

"Oh! not very heinous, mademoiselle," he returned; "a simple abuse of confidence."

"Speak, speak, Colbert; and when you shall have related it, leave us, and go and inform M. d'Artagnan that I have certain orders to give him."

"M. d'Artagnan, sire!" exclaimed La Vallière; "but why send for M. d'Artagnan? I entreat you to tell me?"

"*Pardieu!* in order to arrest this haughty, arrogant Titan, who, true to his menace, threatens to scale my heaven."

"Arrest M. Fouquet, do you say?"

"Ah! does that surprise you?"

"In his own house?"

"Why not? If he be guilty, he is guilty in his own house as anywhere else."

"M. Fouquet, who at this moment is ruining himself for his sovereign."

"In plain truth, mademoiselle, it seems as if you were defending this traitor."

Colbert began to chuckle silently. The King turned round at the sound of this suppressed mirth.

"Sire," said La Vallière, "it is not M. Fouquet I am defending; it is yourself."

"Me! you defend me!"

"Sire, you would be dishonouring yourself, if you were to give such an order."

"Dishonour myself!" murmured the King, turning pale with anger. "In plain truth, mademoiselle, you show a strange persistence in what you say."

"If I do so, sire, my only motive is that of serving your Majesty," replied the noble-hearted girl; "for that I would risk, I would sacrifice my very life, without the slightest reserve."

Colbert seemed inclined to grumble and complain. La Vallière, that timid, gentle lamb, turned round upon him, and with a glance like lightning, imposed silence upon him. "Monsieur," she said, "when the King acts well, whether, in doing so, he does either myself or those who belong to me, an injury, I have nothing to say; but were the King to confer a benefit either upon me or mine, and if he acted badly, I should tell him so."

"But it appears to me, mademoiselle," Colbert ventured to say, "that I too love the King."

"Yes, monsieur, we both love him, but each in a different manner," replied La Vallière, with such an accent that the heart of the young King was powerfully affected by it. "I love him so deeply, that the whole world is aware of it; so purely, that the King himself does not doubt my affection. He is my king and my master; I am the humblest of his servants. But he who touches his honour touches my life. Therefore, I repeat, that they dishonour the King who advise him to arrest M. Fouquet under his own roof."

Colbert hung down his head, for he felt that the King had abandoned him. However, as he bent his head, he murmured, "Mademoiselle, I have only one word to say."

"Do not say it, then, monsieur; for I would not listen to it. Besides, what could you have to tell me? That M. Fouquet has been guilty of certain crimes? I know he has, because the King has said so; and from the moment the King said 'I think so,' I have no occasion for other lips to say, 'I affirm it.' But, were M. Fouquet the vilest of men, I should say aloud, 'M. Fouquet's person is sacred to the King because he is the King's host. Were this house a den of thieves, were Vaux a cave of coiners or robbers, his home is sacred, his palace is inviolable, since his wife is living in it; and that is an asylum which even executioners would not dare to violate.' "

La Vallière paused and was silent. In spite of himself, the King could not but admire her; he was overpowered by the passionate energy of her voice; by the nobleness of the cause she advocated. Colbert yielded, overcome by the inequality of the struggle. At last, the King breathed again more freely, shook his head, and held out his hand to La Vallière. "Mademoiselle," he said gently, "why do you decide against me? Do you know what this wretched fellow will do, if I give him time to breathe again?"

"Is he not a prey which will always be within your grasp?"

"And if he escapes, and takes to flight?" exclaimed Colbert.

"Well, monsieur, it will always remain on record, to the King's eternal honour, that he allowed M. Fouquet to flee; and the more guilty he may have been, the greater will the King's honour and glory appear, when compared with such misery and such shame."

Louis kissed La Vallière's hand, as he knelt before her.

"I am lost," thought Colbert; then suddenly his face brightened up again. "Oh! no, no, not yet," he said to himself.

And while the King, protected from observation by the thick covert of an enormous lime, pressed La Vallière to his breast, with all the ardour of ineffable affection, Colbert tranquilly looked among the papers in his pocket-book, and drew out of it a paper folded in the form of a letter, slightly yellow, perhaps, but which must have been very precious, since the Intendant smiled as he looked at it; he then bent a look full of hatred upon the charming group which the young girl and the King formed together—a group which was revealed for a moment, as the light of the approaching torches shone upon it. Louis noticed the light reflected upon La Vallière's white dress. "Leave me, Louise," he said, "for someone is coming."

"Mademoiselle, mademoiselle, some one is coming," cried Colbert, to expedite the young girl's departure.

Louise disappeared rapidly among the trees; and then, as the King, who had been on his knees before the young girl, was rising from his humble posture, Colbert exclaimed, "Ah! Mademoiselle de la Vallière has let something fall."

"What is it?" inquired the King.

"A paper—a letter—something white; look there, sire."

The King stooped down immediately, and picked up the letter, crumpling it in his hand as he did so; and at the same moment the torches arrived, inundating the darkness of the scene with a flood of light as bright as day.

CHAPTER XXXI

JEALOUSY

The torches we have just referred to, the eager attention which every one displayed, and the new ovation paid to the King by Fouquet, arrived in time to suspend the effect of a resolution which La Vallière had already considerably shaken in Louis XIV's heart. He looked at Fouquet with a feeling almost of gratitude for having given La Vallière an opportunity of showing herself so generously disposed, so powerful in the influence she exercised over his heart. The moment of the last and greatest display had arrived. Hardly had Fouquet conducted the King towards the château, than a mass of fire burst from the dome of Vaux, with a prodigious uproar, pouring a flood of dazzling light on every side, and illumining the remotest corners of the gardens. The fireworks began. Suddenly, just as Louis was on the point of holding it out to Fouquet, he perceived in his hand the paper, which, as he believed, La Vallière had dropped at his feet as she hurried away. The still stronger magnet of love drew the Prince's attention towards the souvenir of his idol; and, by the brilliant light, which increased momentarily in beauty, and drew from the neighbouring villages loud exclamations of admiration, the King read the letter which he supposed was a loving and tender epistle which La Vallière had destined for him. But as he read it, a death-like pallor stole over his face, and an expression of deep-seated wrath, illumined by the many-coloured fires which rose brightly and soaringly around the scene, produced a terrible spectacle, which every one would have shuddered at, could they only have read into his heart, which was torn by the most stormy and most bitter passions. There was no truce for him now, influenced as he was by jealousy and mad passion. From the very moment when the dark truth was revealed to him, every gentler feeling seemed to disappear; pity, kindness of consideration, the religion of hospitality, all were forgotten. In the bitter pang which wrung his heart, he, too weak to hide his feelings, was almost on the point of uttering a cry of alarm, and calling his guards to gather round him. This letter which Colbert had thrown down at the King's feet was the same that had disappeared long ago at Fontainebleau, after the one attempt which Fouquet had made upon La Vallière's heart. Fouquet saw the King's pallor, and was far from guessing the evil; Colbert saw the King's anger, and rejoiced inwardly at the approach of the storm. Fouquet's voice drew the Prince from his wrathful reverie.

"What is the matter, sire?" inquired the Surintendant, with an expression of graceful interest.

Louis made a violent effort over himself, as he replied, "Nothing."

"I am afraid your Majesty is suffering."

"I am suffering, and have already told you so, monsieur; but it is nothing."

And the King, without waiting for the termination of the fireworks, turned towards the château. Fouquet accompanied him, and the whole court followed after them, leaving the remains of the fireworks burning for their own amusement. He had a friendly and kindly smile for the young King, when the latter wished him good night. This, however, was not all the King had to submit to; he was obliged to undergo the usual ceremony, which on that evening was marked by the closest adherence to the strictest etiquette. The next day was the one fixed for the departure; it was but proper that the guests should thank their host, and should show him a little attention in return for the expenditure of his twelve millions. The only remark, approaching to amiability, which the King could find to say to M. Fouquet, as he took leave of him, was in these words, "Monsieur Fouquet, you shall hear from me. Be good enough to desire M. d'Artagnan to come here."

And the blood of Louis XIII, who had so profoundly dissimulated his feelings, boiled in his veins; and he was perfectly ready to get M. Fouquet's throat cut, with the same readiness, indeed, as his predecessor had caused the assassination of Maréchal d'Ancre; and so he disguised the terrible resolution he had formed, beneath one of those royal smiles, which are the lightning flashes indicating *coups d'état*. Fouquet took the King's hand and kissed it; Louis shuddered throughout his whole frame, but allowed M. Fouquet to touch his hand with his lips. Five minutes afterwards, d'Artagnan, to whom the royal order had been communicated, entered Louis XIV's apartment. Aramis and

Philippe were in theirs, still eagerly attentive, and still listening with all their ears. The King did not even give the captain of the musketeers time to approach his arm-chair, but ran forward to meet him. "Take care," he exclaimed, "that no one enters here."

"Very good, sire," replied the captain, whose glance had for a long time past analysed the ravages on the King's countenance. He gave the necessary orders at the door; but, returning to the King, he said, "Is there something fresh the matter, your majesty?"

"How many men have you here?" inquired the King, without making any other reply to the question addressed to him.

"To do what, sire?" replied the musketeer, opening his large, calm eyes.

"To arrest M. Fouquet."

D'Artagnan fell back a step. "To arrest M. Fouquet!" he burst forth.

"Stay," said the King; "do not make his arrest a public affair."

"That will be more difficult."

"Take care of M. Fouquet, until I shall have made up my mind by to-morrow morning."

"That shall be done, sire."

"And return, when I rise in the morning, for further orders; and now leave me to myself."

D'Artagnan quitted the room. The King closed the door with his own hands, and began to walk up and down his apartment at a furious pace, like a wounded bull in an arena, dragging after him the coloured streamers and iron darts. At last he began to take comfort in the expression of his violent feelings.

"Miserable wretch that he is! not only does he squander my finances, but with his ill-gotten plunder he corrupts secretaries, friends, generals, artists, and all, and tries to rob me of the one to whom I am most attached. And that is the reason why that perfidious girl so boldly took his part! Gratitude! and who can tell whether it was not a stronger feeling—love itself?" He gave himself up for a moment to his bitter reflections. "A satyr!" he thought, with that abhorrent hate with which young men regard those more advanced in life, who still think of love. "That man shall fall so low, that when people look at the utter ruin which my anger shall have wrought, they will be forced to confess at least that I am indeed greater than he." The King, who was incapable of mastering his emotions any longer, knocked over with a blow of his fist a small table placed close to his bedside, and in the bitterness of feeling from which he was suffering, almost weeping, and half-suffocated by his passion, he threw himself on his bed, dressed as he was, and bit the sheets in the extremity of his passion, trying to find repose of body at least there. The bed creaked beneath his weight, and with the exception of a few broken sounds, which escaped from his overburdened chest, absolute silence soon reigned in the chamber of Morpheus.

MIM–D

CHAPTER XXXII

HIGH TREASON

The ungovernable fury which took possession of the King at the sight and at the perusal of Fouquet's letter to La Vallière by degrees subsided into a feeling of pain and extreme weariness. Morpheus, the tutelary deity of the apartment, towards whom Louis raised his eyes, wearied by his anger and reddened by his tears, showered down upon him the sleep-inducing poppies with which his hands were filled; so that the King gently closed his eyes and fell asleep. Then it seemed to him, as it often happens in that first sleep, so light and gentle, which raises the body above the couch, the soul above the earth— it seemed to him, we say, as if the god Morpheus, painted on the ceiling, looked at him with eyes resembling human eyes; that something shone brightly, and moved to and fro in the dome above the sleeper; that the crowd of terrible dreams which thronged together in his brain, and which we interrupted for a moment, half revealed a human face, with a hand resting against the mouth, and in an attitude of deep and absorbed meditation. And strange enough, too, this man bore so wonderful a resemblance to the King himself that Louis fancied he was looking at his own face reflected in a mirror; with the exception, however, that the face was saddened by a feeling of the profoundest pity. Then it seemed to him as if the dome gradually retired, escaping from his gaze, and that the figures and attributes painted by Lebrun became darker and darker as the distance became more and more remote. A gentle, easy movement, as regular as that by which a vessel plunges beneath the waves, had succeeded to the immovableness of the bed. Doubtless the King was dreaming, and in this dream the crown of gold, which fastened the curtains together, seemed to recede from his vision, just as the dome, to which it remained suspended, had done, so that the winged genius which, with both its hands, supported the crown, seemed, though vainly so, to call upon the King, who was fast disappearing from it. The bed still sank. Louis, with his eyes open, could not resist the deception of this cruel hallucination. At last, as the light of the royal chamber faded away into darkness and gloom, something cold, gloomy, and inexplicable in its nature seemed to infect the air. No paintings, nor gold, nor velvet hangings, were visible any longer, nothing but walls of a dull grey colour, which the increasing gloom made darker every moment. And yet the bed still continued to descend, and after a minute, which seemed in its duration almost an age to the King, it reached a stratum of air, black and still as death, and then it stopped. The King could no longer see the light in his room, except as from the bottom of a well we can see the light of day. "I am under the influence of a terrible dream," he thought. "It is time to awaken from it. Come! let me wake up."

But when he said, "Come, come! wake up," he perceived that not only was he already awake, but still more, that he had his eyes open also; he then looked all round him. On his right hand and on his left two armed men stood silently, each wrapped in a huge cloak and the face covered with a mask; one of them held a small lamp in his hand, whose glimmering light revealed the saddest picture a King could look upon. Louis could not help saying to himself that his dream still lasted, and that all he had to do to cause it to disappear was to move his arms or to say something aloud; he darted from his bed, and found himself upon the damp, moist ground. Then, addressing himself to the man who held the lamp in his hand, he said,—

"What is this, monsieur, and what is the meaning of this jest?"

"It is no jest," replied in a deep voice the masked figure that held the lantern.

"Do you belong to M. Fouquet?" inquired the King, greatly astonished at his situation.

"It matters very little to whom we belong," said the phantom; "we are your masters now; that is sufficient."

"At least tell me what you want?" exclaimed Louis, folding his arms with a passionate gesture.

"You will know by-and-by," replied the man who held the lamp.

"In the meantime tell me where I am?"

"Look."

Louis looked all around him; but, by the light of the lamp which the masked figure raised for the purpose, he could perceive nothing but the damp walls which glistened here and there with the slimy traces of the snail. "Oh! oh! a dungeon," said the King.

"No, a subterranean passage."

"Which leads—"

"Will you be good enough to follow us?"

He shook his head, and said: "It seems I have fallen into the hands of a couple of assassins. Move on, then."

"Come," replied the figure with the lamp, with a kind of respect in his manner, and leading his prisoner towards a carriage which seemed to be waiting.

"Get in," said the same man, opening the carriage door, and letting down the step. The carriage set off immediately at a quick trot, turned into the road to Paris, and in the forest of Sénart found a relay of horses fastened to trees in the same manner as the first horses had been, and without a postilion. The man on the box changed the horses, and continued to follow the road towards Paris with the same rapidity, and entered the city about three o'clock in the morning. The carriage proceeded along the Faubourg Sainte-Antoine, and, after having called out to the sentinel, "by the King's order," the driver conducted the horses into the circular enclosure of the Bastille, looking out upon the courtyard, called La Cour du Gouvernement. There the horses drew up, reeking with sweat, at the flight of steps, and a sergeant of the guard ran forward. "Go and wake the governor," said the coachman, in a voice of thunder.

With the exception of this voice, which might have been heard at the entrance of the Faubourg Saint-Antoine, everything remained as calm in the carriage as in the prison. Ten minutes afterwards, M. de Baisemeaux appeared in his dressing-gown on the threshold of the door. "What is the matter now?" he asked, "and whom have you brought me there?"

The man with the lantern opened the carriage door, and said two or three words to the one who acted as driver, who immediately got down from his seat, took up a short musket which he kept under his feet, and placed its muzzle on the prisoner's chest.

"And fire at once if he speaks!" added aloud the man who alighted from the carriage.

"Very good!" replied his companion, without any other remark.

With this recommendation, the person who had accompanied the King in the carriage ascended the flight of steps, at the top of which the governor was awaiting him. "Monsieur d'Herblay!" said the latter.

"Hush!" said Aramis. "Let us go into your room."

"Good Heavens! what brings you here at this hour?"

"A mistake, my dear Monsieur de Baisemeaux," Aramis replied quietly. "It appears that you were quite right the other day."

"What about?" inquired the governor.

"About the order of release, my dear friend."

"Tell me what you mean, monsieur — no, monseigneur," said the governor, almost suffocated by surprise and terror.

"It is a very simple affair; you remember, dear M. de Baisémeaux, that an order of release was sent to you."

"Yes, for Marchiali."

"Well, my dear Monsieur de Baisemeaux, it was a mistake; it was discovered at the ministry, so that I now bring you an order from the King to set at liberty — Seldon, that poor Scotch fellow, you know."

"Seldon! are you sure this time?"

"Well, read it yourself," added Aramis, handing him the order.

"Why," said Baisemeaux, "this order is the very same that has already passed through my hands."

"Indeed!"

"It is the very one I assured you I saw the other evening. *Parbleu!* I recognise it by the blot of ink."

"I do not know whether it is that or not; but all I know is, that I bring it for you."

"But, then, about the other?"

"What other?"

"Marchiali?"

"I have got him here with me."

"But that is not enough for me. I require a new order to take him back again."

"Don't talk such nonsense, my dear Baisemeaux; you talk like a child! Where is the order you received respecting Marchiali?"

Baisemeaux ran to his iron chest and took it out. Aramis seized hold of it, coolly tore it in four pieces, held them to the lamp, and burnt them. "Good Heavens! what are you doing?" exclaimed Baisemeaux, in an extremity of terror.

"Look at your position a little quietly, my dear governor," said Aramis, with his imperturbable self-possession, "and you will see how very simple the whole affair is. You no longer possess any order justifying Marchiali's release."

"I am a lost man!"

"Far from it my good fellow, since I have brought Marchiali back to you, and it is just the same as if he had never left."

"Ah!" said the governor, completely overcome by terror.

"And you will hand over this Seldon to me, whose liberation is authorised by this order. Do you understand?"

"I — I —"

"You do understand, I see," said Aramis. "Very good."

Baisemeaux clasped his hands together. "But why, at all events, after having taken Marchiali away from me, do you bring him back again?" cried the unhappy governor, in a paroxysm of terror and completely dumbfounded.

"For a friend such as you are," said Aramis, — "for so devoted a servant, I have no secret;" and he put his mouth close to Baisemeaux's ear, as he said in a low tone of voice, "you know the resemblance between that unfortunate fellow, and — "

"And the King? — yes!"

"Very good; the very first use that Marchiali made of his liberty was to persist — Can you guess what?"

"How is it likely I should guess?"

"To persist in saying that he was the King of France; to dress himself up in clothes like those of the King; and then pretend to assume that he was the King himself."

"Gracious Heavens!"

"That is the reason why I have brought him back again, my dear friend. He is mad, and lets every one see how mad he is."

"What is to be done then?"

"That is very simple; let no one hold any communication with him. You understand, that when his peculiar style of madness came to the King's ears, the King, who had pitied his terrible affliction, and saw how his kindness of heart had been repaid by such black ingratitude, became perfectly furious; so that, now — and remember this very distinctly, dear Monsieur de Baisemeaux, for it concerns you most closely — so that there is now, I repeat, sentence of death pronounced against all those who may allow him to communicate with any one else but me, or the King himself. You understand, Baisemeaux, sentence of death!"

"You need not ask me whether I understand."

"And now let us go down and conduct this poor devil back to his dungeon again."

Baisemeaux ordered the drums to be beaten, and the bells to be rung, as a warning to every one to retire, in order to avoid meeting a prisoner, about whom it was desired to observe a certain mystery. Then, when the passages were free, he went to take the prisoner from the carriage, at whose breast, Porthos, faithful to the directions which had been given him, still kept his musket levelled. "Ah! is that you, miserable wretch?" cried the governor, as soon as he perceived the King. "Very good, very good." And immediately, making the King get out of the carriage, he led him, still accompanied by Porthos, who had not taken off his mask, and Aramis, who again resumed his, up the stairs, to the second Bertaudière, and opened the door of the room in which Philippe for six long years had bemoaned his existence. The King entered into the cell without pronouncing a single word; he was pale and haggard. Baisemeaux shut the door upon him, turned the key twice in the lock, and then returned to Aramis. "It is quite true," he said in a low tone, "that he has a rather strong resemblance to the King; but still, less so than you said."

"So that," said Aramis, "you would not have been deceived by the substitution of the one for the other?"

"What a question!"

"You are a most valuable fellow, Baisemeaux," said Aramis; "and now, set Seldon free."

"Oh, yes. I was going to forget that. I will go and give orders at once."

"Bah! to-morrow will be time enough."

"'To-morrow!'—oh, no. This very minute."

"Well; go off to your own affairs, I shall go away to mine. But it is quite understood, is it not?"

"What is quite understood?"

"That no one is to enter the prisoner's cell, except with an order from the King; an order which I will myself bring."

"Quite so. Adieu, monseigneur."

Aramis turned to his companion. "Now, Porthos, my good fellow, back again to Vaux, and as fast as possible."

"A man is light and easy enough, when he has faithfully served his King; and, in serving him, saved his country," said Porthos. "The horses will be as light as if they had nothing at all behind them. So let us be off." And the carriage, lightened of a prisoner, who might well be—as he in fact was—very heavy for Aramis, passed across the drawbridge of the Bastille, which was raised again immediately behind it.

CHAPTER XXXIII

THE SHADOW OF M. FOUQUET

D'Artagnan, drawing by a gesture peculiar to himself his shoulder-belt over his shoulder, went straight off to M. Fouquet, who, after he had taken leave of his guests, was preparing to retire for the night and to sleep tranquilly after the triumphs of the day. The air was still perfumed or infected, whichever way it may be considered, with the odour of the fireworks. Fouquet, almost entirely alone, was being assisted by his *valet-de-chambre* to undress, when M. d'Artagnan appeared at the entrance of the room. D'Artagnan had never been able to succeed in making himself common at the court; and notwithstanding he was seen everywhere and on all occasions, he never failed to produce an effect wherever and whenever he made his appearance.

"What! M. d'Artagnan?" said Fouquet, who had already taken his right arm out of the sleeve of his doublet.

"At your service," replied the musketeer.

"Come in, my dear M. d'Artagnan."

"Is that your bed, there?"

"Yes; but why do you ask? Are you not satisfied with your own?"

"May I speak frankly to you?"

"Most assuredly."

"Well, then, I am not."

Fouquet started, and then replied, "Will you take my room, Monsieur d'Artagnan?"

"What! deprive you of it, monseigneur? Never!"

"What am I to do then?"

"Allow me to share yours with you."

Fouquet looked at the musketeer fixedly. "Ah! ah!" he said, "you have just left the King."

"I have, monseigneur."

"Come, admit at once that you arrest me," said the Surintendant to the captain.

"Never!" said the latter.

"You intend to look after me, then?"

"Yes, monseigneur, I do, upon my honour."

"Upon your honour!—ah! that is quite another thing! so I am to be arrested in my own house."

"Do not say such a thing."

"On the contrary, I will proclaim it aloud."

"If you do, I shall be compelled to request you to be silent."

"That is quite sufficient, Monsieur d'Artagnan," returned Fouquet, in a cold tone of voice. "It is not idly that you have acquired your reputation as a man of intelligence and full of resources; but with me that is quite superfluous. Let us two come to the point. Grant me a service. Why do you arrest me? What have I done?"

"Oh! I know nothing about what you may have done; but I do not arrest you—this evening, at least!"

"This evening!" said Fouquet, turning pale, "but to-morrow?" ·

"It is not to-morrow just yet, monseigneur. Who can ever answer for the morrow? If you are satisfied with what I have done, and have somewhat recovered from the shock which I prepared you for as much as I possibly could, let us allow the few hours that remain to pass away undisturbed. You are harassed, and require to arrange your thoughts; I beg you, therefore, to go to sleep, or pretend to go to sleep, either on your bed, or in your arm-chair; and when I fall asleep my rest is so sound that a cannon would not wake me."

Fouquet smiled. "I except, however," continued the musketeer, "the case of a door being opened, whether a secret door, or any other; or the case of any one going out of or coming into the room. For anything like that, my ear is as quick and sensitive as possible. Any creaking noise makes me start. It arises, I suppose, from a natural antipathy to anything of the kind. Move about as much as you like; walk up and down in any part of the room; write, efface, destroy, burn—nothing like that will prevent me from going to sleep, or even prevent me from snoring; but do not touch either the key or the handle of the door! for I should start up in a moment, and that would shake my nerves terribly."

"Monsieur d'Artagnan," said Fouquet, "you are certainly the most witty and the most courteous man I ever met with; and you will leave me only one regret; that of having made your acquaintance so late."

D'Artagnan drew a deep sigh, which seemed to say, "Alas! you have perhaps made it too soon." He then settled himself in his arm-chair, while Fouquet, half lying on his bed, and leaning on his arm, was meditating upon his adventure. In this way, both of them, leaving the candles burning, awaited the first dawn of day; and when Fouquet happened to sigh too loudly, d'Artagnan only snored the louder. Not a single visit, not even from Aramis, disturbed their quietude; not a sound, even, was heard throughout the vast palace. Outside, however, the guards on duty, and the patrols of the musketeers, paced up and down; and the sound of their feet could be heard on the gravel walks.

CHAPTER XXXIV

THE MORNING

The young Prince descended from Aramis's room, in the same way the King had descended from the apartment dedicated to Morpheus. The dome gradually and slowly sank down under Aramis's pressure, and Philippe stood beside the royal bed, which had ascended again after having deposited its prisoner in the secret depths of the subterranean passage. Alone, in the presence of all the luxury which surrounded him; alone, in the presence of his power; alone, with the part he was about to be forced to act, Philippe for the first time felt his heart, and mind, and soul expand beneath the influence of a thousand varied emotions, which are the vital throbs of a king's heart.

"I am now face to face with my destiny," said Philippe, with his eyes on fire, and his face lividly white. 'Is it likely to be more terrifying than my captivity has been sad and gloomy? When I am compelled to follow out, at every moment, the sovereign power and authority I have usurped, shall I never cease to listen to the scruples of my heart?"

With these words, Philippe, notwithstanding an instinctive repugnance of feeling, and in spite of the shudder of terror, which mastered his will, threw himself on the royal bed, and forced his muscles to press the still warm place where Louis XIV had lain, while he buried his burning face in the handkerchief still moistened by his brother's tears. With his head thrown back and buried in the soft down of his pillow, Philippe perceived above him the crown of France, suspended, as we have stated, by angels with outspread golden wings.

Towards the morning a shadow, rather than a body, glided into the royal chamber. Philippe expected his approach, and neither expressed nor exhibited any surprise.

"Well, M. d'Herblay?" he said.

"Well, sire, all is done."

"How?"

"Exactly as we expected."

"Did he resist?"

"Terribly! tears and entreaties."

102

"And then?"

"A perfect stupor."

"But at last?"

"Oh! at last, a complete victory, and absolute silence."

"Did the governor of the Bastille suspect anything?"

"Nothing."

"And M. du Vallon?" asked Philippe, in order to change the conversation.

"He will be presented to you to-day, and confidentially will congratulate you on the danger which that conspirator has made you run."

"What is to be done with him?"

"With M. du Vallon?"

"Yes; confer a dukedom on him, I suppose."

At this moment, and in the middle of this idle conversation, under the light tone of which the two conspirators concealed their joy and pride at their mutual success, Aramis heard something which made him prick up his ears.

"What is that?" said Philippe.

"The dawn, sire."

"Well?"

"Well, before you retired to bed last night, you probably decided to do something this morning at the break of day."

"Yes, I told my captain of the musketeers," replied the young man hurriedly, "That I should expect him."

"If you told him that, he will certainly be here, for he is a most punctual man."

"I hear a step in the vestibule."

"It must be he."

"Come, let us begin the attack," said the young King, resolutely.

"Be cautious, for Heaven's sake; to begin the attack, and with d'Artagnan, would be madness. D'Artagnan knows nothing, he has seen nothing; he is a hundred miles from suspecting our mystery in the slightest degree; but if he comes into this room the first this morning, he will be sure to detect something which has taken place, and which he would think his business to occupy himself about."

"But how can I send him away, since I have given him a rendez-vous?" observed the Prince, impatient to measure swords with so redoubtable an antagonist.

"I will take care of that," replied the Bishop, "and in order to begin, I am going to strike a blow which will completely stupefy our man."

"He too is striking a blow, for I hear him at the door," added the Prince, hurriedly.

And, in fact, a knock at the door was heard at that moment. Aramis was not mistaken; for it was indeed d'Artagnan who adopted that mode of announcing himself.

We have seen how he passed the night in philosophising with M. Fouquet, but the musketeer was very wearied, even of feigning to fall asleep, and as soon as the dawn illumined with its pale blue light the sumptuous cornices of the Surintendant's room, d'Artagnan rose from his arm-chair, arranged his sword, brushed his coat and hat with his sleeve like a private soldier getting ready for inspection.

"Are you going out?" said Fouquet.

"Yes, monseigneur. Are you?"

"No, I shall remain."

"You give me your word?"

"Certainly."

"Very good. Besides, my only reason for going out is to try to get that reply—you know what I mean?"

And with these words, pronounced with the most affectionate graciousness of manner, the captain took leave of Fouquet in order to wait upon the King.

D'Artagnan did not think himself so good a prophet. It was written that the day would pass away and realise all the predictions that had been made in the morning. He had accordingly knocked, as we have seen, at the King's door. The door opened. The captain thought that it was the King who had just opened it himself; and this supposition was not altogether inadmissible, considering the state of agitation in which he had left Louis XIV the previous evening; but instead of his royal master, whom he was on the point of saluting with the greatest respect, he perceived the long, calm features of Aramis. So extreme was his surprise, that he could hardly refrain from uttering a loud exclamation. "Aramis!" he said.

"Good morning, dear d'Artagnan," replied the prelate coldly.

"You here," stammered the musketeer.

"His Majesty desires you to report that he is still sleeping, after having been greatly fatigued during the whole night."

"Ah!" said d'Artagnan, who could not understand how the Bishop of Vannes, who had been so indifferent a favourite the previous evening, had become in half a dozen hours the largest mushroom of fortune which had ever sprung up in a sovereign's bedroom.

"And then," continued the Bishop, "as an answer to what you were coming to ask the King, my dear d'Artagnan, here is an order of His Majesty, which you will be good enough to attend to forthwith, for it concerns M. Fouquet."

D'Artagnan took the order which was held out to him.

"To be set at liberty!" he murmured. "Ah!" and he uttered a second "Ah!" still more full of intelligence than the former; for this order explained Aramis's presence with the King, and that Aramis, in order to have obtained Fouquet's pardon, must have made considerable progress in the royal favour, and that this favour explained, in its tenor, the hardly conceivable assurance with which M. d'Herblay issued the orders in the King's name. For d'Artagnan it was quite sufficient to have understood something in order to understand everything. He bowed and withdrew a couple of steps, as if he were about to leave.

"I am going with you," said the Bishop.

"Where to?"

"To M. Fouquet; I wish to be a witness of his delight."

"I will lead the way, monseigneur," said d'Artagnan and he conducted Aramis to Fouquet's apartments.

CHAPTER XXXV

THE KING'S FRIEND

Fouquet was waiting with anxiety. When he saw d'Artagnan return, and when he perceived the Bishop of Vannes behind him, he could hardly restrain from his delight; it was fully equal to his previous uneasiness. The mere sight of Aramis was a complete compensation to the Surintendant for the unhappiness he had undergone in being arrested. The prelate was silent and grave; d'Artagnan completely bewildered by such an accumulation of events.

"Well, captain; so you have brought M. d'Herblay to me."

"And something better still, monseigneur."

"What is that?"

"Liberty."

"I am free!"

"Yes: by the King's order."

Fouquet resumed his usual serenity, that he might interrogate Aramis with his look.

"Oh! yes, you can thank the Bishop of Vannes," pursued d'Artagnan, "for it is indeed to him that you owe the change that has taken place in the King."

"Oh!" said Fouquet, more humiliated at the service than grateful at its success.

D'Artagnan fancied he perceived that these two men had something to say to each other; he, therefore, bowed to Fouquet, and then to Aramis,—to the latter with a slight admixture of ironical respect,—and disappeared.

No sooner had he left, than Fouquet, whose impatience had hardly been able to wait for that moment, darted towards the door to close it, and then returning to the Bishop, he said, "My dear d'Herblay, I think it now high time you should explain to me what has passed, for, in plain and honest truth, I do not understand anything."

"We will explain all that to you," said Aramis, sitting down, and making Fouquet sit down also.

"Do you remember those receipts for thirteen millions which M. de Mazarin contrived to get stolen from you?"

"Yes, of course!"

"Well, you are already pronounced to be a public robber."

"Good heavens!"

"Oh! that is not all. Do you also remember that letter you wrote to La Vallière?"

"Alas, yes!"

"And that proclaims you a traitor and suborner."

"Why should he have pardoned me, then?"

"We have not yet arrived at that part of our argument."

"You are killing me with impatience, d'Herblay. Am I still Surintendant?"

"As long as you like."

"But what extraordinary empire have you so suddenly acquired over his Majesty's mind?"

"Ah! that is it."

"You have something particular then, between you?"

"Yes."

"A secret, perhaps?"

"Yes, a secret."

"A secret of such a nature as to change his Majesty's interests?"

"You are, indeed, a man of superior intelligence, monseigneur, and have made a very accurate guess. I have, in fact, discovered a secret, of a nature to change the interests of the King of France."

"Ah!" said Fouquet, with the reserve of a man who does not wish to ask any questions.

"Do you remember," said the Bishop, casting down his eyes, "the birth of Louis XIV?"

"As it were yesterday."

"Have you heard anything particular respecting his birth?"

"Nothing."

"That is where my secret begins." Aramis thereupon related the facts regarding the birth of Philippe and the incidents that took place during the previous night that ended in the substitution of the watchers and the imprisonment of Louis in the Bastille.

Fouquet uttered a thick, smothered cry, as if he had been struck by some invisible blow, and clasping his head between his clenched hands, he murmured: "You did that?"

"Cleverly enough, too; what do you think of it?"

"You dethroned the King? imprisoned him, too?"

"Yes, that has been done."

"And such an action has been committed here at Vaux?"

"Yes, here, at Vaux, in the Chamber of Morpheus. It would almost seem that it had been built in anticipation of such an act."

"And at what time did it occur?"

"Last night, between twelve and one o'clock."

Fouquet made a movement as if he were on the point of springing upon Aramis; he restrained himself. "At Vaux! under my roof!" he said, in a half-strangled voice.

"I believe so! for it is still your house, and is likely to continue so, since M. Colbert cannot rob you of it now."

"It was under my roof, then, monsieur, that you committed this crime?"

"This crime!" said Aramis stupefied.

"This abominable crime!" pursued Fouquet, becoming more and more excited; "this crime more execrable than an assassination! this crime which dishonours my name for ever, and entails upon me the horror of posterity!"

"You are not in your senses, monsieur," replied Aramis, in an irresolute tone of voice; "you are speaking too loudly; take care!"

"I will call out so loudly that the whole world shall hear me."

"Monsieur Fouquet, take care."

Fouquet turned round towards the prelate, whom he looked at full in the face. "You have dishonoured me," he said, "in committing so foul an act of treason, so heinous a crime upon my guest, upon one who was peacefully reposing beneath my roof. Oh! woe, woe, is me!"

"Woe to the man, rather, who beneath your roof meditated the ruin of your fortune, your life. Do you forget that?"

"He was my guest, my sovereign."

Aramis rose, his eyes literally bloodshot, his mouth trembling convulsively. "Have I a man out of his senses to deal with," he said.

"A man who would sooner, oh! far sooner, die; who would kill you, even, rather than allow you to complete his dishonour."

Aramis raised his head gently, and a glimmer of hope might be seen once more to animate his eyes. "Reflect, monseigneur," he said, "upon everything we have to expect. As the matter now stands, the King is still alive, and his imprisonment saves your life."

"Yes," replied Fouquet, "you may have been acting on my behalf, but I will not, do not accept your services. But first of all, I do not wish your ruin. You will leave this house."

Aramis stifled the exclamation which almost escaped his broken heart.

"I am hospitable towards all who are dwellers beneath my roof," continued Fouquet, with an air of inexpressible majesty; "you will not be more fatally lost, than he whose ruin you have consummated."

"You will be so," said Aramis, in a hoarse, prophetic voice; "you will be so, believe me."

"I accept the augury, Monsieur d'Herblay; but nothing shall prevent me, nothing shall stop me. You will leave Vaux—you must leave France; I give you four hours to place yourself out of the King's reach."

"Four hours?" said Aramis scornfully and incredulously.

"Upon the word of Fouquet, no one shall follow you before the expiration of that time. You will therefore have four hours' advance of those whom the King may wish to despatch after you."

"Four hours!" repeated Aramis, in a thick, smothered voice.

"It is more than you will need to get on board a vessel and flee to Belle-Isle, which I give you as a place of refuge."

"Ah!" murmured Aramis.

"Belle-Isle is as much mine for you, as Vaux is mine for the King. Go, d'Herblay, go! as long as I live, not a hair of your head shall be injured."

"Thank you," said Aramis, with a cold irony of manner.

"Go at once then, and give me your hand, before we both hasten away; you to save your life, I to save my honour."

Aramis withdrew from his breast the hand he had concealed there; it was stained with blood. He had dug his nails into his flesh, as if in punishment for having nursed so many projects, more vain, insensate, and fleeting than the life of man himself. Fouquet was horror-stricken, and then his heart smote him with pity. He threw open his arms as if to embrace him.

"I had no arms," murmured Aramis, as wild and terrible in his wrath as the shade of Dido. And then, without touching Fouquet's hand, he turned his head aside, and stepped back a pace or two. His last word was an imprecation, his last gesture a curse, which his blood-stained hand seemed to invoke, as it sprinkled on Fouquet's face a few drops of blood which flowed from his breast. And both of them darted out of the room by the secret staircase which led down to the inner courtyard. Fouquet ordered his best horses, while Aramis paused at the foot of the staircase which led to Porthos's apartment. He reflected profoundly and for some time, while Fouquet's carriage left the stone-paved courtyard at full gallop.

And Aramis, apprehensive of meeting any one to whom his hurried movements might appear suspicious, ascended the staircase without being perceived. Porthos, so recently returned from Paris, was already in a profound sleep; his huge body forgot its fatigue, as his mind forgot its thoughts. Aramis entered, light as a shadow, and placed his nervous grasp on the giant's shoulder. "Come, Porthos," he cried, "come."

Porthos obeyed, rose from his bed, opened his eyes, even before his intelligence seemed to be aroused.

"We are going off," said Aramis.

"Ah!" returned Porthos.

"We shall go mounted, and faster than we have ever gone in our lives."

"Ah!" repeated Porthos.

"Dress yourself, my friend."

And he helped the giant to dress himself, and thrust his gold and diamonds into his pocket. Whilst he was thus engaged, a slight noise attracted his attention, and on looking up he saw d'Artagnan watching them through the half-open door. Aramis started.

"What the devil are you doing there in such an agitated manner?" said the musketeer.

"Hush!" said Porthos.

"We are going off on a mission of great importance," added the Bishop.

"You are very fortunate," said the musketeer.

"Oh, dear me!" said Porthos, "I feel so wearied; I would far sooner have been fast asleep. But the service of the King——"

"Have you seen M. Fouquet," said Aramis to d'Artagnan.

"Yes, this very minute, in a carriage."

"What did he say to you?"

"'Adieu'; nothing more."

"Come, Porthos, are you ready? Let us go."

They embraced d'Artagnan. Then the two fugitives mounted their horses beneath the captain of the musketeer's eyes, who held Porthos's stirrup for him, and gazed after them until they were out of sight.

"On any other occasion," thought the Gascon, "I should say that those gentlemen are making their escape; but in these days politics seem so changed that that is what is termed going on a mission. I have no objection; let me attend to my own affairs, that is quite enough;" and he philosophically entered his apartments.

CHAPTER XXXVI

SHOWING HOW THE COUNTERSIGN WAS RESPECTED AT THE BASTILLE

Fouquet tore along as fast as his horses could drag him. On his way he trembled with horror at the idea of what had just been revealed to him.

"What must have been," he thought, "the youth of those extraordinary men, who, even as age is stealing fast upon them, still are able to conceive such plans, and can carry them out without flinching?"

Travelling at the rate of five leagues and a half the hour, the Surintendant arrived at the Bastille.

Baisemeaux recognised Fouquet immediately. The latter followed the governor to his official residence. Baisemeaux was already trembling with shame and uneasiness. Aramis's early visit, from that moment, seemed to possess consequences which a functionary such as he (Baisemeaux) was, was perfectly justified in apprehending. It was quite another thing, however, when Fouquet, in a sharp tone of voice, and with an imperious look, said, "You have seen M. d'Herblay this morning?"

"Yes, monseigneur."

"And are you not horrified at the crime of which you have made yourself an accomplice?"

"Well," thought Baisemeaux, "good so far"; and then he added, aloud, "But what crime, monsieur, do you allude to?"

"That for which you can be quartered alive, monsieur,—do not forget that! But this it not a time to show anger. Conduct me immediately to the prisoner."

"To what prisoner?" said Baisemeaux tremblingly.

"You pretend to be ignorant? Very good—it is the best thing for you, perhaps, to do; for if, in fact, you were to admit your participation in it, it would be all over with you. I wish, therefore, to seem to believe in your assumption of ignorance."

"I entreat you, monseigneur——"

"That will do. Lead me to the prisoner."

"To Marchiali?"

"Who is Marchiali?"

"The prisoner who was brought back this morning by M. d'Herblay."

"He is called Marchiali?" said the Surintendant, his conviction somewhat shaken by Baisemeaux's cool manner.

"Yes, monseigneur; that is the name under which he was inscribed here."

Fouquet looked steadily at Baisemeaux, as if he would read his very heart; and perceived, with that clear-sightedness which men possess who are accustomed to the exercise of power, that the man was speaking with the most perfect sincerity. Besides, in observing his face for a few moments, he could not believe that Aramis would have chosen such a confidant.

"It is the prisoner," said the Surintendant to him, "whom M. d'Herblay carried away the day before yesterday?"

"Yes, monseigneur."

"And whom he brought back this morning?" added Fouquet, quickly: for he understood immediately the mechanism of Aramis's plan.

"Precisely, monseigneur."

"And his name is Marchiali, you say?"

"Yes, Marchiali. If monseigneur has come here to remove him, so much the better, for I was going to write about him."

"What has he done, then?"

"Ever since this morning he has annoyed me extremely. He has had such terrible fits of passion, as almost to make me believe that he would bring the Bastille itself down about our ears."

"I will soon relieve you of his presence," said Fouquet.

"Ah! so much the better."

"Conduct me to his prison."

"Come with me to the keep, monseigneur, you shall see Marchiali."

Fouquet darted out of the room, followed by Baisemeaux as he wiped the perspiration from his face. "What a terrible morning!" he said; "what a disgrace!"

"Walk faster," replied Fouquet.

Baisemeaux bowed his head, took the keys, and unaccompanied, except by the minister, ascended the staircase. The higher they advanced up the spiral staircase, certain smothered murmurs became distinct cries and fearful imprecations. "What is that?" asked Fouquet.

"That is your Marchiali," said the governor; "that is the way these madmen call out."

And he accompanied that reply with a glance more indicative of injurious allusions, as far as Fouquet was concerned, than of politeness. The latter trembled; he had just recognised in one cry more terrible than any that had preceded it the King's voice. He paused on the staircase, snatching the bunch of keys from Baisemeaux, who thought this new madman was going to dash out his brains with one of them. "Ah!" he cried, "M. d'Herblay did not say a word about that."

"Give me the keys at once!" cried Fouquet, tearing them from his hand. "Which is the key of the door I am to open?"

"That one."

A fearful cry, followed by a violent blow against the door, made the whole staircase resound with the echo. "Leave this place," said Fouquet to Baisemeaux, in a threatening voice.

"I ask nothing better," murmured the latter, "there will be a couple of madmen face to face, and the one will kill the other, I am sure."

"Go!" repeated Fouquet. "If you place your foot in this staircase before I call you, remember that you shall take the place of the meanest prisoner in the Bastille."

"This job will kill me, I am sure it will," muttered Baisemeaux, as he withdrew with tottering steps.

The prisoner's cries became more and more terrible. When Fouquet had satisfied himself that Baisemeaux had reached the bottom of the staircase, he inserted the key in the first lock. It was then that he heard the hoarse, choking voice of the King, crying out, in a frenzy of rage, "Help! help! I am the King." The key of the second door was not the same as the first, and Fouquet was obliged to look for it on the bunch. The King, however, furious, and almost mad with rage and passion, shouted at the top of his voice, "It was M. Fouquet who brought me here. Help me against M. Fouquet! I am the King! Help the King against M. Fouquet!"

Fouquet at last succeeded in finding the key. The door flew open.

CHAPTER XXXVII

THE KING'S GRATITUDE

The two men were on the point of darting towards each other when they suddenly and abruptly stopped, as a mutual recognition took place, and each uttered a cry of horror.

"Have you come to assassinate me, monsieur?" said the King, when he recognised Fouquet.

"Sire," said Fouquet, in a voice trembling with emotion, "do you not recognise the most faithful of your friends?"

"A friend—you!" repeated Louis, gnashing his teeth in a manner which betrayed his hate and desire for speedy vengeance.

"The most respectful of your servants," added Fouquet, throwing himself on his knees.

Louis recalled to himself by the change of situation, looked at himself, and ashamed of the disordered state of his apparel, ashamed of his conduct, and ashamed of the air of pity and protection that was shown towards him, drew back. Fouquet did not understand this movement; he did not perceive that the King's feeling of pride would never forgive him for having been a witness of such an exhibition of weakness.

"Come, sire," he said, "you are free."

"Free?" repeated the King. "Oh! you set me at liberty, then, after having dared to lift up your hand against me."

"You do not believe that!" exclaimed Fouquet indignantly; "you cannot believe me to be guilty of such an act."

And rapidly, warmly even, he related the whole particulars of the intrigue, the details of which are already known to the reader.

"But where are these persons, then?" murmured the King.

"At Vaux."

"At Vaux! and you suffer them to remain there!"

"My most pressing duty seemed to be your Majesty's release. I have accomplished that duty; and now, whatever your Majesty may command, shall be done. I await your orders. Their chief—the very soul of the enterprise, having been unmasked by me, the whole plan seems to me to have miscarried."

"You have unmasked this false prince also?"

"No, I have not seen him."

"Whom have you seen, then?"

"The leader of the enterprise, not that unhappy young man; the latter is merely an instrument, destined through his whole life to wretchedness, I plainly perceive."

"Most certainly."

"It is M. l'Abbé d'Herblay, Bishop of Vannes."

"Your friend."

"He was my friend, sire," replied Fouquet nobly.

"An unfortunate circumstance for you," said the King, in a less generous tone of voice.

"Your Majesty will put these men to death!" cried Fouquet.

"To the very meanest of them."

"Sire," said the Surintendant with firmness, as he raised his head proudly, "your Majesty will take the life, if you please, of your brother Philippe of France; that concerns you alone, and you will doubtless consult the Queen-Mother upon the subject. Whatever she may command will be perfectly correct. I do not wish to mix myself up in it, not even for the honour of your crown, but I have a favour to ask of you, and I beg to submit it to you."

"Speak," said the King, in no little degree agitated by his minister's last words. "What do you require?"

"The pardon of M. d'Herblay and M. du Vallon."

"Never, as long as I live," replied the inflexible King. "Do me the kindness not to speak of it again."

"Your Majesty shall be obeyed."

"And you will bear me no ill will for it?"

"Oh! no, sire; for I anticipated it as being most likely."

"You had 'anticipated' that I should refuse to forgive those gentlemen?"

"Certainly; and all my measures were taken in consequence."

"What do you mean to say?" cried the King, surprised.

"M. d'Herblay came, as may be said, to deliver himself into my hands. M. d'Herblay left to me the happiness of saving my King and my country. I could not condemn M. d'Herblay to death; nor could I, on the other hand, expose him to your Majesty's most justifiable wrath; it would have been just the same as if I had killed him myself."

"Well; and what have you done?"

"Sire, I gave M. d'Herblay the best horses in my stables, and four hours' start over all those your Majesty might, probably, despatch after him. After having galloped as hard as possible, with the four hours' start, before your musketeers, he will reach my château of Belle-Isle, where I have given him a safe asylum."

"That may be! But you forget that you have made me a present of Belle-Isle."

"But not for you to arrest my friends."

"You take it back again, then?"

"As far as that goes — yes, sire."

"My musketeers will capture it, and the affair will be at an end."

"Neither your musketeers, nor your whole army could take Belle-Isle," said Fouquet coldly. "Belle-Isle is impregnable."

The King became perfectly livid; a lightning flash seemed to dart from his eyes. Fouquet felt that he was lost, but he was not one to shrink when the voice of honour spoke loudly within him. He bore the King's wrathful gaze; the latter swallowed his rage, and after a few moments' silence, said, "Are you going to return to Vaux?"

"I am at your Majesty's orders," replied Fouquet, with a low bow; "but I think that your Majesty can hardly dispense with changing your clothes previous to appearing before your court."

"We shall pass by the Louvre," said the King. "Come." And they left the prison, passing before Baisemeaux, who looked completely bewildered as he saw Marchiali once more leave; and, in his helplessness, tore out the few remaining hairs he had left.

CHAPTER XXXVIII

THE FALSE KING

In the meantime, usurped royalty was playing out its part bravely at Vaux. Philippe gave orders for a full reception at his *petit lever*. He determined to give this order notwithstanding the absence of M. d'Herblay, who did not return, and our readers know for what reason. But the Prince, not believing that absence could be prolonged, wished, as all rash spirits do, to try his valour and his fortune when far from all protection and all counsel. Philippe opened his folding doors, and several persons entered silently. His own memory and the notes of Aramis announced everybody to him, first of all Anne of Austria, to whom Monsieur gave his hand, and then Madame with M. de Saint-Aignan. He smiled at seeing these countenances, but trembled on recognising his mother. That figure so noble, so imposing, ravaged by pain, pleaded in his heart the cause of that famous Queen who had immolated a child to reasons of State. He found his mother still handsome. He knew that Louis XIV loved her, and he promised himself to love her likewise, and not to prove a cruel chastisement for her old age. He contemplated his mother with a tenderness easily to be understood. The latter had usurped nothing over him, had cast no shade over his life. He bowed with a friendly air to Saint-Aignan, who was all reverences and smiles, and tremblingly held out his hand to Henrietta, his sister-in-law, whose beauty struck him; but he saw in the eyes of the Princess an expression of coldness which would facilitate, as he thought, their future relations.

The only visit he dreaded at this moment was that of the Queen; his heart—his mind—had just been shaken by so violent a trial, that, in spite of their firm temperament, they would not, perhaps, support another shock. Happily the Queen did not come. Then commenced, on the part of Anne of Austria, a political dissertation upon the welcome M. Fouquet had given to the house of France.

"Well, my son," said she, "are you convinced with regard to M. Fouquet?"

"Saint-Aignan," said Philippe, "have the goodness to go and inquire after the Queen."

At these words, the first Philippe had pronounced aloud, the slight difference that there was between his voice and that of the King was sensible to maternal ears, and Anne of Austria looked earnestly at her son. Saint-Aignan left the room, and Philippe continued.

"Madame, I do not like to hear M. Fouquet ill-spoken of, you know I do not—and you have even spoken well of him yourself."

"That is true; therefore I only question you on the state of your sentiments with respect to him."

"Sire," said Henrietta, "I, on my part, have always liked M. Fouquet. He is a man of good taste—he is a superior man."

"A Surintendant who is never sordid or niggardly," added Monsieur; "and who pays in gold all the orders I have on him."

"Every one in this thinks too much of himself, and nobody for the State," said the old Queen. "M. Fouquet, it is a fact, M. Fouquet is ruining the State."

"What is your Majesty looking for?" said Henrietta, seeing the King's eyes constantly turning towards the door, and wishing to let fly a little poisoned arrow at his heart, supposing he was so anxiously expecting either La Vallière or a letter from her.

"My sister," said the young man, who had divined her thought, thanks to that marvellous perspicuity of which fortune was from that time about to allow him the exercise, "my sister, I am expecting a most distinguished man, a most able counsellor, whom I wish to present to you all, recommending him to your good graces. Ah! come in then, d'Artagnan."

"What does your Majesty wish?" said d'Artagnan, appearing.

"Where is monsieur the Bishop of Vannes, your friend?"

"Why, sire——"

"I am waiting for him, and he does not come. Let him be sought for."

D'Artagnan remained for an instant stupefied; but soon, reflecting that Aramis had left Vaux secretly with a mission from the King, he concluded that the King wished to preserve the secret of it. "Sire," replied he, "does your Majesty absolutely require M. d'Herblay to be brought to you?"

"Absolutely is not the word," said Philippe; "I do not want him so particularly as that; but if he can be found——"

"I thought so," said d'Artagnan to himself.

"What is all that noise?" said Philippe, turning round towards the door of the second staircase.

And a voice was heard, saying: "This way! this way! A few steps more, sire!"

"The voice of M. Fouquet," said d'Artagnan, who was standing close to the Queen-Mother.

"Then M. d'Herblay cannot be far off," added Philippe.

But he then saw what he little thought to see so near to him. All eyes were turned towards the door at which M. Fouquet was expected to enter; but it was not M. Fouquet who entered. A terrible cry resounded from all corners of the chamber, a painful cry uttered by the King and all present. The half-closed shutters only admitted the entrance of an uncertain light passing through large velvet curtains lined with silk. In this soft shade, the eyes were by degrees dilated, and every one present saw others rather with trust than with positive sight. There could not, however, escape, in these circumstances, one of the surrounding details; and the new object which presented itself appeared as luminous as if it had been enlightened by the sun. The Queen-Mother, who perceived Louis XIV, and who held the hand of Philippe, uttered the cry of which we have spoken, as if she had beheld a phantom. Monsieur was bewildered, and kept turning his head in astonishment from one to the other. Madame made a step forward, thinking she saw the form of her brother-in-law reflected in a glass. And, in fact, the illusion was possible. The two princes, both pale as death—for we renounce the hope of being able to describe the fearful state of Philippe—both trembling, and, clenching their hands convulsively, measured each other with their looks, and darted their eyes like poniards, into each other. Mute, panting, bending forward, they appeared as if about to spring upon an enemy. The unheard-of resemblance of countenance, gesture, shape, height, even to the resemblance of costume, produced by chance—for Louis XIV had been to the Louvre and put on a violet-coloured dress—the perfect analogy of the two princes, completed the consternation of Anne of Austria. And yet she did not at once guess the truth. There are misfortunes in life that no one will accept; people would rather believe in the supernatural and the impossible. Suddenly Louis XIV, more impatient and more accustomed to command, ran to one of the shutters, which he opened, tearing the curtains in his eagerness. A flood of living light entered the chamber, and made Philippe draw back to the alcove. Louis seized upon this movement with eagerness, and addressing himself to the Queen,—

"My mother," said he, "do you not acknowledge your son, since every one here has forgotten his King!" Anne of Austria started, and raised her arms towards Heaven, without being able to articulate a single word.

"My mother," said Philippe, with a calm voice, "do you not acknowledge your son?" And this time, in his turn, Louis drew back.

As to Anne of Austria, struck in both head and heart with remorse, she lost her equilibrium. No one aiding her, for all were petrified, she sank back in her chair, breathing a weak, trembling sigh. Louis could not endure this spectacle and this affront. He bounded towards d'Artagnan, upon whom the vertigo was beginning to gain, and who staggered as he caught at the door for support.

"Captain!" said he, "look us in the face and say which is the paler, he or I!"

This cry roused d'Artagnan, and stirred in his heart the fibre of obedience. He shook his head, and, without more hesitation, he walked straight up to Philippe, upon whose shoulder he laid his hand, saying, "Monsieur, you are my prisoner!"

Philippe did not raise his eyes towards Heaven, nor stir from the spot, where he seemed nailed to the floor, his eye intensely fixed upon the King his brother. He reproached him by a sublime silence with all his misfortune past, with all his tortures to come. Philippe approached Anne of Austria, and said to her, in a soft and nobly agitated voice,—

"If I were not your son, I should curse you, my mother, for having rendered me so unhappy."

D'Artagnan felt a shudder pass through the marrow of his bones. He bowed respectfully to the young Prince, and said, as he bent, "Excuse me, monseigneur, I am but a soldier, and my oaths are his who has just left the chamber."

"Thank you, M. d'Artagnan. But what is become of M. d'Herblay?"

"M. d'Herblay is in safety, monseigneur," said a voice behind them; "and no one, while I live and am free, shall cause a hair to fall from his head."

"Monsieur Fouquet!" said the Prince, smiling sadly.

"Pardon me, monseigneur," said Fouquet, kneeling, "but he who is just gone out from hence was my guest."

"Here are," murmured Philippe, with a sigh, "brave friends and good hearts. They make me regret the world. On, M. d'Artagnan, I follow you."

At the moment the captain of the musketeers was about to leave the room with his prisoner, Colbert appeared, and, after remitting an order from the King to d'Artagnan, retired. D'Artagnan read the paper, and then crushed it in his hand with rage.

"What is it?" asked the Prince.

"Read, monseigneur," replied the musketeer.

Philippe read the following words, hastily traced by the hand of the King:—"M. d'Artagnan will conduct the prisoner to the Iles Sainte-Marguerite. He will cover his face with an iron visor, which the prisoner cannot raise without peril of his life."

"That is just," said Philippe, with resignation, "I am ready."

"Aramis was right," said Fouquet, in a low voice to the musketeer; "this one is quite as much of a king as the other."

"More!" replied d'Artagnan. "He only wants you and me."

CHAPTER XXXIX

IN WHICH PORTHOS THINKS HE IS PURSUING A DUCHY

Aramis and Porthos, having profited by the time granted them by Fouquet, did honour to the French cavalry by their speed. Porthos did not clearly understand for what kind of mission he was forced to display so much velocity; but as he saw Aramis spurring on furiously, he, Porthos, spurred on in the same manner.

Thus travelled they on for eight long hours, and then arrived at Orleans. It was four o'clock in the afternoon. Aramis, on observing this, judged that nothing demonstrated pursuit to be possible. It would be without example that a troop capable of taking him and Porthos should be furnished with relays sufficient to perform forty leagues in eight hours. Thus, admitting pursuit, which was not at all manifest, the fugitives were five hours in advance of their pursuers.

Aramis thought that there might be no imprudence in taking a little rest, but that to continue would make the matter more certain. Twenty leagues more, performed with the same rapidity, twenty more leagues devoured, and no one, not even d'Artagnan, could overtake the enemies of the King. Aramis felt obliged, therefore, to inflict upon Porthos the pain of mounting on horseback again. They rode on till seven o'clock in the evening, and had only one post more between them and Blois. But here a diabolical accident alarmed Aramis greatly. There were no horses at the post. The prelate asked himself by what infernal machination his enemies had succeeded in depriving him of the means of going farther,—he who never recognised chance as a deity, he who found a cause for every result, he preferred believing that the refusal of the postmaster, at such an hour in such a country, was the consequence of an order emanating from above; an order given with a view of stopping short the king-maker in the midst of his flight. But at the moment he was about to fly into a passion, so as to procure either a horse or an explanation, he was struck with the recollection that the Comte de la Fère lived in the neighbourhood.

"I am not travelling," said he; "I do not want horses for a whole stage. Find me two horses to go and pay a visit to a nobleman of my acquaintance who resides near this place."

"What nobleman?" asked the postmaster.

"M. le Comte de la Fère."

"Oh!" replied the postmaster, uncovering with respect, "a very worthy nobleman. But, whatever may be my desire to make myself agreeable to him, I cannot furnish you with horses, for all mine are engaged by M. le Duc de Beaufort."

"Indeed!" said Aramis, much disappointed.

"Only," continued the postmaster, "if you will put up with a little carriage I have, I will harness an old blind horse, who has still his legs left, and will draw you to the house of M. le Comte de la Fère."

And he himself harnessed the old horse to the creaking carriage.

They arrived at Athos's dwelling about nine o'clock in the evening. Athos and Raoul were, as usual, conversing, and walking backwards and forwards in the long alley of limes in the park, when the bell which served to announce to the Comte either the hour of dinner or the arrival of a visitor was rung; and, without attaching any importance to it, he turned towards the house with his son; and at the end of the alley they found themselves in the presence of Aramis and Porthos.

CHAPTER XL

THE LAST ADIEUX

Raoul uttered a cry, and affectionately embraced Porthos. Aramis and Athos embraced like old men; and this embrace itself being a question for Aramis, he immediately said, "My friend, we have not long to remain with you."

"Ah!" said the Comte.

"Only time to tell you of my good fortune," interrupted Porthos.

"Ah!" said Raoul.

Athos looked silently at Aramis, whose sombre air had already appeared to him very little in harmony with the good news Porthos spoke of.

"What is the good fortune that has happened to you? Let us hear it," said Raoul, with a smile.

"The King has made me a duke," said the worthy Porthos, with an air of mystery, in the ear of the young man, "a duke by brevet."

But the asides of Porthos were always loud enough to be heard by everybody. His murmurs were in the diapason of ordinary roaring. Athos heard him, and uttered an exclamation which made Aramis start. The latter took Athos by the arm, and, after having asked Porthos's permission to say a word to his friend in private, "My dear Athos," he began, "you see me overwhelmed with grief."

"With grief, my dear friend?" cried the Comte; "oh, what!"

"In two words. I have raised a conspiracy against the King; that conspiracy has failed, and, at this moment, I am doubtless pursued."

"You are pursued!—a conspiracy! Eh, my friend, what do you tell me?"

"A sad truth. I am entirely ruined."

"Well, but Porthos—this title of duke—what does all that mean?"

"That is the subject of my severest pain; that is the deepest of my wounds. I have, believing in an infallible success, drawn Porthos into my conspiracy. He has thrown himself into it, as you know he would do, with all his strength, without knowing what he was about; and now, he is as much compromised as myself—as completely ruined as I am."

"Good God!" And Athos turned towards Porthos, who was smiling complacently.

"I must make you acquainted with the whole. Listen to me," continued Aramis; and he related the history as we know it. Athos, during the recital, several times felt the sweat break from his forehead. "It was a great idea," said he, "but a great error."

"For which I am punished, Athos."

"Therefore, I will not tell you my entire thought."

"Tell it, nevertheless."

"It is a crime."

"Capital. I know it is. *Lése-majesté*."

"Porthos! poor Porthos!"

"What would you advise me to do? Success, as I have told you, was certain."

"M. Fouquet is an honest man."

"And I am a fool for having so ill judged of him," said Aramis. "Oh! the wisdom of man! Oh, vast millstone which grinds the world! and which is one day stopped by a grain of sand which has fallen, no one knows how, in its wheels."

"Say, by a diamond, Aramis. But the thing is done. How do you think of acting?"

"I am taking away Porthos. The King will never believe that that worthy man has acted innocently. He never can believe that Porthos has thought he was serving the King whilst acting as he has done.

118

His head would pay for my fault. It shall not be so."

"You are taking him away; whither?"

"To Belle-Isle, at first. That is an impregnable place of refuge. Then I have the sea, and a vessel to pass over into England, where I have many relations."

"You? in England?"

"Yes, or else into Spain, where I have still more."

"But, our excellent Porthos! you ruin him, for the King will confiscate all his property."

"All is provided for. I know how, when once in Spain, to reconcile myself with Louis XIV, and restore Porthos to favour."

"You have credit, seemingly, Aramis," said Athos, with a discreet air.

"Much; and at the service of my friends."

These words were accompanied by a warm pressure of the hand.

"Thank you," replied the Comte.

"And while we are on that head," said Aramis, "you also are a malcontent; you also, Raoul, have griefs to lay to the King. Follow our example; pass over into Belle-Isle."

"No; for my part I prefer having something to reproach the King with; it is a pride natural to my race to pretend to a superiority over royal races. Doing what you propose, I should become the obliged of the King; I should certainly be a gainer on that ground, but I should be a loser in my conscience.—No, thank you!"

"Then, give me two things, Athos,—your absolution."

"Oh! I give it you if you have really wished to avenge the weak and the oppressed against the oppressor."

"That is sufficient for me," said Aramis, with a blush which was lost in the obscurity of the night. "And now, give me your two best horses to gain the second post, as I have been refused any under the pretext of the Duc de Beaufort being travelling in this country."

"You shall have the two best horses, Aramis; and I again recommend Porthos strongly to you."

Raoul was gone out to give orders for the saddling of the horses. The group was already divided. Athos saw his two friends on the point of departure, and something like a mist passed before his eyes, and weighed upon his heart.

"It is strange," thought he; "whence comes the inclination I feel to embrace Porthos once more?" At that moment Porthos turned round, and he came towards his old friend with open arms. This last endearment was tender as in youth, as in times when the heart was warm and life happy. And then Porthos mounted his horse. Aramis came back once more to throw his arms round the neck of Athos. The latter watched them along the high road, elongated by the shade, in their white cloaks. Like two phantoms, they seemed to be enlarged on departing from the earth, and it was not in the mist, but in the declivity of the ground that they disappeared. At the end of the perspective, both seemed to have given a spring with their feet, which made them vanish as if evaporated into the clouds.

All at once a noise of horses and voices, from the extremity of the road to Blois, attracted their attention that way. Flambeaux-bearers shook their torches merrily among the trees of their route, and turned round, from time to time, to avoid distancing the horsemen who followed them. These flames, this noise, this dust of a dozen richly caparisoned horses, formed a strange contrast in the middle of the night with the melancholy funeral disappearance of the two shadows of Aramis and Porthos. Athos went towards the house: but he had hardly reached the parterre, when the entrance gate appeared in a blaze; all the flambeaux stopped and appeared to enflame the road. A cry was heard of "M. le Duc de Beaufort"—and Athos sprang towards the door of his house. But the Duc had already alighted from his horse, and was looking around him.

"I am here, monseigneur," said Athos.

"Ah! good evening, dear Comte," said the Prince, with that frank cordiality which won him so many hearts. "Is it too late for a friend?"

"Ah! my dear Prince—come in!" said the Comte.

And, M. de Beaufort leaning on the arm of Athos, they entered the house, followed by Raoul, who walked respectfully and modestly among the officers of the Prince, with several of whom he was acquainted.

CHAPTER XLI

MONSIEUR DE BEAUFORT

The Prince turned round at the moment when Raoul, in order to leave him alone with Athos, was shutting the door, and preparing to go with the other officers into an adjoining apartment.

"Is that the young man I have heard M. le Prince speak so highly of?" asked M. de Beaufort.

"It is, monseigneur."

"*Ma foi!* he is tall and handsome!" continued the Duke. "Will you give him to me, monseigneur, if I ask him of you?"

"How am I to understand you, monseigneur?" said Athos.

"I am going to become an African Prince,—a Bedouin gentleman. The King is sending me to make conquests among the Arabs."

"What do you tell me, monseigneur?"

"Strange, is it not? I, Parisian of the Parisians,—I, who have reigned in the faubourgs, and have been called King of the *Halles*,—I am going to pass from the Place Maubert to the minarets of Gigelli; I become from a *Frondeur* an adventurer!"

"Oh, monseigneur, if you did not yourself tell me that——"

"And can you believe, just and simple man as you are, that if I go into Africa for this ridiculous motive, I will not endeavour to come out of it without ridicule? Will I not give the world cause to speak of me? And to be spoken of, nowadays, when there are M. le Prince, M. de Turenne, and many others, my contemporaries, I, admiral of France, grandson of Henry IV, King of Paris, have I anything left but to get myself killed? *Cordieu!* I will be talked of, I tell you; I shall be killed, whether or not; if not there, somewhere else."

"Why, monseigneur, this is only exaggeration; and hitherto you have demonstrated nothing of that kind but in bravery."

"But, what is this, Comte, only one glass?"

"I should not think of drinking with your Highness, unless your Highness permitted me," replied Athos, with noble humility.

"*Cordieu!* you were right to bring only one glass, we will both drink out of it, like two brothers in arms. Begin, Comte."

"Do me the honour," said Athos, gently putting back the glass.

"You are a charming friend," replied the Duc de Beaufort, who drank, and passed the goblet to his companion. "But that is not all," continued he, "I am still thirsty, and I wish to do honour to this handsome young man who stands here. I carry good luck with me, Vicomte," said he to Raoul; "wish for something while drinking out of my glass, and the plague stifle me if what you wish does not come to pass!" He held the goblet to Raoul, who hastily moistened his lips, and replied with the same promptitude:

"I have wished for something, monseigneur." His eyes sparkled with a gloomy fire, and the blood mounted to his cheeks; he terrified Athos, if only with his smile.

"And what have you wished for?" replied the Duc, sinking back into his chair, whilst with one hand he returned the bottle of Grimaud, and with the other gave him a purse.

"Will you promise me, monseigneur, to grant me what I wish for?"

"*Pardieu!* That is agreed upon!"

"I wished, Monsieur le Duc, to go with you."

"Well! *mordieu!*" cried the Duc, "the young Vicomte is right! What can he do here? He will rot with grief."

Raoul blushed, and the excitable Prince continued: "War is a distraction; we gain everything by it; we can only lose one thing by it: life;—then so much the worse!"

"That is to say, memory," said Raoul eagerly; "and that is to say, so much the better."

"Well, come," said the Duc, "let us see! Shall he go, or shall he not? If he goes, Comte, he shall be my aide-de-camp, my son."

"Monseigneur!" cried Raoul, bending his knee.

"Monseigneur!" cried Athos, taking the hand of the Duc; "Raoul shall do just as he likes."

"Oh! no, monsieur, just as you like," interrupted the young man.

"Comte, I shall set off in two days for Toulon," said M. de Beaufort. "Will you meet me there in a fortnight?"

"I will have the honour of thanking you there, my Prince, for all your kindnesses," replied the Comte.

"Here is your commission," said the Prince to Raoul. "I had prepared it, reckoning upon you. You will go on before me as far as Antibes."

"Yes, monseigneur."

CHAPTER XLII

THE SILVER DISH

The journey passed off pretty well. Athos and his son traversed France at the rate of fifteen leagues per day; sometimes more, sometimes less, according to the intensity of Raoul's grief. Athos learned that d'Artagnan had been seen at Antibes, and the Comte was eager to see his old friend before Raoul was due to embark. Raoul was much affected at not meeting with d'Artagnan. His affectionate heart longed to take a farewell and receive consolation from that heart of steel. Athos knew from experience that d'Artagnan became impenetrable when engaged in any serious affair, whether on his own account, or in the service of the King. He even feared to offend his friend, or thwart him by too pressing inquiries. And yet when Raoul commenced his labour of classing the flotilla, and got together the lighters to send them to Toulon, one of the fishermen told the Comte that his boat had been laid up to refit since a trip he had made on account of a gentleman who was in great haste to embark. Athos, believing that this man was telling a falsehood in order to be left at liberty to fish, and so gain more money when all his companions were gone, insisted upon having the details. The fisherman informed him that six days previously a man had come in the night to hire his boat, for the purpose of visiting the island of St. Honorat. The price was agreed upon, but the gentleman had arrived with an immense carriage case, which he insisted upon embarking, in spite of all the difficulties which opposed themselves to that operation. The fisherman had wished to retract. He had even threatened, but his threats had procured him nothing but a shower of blows from the gentleman's cane, which fell upon his shoulders sharp and long. Swearing and grumbling, he had recourse to the syndic of his brotherhood at Antibes, who administer justice among themselves and protect each other; but the gentleman had exhibited a certain paper, at the sight of which the syndic, bowing to the very ground, had enjoined obedience from the fisherman, and abused him for having been refractory. They then departed with the freight.

"But all this does not tell us," said Athos, "how you have injured your boat."

"This is the way. I was steering towards St. Honorat as the gentleman had desired me; but he changed his mind, and pretended that I could not pass to the south of the abbey."

"And why not?"

"Because, monsieur, there is in front of the square tower of the Benedictines, towards the southern point, the bank of the *Moines.*"

"A rock?" asked Athos.

"Level with the water, and below the water; a dangerous passage, but one I have cleared a thousand times; the gentlemen required me to land him at Sainte-Marguerite's."

"Well?"

"Well, monsieur!" cried the fisherman, with his Provençal accent, "a man is a sailor, or he is not; he knows his course, or he is nothing but a fresh-water lubber. I was obstinate, and wished to try the channel. The gentleman took me by the collar, and told me quietly he would strangle me. My mate armed himself with a hatchet, and so did I. We had the affront of the night before to pay him out for. But the gentleman drew his sword, and used it in such an astonishingly rapid manner, that we neither of us could get near him. I was about to hurl my hatchet at his head, and I had a right to do so, hadn't I, monsieur? for a sailor aboard is master, as a citizen is in his chamber; I was going, then, in self-defence, to cut the gentleman in two, when all at once—believe me or not, monsieur—the great carriage case opened of itself, I don't know how, and there came out of it a sort of a phantom, his head covered with a black helmet and a black mask, something terrible to look upon, which came towards me threatening with its fists."

"And that was——" said Athos.

"That was the devil, monsieur; for the gentleman, with great glee, cried out on seeing him: 'Ah! thank you, monseigneur!'"

"A strange story!" murmured the Comte, looking at Raoul.

"And what did you do?" asked the latter of the fisherman.

"You must know, monsieur, that two poor men, such as we are, could be no match for two gentlemen; but when one of them is the devil we had no chance! My companion and I did not stop to consult one another; we made but one jump into the sea, for we were within seven or eight hundred feet of the shore."

"Well, and then?"

"Why, and then, monsieur, as there was a little wind from the south-west, the boat drifted into the sands of Sainte-Marguerite's."

"Oh!—but the two travellers?"

"Bah! you need not be uneasy about them! It was pretty plain that one was the devil, and protected the other; for when we recovered the boat, after she got afloat again, instead of finding these two creatures injured by the shock, we found nothing, not even the carriage or the case."

"Very strange! very strange!" repeated the Comte. "But since that, what have you done, my friend?"

"I made my complaint to the governor of Sainte-Marguerite's, who brought my finger under my nose by telling me if I plagued him with such silly stories he would have me flogged."

"What! did the governor say so?"

"Yes, monsieur; and yet my boat was injured, seriously injured, for the prow is left upon the point of Sainte-Marguerite's, and the carpenter asks a hundred and twenty livres to repair it."

"Very well," replied Raoul; "you will be exempted from the service. Go."

"We will go to Sainte-Marguerite's, shall we?" said the Comte to Bragelonne, as the man walked away.

"Yes, monsieur, for there is something to be cleared up; that man does not seem to me to have told the truth."

That same day they set out for Sainte-Marguerite's, on board a lugger, come from Toulon under orders. The impression they felt on landing was a singularly pleasing one. The isle was full of flowers and fruits. Flat, offering nothing but a tiny bay for the convenience of embarkation, and under the protection of the governor, who went shares with them, smugglers made use of it as a provisional depot, at the expense of not killing the game or devastating the garden. With this compromise, the governor was in a situation to be satisfied with a garrison of eight men to guard his fortress, in which twelve cannons accumulated their coats of mouldy green. The governor was a sort of happy farmer, harvesting wines, figs, oil, and oranges, preserving his citrons and lemons within his sunny casemates.

Athos and Raoul wandered for some time round the fences of the garden without finding any one to introduce them to the governor. They ended by making their own way into the garden. All at once they heard some one call out, and raising their heads, perceived in the frame of the bars of a window something of a white colour, like a hand that was waved backwards and forwards—something shining, like a polished weapon struck by the rays of the sun. And before they were able to ascertain what it was they saw, a luminous train, accompanied by a hissing sound in the air, called their attention from the donjon to the ground. A second dull noise was heard from the ditch, and Raoul ran to pick up a silver plate which was rolling along the dry sand. The hand which had thrown this plate made a sign to the two gentlemen, and then disappeared. Athos and Raoul, approaching each other, commenced an attentive examination of the dusty plate, and they discovered, in characters traced upon the bottom of it with the point of a knife, this inscription:

"I am the brother of the King of France—a prisoner to-day—a madman to-morrow. French gentlemen and Christians, pray to God for the soul and the reason of the son of your masters."

The plate fell from the hands of Athos whilst Raoul was endeavouring to make out the meaning of these dismal words. At the same instant they heard a cry from the top of the donjon. As quick as lightning, Raoul bent down his head and forced down that of his father likewise. A musket barrel glittered from the crest of the wall. A white smoke floated like a plume from the mouth of the musket, and a ball was flattened against a stone within six inches of the two gentlemen.

"Cordieu!" cried Athos. "What are people assassinated here? Come down, cowards as you are!"

"Yes, come down!" cried Raoul, furiously shaking his fist at the castle.

One of the assailants—he who was about to fire—replied to these cries by an exclamation of surprise; and, as his companion, who wished to continue the attack, had seized his loaded musket, he who had cried out, threw up the weapon, and the ball flew into the air. Athos and Raoul seeing them disappear from the platform, expected they would come to them, and waited with a firm demeanour. Five minutes had not elapsed, when a stroke upon a drum called the eight soldiers of the garrison to arms, and they showed themselves on the other side of the ditch with their muskets in hand. At the head of these men was an officer, whom Athos and Raoul recognised as the one who had fired the first musket. The man ordered the soldiers to "make ready."

"We are going to be shot!" cried Raoul; "but, sword in hand, at least, let us leap the ditch! We shall kill at least two of these scoundrels when their muskets are empty." And, suiting the action to the word, Raoul was springing forward, followed by Athos, when a well-known voice resounded behind them—"Athos! Raoul!"

"D'Artagnan!" replied the two gentlemen.

"Recover arms! *Mordioux!*" cried the captain to the soldiers, "I was sure I could not be mistaken."

"What is the meaning of this?" asked Athos. "What! were we to be shot without warning?"

"It was I who was going to shoot you, and if the governor missed you, I should not have missed you, my dear friends. How fortunate it is that I am accustomed to take a long aim, instead of firing the instant I raise my weapon! I thought I recognised you! Ah! my dear friends, how fortunate!" and d'Artagnan wiped his brow, for he had run fast, and emotion with him was not feigned.

"How!" said Athos. "And is the gentleman who fired at us the governor of the fortress?"

"In person."

"And why did he fire at us? What have we done to him?"

"*Pardieu!* you received what the prisoner threw to you?"

"That is true."

"That plate—the prisoner has written something on the bottom of it, has he not?"

"Yes."

"Good Heavens! I was afraid he had."

And d'Artagnan, with all the marks of mortal disquietude, seized the plate to read the inscription. When he had read it, a fearful pallor spread over his countenance. "Oh! Good Heavens!" repeated he. "Silence!—Here is the governor."

"Invite these gentlemen to come to the fortress," said he.

"That I will willingly do. I was about to propose it to you." The fact is, the captain had quite another idea, and would have wished his friends a hundred leagues off. But he was obliged to make the best of it. They all turned towards the entrance of the fort, and the incident being exhausted, the eight soldiers returned to their delightful leisure for a moment disturbed by this unexpected adventure.

CHAPTER XLIII

CAPTIVE AND JAILERS

When they had entered the fort, and whilst the governor was making some preparations for the reception of his guests—"Come," said Athos, "let us have a word of explanation whilst we are alone."

"It is simply this," replied the musketeer. "I have conducted hither a prisoner, who the King commands shall not be seen. You came here, he has thrown something to you through the lattice of his window; I was at dinner with the governor, I saw the object thrown, and I saw Raoul pick it up. It does not take long to understand this. I understood it; and I thought you in intelligence with my prisoner. And then——"

"And then—you commanded us to be shot."

"*Ma foi!* I admit it; but if I was the first to seize a musket, fortunately I was the last to take aim at you."

"If you had killed me, d'Artagnan, I should have had the good fortune to die for the royal house of France, and it would be an honour to die by your hand—you, its noblest and most loyal defender."

"What the devil, Athos, do you mean by the royal house?" stammered d'Artagnan. "You don't mean that you, a well-informed and sensible man, can place any faith in the nonsense written by an idiot?"

"I do believe in it."

"With so much the more reason, my dear Chevalier, from your having orders to kill all those who do believe in it," said Raoul.

"That is because," replied the captain of the musketeers,—"because every calumny, however absurd it may be, has the almost certain chance of becoming popular."

"No, d'Artagnan," replied Athos promptly; "but because the King is not willing that the secret of his family should transpire among the people, and cover with shame the executioners of the son of Louis XIII."

"Do not talk in such a childish manner, Athos, or I shall begin to think you have lost your senses. Besides, explain to me how it is possible Louis XIII should have a son in the Isle of Sainte-Marguerite?"

"A son whom you have brought hither masked, in a fishing boat," said Athos. "Why not?"

D'Artagnan was brought to a pause.

"Ah! ah!" said he; "whence do you know that a fishing boat—"

"Brought you to Sainte-Marguerite's with the carriage containing the prisoner—with a prisoner whom you styled monseigneur. Oh! I am acquainted with all that," resumed the Comte. D'Artagnan bit his moustache.

"If it were true," said he, "that I had brought hither in a boat, and with a carriage, a masked prisoner, nothing proves that this prisoner must be a prince—a prince of the house of France?"

"Oh! ask that of Aramis," replied Athos coolly.

"Of Aramis!" cried the musketeer, quite at a stand. "Have you seen Aramis?"

"After his discomfiture at Vaux, yes; I have seen Aramis, a fugitive, pursued, ruined; and Aramis has told me enough to make me believe in the complaints that this unfortunate young man cut upon the bottom of the plate."

D'Artagnan's head sank upon his breast with confusion. "This is the way," said he, "in which God turns to nothing that which men call their wisdom! A fine secret must that be of which twelve or fifteen persons hold the tattered fragments! Athos, cursed be the chance which has brought you face to face with me in this affair! for now—"

"Well!" said Athos, with his customary mild severity, "is your secret lost because I know it? Consult your memory, my friend. Have I not borne secrets as heavy as this?"

"You have never borne one so dangerous," replied d'Artagnan, in a tone of sadness. "I have something like a sinister idea that all who are concerned with this secret will die, and die unfortunately."

"And now," said the musketeer, "answer me the question put to you by that black-looking Saint-Mars: 'What did you come to do at the Lerin Isles?'"

"To bid you farewell."

"Bid me farewell! What do you mean by that? Is Raoul going anywhere?"

"Yes."

"Then I will lay a wager it is with M. de Beaufort?"

"With M. de Beaufort it is, my dear friend; you always guess rightly."

"From habit."

Later, as they re-entered the fort, the sea rose with that rapid, gusty vehemence which characterises the Mediterranean; the ill humour of the element became a tempest. Something shapeless, and tossed about violently by the waves, appeared just off the coast.

"What is that?" said Athos — "a wrecked boat?"

"No, it is not a boat," said d'Artagnan.

"Pardon me," said Raoul, "there is a barque gaining the port rapidly."

"Yes, there is a barque in the creek, which is prudently seeking shelter here; but that which Athos points to in the sand is not a boat at all — it has run aground."

"Yes, yes, I see it."

"It is the carriage which I threw into the sea, after landing the prisoner."

"Well!" said Athos, "if you will take my advice, d'Artagnan, you will burn that carriage, in order that no vestige of it may remain, without which the fishermen of Antibes, who have believed they had to do with the devil, will endeavour to prove that your prisoner was but a man."

CHAPTER XLIV

PROMISES

Scarcely had d'Artagnan re-entered his apartment with his two friends, than one of the soldiers of the fort came to inform him that the governor was seeking for him. The barque which Raoul had perceived at sea, and which appeared so eager to gain the port, came to Sainte-Marguerite with an important despatch for the captain of the musketeers. On opening it, d'Artagnan recognised the writing of the King: "I should think," said Louis XIV, "you will have completed the execution of my orders, Monsieur d'Artagnan; return then immediately to Paris, and join me at the Louvre."

"There is the end of my exile," cried the musketeer with joy; "God be praised, I am no longer a jailer!" And he showed the letter to Athos.

The three friends quitted the little isle, after paying their respects to the governor, and by the last flashes of the departing tempest they

127

took their farewell of the white walls of the fort. D'Artagnan parted from his friends that same night, after having seen fire set to the carriage upon the shore, by the orders of Saint-Mars, according to the advice the captain had given him.

Athos and Raoul returned to Toulon, which began to be filled with the noise of carriages, with the noise of arms, with the noise of neighing horses. The trumpeters sounded their spirited marches; the drummers signalised their strength; the streets were overflowing with soldiers, servants, and trades-people. The Duc de Beaufort was everywhere, superintending the embarkation with the zeal and interest of a good captain. He encouraged even the most humble of his companions; he scolded his lieutenants, even those of the highest rank. Artillery, provisions, baggage, he insisted upon seeing all himself. He examined the equipment of every soldier; he assured himself of the health and soundness of every horse. It was plain that, light, boastful, egotistical in his hotel, the gentleman became the soldier again—the high noble, a captain—in face of the responsibility he had accepted. And yet, it must be admitted that, whatever was the care with which he presided over the preparations for departure, it was easy to perceive careless precipitation, and the absence of all the precaution which make the French soldier the first soldier in the world, because in that world, he is the one most abandoned to his own physical and moral resources. All things having satisfied, or appearing to have satisfied, the admiral, he paid his compliments to Raoul, and gave the last orders for sailing, which was ordered the next morning at daybreak. He invited the Comte and his son to dine with him; but they, under a pretext of the service, kept themselves apart. Gaining their hostelry, situated under the trees of the great Place, they took their repast in haste, and Athos led Raoul to the rocks which dominate the city, vast grey mountains, whence the view is infinite, and embraces a liquid horizon, which appears, so remote is it, on a level with the rocks themselves. The night was fine, as it always is in these happy climates. The moon, rising behind the rocks, unrolled, like a silver sheet, upon the blue carpet of the sea. In the road manœuvred silently the vessels which had just taken their rank to facilitate the embarkation. The sea, loaded with phosphoric light, opened beneath the hulls of the barques which transported the baggage and munitions; every dip of the prow ploughed up this gulf of white flames; and from every oar dropped liquid diamonds. The sailors, rejoicing in the largesses of the admiral, were heard murmuring their slow and artless songs. Sometimes, the grinding of the chains was mixed with the dull noise of shot falling into the holds. These harmonies, and this spectacle, oppress the heart like fear, and dilate it like hope. All this life speaks of death. Athos had seated himself with his son, upon the moss, among the brambles of the promontory. Around their heads passed and repassed large bats, carried along in the fearful whirl of their blind chase. The feet of Raoul were across the edge of the cliff, and bathed in that void which is peopled by vertigo, and provokes to annihilation.

At that moment the drums suddenly rolled, and the clarions filled the air with their inspiring notes. The regiments destined for the expedition began to debouch from the city. They advanced to the number of five, each composed of forty companies. Royals marched first, distinguished by their white uniform, faced with blue. The regimental colours, quartered crosswise, violet and dead-leaf, with a sprinkling of golden fleurs-de-lis, left the white-coloured flag, with its fleur-de-lised cross, to dominate over the whole. Musketeers, at the wings, with their forked sticks and their muskets on their shoulders; pikemen in the centre, with their lances, fourteen feet in length, marched gaily towards the transports, which carried them in detail to the ships. The regiments of Picardy, Navarre, Normandy, and Royal Vaisseau followed after. M. de Beaufort had known well how to select his troops. He himself was seen closing the march with his staff — it would take a full hour before he could reach the sea. Raoul with Athos turned his steps slowly towards the beach, in order to take his place when the Prince embarked. Grimaud, boiling with the ardour of a young man, superintended the embarkation of Raoul's baggage in the admiral's vessel. Athos, with his arm passed through that of the son he was about to lose, absorbed in melancholy meditation, was deaf to the noise around him. An officer came quickly towards them to inform Raoul that M. de Beaufort was anxious to have him by his side.

"Have the kindness to tell the Prince," said Raoul, "that I request he will allow me this hour to enjoy the company of my father."

"No, no," said Athos, "an aide-de-camp ought not thus to quit his general. Please to tell the Prince, monsieur, that the Vicomte will join him immediately." The officer set off at a gallop.

"Whether we part here or part there," added the Comte, "it is no less a separation." He carefully brushed the dust off his son's coat, and passed his hand over his hair as they walked along. "But, Raoul," said he, "you want money. M. de Beaufort's train will be splendid, and I am certain it will be agreeable to you to purchase horses and arms, which are very dear things in Africa. Now, as you are not actually in the service of the King, or M. de Beaufort, and are simply a volunteer, you must not reckon upon either pay or largesses. But I should not like you to want for anything at Gigelli. Here are two hundred pistoles; if you would please me, Raoul, spend them."

Raoul pressed the hand of his father, and, at the turning of a street, they saw M. de Beaufort, mounted upon a magnificent white horse, which replied by graceful curvets to the applauses of the women of the city. The Duc called Raoul, and held out his hand to the Comte. He spoke to him for some time, with such a kindly expression, that the heart of the poor father even felt a little comforted. It was, however, evident to both father and son that their walk was directed to nothing less than a punishment. There was a terrible moment — that at which, in quitting the sands of the shore, the soldiers and sailors exchanged the last kisses with their families and friends; a supreme moment, in which, notwithstanding the clearness of the heavens, the warmth of the sun, the perfumes of the air, and the rich life that was circulating in their veins, everything appeared black, everything appeared bitter, everything created doubts of a God, whilst speaking by the mouth, even, of God. It was customary for the admiral and his suite to embark the last; the cannon waited to announce, with its formidable voice, that the leader had placed his foot on board his vessel. Athos, forgetful of both the admiral and the fleet, and of his own dignity as a strong man, opened his arms to his son, and pressed him, convulsively, to his heart.

"Accompany us on board," said the Duc, very much affected; "you will gain a good half-hour."

"No," said Athos, "my farewell is spoken. I do not wish to speak a second."

"Then, Vicomte, embark—embark quickly!" added the Prince, wishing to spare the tears of these two men, whose hearts were bursting. And paternally, tenderly, very much as Porthos might have done, he took Raoul in his arms and placed him in the boat; the oars of which at a signal immediately were dipped in the waves. Himself, forgetful of ceremony, he jumped into his boat, and pushed it off with a vigorous foot. "Adieu!" cried Raoul.

Towards midday, when the sun devoured space, and scarcely the tops of the masts dominated the incandescent line of the sea, Athos perceived a soft aerial shadow rise, and vanish as soon as seen. This was the smoke of a cannon, which M. de Beaufort ordered to be fired as a last salute to the coast of France. The point was buried in its turn beneath the sky, and Athos returned painfully and slowly to his hostelry.

CHAPTER XLV

AMONG WOMEN

D'Artagnan, riding fast, thinking as constantly, alighted from his horse in Paris, fresh and tender in his muscles as the athlete preparing for the gymnasium. The King did not expect him so soon, and had just departed for the chase towards Meudon. D'Artagnan, instead of riding after the King, as he would formerly have done, took off his boots, had a bath, and waited till His Majesty should return dusty and tired. He occupied the interval of five hours in taking, as people say, the air of the house, and in arming himself against all ill chances. He learned that the King, during the last fortnight, had been gloomy; that the Queen-Mother was ill and much depressed; that Monsieur, the King's brother, was exhibiting a devotional turn; that Madame had the vapours; and that M. de Guiche was gone to one of his estates. He learned that M. Colbert was radiant; that M. Fouquet consulted a fresh physician every day, who still did not cure him, and that his principal complaint was one which physicians do not usually cure, unless they are political physicians. The King, d'Artagnan was told, behaved in the kindest manner to M. Fouquet, and did not allow him ever to be out of his sight; but the Surintendant, touched to the heart, like one of those fine trees which a worm has punctured, was declining daily, in spite of the royal smile, that sun of court trees. D'Artagnan learned that Mademoiselle de la Vallière had become indispensable to the King; that the King, during his sporting excursions, if he did not take her with him, wrote to her frequently—no longer verses, but, what was much worse, prose, and that whole pages at a time. Thus, as the poetical Pleiad of the day said, the *first King in the world* was seen descending from his horse *with an ardour beyond compare,* and on the crown of his hat scrawling bombastic phrases, which M. de Saint-Aignan, aide-de-camp in perpetuity, carried to La Vallière at the risk of foundering his horses. During this time, deer and pheasants were left to the free enjoyments of their nature, hunted so lazily, that, it was said, the art of venery ran great risk of degenerating at the court of France. D'Artagnan then thought of the wishes of poor Raoul, and as he loved to philosophise a little occasionally, he resolved to profit by the absence of the King to have a minute's talk with Mademoiselle de la Vallière. This was a very easy affair: while the King was hunting, Louise was walking with some other ladies in one of the galleries of the Palais Royal, exactly where the captain of the musketeers had some guards to inspect. D'Artagnan did not doubt, that if he could but open the conversation upon Raoul, Louise might give him grounds for writing a consolatory letter to the poor exile; and hope, or at least consolation for Raoul, in the state of heart in which he had left him, was life, to two men who were very dear to our captain. He directed his course, therefore, to the spot where he knew he should find Mademoiselle de la Vallière. D'Artagnan found La Vallière the centre of a circle. In her apparent solitude, the King's favourite received, like a queen, more perhaps than the Queen, a homage of which Madame had been so proud, when all the King's looks were directed to her and commanded the looks of the courtiers. D'Artagnan, although no squire of dames, received, nevertheless, civilities and attentions from the ladies; he was polite, as a brave man always is, and his terrible reputation had conciliated as much friendship among the men as admiration among the women. On seeing him enter, therefore, they immediately accosted him: and, as is not infrequently the case with fair ladies, opened the attack by questions: "Where *had* he been? What *had* become of him so long? Why had they not seen him as usual make his fine horse curvet in such beautiful style, to the delight and astonishment of the curious, from the King's balcony?"

He replied that he had just come from the land of oranges. This set all the ladies laughing. Those were times in which everybody travelled, but in which, notwithstanding, a journey of a hundred leagues was a problem often solved by death.

"'From the land of oranges?'" cried Mademoiselle de Tonnay-Charente. "From Spain?"

"Eh! eh!" said the musketeer.

"From Malta?" said Montalais.

"*Ma foi!* You are coming very near, ladies."

"Is it an island?" asked La Vallière.

"Mademoiselle," said d'Artagnan; "I will not give you the trouble of seeking any further; I come from the country where M. de Beaufort is, at this moment, embarking for Algiers."

"Have you seen the army?" said several warlike fair ones.

"As plainly as I see you," replied d'Artagnan.

"And the fleet?"

"Yes; I saw everything."

"Have we any of us any friends there?" said Mademoiselle de Tonnay-Charente coldly, but in a manner to attract attention to a question that was not without a calculated aim.

"Why," replied d'Artagnan, "yes; there were M. de la Guillitière, M. de Manchy, M. de Bragelonne——"

La Vallière became pale. "M. de Bragelonne!" cried the perfidious Athenaïs. "Eh, what! — is he gone to the wars? — he!"

Montalais trod upon her toe, but in vain.

But making La Vallière pale did not satisfy Athenaïs; she determined to make her blush likewise. Resuming the conversation without pause, "Do you know, Louise," said she, "that that is a great sin on your conscience?"

"What sin, mademoiselle?" stammered the unfortunate girl, looking round her for support, without finding it.

"Eh! — why?" continued Athenaïs, "the poor young man was affianced to you; he loved you, you cast him off."

"Well, and that is a right every honest woman has," said Montalais, in an affected tone. "When we know we cannot constitute the happiness of a man, it is much better to cast him off."

"Cast him off! or refuse him! — that's all very well," said Athenaïs, "but that is not the sin Mademoiselle de la Vallière has to reproach herself with. The actual sin, is sending poor Bragelonne to the wars; and to wars in which death is to be met with." Louise pressed her hand over her icy brow. "And if he dies," continued her pitiless tormentor, "you will have killed him. That is the sin."

Louise, half-dead, caught at the arm of the captain of the musketeers, whose face betrayed unusual emotion. "You wished to speak with me, Monsieur d'Artagnan," said she, in a voice broken by anger and pain. "What had you to say to me?"

D'Artagnan made several steps along the gallery, holding Louise on his arm; then, when they were far enough removed from the others — "What I had to say to you, mademoiselle," replied he, "Mademoiselle de Tonnay-Charente has just expressed; roughly, and unkindly, it is true, but still in its entirety."

She uttered a faint cry; and, struck to the heart by this new wound, she went on her way, like one of those poor birds which, struck to death, seeks the shade of the thicket to die in. She disappeared at one door, at the moment the King was entering by another. The first glance of the King was directed towards the empty seat of his mistress. Not perceiving La Vallière, a frown came over his brow; but as soon as he saw d'Artagnan, who bowed to him — "Ah! monsieur!" cried he, "you *have* been diligent! I am much pleased with you." This was the superlative expression of royal satisfaction. Many men would have been ready to lay down their lives for such a speech from the King. The maids of honour and the courtiers, who had formed a respectful circle round the King on his entrance, drew back, on observing he wished to speak privately with the captain of the musketeers. The King led the way out of the gallery, after having again, with his eyes, sought everywhere for La Vallière, whose absence he could not account for. The moment they were out of the reach of curious ears, "Well! Monsieur d'Artagnan," said he, "the prisoner?"

"Is in his prison, sire."

"What did he say on the road?"

"Nothing, sire."

"What did he do?"

"There was a moment at which the fisherman—who took me in his boat to Sainte-Marguerite—revolted, and did his best to kill me. The —the prisoner defended me instead of attempting to fly."

The King became pale. "Enough!" said he; and d'Artagnan bowed. Louis walked about his cabinet with hasty steps. "Were you at Antibes," said he, "when Monsieur de Beaufort came there?"

"No, sire; I was setting off when Monsieur le Duc arrived."

"Ah!" which was followed by a fresh silence. "Whom did you see there?"

"A great many persons," said d'Artagnan coolly.

The King perceived that he was unwilling to speak. "I have sent for you, captain, to desire you to go and prepare my lodgings at Nantes."

"At Nantes!" cried d'Artagnan.

"In Bretagne."

"Yes, sire, it is in Bretagne. Will your Majesty make so long a journey as to Nantes?"

"The States are assembled there," replied the King. "I have two demands to make of them: I wish to be there."

"When shall I set out?" said the captain.

"This evening—to-morrow—to-morrow evening; for you must stand in need of rest."

"I have rested, sire."

"That is well. Then between this and to-morrow evening, when you please."

D'Artagnan bowed as if to take his leave; but, perceiving the King very much embarrassed, "Will your Majesty," said he, stepping two paces forward, "take the court with you?"

"Certainly I shall."

"Then your Majesty will, doubtless, want the musketeers?" And the eye of the King sank beneath the penetrating glance of the captain.

"Take a brigade of them," replied Louis.

"Is that all? Has your Majesty no other orders to give me?"

"No—ah—yes."

"I am all attention, sire."

"At the castle of Nantes, which I hear is very ill arranged, you will adopt the practice of placing musketeers at the door of each of the principal dignitaries I shall take with me."

"Of the principal?"

"Yes."

"For instance, at the door of M. de Lyonne?"

"Yes."

"And of Monsieur le Surintendant?"

"Without doubt."

"Very well, sire. By to-morrow I shall have set out."

"Oh, yes; but one more word, Monsieur d'Artagnan. At Nantes you will meet with M. le Duc de Gesvres, captain of the guards. Be sure that your musketeers are placed before his guards arrive. Precedence always belongs to the first comer."

"Yes, sire."

"And if M. de Gesvres should question you?"

"Question me, sire! Is it likely that M. de Gesvres should question me?" And the musketeer, turning cavalierly on his heel, disappeared. "To Nantes!" said he to himself, as he descended the stairs. "Why did he not dare to say, from thence to Belle-Isle?"

CHAPTER XLVI

HOW KING LOUIS XIV PLAYED HIS LITTLE PART

Fouquet, on his arrival at Nantes, got into a carriage which the city sent to him, we know not why or how, and he repaired to *la Maison de Nantes,* escorted by a vast crowd of people, who for several days had been boiling with the expectation of a convocation of the States. A report was spread during the night, that the King was coming in great haste upon post horses, and that he would arrive within ten or twelve hours at latest. The people, while waiting for the King, were greatly rejoiced to see the musketeers, freshly arrived with Monsieur d'Artagnan, their captain, and quartered in the castle, of which they occupied all the posts, in quality of guard of honour.

The King was entering the city, which soon resounded with the cannon from the ramparts, and from a vessel which replied from the lower part of the river. Fouquet's brow darkened; he called his *valets de chambre,* and dressed in ceremonial costume. From his window, behind the curtains, he could see the eagerness of the people, and the movement of a large troop, which had followed the Prince, without its being to be guessed how. The King was conducted to the castle in great pomp, and Fouquet saw him dismount under the portcullis, and speak something in the ear of d'Artagnan, who held his stirrup. D'Artagnan, when the King had passed under the arch, directed his steps towards the house Fouquet was in, but so slowly, and stopping so frequently to speak to his musketeers, drawn up as a hedge, that it might be said he was counting the seconds, or the steps, before accomplishing his message. Fouquet opened the window to speak to him in the court.

"Ah!" cried d'Artagnan, on perceiving him, "are you still there, monseigneur?"

The Surintendant sighed deeply. "Good Heavens! yes, monsieur," replied he. "The arrival of the King has interrupted me in the projects I had formed."

"Oh! then you know that the King has arrived?"

"Yes, monsieur, I have seen him; and this time you come from him——"

"To inquire after you, monseigneur; and to beg you to have the kindness to repair to the castle."

Fouquet heaved a last sigh, got into his carriage, so great was his weakness, and went to the castle, escorted by d'Artagnan.

It was two o'clock in the afternoon. The King, full of impatience, went to his cabinet on the terrace, and kept opening the door of the corridor, to see what his secretaries were doing.

Then the summons of the bell recalled Rose, whose hour it was.

"See, if M. d'Artagnan has returned."

"Not yet, sire."

"It is very strange!" murmured the King.

He had not finished these words when a much rougher voice than that of the King was heard.

"D'Artagnan!" cried the King, with evident joy. "In the first place, let me see the result of your commission, monsieur; you may repose afterwards."

D'Artagnan, who was just passing through the door, stopped at the voice of the King. "I have arrested M. Fouquet, sire."

"You took plenty of time about it," said the King sharply.

D'Artagnan looked at the King.

"Where is M. Fouquet at this moment?" asked Louis, after a short silence.

"M. Fouquet, sire," replied d'Artagnan, "is in the iron cage that M. Colbert had prepared for him, and is going, as fast as four vigorous horses can drag him, towards Angers."

"Monsieur d'Artagnan," said the King, "give twenty of your musketeers to M. de Saint-Aignan, to form a guard for M. Fouquet. And from Angers," continued the King, "they will conduct the prisoner to the Bastille, in Paris."

D'Artagnan was about to retire; but the King stopped him.

"Monsieur," said he, "you will go immediately, and take possession of the isle and fief of Belle-Isle-en-Mer."

"Yes, sire. Alone?"

"You will take a sufficient number of troops to prevent delay, in case the place should be contumacious."

A murmur of adulatory incredulity arose from the group of courtiers. "That is to be done," said d'Artagnan.

"I saw the place in my infancy," resumed the King, "and I do not wish to see it again. You have heard me? Go, monsieur, and do not return without the keys of the place."

Colbert went up to d'Artagnan. "A commission which, if you carry it out well," said he, "will be worth a marshal's baton to you."

"Why do you employ the words, 'if you carry it out well'?"

"Because it is difficult."

"Ah! in what respect?"

"You have friends in Belle-Isle, Monsieur d'Artagnan; and it is not an easy thing for men like you to march over the bodies of their friends to obtain success."

CHAPTER XLVII

BELLE-ISLE-EN-MER

At the extremity of the mole, which the furious sea beats at evening tide, two men, holding each other by the arm, were conversing in an animated and expansive tone. Every one has already perceived that those two men were our proscribed heroes, Porthos and Aramis, who had taken refuge in Belle-Isle since the ruin of their hopes, since the discomfiture of the vast plan of M. d'Herblay.

"It is of no use you saying anything to the contrary, my dear Aramis," repeated Porthos, inhaling vigorously the saline air with which he filled his powerful chest. "It is of no use, Aramis. The disappearance of all the fishing-boats that went out two days ago, is not an ordinary circumstance. There has been no storm at sea; the weather has been constantly calm, not even the lightest gale; and even if we had had a tempest, all our boats would not have foundered. I repeat, it is strange. This complete disappearance astonishes me, I tell you."

"True," murmured Aramis. "You are right, friend Porthos; it is true, there is something strange in it."

"And, further," added Porthos, whose ideas the assent of the Bishop of Vannes seemed to enlarge; "and, further, have you remarked, that if the boats have perished, not a single plank has been washed ashore?"

"I have remarked that as well as you."

"Have you remarked, besides, that the two only boats we had left in the whole island, and which I sent in search of the others ——"

Aramis here interrupted his companion by a cry, and by so sudden a movement, that Porthos stopped as if he were stupefied. "What do you say, Porthos! What! – You have sent the two boats ——"

"In search of the others! Yes; to be sure I have," replied Porthos, quite simply.

"Unhappy man! What have you done? Then we are indeed lost," cried the Bishop.

"Lost! – what did you say?" exclaimed the terrified Porthos. "How lost? Aramis. How are we lost?"

Aramis bit his lips. "Nothing! nothing! Your pardon. I meant to say ——"

"What?"

"Porthos, what is that yonder?" interrupted Aramis, rising suddenly, and pointing out to his friend a black spot upon the empurpled line of the water.

"A bark!" said Porthos; "yes, it is a bark! Ah! we shall have some news at last."

"There are two!" cried the Bishop, on discovering another mast; "two! three! four!"

"Five!" said Porthos, in his turn. "Six! seven! Ah! *mon Dieu! mon Dieu!* It is a whole fleet!"

An old fisherman passed. "Are those our barks yonder?" asked Aramis.

The old man looked steadily into the horizon.

"No, monseigneur," replied he, "they are lighter boats in the King's service."

"Boats in the royal service?" replied Aramis, starting. "How do you know that?" said he.

"By the flag."

"Ah!" said Aramis.

"*Vivat!*" cried Porthos, "they are sending us reinforcements; don't you think they are, Aramis?"

"Probably."

"Unless it is the English coming."

"By the Loire? That would have an ill look, Porthos, for they must have come through Paris."

"You are right; they are reinforcements decidedly, or provisions."

Aramis leant his head upon his hands, and made no reply. Then, all at once,—"Porthos," said he, "have the alarm sounded."

"The alarm! do you think of such a thing?"

"Yes, and let the cannoniers mount to their batteries, let the artillery men be at their pieces, and be particularly watchful of the coast batteries."

Porthos opened his eyes to their widest extent. He looked attentively at his friend, to convince himself he was in his proper senses.

"I will do it, my dear Porthos," continued Aramis, in his most bland tone; "I will go and have these orders executed myself, if you do not go, my friend."

"Well! I will go instantly!" said Porthos, who went to execute the orders, casting all the while looks behind him, to see if the Bishop of Vannes were not deceived; and if, on returning to more rational ideas, he would not recall him. The alarm was sounded, the trumpets brayed, the drums rolled; the great bell of the belfry was put in motion. The dikes and moles were quickly filled with the curious and soldiers; the matches sparkled in the hands of the artillerymen, placed behind the large cannon bedded in their stone carriages. When every man was at his post, when all the preparations for the defence were made: "Permit me, Aramis, to try and comprehend," whispered Porthos timidly, in Aramis's ear.

"My dear friend, you will comprehend but too soon," murmured M. d'Herblay, in reply to this question of his lieutenant.

"The fleet which is coming yonder, with sails unfurled, straight towards the port of Belle-Isle, is a royal fleet, is it not?"

"But as there are two kings in France, Porthos, to which of these two kings does this fleet belong?"

"Oh! you open my eyes," replied the giant, stunned by this argument.

And Porthos, for whom the reply of his friend had just opened the eyes, or rather thickened the bandage which covered his sight, went with his best speed to the batteries to overlook his people, and exhort every one to do his duty. It was quite night when one of these vessels, which had created such a sensation among the inhabitants of Belle-Isle, was moored within cannon-shot of the place. It was soon seen, notwithstanding the darkness, that a sort of agitation reigned on board this vessel, from the side of which a skiff was lowered, of which the three rowers, bending to their oars, took the direction of the port, and in a few instants struck land at the foot of the fort. The commander of this yawl jumped on shore. He had a letter in his hand, which he waved in the air, and seemed to wish to communicate with somebody. This man was soon recognised by several soldiers, as one of the pilots of the island. He was the skipper of one of the two barques kept back by Aramis, and which Porthos, in his anxiety with regard to the fate of the fishermen who had disappeared for two days, had sent in search of the missing boats. He asked to be conducted to M. d'Herblay. Two soldiers, at a signal from the sergeant, placed him between them, and escorted him. Aramis was upon the quay. The envoy presented himself before the Bishop of Vannes. The darkness was almost complete, notwithstanding the flambeaux borne at a small distance by the soldiers who were following Aramis in his rounds.

"Well, Jonathan, from whom do you come?"

"Monseigneur, from those who captured me."

"Who captured you?"

"You know, monseigneur, we set out in search of our comrades?"

"Yes; and afterwards?"

"Well! monseigneur, within a short league we were captured by a cutter belonging to the King."

"Humph!" said Aramis, "then I suppose it is the royal fleet blockading the coasts?"

"Yes, monseigneur."

"Who commands it?"

"The captain of the King's musketeers."

"D'Artagnan?"

"D'Artagnan!" exclaimed Porthos.

"I believe that is the name."

"And did he give you this letter?"

"Yes, monseigneur."

"Bring the flambeaux nearer."

"It is his writing," said Porthos.

Aramis eagerly read the following lines:

"Order of the King to take Belle-Isle; or to put the garrison to the sword, if they resist; order to make prisoners of all the men of the garrison; signed, D'ARTAGNAN, who, the day before yesterday, arrested M. Fouquet, for the purpose of his being sent to the Bastille."

Aramis turned pale, and crushed the paper in his hands.

"What is it?" asked Porthos.

"Nothing, my friend, nothing."

"What shall I do?" asked Jonathan.

"You will return on board this captain's vessel."

"Yes, monseigneur."

"And tell him that we beg he will himself come into the island."

"Ah! I comprehend!" said Porthos.

"Yes, monseigneur," replied Jonathan; "but if the captain should refuse to come to Belle-Isle?"

"If he refuses, as we have cannon, we will make use of them."

"What! against d'Artagnan?"

"If it is d'Artagnan, Porthos, he will come. Go, Jonathan, go!"

"*Ma foi!* I no longer comprehend anything," murmured Porthos.

"I will make you comprehend all, my dear friend; the time for it is come; sit down upon this gun-carriage, open your ears, and listen well to me."

"Oh! *pardieu!* I shall listen, no fear of that."

"May I depart, monseigneur?" cried Jonathan.

"Yes, begone, and bring back an answer. Allow the canoe to pass, you men there!" And the canoe pushed off to regain the fleet.

Aramis took Porthos by the hand, and explained all to him.

CHAPTER XLVIII

THE EXPLANATIONS OF ARAMIS

"So then," said Porthos, when Aramis had concluded his narrative, "so then, it seems, I have quite fallen out with Louis XIV?"

"Oh! I will settle all that, my good friend, I will settle all that. I will take it upon myself alone!"

"Aramis!"

"No, no, Porthos, I conjure you, let me act. No false generosity! No inopportune devotedness! You knew nothing of my projects. You have done nothing of yourself. With me it is different. I am alone the author of the plot. I stood in need of my inseparable companion: I called upon you, and you came to me, in remembrance of our ancient device, 'All for one, one for all.' My crime was being an egotist."

"Now, that is a word I like," said Porthos; "and seeing that you have acted entirely for yourself, it is impossible for me to blame you; it is natural."

And upon this sublime reflection, Porthos pressed the hand of his friend cordially.

In presence of this ingenuous greatness of soul, Aramis felt himself little. It was the second time he had been compelled to bend before real superiority of heart, much more powerful than splendour of mind. He replied by a mute and energetic pressure to the kind endearment of his friend.

"Now," said Porthos, "that we have come to an explanation, now that I am perfectly aware of our situation with respect to Louis XIV, I think, my friend, it is time to make me comprehend the political intrigue of which we are the victims."

"My dear friend," said Aramis, smiling with a strong shade of sadness, "do not let us reason like children; let us be men in council and execution—But, hark! I hear a hail for landing at the port. Attention, Porthos, serious attention!"

"It is d'Artagnan, no doubt," said Porthos, in a voice of thunder, approaching the parapet.

"Yes, it is I," replied the captain of the musketeers, running lightly up the steps of the mole, and gaining rapidly the little esplanade upon which his two friends waited for him. As soon as he came towards them, Porthos and Aramis observed an officer who followed d'Artagnan, treading apparently in his very steps. The captain stopped upon the stairs of the mole, when half-way up. His companion imitated him.

"Make your men draw back," cried d'Artagnan to Porthos and Aramis; "let them retire out of hearing." The order being given by Porthos, was executed immediately. Then d'Artagnan, turning towards him who followed him:

"Monsieur," said he, "we are no longer here on board the King's fleet, where, in virtue of your order, you spoke so arrogantly to me just now."

"Monsieur," replied the officer, "I did not speak arrogantly to you; I simply, but rigorously, obeyed what I had been commanded. I have been directed to follow you. I follow you. I am directed not to allow you to communicate with any one without taking cognisance of what you do; I mix myself, therefore, with your communications."

D'Artagnan trembled with rage, and Porthos and Aramis, who heard this dialogue, trembled likewise, but with uneasiness and fear. D'Artagnan, biting his moustache with that vivacity which denoted in him the state of an exasperation closely to be followed by a terrible explosion, approached the officer.

"Monsieur," said he, in a low voice, so much the more impressive, that affecting a calm it threatened a tempest — "Monsieur, when I sent a canoe hither, you wished to know what I wrote to the defenders of Belle-Isle. You produced an order to that effect; and, in my turn, I instantly showed you the note I had written. When the skipper of the boat sent by me returned, when I received the reply of these two gentlemen (and he pointed to Aramis and Porthos), you heard every word of what the messenger said. All that was plainly in your orders, all that was well executed, very punctually, was it not?"

"Yes, monsieur," stammered the officer; "yes, without doubt, but — "

"Monsieur," continued d'Artagnan, growing warm — "Monsieur, when I manifested the intention of quitting my vessel to cross to Belle-Isle, you required to accompany me; I did not hesitate; I brought you with me. You are now at Belle-Isle, are you not?"

"Yes, monsieur, but — "

"But — the question no longer is of M. Colbert, who has given you that order, or of whomsoever in the world you are following the instructions: the question now is of a man who is a clog upon M. d'Artagnan, and who is alone with M. d'Artagnan upon steps whose feet are bathed by thirty feet of salt water; a bad position for that man, a bad position, monsieur! I warn you."

Porthos and Aramis, mute and trembling at the top of the parapet, cried to the musketeer, "Dear d'Artagnan, take care!"

D'Artagnan made them a sign to keep silence, raised his foot with a terrifying calmness to mount the stairs, and turned round, sword in hand, to see if the officer followed him. The officer made a sign of the cross and stepped up. Porthos and Aramis, who knew their d'Artagnan, uttered a cry, and rushed down to prevent the blow they thought they already heard. But, d'Artagnan, passing his sword into his left hand, —

"Monsieur," said he to the officer, in an agitated voice, "you are a brave man. You ought better to comprehend what I am going to say to you now than that which I have just said to you."

"Speak, Monsieur d'Artagnan, speak," replied the brave officer.

"These gentlemen we have just seen, and against whom you have orders, are my friends."

"I know they are, monsieur."

"You can understand if I ought to act towards them as your instructions prescribe."

"I understand your reserves."

"Very well; permit me, then, to converse with them without a witness."

"Monsieur d'Artagnan, if I yielded to your request, if I did that which you beg me to do, I should break my word; but if I do not do it, I shall disoblige you. I prefer the one to the other. Converse with your friends, and do not despise me, monsieur, for doing for the sake of you, whom I esteem and honour; do not despise me for committing for you, and you alone, an unworthy act." D'Artagnan, much agitated, passed his arms rapidly round the neck of the young man, and went up to his friends. The officer, enveloped in his cloak, sat down on the damp weed-covered steps.

"Well!" said d'Artagnan to his friends, "such is my position; judge for yourselves." They all three embraced. All three pressed each other in their arms as in the glorious days of their youth.

"What is the meaning of all these rigours?" said Porthos.

"You ought to have some suspicions of what it is," said d'Artagnan.

"Not much, I assure you, my dear captain; for, in fact, I have done nothing, no more has Aramis," hastened the worthy baron to say.

D'Artagnan darted a reproachful look at the prelate, which penetrated that hardened heart.

"Dear Porthos!" cried the Bishop of Vannes.

"You see what has been done against you," said d'Artagnan; "interception of all that is coming to or going from Belle-Isle. Your boats are all seized. If you had endeavoured to fly, you would have fallen into the hands of the cruisers which plough the sea in all directions on the watch for you. The King wants you to be taken, and he will take you." And d'Artagnan tore several hairs from his grey moustache. Aramis became sombre, Porthos angry.

"My idea was this," continued d'Artagnan; "to make you both come on board, to keep you near me, and restore you your liberty. But now, who can say that when I return to my ship, I may not find a superior; that I may not find secret orders which will take from me my command, and give it to another, who will dispose of me and you without hopes of help?"

"We must remain at Belle-Isle," said Aramis resolutely; "and I assure you, for my part, I will not surrender easily." Porthos said nothing. D'Artagnan remarked the silence of his friend.

"I have another trial to make of this officer, of this brave fellow who accompanies me, and whose courageous resistance makes me very happy; for it denotes an honest man, who, although an enemy, is a thousand times better than a complaisant coward. Let us try to learn from him what he has the right of doing, and what his orders permit or forbid."

"Let us try," said Aramis.

D'Artagnan came to the parapet, leaned over towards the steps of the mole, and called the officer, who immediately came up. "Monsieur," said d'Artagnan, after having exchanged the most cordial courtesies, natural between gentlemen, who know and appreciate each other worthily—"monsieur, if I wished to take away these gentlemen, what would you do?"

"I should not oppose it, monsieur; but having direct orders, formal orders to take them under my guard, I should detain them."

"Ah!" said d'Artagnan.

"That's all over," said Aramis gloomily. Porthos did not stir.

"But still take Porthos," said the Bishop of Vannes; "he can prove to the King, I will help him in doing so, and you also can, Monsieur d'Artagnan, that he has had nothing to do in this affair."

"Hum!" said d'Artagnan. "Will you come? Will you follow me, Porthos? The King is merciful."

"I beg to reflect," said Porthos nobly.

"You will remain here, then?"

"Until fresh orders," cried Aramis, with vivacity.

"Until we have had an idea," resumed d'Artagnan; "and I now believe that will not be long first, for I have one already."

"Let us say adieu, then," said Aramis; "but in truth, my good Porthos, you ought to go."

"No!" said the latter laconically.

"As you please," replied Aramis, a little wounded in his nervous susceptibility at the morose tone of his companion. "Only I am re-assured by the promise of an idea from d'Artagnan, an idea I fancy I have divined."

"Let me see," said the musketeer, placing his ear near Aramis's mouth. The latter spoke several words rapidly to which d'Artagnan replied, "That is it, precisely."

"Infallible, then!" cried Aramis.

"During the first emotion that this resolution will cause, take care of yourself, Aramis."

"Oh! don't be afraid."

"Now, monsieur," said d'Artagnan to the officer, "thanks, a thousand thanks! You have made yourself three friends for life."

"Yes," added Aramis. Porthos alone said nothing, but merely bowed.

D'Artagnan having tenderly embraced his two old friends, left Belle-Isle with the inseparable companion M. Colbert had given him. Thus, with the exception of the explanation with which the worthy Porthos had been willing to be satisfied, nothing had changed in appearance in the fate of the one or the other. "Only," said Aramis, "there is d'Artagnan's idea."

D'Artagnan did not return on board without examining to the bottom the idea he had discovered. Now, we know that when d'Artagnan did examine, according to custom, daylight pierced through. As to the officer, becoming mute again, he left him full measure to meditate. Therefore, on putting his foot on board his vessel, moored within cannon-shot of the island, the captain of the musketeers had already got together all his means, offensive and defensive.

He immediately assembled his council, which consisted of the officers serving under his orders. These were eight in number: a chief of the maritime forces; a major directing the artillery; an engineer, the officer we are acquainted with, and four lieutenants. Having assembled them in the chamber of the poop, d'Artagnan arose, took off his hat, and addressed them thus:

"Gentlemen, I have been to reconnoitre Belle-Isle-en-Mer, and I have found it a good and solid garrison; moreover, preparations are made for a defence that may prove troublesome. I therefore intend to send for two of the principal officers of the place, that we may converse with them. Having separated them from their troops and their cannon, we shall be better able to deal with them; particularly with good reasoning. Is this your opinion, gentlemen?"

The officers looked at each other as if to read their opinions in their eyes, with the intention of evidently acting, after they should have agreed, according to the desire of d'Artagnan. And already the latter saw with joy that the result of their consent would be sending a barque to Porthos and Aramis, when the King's officer drew from his pocket a folded paper, which he placed in the hands of d'Artagnan.

D'Artagnan, full of mistrust, unfolded the paper, and read these words:

"Prohibition to M. d'Artagnan to assemble any council whatever, or to deliberate in any way before Belle-Isle be surrendered and the prisoners shot. Signed, Louis."

D'Artagnan repressed the movement of impatience that ran through his whole body, and, with a gracious smile, —

"That is well, monsieur," said he; "the King's orders shall be complied with."

CHAPTER XLIX

RESULT OF THE IDEAS OF THE KING, AND THE IDEAS OF D'ARTAGNAN

The blow was direct. It was severe, mortal. D'Artagnan, furious at having been anticipated by an idea of the King's, did not, however, yet despair; and, reflecting upon the idea he had brought back from Belle-Isle, he augured from it a new means of safety for his friends.

"Gentlemen," said he suddenly, "since the King has charged some other than myself with his secret orders, it must be because I no longer possess his confidence, and I should be really unworthy of it, if I had the courage to hold a command subject to so many injurious suspicions. I will go then immediately and carry my resignation to the King. I give it before you all, enjoining you all to fall back with me upon the coast of France, in such a way as not to compromise the safety of the forces His Majesty has confided to me. For this purpose, return all to your posts; within an hour we shall have the ebb of the tide. To your posts, gentlemen! I suppose," added he, on seeing that all prepared to obey him, except the surveillant officer, "you have no orders to object, this time?"

And d'Artagnan almost triumphed while speaking these words. This plan was the safety of his friends. The blockade once raised, they might embark immediately and set sail for England or Spain, without fear of being molested. Whilst they were making their escape, d'Artagnan would return to the King; would justify his return by the indignation which the mistrusts of Colbert had raised in him; he would be sent back with full powers, and he would take Belle-Isle, that is to say, the cage, after the birds had flown. But to this plan the officer opposed a second order of the King's. It was thus conceived:

"From the moment M. d'Artagnan shall have manifested the desire of giving in his resignation, he shall no longer be reckoned leader of the expedition, and every officer placed under his orders shall be held to no longer obey him. Moreover, the said Monsieur d'Artagnan having lost that quality of leader of the army sent against Belle-Isle, shall set out immediately for France, in company of the officer who will have remitted the message to him, and who will consider him as a prisoner for whom he is answerable."

Brave and careless as he was, d'Artagnan turned pale. Everything had been calculated with a depth which, for the first time in thirty years, had recalled to him the solid foresight and the inflexible logic of the great Cardinal. He leant his head on his hand, thoughtful, scarcely breathing. "If I were to put this order into my pocket," thought he, "who would know it, or who would prevent my doing it? Before the King had had time to be informed, I should have saved those poor fellows yonder. Let us exercise a little audacity! My head is not one of those which the executioner strikes off for disobedience. We will disobey!" But at the moment he was about to adopt this plan, he saw the officers around him reading similar orders which the infernal agent of the thoughts of Colbert had just distributed to them. The case of disobedience had been foreseen, as the others had been.

"Monsieur," said the officer, coming up to him, "I await your good pleasure to depart."

"I am ready, monsieur," replied d'Artagnan, grinding his teeth.

The officer immediately commanded a canoe to receive M. d'Artagnan and himself. At sight of this he became almost mad with rage.

"How," stammered he, "will you carry on the direction of the different corps?"

"When you are gone, monsieur," replied the commander of the fleet, "it is to me the direction of the whole is committed."

"Then, monsieur," rejoined Colbert's man, addressing the new leader, "it is for you that this last order that has been remitted to me is intended. Let us see your powers."

"Here they are," said the sea officer, exhibiting a royal signature.

"Here are your instructions," replied the officer, placing the folded paper in his hands; and turning towards d'Artagnan, "Come, monsieur," said he in an agitated voice (such despair did he behold in that man of iron), "do me the favour to depart at once."

"Immediately!" articulated d'Artagnan feebly, subdued, crushed by implacable impossibility.

And he let himself slide down into the little boat, which started, favoured by wind and tide, for the coast of France. The King's guards embarked with him. The musketeer still preserved the hope of reaching Nantes quickly, and of pleading the cause of his friends eloquently enough to incline the King to mercy. The barque flew like a swallow. D'Artagnan distinctly saw the land of France profiled in black against the white clouds of night.

"Ah! monsieur," said he, in a low voice, to the officer, to whom, for an hour, he had ceased speaking, "what would I give to know the instructions for the new commander! They are all pacific, are they not? and——"

He did not finish; the sound of a distant cannon rolled over the waters, then another, and two or three still louder. D'Artagnan shuddered.

"The fire is opened upon Belle-Isle," replied the officer. The canoe had just touched the soil of France.

CHAPTER L

THE ANCESTORS OF PORTHOS

When d'Artagnan had quitted Aramis and Porthos, the latter returned to the principal fort to converse with the greater liberty. Porthos, still thoughtful, was a constraint upon Aramis, whose mind had never felt itself more free.

"Dear Porthos," said he suddenly, "I will explain d'Artagnan's idea to you."

"What idea, Aramis?"

"An idea to which we shall owe our liberty within twelve hours."

"Ah! indeed!" said Porthos, much astonished. "Let us see it."

"Did you remark, in the scene our friend had with the officer that certain orders restrained him with regard to us?"

"Yes, I did remark that."

"Well! d'Artagnan is going to give in his resignation to the King, and during the confusion which will result from his absence, we will get away, or rather you will get away, Porthos, if there is a possibility of flight only for one."

Here Porthos shook his head and replied: "We will escape together, Aramis, or we will remain here together."

"You are a generous heart," said Aramis, "only your melancholy uneasiness afflicts me."

"I am not uneasy," said Porthos.

"Then you are angry with me."

"I am not angry with you."

"Then why, my friend, do you put on such a dismal countenance?"

"I will tell you: I feel fatigued. It is the first time, and there is a custom in our family."

"What is it, my friend?"

"My grandfather was a man twice as strong as I am."

"Indeed!" said Aramis; "then your grandfather must have been Samson himself."

"No; his name was Antoine. Well! he was about my age, when setting out one day for the chase, he felt his legs weak, he who had never known this before."

"What was the meaning of that fatigue, my friend?"

"Nothing good, as you will see; for having set out, complaining still of the weakness of his legs, he met a wild boar, which made head against him; he missed him with his arquebuse, and was ripped up by the beast, and died directly."

"There is no reason in that why you should alarm yourself, dear Porthos."

"Oh! you will see. My father was as strong again as I am. He was a rough soldier, under Henry III and Henry IV; his name was not Antoine, but Gaspard, the same as M. de Coligny. Always on horseback, he had never known what lassitude was. One evening, as he rose from table, his legs failed him."

"He had supped heartily, perhaps," said Aramis, "and that was why he staggered."

"Bah! A friend of M. de Bassompierre, nonsense! No, no, he was astonished at feeling this lassitude, and said to my mother, who laughed at him, 'Would not one believe I was going to meet with a wild boar, as the late M. du Vallon, my father, did?'"

"Well?" said Aramis.

"Well! having this weakness, my father insisted upon going down into the garden instead of going to bed; his foot slipped on the first stair; the staircase was steep; my father fell against a stone angle in which an iron hinge was fixed. The hinge opened his temple; and he lay dead upon the spot."

Aramis raised his eyes to his friend: "These are two extraordinary circumstances," said he; "let us not infer that there may succeed a third. It is not becoming in a man of your strength to be superstitious, my brave Porthos. Besides, when were your legs seen to fail? Never have you been so firm, so superb; why, you could carry a house on your shoulders."

"At this moment," said Porthos, "I feel myself pretty active; but at times I vacillate, I sink; and lately this phenomenon, as you say, has occurred four times. I will not say that this frightens me, but it annoys me. Life is an agreeable thing. I have money; I have fine estates; I have horses that I love; I have also friends I love: d'Artagnan, Athos, Raoul, and you."

The admirable Porthos did not even take the trouble to dissimulate to Aramis the rank he gave him in his friendship. Aramis pressed his hand: "We will still live many years," said he, "to preserve in the world specimens of rare men. Trust yourself to me, my friend; we have no reply from d'Artagnan; that is a good sign. He must have given orders to get the vessels together and clear the seas. On my part I have just issued directions that a barque should be rolled upon rollers to the mouth of the great cavern of Locmaria, which you know, where we have so often laid wait for foxes."

"Yes, and which terminates at the little creek by a trench which we discovered the day that splendid fox escaped that way."

"Precisely. In case of misfortunes, a barque is to be concealed for us in that cavern; indeed, it must be there by this time. We will wait for a favourable moment, and, during the night, to sea!"

"That is a good idea; what shall we gain by it?"

"We shall gain by it—that nobody knows that grotto, or rather its issue, except ourselves and two or three hunters of the island; we shall gain by it—that if the island is occupied, the scouts, seeing no barque upon the shore, will never imagine we can escape, and will cease to watch."

All at once a cry resounded in their ears: "To arms! to arms!"

This cry, repeated by a hundred voices, brought to the chamber where the two friends were conversing, surprise to the one, and uneasiness to the other. Aramis opened the window; he saw a crowd of people running with flambeaux. Women were seeking places of safety, the armed population were hastening to their posts.

"The fleet! the fleet!" cried a soldier, who recognised Aramis.

"The fleet?" repeated the latter.

"Within half cannon-shot," continued the soldier.

"To arms!" cried Aramis.

"To arms!" repeated Porthos formidably. And both rushed forth towards the mole, to place themselves within the shelter of the batteries. Boats, laden with soldiers, were seen approaching; they took three directions, for the purpose of landing at three points at once.

"What must be done?" said an officer of the guard.

"Stop them; and if they persist, fire!" said Aramis.

Five minutes after the cannonade commenced. These were the shots that d'Artagnan had heard as he landed in France. But the boats were too near the mole to allow the cannon to aim correctly. They landed, and the combat commenced hand to hand.

"What's the matter, Porthos?" said Aramis to his friend.

"Nothing! nothing!—only my legs; it is really incomprehensible! —they will be better when we charge." In fact, Porthos and Aramis did charge with such vigour; they so thoroughly animated their men, that the royalists re-embarked precipitately, without gaining anything but the wounds they carried away.

"Eh! but, Porthos," cried Aramis, "we must have a prisoner, quick! quick!" Porthos bent over the stair of the mole, and seized by the nape of the neck one of the officers of the royal army who was waiting to embark till all his people should be in the boat. The arm of the giant lifted up his prey, which served him as a buckler, as he recovered himself, without a shot being fired at him.

"Here is a prisoner for you," said Porthos coolly to Aramis.

"Well!" cried the latter, laughing, "have you not calumniated your legs?"

"It was not with my legs I took him," said Porthos; "It was with my arms."

CHAPTER LI

THE SON OF BISCARRAT

The Bretons of the Isle were very proud of this victory; Aramis did not encourage them in the feeling.

"What will happen," said he to Porthos, when everybody was gone home, "will be that the anger of the King will be roused by the account of the resistance, and that these brave people will be decimated or shot when they are taken, which cannot fail to take place."

"From which it results then," said Porthos, "that what we have done is of no use."

"For the moment it may be of some," replied the Bishop, "for we have a prisoner from whom we shall learn what our enemies are preparing to do."

"Yes, let us interrogate the prisoner," said Porthos, "and the means of making him speak are very simple. We are going to supper; we will invite him to join us; when he drinks he will talk."

This was done. The officer was at first rather uneasy, but became reassured on seeing what sort of men he had to deal with. He gave, without having any fear of compromising himself, all the details imaginable of the resignation and departure of d'Artagnan. He explained how, after that departure, the new leader of the expedition had ordered a surprise upon Belle-Isle. There his explanations stopped. Aramis and Porthos exchanged a glance which evinced their despair. No more dependence to be placed upon the brave imagination of d'Artagnan; consequently, no more resources in the event of defeat. Aramis, continuing his interrogations, asked the prisoner what the leaders of the expedition contemplated doing with the leaders of Belle-Isle.

"The orders are," replied he, "to kill during the combat, and hang afterwards."

Porthos and Aramis looked at each other again, and the colour mounted to their faces.

"One more cup of wine to your health," said Porthos, drinking himself. From one subject to another the chat with the officer was prolonged. He was an intelligent gentleman, and suffered himself to be led away by the charm of Aramis's wit, and Porthos's cordial *bonhomie*.

"Pardon me," said he, "if I address a question to you; but men who are in their sixth bottle have a clear right to forget themselves a little."

"Address it!" said Porthos; "address it!"

"Speak," said Aramis.

"Were you not, gentlemen, both in the musketeers of the late King?"

148

"Yes, monsieur, and of the best of them, if you please," said Porthos.

"That is true; I should say even the best of all soldiers, messieurs, if I did not fear to offend the memory of my father."

"Of your father?" cried Aramis.

"Do you know what my name is?"

"*Ma foi!* no, monsieur; but you can tell us, and——"

"I am called Georges de Biscarrat."

"Oh!" cried Porthos in his turn, "Biscarrat! Do you remember that name, Aramis?"

"Biscarrat!" reflected the Bishop. "It seems to me——"

"Try to recollect, monsieur," said the officer.

"*Pardieu!* that won't take me long," said Porthos. "Biscarrat—called Cardinal—one of the four who interrupted us the day on which we formed our friendship with d'Artagnan, sword in hand."

"Precisely, gentlemen."

"The only one," cried Aramis eagerly, "we did not wound."

"Consequently, a good blade," said the prisoner.

"That's true! very true!" exclaimed both the friends together. "*Ma foi!* Monsieur Biscarrat, we are delighted to make the acquaintance of such a brave man's son."

Biscarrat pressed the hands held out to him by the two ancient musketeers.

"Cannon!" said Porthos suddenly.

"Cannon and musketry too!" cried the Bishop.

On hearing at a distance, among the rocks, these sinister reports of combat which they thought had ceased, "What can that be?" asked Porthos.

"Eh! *pardieu!*" cried Aramis; "this is just what I expected."

"What is that?"

"The attack made by you was nothing but a feint; is not that true, monsieur? And whilst your companions allowed themselves to be repulsed, you were certain of effecting a landing on the other side of the island."

"Oh! several, monsieur."

"Monsieur de Biscarrat," said the Bishop of Vannes, with a singular accent of nobleness and courtesy, "Monsieur de Biscarrat, be kind enough to resume your liberty."

The worthy officer, then jumping upon a horse given him by Aramis, departed in the direction of the sound of the cannon, and which, by bringing the crowd into the fort, had interrupted the conversation of the two friends and their prisoner. Aramis watched his departure, and when left alone with Porthos, "Well, do you comprehend?" said he.

"I comprehend. We are going to escape by the cavern."

"If you please," replied Aramis joyously. "Forward, my friend, Porthos; our boat awaits us, and the King has not caught us yet."

CHAPTER LII

THE GROTTO OF LOCMARIA

The cavern of Locmaria was sufficiently distant from the mole to render it necessary for our friends to husband their strength to arrive there. Besides, night was advancing; midnight had struck at the fort. Porthos and Aramis were loaded with money and arms. They walked then, across the heath, which is between the mole and the cavern, listening to every noise, and endeavouring to avoid ambushes. At length, after a rapid course, frequently interrupted by prudent stoppages, they reached the deep grottos, into which the foreseeing Bishop of Vannes had taken care to have rolled upon cylinders a good barque capable of keeping the sea at this fine season.

"My good friend," said Porthos, after having respired vigorously, "we are arrived, it seems. But I thought you spoke of three men, three servants who were to accompany us. I don't see them—where are they?"

"Why should you see them, dear Porthos?" replied Aramis. "They are certainly waiting for us in the cavern, and, no doubt, are resting for a moment, after having accomplished their rough and difficult task."

Aramis stopped Porthos, who was preparing to enter the cavern. "Will you allow me, my friend," said he to the giant, "to pass in first? I know the signal I have given to these men; who, not hearing it, would be very likely to fire upon you or slash away with their knives in the dark."

"Go on, then, Aramis; go on—go first; you are all wisdom and prudence; go on. Ah! there is that fatigue again, of which I spoke to you. It has just seized me again."

Aramis left Porthos sitting at the entrance of the grotto, and bowing his head, he penetrated into the interior of the cavern, imitating the cry of the owl. A little plaintive cooing, a scarcely distinct cry, replied from the depths of the cave. Aramis pursued his way cautiously, and soon was stopped by the same kind of cry as he had first uttered, and this cry sounded within ten paces of him.

"Are you there, Yves?" said the Bishop.

"Yes, monseigneur; Goenne is here likewise. His son accompanies us."

"That is well. Are all things ready?"

"Yes, monseigneur."

"Go to the entrance of the grottos my good Yves, and you will there find the Seigneur de Pierrefonds, who is resting after the fatigue of our journey. And if he should happen not to be able to walk, lift him up, and bring him hither to me."

The three men obeyed. But the recommendation given to his servants was useless. Porthos, refreshed, had already himself commenced the descent, and his heavy step resounded amongst the cavities, formed and supported by columns of silex and granite. As soon as the Seigneur de Bracieux had rejoined the Bishop, the Bretons lighted a lantern with which they were furnished, and Porthos assured his friend that he felt as strong as ever.

"Let us visit the canoe," said Aramis, "and satisfy ourselves at once what it will hold."

"Do not go too near with the light," said Yves; "for, as you desired me, monseigneur, I have placed under the bench of the poop, in the coffer you know of, the barrel of powder, and the musket charges that you sent me from the fort."

"Very well," said Aramis; and, taking the lantern himself, he examined minutely all parts of the canoe, with the precautions of a man who is neither timid nor ignorant in the face of danger. When Aramis appeared satisfied with the result of his inspection, "Let us consult, Porthos," said he, "to know if we must endeavour to get the barque out by the unknown extremity of the grotto, following the descent and the shade of the cavern, or whether it be better in the open air, to make it slide upon the rollers, through the bushes, levelling the road of the little beach, which is but twenty feet high, and gives at its foot, in the tide, three or four fathoms of good water upon a sound bottom."

"It must be as you please, monseigneur," replied Yves, respectfully; "but I don't believe that by the slope of the cavern, and in the dark, in which we shall be obliged to manoeuvre our boat, the road will be so convenient as in the open air. I know the beach well, and can certify that it is as smooth as a grass plat in a garden; the interior of the grotto, on the contrary, is rough; without again reckoning, monseigneur, that at the extremity we shall come to the trench which leads to the sea, and perhaps the canoe will not pass down it."

"I have made my calculations," said the Bishop, "and I am certain it would pass."

"So be it; I wish it may, monseigneur," continued the skipper; "but your greatness knows very well that to make it reach the extremity of the trench, there is an enormous stone to be lifted—that under which the fox always passes, and which closes the trench up like a door."

"That can be raised," said Porthos, "that is nothing."

"Oh! I know that monseigneur has the strength of ten men," replied Yves; "but that is giving monseigneur a great deal of trouble."

"I think the skipper may be right," said Aramis; "let us try the open-air passage."

"The more so, monseigneur," continued the fisherman, "that we should not be able to embark before day, it would require so much labour, and that as soon as daylight appears, a good vedette placed outside the grotto would be necessary, indispensable even, to watch the manoeuvres of the lighters or the cruisers that are upon the lookout for us."

"Yes, yes, Yves, your reasons are good; we will go by the beach."

And the three robust Bretons went to the boat, and were beginning to place their rollers underneath it to put it in motion, when the distant barking of dogs was heard, proceeding from the interior.

Aramis darted out of the grotto, followed by Porthos. Dawn just tinted with purple and white the waves and the plain; through the dim light the young, melancholy firs waved their tender branches over the pebbles, and long flights of crows were skimming with their black wings over the thin fields of buck-wheat. In a quarter of an hour it would be clear daylight; the awakened birds joyously announced it to all nature. The barking which had been heard, which had stopped the three fishermen engaged in moving the boat, and had brought Aramis and Porthos out of the cavern, was prolonged in a deep gorge within about a league of the grotto.

"It is a pack of hounds," said Porthos; "the dogs are upon a scent."

"Who can be hunting at such a moment as this?" said Aramis.

"And this way particularly," continued Porthos, "this way, where they may expect the army of the royalists."

"In common prudence," said Aramis, "let us go back into the grotto; the voices evidently draw nearer; we shall soon know what we have to trust to."

They re-entered, but had scarcely proceeded a hundred steps in the darkness, when a noise like the hoarse sigh of a creature in distress resounded through the cavern, and breathless, rapid, terrified, a fox passed like a flash of lightning before the fugitives, leaped over the boat and disappeared, leaving behind it its sour scent, which was perceptible for several seconds under the low vaults of the cave.

"The fox!" cried the Bretons, with the joyous surprise of hunters.

"Accursed chance!" cried the Bishop, "our retreat is discovered."

As if to confirm the words of Aramis, they heard the yelping pack come with frightful swiftness upon the trail of the animal. Six fox-hounds burst out at once upon the little heath, with a cry resembling the noise of a triumph.

"There are the dogs plain enough!" said Aramis, posted on the look-out behind a chink between two rocks; "now, who are the huntsmen?"

Porthos applied his eye to the slit, and saw at the summit of a hillock a dozen horsemen urging on their horses in the track of the dogs, shouting "*Taïaut! taïaut!*"

"The guards!" said he.

"Yes, my friend, the King's guards."

"The King's guards! do you say, monseigneur!" cried the Bretons, becoming pale in their turns.

"And Biscarrat at their head, mounted upon my grey horse," continued Aramis.

The hounds at the same moment rushed into the grotto like an avalanche, and the depths of the cavern were filled with their deafening cries.

"Ah! the devil!" said Aramis, resuming all his coolness at the sight of the certain inevitable danger. "I am perfectly satisfied we are lost, but we have at least one chance left. If the guards who follow their hounds happen to discover there is an issue to the grotto, there is no more help for us, for on entering they must see both us and our boat. The dogs must not go out of the cavern. The masters must not enter."

"That is clear," said Porthos.

"You understand," added Aramis, with the rapid precision of command; "there are six dogs which will be forced to stop at the great stone under which the fox has glided—but at the too narrow opening of which they shall be themselves stopped and killed."

The Bretons sprang forward knife in hand. In a few minutes there was a lamentable concert of growls, and mortal howlings—and then, nothing.

"That's well!" said Aramis, coolly, "now for the masters!"

"What is to be done with them?" said Porthos.

"Wait their arrival, conceal ourselves, and kill them."

"Kill them!" replied Porthos.

"There are sixteen," said Aramis, "at least, up at present."

"And well armed," added Porthos, with a smile of consolation.

"It will last about ten minutes," said Aramis. "To work!"

And with a resolute air he took up a musket, and placed his hunting knife between his teeth.

"Yves, Goenne, and his son," continued Aramis, "will pass the muskets to us. You, Porthos, will fire when they are close. We shall have brought down eight before the others are aware of anything—that is certain; then, all, there are five of us; we will despatch the other eight, knife in hand."

"And poor Biscarrat?" said Porthos.

Aramis reflected a moment—"Biscarrat the first," replied he coolly; "He knows us."

CHAPTER LIII

THE GROTTO

Biscarrat, better mounted than his companions, arrived the first at the opening of the grotto, and comprehended that the fox and the dogs were all engulfed in it.

"Well?" asked the young men, coming up, out of breath, and unable to understand the meaning of his inaction.

"Well! I cannot hear the dogs; they and the fox must be all engulfed in this cavern."

"What the devil can have become of them?" asked the young men in chorus. And every master called his dog by name, whistled to him in his favourite note, without a single one replying to either the call or the whistle.

"It is perhaps an enchanted grotto," said Biscarrat; "let us see." And jumping from his horse, he made a step into the grotto.

"Stop! stop! I will accompany you," said one of the guards, on seeing Biscarrat disappear in the shade of the cavern's mouth.

"No," replied Biscarrat, "there must be something extraordinary in the place—don't let us risk ourselves all at once. If in ten minutes you do not hear of me you can come in, but not all at once."

Biscarrat entered then alone, and advanced through the darkness till he came in contact with the muzzle of Porthos's musket. The resistance which his chest met with astonished him. He naturally raised his hand and laid hold of the icy barrel. At the same instant, Yves lifted a knife against the young man which was about to fall upon him with all the force of a Breton's arm, when the iron wrist of Porthos stopped it half-way. Then, like low, muttering thunder, his voice growled in the darkness; "I will not have him killed."

Biscarrat found himself between a protection and a threat, the one almost as terrible as the other. However brave the young man might be, he could not prevent a cry escaping him, which Aramis immediately suppressed by placing a handkerchief over his mouth. "Monsieur de Biscarrat," said he, in a low voice, "we mean you no harm, and you must know that, if you have recognised us; but, at the first word, the first sigh, or the first breath, we shall be forced to kill you as we have killed your dogs."

"Yes, I recognise you, gentlemen," said the officer in a low voice. "But why are you here—what are you doing here? Unfortunate men! I thought you were in the fort?"

"And you, monsieur, you were to obtain conditions for us, I think?"

"I did all I was able, messieurs, but——"

"But what?"

"But there are positive orders."

"To kill us?" Biscarrat made no reply. It would have cost him too much to speak of the cord to gentlemen. Aramis understood the silence of the prisoner.

"Monsieur Biscarrat," said he, "you would be already dead if we had not had regard for your youth and our ancient association with your father; but you may yet escape from the place by swearing that you will not tell your companions what you have seen."

"I will not only swear that I will not speak of it," said Biscarrat, "but I still further swear that I will do everything in the world to prevent my companions from setting foot in the grotto."

"Biscarrat! Biscarrat!" cried several voices from the outside, coming like a whirlwind into the cave.

"Reply," said Aramis.

"Here am I!" cried Biscarrat.

"Now, begone; we depend upon your loyalty." And he left his hold of the young man, who hastily returned towards the light.

"Biscarrat! Biscarrat!" cried the voices, still nearer. And the shadows of several human forms projected into the interior of the grotto.

Biscarrat rushed to meet his friends, in order to stop them, and met them just as they were adventuring into the cave.

Biscarrat made a last effort to stop his friends, but it was useless. In vain he threw himself before the most rash; in vain he clung to the rocks to bar the passage; the crowd of young men rushed into the cave, in the steps of the officer who had spoken last, but who had sprung in first, sword in hand, to face the unknown danger. Biscarrat, repulsed by his friends, not able to accompany them without passing in the eyes of Porthos and Aramis for a traitor and a perjurer, with painfully attentive ear and still supplicating hands leant against the rough side of a rock which he thought must be exposed to the fire of the musketeers. As to the guards, they penetrated farther and farther, with cries that grew weaker as they advanced. All at once, a discharge of musketry, growling like thunder, exploded beneath the vault. Two or three balls were flattened against the rock where Biscarrat was leaning. At the same instant, cries, howlings, and imprecations burst forth, and the little troop of gentlemen reappeared — some pale, some bleeding — all enveloped in a cloud of smoke, which the outward air seemed to draw from the depths of the cavern. "Biscarrat! Biscarrat!" cried the fugitives, "you knew that was an ambuscade in that cavern, and you have not warned us! Biscarrat, you are the cause that four of us have been killed! Woe be to you, Biscarrat!"

Biscarrat, with hair on end, haggard eyes, and bewildered head, advanced towards the interior of the cavern, saying, "You are right. Death to me, who have allowed my companions to be assassinated. I am a base wretch!" And throwing away his sword, for he wished to die without defending himself, he rushed head foremost into the cavern. The others followed him. The eleven who remained out of sixteen imitated his example; but they did not go farther than the first. A second discharge laid five upon the icy sand; and, as it was impossible to see whence this murderous thunder issued, the others fell back with a terror that can be better imagined than expressed. But, far from flying, as the others had done, Biscarrat remained safe and sound, seated on a fragment of rock, and waited. There were only six gentlemen left.

"Where is Biscarrat?" The young men looked round them, and saw that Biscarrat did not answer.

"He is dead!" said two or three voices.

"Oh! no," replied another; "I saw him through the smoke, sitting quietly on a rock. He is in the cavern; he is waiting for us."

"He must know who are there."

"And how should he know them?"

"He was taken prisoner by the rebels."

"Good!" said an officer. "We have no longer any need of him; here are reinforcements coming."

In fact, a company of the guards, left in the rear by their officers, whom the ardour of the chase had carried away — from seventy-five to eighty men — arrived in good order, led by their captain and the first lieutenant. The five officers hastened to meet their soldiers; and, in a language, the eloquence of which may be easily imagined, they related the adventure, and asked for aid. The captain interrupted them: "Where are your companions?" demanded he.

"Dead!"

"But there were sixteen of you."

"Ten are dead. Biscarrat is in the cavern, and we are five."

"Biscarrat is then a prisoner?"

"Probably."

"No, for here he is — look." In fact, Biscarrat, appeared at the opening of the grotto.

"He makes us a sign to come on," said the officer. "Come on!"

"Come on!" cried all the troop. And they advanced to meet Biscarrat.

"Monsieur," said the captain, addressing Biscarrat, "I am assured that you know who the men are in that grotto, and who make such a desperate defence. In the King's name I command you to declare what you know."

"Captain," said Biscarrat, "you have no need to command me; my word has been restored to me this very instant; and I come in the name of these men."

"Tell me who they are?"

"To tell you they are determined to defend themselves to the death, unless you grant them good terms."

"How many are there of them, then?"

"There are two," said Biscarrat.

"Two men—and they have killed ten in two discharges! That is impossible, Monsieur Biscarrat!"

And he marched first as far as the opening of the grotto. There he halted. The object of this halt was to give to Biscarrat and his companions time to describe to him the interior of the grotto. Then, when he believed he had a sufficient acquaintance with the places, he divided his company into three bodies, which were to enter successively, keeping up a sustained fire in all directions.

"Captain," said Biscarrat, "I beg to be allowed to march at the head of the first platoon."

"So be it," replied the captain; "you have all the honour of it. That is a present I make you."

"Thanks!" replied the young man, with all the firmness of his race.

"Take your sword, then."

"I shall go as I am, captain," said Biscarrat, "for I do not go to kill, I go to be killed."

And placing himself at the head of the first platoon with his head uncovered and his arms crossed,—"March, gentlemen!" said he.

CHAPTER LIV

AN HOMERIC SONG

It is time to pass into the other camp, and to describe at once the combatants and the field of battle. Aramis and Porthos had gone to the grotto of Locmaria with the expectation of finding there their canoe ready armed, as well as the three Bretons, their assistants; and they at first hoped to make the barque pass through the little issue of the cavern, concealing in that fashion both their labours and their flight. The arrival of the fox and the dogs had obliged them to remain concealed. The grotto extended the space of about two hundred yards, to that little slope dominating a creek. The first entrance to the cavern was by a moderate descent, above which heaped-up rocks formed a low arcade; the interior, very unequal as to the ground, dangerous from the rocky inequalities of the vault, was subdivided into several compartments which commanded each other and joined each other by means of several rough, broken steps, fixed right and left, in enormous natural pillars. At the third compartment, the vault was so low, the passage so narrow, the barque would scarcely have passed without touching the two sides; nevertheless, in a moment of despair, wood softens and stone becomes compliant under the breath of human will. Such was the thought of Aramis, when, after having fought the fight, he decided upon flight—a flight certainly dangerous, since all the assailants were not dead; and that, admitting the possibility of putting the barque to sea, they would have to fly in open day, before the conquered, so interested on recognising their small number, in pursuing their conquerors. Then the two discharges had killed ten men. Aramis, habituated to the windings of the cavern, went to reconnoitre them one by one—counted them, for the smoke prevented seeing outside; and he immediately commanded that the canoe should be rolled as far as the great stone, the closure of the liberating issue. Porthos collected all his strength, took the canoe up in his arms and raised it up, whilst the Bretons made it run rapidly along the rollers. They had descended into the third compartment; they had arrived at the stone which walled up the outlet. Porthos seized this gigantic stone at its base, applied to it his robust shoulder, and gave a heave which made this wall crack. A cloud of dust fell from the vault with the ashes of ten thousand generations of sea-birds, whose nests stuck like cement to the rock. At the third shock the stone gave way; it oscillated for a minute. Porthos, placing his back against the neighbouring rock, made an arch with his foot, which drove the block out of the calcareous masses which served for hinges and cramps. The stone fell, and daylight was visible, brilliant, radiant, which rushed into the cavern by the opening, and the blue sea appeared to the delighted Bretons. They then began to lift the barque over the barricade. Twenty more yards, and it might glide into the ocean. It was during this time, that the company arrived, was drawn up by the captain, and disposed for either an escalade or an assault. Aramis watched over everything, to favour the labours of his friends. He saw the reinforcements, he counted the men, he convinced himself at a single glance of the insurmountable peril to which a fresh combat would expose them. To escape by sea, at the moment the cavern was about to be invaded, was impossible. In fact, the daylight which had just been admitted to the last two compartments had exposed to the soldiers the barque being rolled towards the sea, the two rebels within musket shot, and one of their discharges would riddle the boat if it did not kill the five navigators. Aramis, digging his hands into his grey hair with rage, invoked the assistance of God and the assistance of the demon. Calling to Porthos, who was working alone more than all the rollers—whether of flesh or of wood—"My friend," said he, "our enemies have just received a reinforcement."

"Ah! ah!" said Porthos quietly, "what is to be done, then?"

"These people are coming down into the grotto."

"Yes."

"We could kill about fifteen of them, but not more."

"How many are there in all?" asked Porthos.

"They have received a reinforcement of seventy-five men."

"Seventy-five and five, eighty. Ah! ah!" said Porthos.

"If they fire all at once they will riddle us with balls."

"Certainly they will."

"We two will keep the powder, the balls, and the muskets here."

"But only two, my dear Aramis — we shall never fire three shots together," said Porthos innocently, "the defence by musketry is a bad one."

"Find a better, then."

"I have found one," said the giant eagerly; "I will place myself in ambuscade behind the pillar with this iron bar, and invisible, unattackable if they come on in floods. I can let my bar fall upon their skulls, thirty times in a minute. *Hein!* what do you think of the project? You smile!"

"Excellent, dear friend, perfect! I approve it greatly; only you will frighten them, and half of them will remain outside to take us by famine. What we want my good friend, is the entire destruction of the troop; a single man left standing ruins us."

"You are right, my friend, but how can we attract them, pray?"

"By not stirring, my good Porthos."

"Well! we won't stir, then; but when they shall be all together ——"

"Then leave it to me! I have an idea."

"If it is thus, and your idea be a good one — and your idea is most likely to be good — I am satisfied."

"To your ambuscade, Porthos, and count how many enter."

"But you, what will you do?"

"Don't trouble yourself about me; I have a task to perform."

"I think I can hear cries."

"It is they. To your post. Keep within reach of my voice and hand."

Porthos took refuge in the second compartment, which was absolutely black with darkness. Aramis glided into the third; the giant held in his hand an iron bar of about fifty pounds weight. Porthos handled this lever, which had been used in rolling the barque, with marvellous facility. During this time, the Bretons had pushed the barque to the beach. In the enlightened compartment, Aramis, stooping and concealed, was busied in some mysterious manoeuvre. A command was given in a loud voice. It was the last order of the captain commandant. Twenty-five men jumped from the upper rocks into the first compartment of the grotto, and having taken their ground, began to fire. The echoes growled, the hissing of the balls cut the air, an opaque smoke filled the vault.

"To the left! to the left!" cried Biscarrat, who, in his first assault, had seen the passage to the second chamber, and who, animated by the smell of powder, wished to guide his soldiers in that direction. The troop accordingly precipitated themselves to the left — the passage gradually growing narrower. Biscarrat, with his hands stretched forward, devoted to death, marched in advance of the muskets. "Come on!" exclaimed he, "I see daylight!"

"Strike, Porthos!" cried the sepulchral voice of Aramis.

Porthos heaved a heavy sigh — but he obeyed. The iron bar fell full and direct upon the head of Biscarrat, who was dead before he had ended his cry. Then the formidable lever rose ten times in ten seconds, and made ten corpses. The soldiers could see nothing; they heard sighs and groans; they stumbled over dead bodies, but as they had no conception of the cause of all this, they came forward jostling each other. The implacable bar, still falling, annihilated the first platoon, without a single sound having warned the second which was quietly advancing, only this second platoon, commanded by the captain, had broken a thin fir, growing on the shore, and, with its resinous branches twisted together, the captain had made a flambeau. On arriving at the compartment where Porthos, like the exterminating angel had destroyed all he touched, the first rank drew back in terror. No firing had replied to that of the guards, and yet their way was stopped by a heap of dead bodies—they literally walked in blood. Porthos was still behind his pillar. The captain, on enlightening with the trembling flame of the fir this frightful carnage, of which he in vain sought the cause, drew back towards the pillar, behind which Porthos was concealed. Then a gigantic hand issued from the shade, and fastened on the throat of the captain, who uttered a stifled rattle; his outstretched arms beating the air, the torch fell and was extinguished in blood. A second after the corpse of the captain fell close to the extinguished torch, and added another body to the heap of dead which blocked up the passage. From an unreflective, instinctive, mechanical feeling, the lieutenant cried, —"Fire!"

Immediately a volley of musketry flamed, thundered, roared in the cavern, bringing down enormous fragments from the vaults. The cavern was lighted for an instant by this discharge, and then immediately returned to a darkness rendered still thicker by the smoke. To this succeeded a profound silence, broken only by the steps of the third brigade, now entering the cavern.

CHAPTER LV

THE DEATH OF A TITAN

At the moment when Porthos, more accustomed to the darkness than all these men coming from open daylight, was looking round him to see if in this night Aramis were not making him some signal, he felt his arm gently touched, and a voice low as a breath murmured in his ear, "Come."

And amidst the noise of the third brigade, which continued to advance, amidst the imprecations of the guards left alive, of the dying, rattling their last sigh, Aramis and Porthos glided imperceptibly along the granite walls of the cavern. Aramis led Porthos into the last but one compartment, and showed him, in a hollow of the rocky wall, a barrel of powder weighing from seventy to eighty pounds, to which he had just attached a match. "My friend," said he to Porthos, "you will take this barrel, the match of which I am going to set fire to, and throw it amidst our enemies; can you do so?"

"Parbleu!" replied Porthos; and he lifted the barrel with one hand. "Light it!"

159

"Stop," said Aramis, "till they are all massed together, and then, my Jupiter, hurl your thunder-bolt among them."

"Light it," repeated Porthos.

"On my part," continued Aramis, "I will join our Bretons, and help them to get the canoe to the sea. I will wait for you on the shore; launch it strongly, and hasten to us."

"Light it," said Porthos, a third time.

"But do you understand me?"

"*Parbleu!*" said Porthos again, with laughter that he did not even attempt to restrain; "when a thing is explained to me I understand it; begone, and give me the light."

Aramis gave the burning match to Porthos, who held out his arm to him, his hands being engaged. Aramis pressed the arm of Porthos with both his hands, and fell back to the outlet of the cavern where the three rowers awaited him.

Porthos, left alone, applied the spark bravely to the match. The spark—a feeble spark, first principle of a conflagration—shone in the darkness like a fire-fly, then was deadened against the match which it enflamed, Porthos enlivening the flame with his breath. The smoke was a little dispersed, and by the light of the sparkling match, objects might, for two seconds, be distinguished.

Then the arm of the giant swung round; then was seen to pass through the air, like a falling star, the train of fire. The barrel, hurled a distance of thirty feet, cleared the barricade of dead bodies, and fell midst a group of shrieking soldiers, who threw themselves on their faces. The officer had followed the brilliant train in the air; he endeavoured to precipitate himself upon the barrel and tear out the match before it reached the powder it contained. Useless devotedness! the air had made the flame attached to the conductor more active; the match, which at rest might have burnt five minutes, was consumed in thirty seconds, and the infernal work exploded. Furious vortices, hissings of sulphur and nitre, devouring ravages of the fire which caught to objects, the terrible thunder of the explosion, this is what the second which followed the two seconds we have described, disclosed in that cavern, equal in horrors to a cavern of demons. The rock split like planks of deal under the axe. A jet of fire, smoke, and debris sprang up from the middle of the grotto, enlarging as it mounted. The large walls of silex tottered and fell upon the sand, and the sand itself, an instrument of pain when launched from its hardened bed, riddled the face with its myriads of cutting atoms. Cries, howlings, imprecations, and existences—all were extinguished in one immense crash.

As to Porthos, after having hurled the barrel of powder amidst his enemies, he had fled as Aramis had directed him to do, and had gained the last compartment, into which air, light, and sunshine penetrated through the opening. Therefore, scarcely had he turned the angle which separated the third compartment from the fourth when he perceived at a hundred paces from him the barque dancing on the waves; there were his friends, there was liberty, there was life after victory. Six more of his formidable strides, and he would be out of the vault; out of the vault! two or three vigorous springs and he would reach the canoe. Suddenly he felt his knees give way; his knees appeared powerless, his legs to yield under him.

"Oh! oh!" murmured he, "there is my fatigue seizing me again! I can walk no further! What is this?"

Aramis perceived him through the opening, and unable to conceive what could induce him to stop thus— "Come on, Porthos! Come on!" cried he; "come quickly."

"Oh!" replied the giant, making an effort which acted upon every muscle of his body— "oh, but I cannot." While saying these words he fell upon his knees, but with his robust hands he clung to the rocks, and raised himself up again.

"Quick! quick!" repeated Aramis, bending forward towards the shore, as if to draw Porthos towards him with his arms.

"Here I am," stammered Porthos, collecting all his strength to make one step more.

"In the name of Heaven! Porthos, make haste! the barrel will blow up!"

"Make haste, monseigneur!" shouted the Bretons to Porthos, who was floundering as in a dream.

But there was no longer time; the explosions resounded, the earth gaped, the smoke which rushed through the large fissures obscured the sky.

This frightful shock seemed to restore to Porthos the strength he had lost; he arose, himself a giant among these giants. But at the moment he was flying between the double hedge of granite phantoms, these latter, which were no longer supported by the corresponding links, began to roll with a crash around this Titan, who looked as if precipitated from heaven amidst rocks which he had just been launching at it. Porthos felt the earth beneath his feet shaken by this long rending. He extended his vast hands to the right and left to repulse the falling rocks. A gigantic block was held back by each of his extended hands; he bent his head and a third granite mass sank between his two shoulders. For an instant the arms of Porthos had given way, but the Hercules united all his forces, and the two walls of the prison in which he was buried fell back slowly and gave him place. For an instant he appeared in this frame of granite like the ancient angel of chaos, but in pushing back the lateral rocks, he lost his point of support for the monolith, which weighed upon his strong shoulders, and the monolith, weighing upon him with all its weight, brought the giant down upon his knees. The lateral rocks, for an instant pushed back, drew together again, and added their weight to the primitive weight which would have been sufficient to crush ten men. The giant fell without crying for help; he fell while answering Aramis with words of encouragement and hope, thanks to the powerful arch of his hands, for an instant, he might believe that, like Enceladus, he should shake off the triple load. But, by degrees, Aramis saw the block sink; the hands strung for a last effort, gave way, the extended shoulders sank wounded and torn, and rock continued to lower gradually.

"Porthos! Porthos!" cried Aramis, tearing his hair. "Porthos! where are you? Speak!"

"There, there!" murmured Porthos, with a voice growing evidently weaker, "Patience! patience!"

Scarcely had he pronounced these words, when the impulse of the fall augmented the weight; the enormous rock sank down, pressed by the two others which sank in from the sides, and, as it were, swallowed up Porthos in a sepulchre of broken stones. On hearing the dying voice of his friend, Aramis had sprung to land. Two of the Bretons followed him, with each a lever in his hand—one being sufficient to take care of the barque. The last rattles of the valiant struggler guided them amidst the ruins. Aramis, animated, active, and young, as at twenty, sprang towards the triple mass, and with his hands, delicate as those of a woman, raised by a miracle of vigour a corner of the immense sepulchre of granite. Then he caught a glimpse, in the darkness of that grave, of the still brilliant eye of his friend, to whom the momentary lifting of the mass restored that moment of respiration. The two men came rushing in, grasped their iron levers, united their triple strength, not merely to raise it, but to sustain it. All was useless. The three men slowly gave way with cries of grief, and the rough voice of Porthos, seeing them exhaust themselves in a useless struggle, murmured in a jeering tone those supreme words which came to his lips with the last respiration, "Too heavy."

After which the eye darkened and closed, the face became pale, the hand whitened, and the Titan sank quite down, breathing his last sigh. With him sank the rock, which, even in his agony, he had still held up. The three men dropped the levers, which rolled upon the tumulary stone. Then, breathless, pale, his brow covered with sweat, Aramis listened, his breast oppressed, his heary ready to break.

Nothing more! The giant slept the eternal sleep, in the sepulchre which God had made to his measure.

CHAPTER LVI

THE EPITAPH OF PORTHOS

Aramis, silent, icy, trembling like a timid child, arose shivering from the stone. A Christian does not walk upon tombs. But though capable of standing, he was not capable of walking. It might be said that something of dead Porthos had just died within him. His Bretons surrounded him; Aramis yielded to their kind exertions, and the three sailors, lifting him up, carried him into the canoe. Then having laid him down upon the bench near the rudder, they took to their oars, preferring to get off by rowing to hoisting a sail, which might betray them.

Of all that levelled surface of the ancient grotto of Locmaria, of all that flattened shore, one single little hillock attracted their eyes. Aramis never removed his from it; and, at a distance out in the sea, in proportion as the shore receded, the menacing and proud mass of rock seemed to draw itself up, as formerly Porthos used to draw himself up, and raise a smiling and invincible head towards heaven, like that of the honest and valiant friend, the strongest of the four, and yet the first dead.

Aramis, still pale, still icy, his heart upon his lips, Aramis looked, even till with the last ray of daylight, the shore faded on the horizon. Not a word escaped his lips, not a sigh rose from his deep breast. The superstitious Bretons looked at him trembling. That silence was not of a man, it was of a statue. In the meantime, with the first grey lines that descended from the heavens, the canoe had hoisted its little sail, which, swelling with the kisses of the breeze, and carrying them rapidly from the coast, made brave way with its head towards Spain, across the terrible gulf of Gascony, so rife with tempests. But scarcely half an hour after the sail had been hoisted, the rowers became inactive, reclining upon their benches, and making an eyeshade with their hands, pointed out to each other a white spot which appeared on the horizon as motionless as is in appearance a gull rocked by the insensible respiration of the waves. But that which might have appeared motionless to ordinary eyes was moving at a quick rate to the experienced eye of the sailor; that which appeared stationary on the ocean was cutting a rapid way through it. For some time, seeing the profound torpor in which their master was plunged, they did not dare to rouse him, and satisfied themselves with exchanging their conjectures in a low, disturbed voice. Aramis, in fact, so vigilant, so active — Aramis, whose eye, like that of the lynx, watched without ceasing, and saw better by night than by day — Aramis seemed to sleep in the despair of his soul. An hour passed thus, during which daylight gradually disappeared, but during which also the sail in view gained so swiftly on the barque, that Goenne, one of the three sailors, ventured to say aloud, —

"Monseigneur, we are being chased!"

Aramis made no reply; the ship still gained upon them. Then, of their own accord, two of the sailors, by the direction of the skipper Yves, lowered the sail, in order that that single point which appeared above the surface of the waters should cease to be a guide to the eye of the enemy who was pursuing them. On the part of the ship in sight, on the contrary, two more small sails were run up at the extremities of the masts. Unfortunately, it was the time of the finest and longest days of the year, and the moon in all her brilliancy succeeded to this inauspicious daylight. The corvette, which was pursuing the little barque before the wind, had then still half an hour of twilight, and a whole night almost as light as day.

The oars dropped from the hands of the sailors, and the barque, ceasing to make way, rocked motionless on the summits of the waves. Night came on, but the vessel still approached nearer. It might be said it redoubled its speed with the darkness. From time to time, as a bloody-necked vulture rears its head out of its nest, the formidable Greek fire darted from its sides, and cast its flame into the ocean like an incandescent snow. At last it came within musket-shot. All the men were on deck, arms in hand; the cannoniers were at their guns, and matches were burning. It might be thought they were about to board a frigate and to combat a crew superior in number to their own, and not to take a canoe manned by four people.

"Surrender!" cried the commander of the corvette, with the aid of the speaking trumpet.

The sailors looked at Aramis. Aramis made a sign with his head. Yves waved a white cloth at the end of a gaff. This was like striking their flag. The vessel came on like a racehorse. It launched a fresh Greek fire which fell within twenty paces of the little canoe, and threw a stronger light upon them than the most ardent ray of the sun could have done.

"At the first sign of resistance," cried the commander of the corvette, "fire!" And the soldiers brought their muskets to the present.

"Did not we say we surrendered?" said Yves.

"Living! living, captain!" cried some highly excited soldiers. "They must be taken living."

"Well, yes—living," said the captain. Then turning towards the Bretons, "Your lives are all safe, my friends!" cried he, "except the Chevalier d'Herblay."

"We accept," repeated the sailors: "but what security have we?"

"The word of a gentleman," said the officer. "By my rank and by my name I swear, that all but M. le Chevalier d'Herblay shall have their lives spared. I am lieutenant of the King's frigate the *Pomona*, and my name is Louis Constant de Pressigny."

With a rapid gesture, Aramis—already bent over the side of the barque towards the sea—raised his head, drew himself up, and with a flashing eye, and a smile upon his lips, "Throw out the ladder, messieurs," said he, as if the command had belonged to him. He was obeyed. Then Aramis, seizing the rope-ladder, instead of the terror which was expected to be displayed upon his countenance, the surprise of the sailors of the corvette was great, when they saw him walk straight up to the commander, with a firm step, look at him earnestly, make a sign to him with his hand, a mysterious and unknown sign, at the sight of which the officer turned pale, trembled, and bowed his head. Without saying a word, Aramis then raised his hand close to the eyes of the commander, and showed him the collet of a ring which he wore on the ring-finger of his left hand. And while making this sign, Aramis, draped in cold, silent, and haughty majesty, had the air of an emperor giving his hand to be kissed. The commandant, who for a moment had raised his head, bowed a second time with marks of the most profound respect. Then stretching his hand out towards the poop, that is to say, towards his own cabin, he drew back to allow Aramis to go first. The three Bretons, who had come on board after their Bishop, looked at each other, stupefied. The crew were struck with silence. Five minutes after, the commander called the second lieutenant, who returned immediately, and gave directions for the head to be put towards Corunna. Whilst the order was being executed Aramis reappeared upon the deck, and took a seat near the bulwarks. The night had fallen, the moon had not yet risen, and yet Aramis looked incessantly towards Belle-Isle. Yves then approached the captain, who had returned to take his post in the stern, and said, in a low and humble voice, "What course are we to follow, captain?"

"We take what course monseigneur pleases," replied the officer.

Aramis passed the night leaning upon the bulwarks. Yves, on approaching him the next morning, remarked, that "the night must have been very humid, for the wood upon which the Bishop's head had rested, was soaked with dew." Who knows!—that dew was, perhaps, the first tears that had ever fallen from the eyes of Aramis!

What epitaph would have been worth that? Good Porthos!

CHAPTER LVII

KING LOUIS XIV

D'Artagnan was not accustomed to resistances like that he had just experienced. He returned, profoundly irritated, to Nantes. Irritation with this vigorous man vented itself in an impetuous attack, which few people, hitherto, were they King, were they giants, had been able to resist. D'Artagnan, trembling with rage, went straight to the castle, and asked to speak to the King.

The King was seated in his cabinet, with his back turned towards the door of entrance. In front of him was a mirror, in which, while turning over his papers, he could see with a glance those who came in. He did not take any notice of the entrance of d'Artagnan, but laid over his letters and plans the large silk cloth which he made use of to conceal his secrets from the importunate. D'Artagnan understood his play, and kept in the background; so that, at the end of a minute, the King, who heard nothing and saw nothing but with the corner of his eye, was obliged to cry, "Is not M. d'Artagnan there?"

"I am here, sire," replied the musketeer, advancing.

"Well, monsieur," said the King, fixing his clear eye upon d'Artagnan, "what have you to say to me?"

"I, sire!" replied the latter, who watched the first blow of his adversary to make a good retort; "I have nothing to say to your Majesty, unless it be that you have caused me to be arrested, and here I am."

The King was going to reply that he had not had d'Artagnan arrested, but the sentence appeared too much like an excuse, and he was silent. D'Artagnan likewise preserved an obstinate silence.

"Monsieur," at length resumed the King, "what did I charge you to go and do at Belle-Isle? Tell me, if you please."

The King while speaking these words looked fixedly at his captain. Here d'Artagnan was too fortunate; the King seemed to place the game in his hands.

"I believe," replied he, "that your Majesty does me the honour to ask what I went to Belle-Isle to do?"

"Yes, monsieur."

"Well! sire, I know nothing about it; it is not of me that question should be asked, but of that infinite number of officers of all kinds, to whom have been given an infinite number of orders of all kinds, whilst to me, head of the expedition, nothing precise was ordered."

The King was wounded; he showed it by his reply. "Monsieur," said he, "orders have only been given to such as were judged faithful. You have ill-served me, monsieur, by taking part with my enemies against me."

"Who are your enemies, sire?"

"The men I sent you to fight with."

"Two men the enemies of the whole of your Majesty's army! That is incredible!"

Almost at the same moment an officer entered and placed a despatch in the hands of the King, who, in his turn, changed colour while reading it.

"Monsieur," said he, "what I learn here you would know later; it is better I should tell you, and that you should learn it from the mouth of your King. A battle has taken place at Belle-Isle."

"Oh! ah!" said d'Artagnan, with a calm air, though his heart beat enough to break through his chest. "Well, sire!"

"Well, monsieur—and I have lost a hundred and ten men."

A beam of joy and pride shone in the eyes of d'Artagnan. "And the rebels?" said he.

"The rebels have fled," said the King.

D'Artagnan could not restrain a cry of triumph. "Only," added the King, "I have a fleet which closely blockades Belle-Isle, and I am certain no barque can escape."

"So that," said the musketeer, brought back to his dismal ideas, "if these two gentlemen are taken——"

"They will be hanged," said the King quietly.

"And do they know it?" replied d'Artagnan, repressing his trembling.

"They know it, because you must have told them yourself; and all the country knows it."

"Then, sire, they will never be taken alive, I will answer for that."

"Ah!" said the King negligently, and taking up his letter again. "Very well, they will be had dead then, Monsieur d'Artagnan, and that will come to the same thing, since I should only take them to have them hanged."

D'Artagnan wiped the sweat which flowed from his brow.

"I have told you," pursued Louis XIV, "that I would one day be an affectionate, generous, and constant master. You are now the only man of former times worthy of my anger or my friendship. I will not be sparing of either to you, according to your conduct. I am master at home, Captain d'Artagnan, and I shall have servants who, wanting, perhaps, your genius, will carry devotedness and obedience up to heroism. Of what consequence, I ask you, of what consequence is it that God has given no genius to arms and legs? It is to the head he has given it, and the head, you know, all the rest obey. I am the head."

D'Artagnan started. Louis XIV continued as if he had seen nothing, although this emotion had not at all escaped him. "Now let us conclude between us two that bargain which I promised to make with you one day when you found me very little at Blois. Do me justice, monsieur, when you think that I do not make any one pay for the tears of shame I then shed. Look around you; lofty heads have bowed. Bow yours, or choose the exile that will best suit you. Perhaps, when reflecting upon it, you will find that this king is a generous heart, who reckons sufficiently upon your loyalty to allow you to leave him dissatisfied, when you possess a great state secret. You are a brave man; I know you to be so. Why have you judged me prematurely? Judge me from this day forward, d'Artagnan, and be as severe as you please."

D'Artagnan remained bewildered, mute, undecided for the first time in his life. He had just found an adversary worthy of him. This was no longer trick, it was calculation; it was no longer violence, it was strength; it was no longer passion, it was will; it was no longer boasting, it was council. This young man who had brought down Fouquet, and could do without d'Artagnan, deranged all the somewhat headstrong calculations of the musketeer.

"Come, let us see what stops you," said the King kindly. "You have given in your resignation: shall I refuse to accept it? I admit that it may be hard for an old captain to recover his good humour."

"Oh!" replied d'Artagnan in a melancholy tone, "that is difficult, but I have got over greater difficulties than that. I will do it. Why should I do it? Because I love money?—I have enough. Because I am ambitious?—my career is bounded. Because I love the court? No. I will remain because I have been accustomed for thirty years to go and take the orderly word of the King, and to have said to me, 'Good-evening, d'Artagnan,' with a smile I did not beg for! That smile I will beg for! Are you content, sire?" And d'Artagnan bowed his silvered head, upon which the smiling King placed his white hand, with pride.

"Thanks, my old servant, my faithful friend," said he. "As reckoning from this day, I have no longer any enemies in France; it remains with me to send you to a foreign field to gather your marshal's baton. Depend upon me for finding you an opportunity. In the meanwhile, eat of my best bread, and sleep tranquilly."

"That is all kind and well!" said d'Artagnan, much agitated. "But those poor men at Belle-Isle? One of them, in particular—so good! so brave! so true!"

"Do you ask their pardon of me?"

"Upon my knees, sire."

"Well, then, go, and take it to them, if it be still time. But do you answer for them?"

"With my life, sire!"

"Go then. To-morrow I set out for Paris. Return by that time, for I do not wish you to leave me in future."

"Be assured of that, sire," said d'Artagnan, kissing the royal hand.

And, with a heart swelling with joy, he rushed out of the castle on his way to Belle-Isle.

CHAPTER LVIII

D'ARTAGNAN'S NEWS

The King had returned to Paris and with him d'Artagnan, who, in twenty-four hours, having made with the greatest care all possible inquiries at Belle-Isle, had learned nothing of the secret so well kept by the heavy rock of Locmaria; which had fallen on the heroic Porthos.

Scarcely was the King reinstalled in Paris, when his captain of the musketeers presented himself before him. D'Artagnan was pale and looked unhappy. The King, at the first glance, perceived the change in a countenance generally so unconcerned. "What is the matter, d'Artagnan?" said he.

"Sire, a great misfortune has happened to me."

"Good heavens! what is that?"

"Sire, I have lost one of my friends, M. du Vallon, in the affair of Belle-Isle."

And while speaking these words, d'Artagnan fixed his falcon eye upon Louis XIV to catch the first feeling that would show itself.

"I knew it," replied the King quietly.

"You knew it, and did not tell me!" cried the musketeer.

"To what good? Your grief, my friend, is so respectable. It was my duty to treat it kindly. To have informed you of this misfortune, which I knew would pain you so greatly, d'Artagnan, would have been, in your eyes, to have triumphed over you. Yes, I knew that M. du Vallon had buried himself beneath the rocks of Locmaria; I knew that M. d'Herblay had taken one of my vessels with its crew, and had compelled it to convey him to Bayonne."

. "But, sire, how could you know?"

"How do you yourself know, d'Artagnan?"

"By this letter, sire, which M. d'Herblay, free and out of danger, writes me from Bayonne."

"Look here," said the King, drawing from a casket placed upon the table close to the seat upon which d'Artagnan was leaning, "here is a letter copied exactly from that of M. d'Herblay. Here is the very letter which Colbert placed in my hands a week before you received yours. I am well served, you may perceive."

"Yes, sire," murmured the musketeer, "you were the only man whose fortune was capable of dominating the fortunes and strength of my two friends. You have used it, sire, but you will not abuse it, will you?"

"D'Artagnan," said the King, with a smile beaming with kindness, "I could have M. d'Herblay carried off from the territories of the King of Spain, and brought here alive to inflict justice upon him. But, d'Artagnan, be assured I will not yield to this first and natural impulse. He is free; let him continue free."

"Oh, sire! you will not always remain so clement, so noble, so generous as you have shown yourself with respect to me and M. d'Herblay; you will have about you counsellors who will cure you of that weakness."

"No, d'Artagnan, you are mistaken when you accuse my council of urging me to pursue rigorous measures. The advice to spare M. d'Herblay comes from Colbert himself."

"Oh, sire!" said d'Artagnan, extremely surprised.

"As for you," continued the King, with a kindness very uncommon with him, "I have several pieces of good news to announce to you; but you shall know them, my dear captain, the moment I have made my accounts all straight. I have said that I wished to make, and would make, your fortune; that promise will soon be a reality."

"A thousand times thanks, sire!"

CHAPTER LIX

THE VISION OF ATHOS

While all these affairs were separating for ever the four musketeers, formerly bound together in a manner that seemed indissoluble, Athos, left alone after the departure of Raoul, began to pay his tribute to that anticipated death which is called the absence of those we love. Returned to his house at Blois, no longer having even Grimaud to receive a poor smile when he passed through the parterre, Athos daily felt the decline of the vigour of a nature which for so long a time had appeared infallible. Age, which had been kept back by the presence of the beloved object, now came on, with its attendant pains and inconveniences. The Comte de la Fère, who had remained a young man up to his sixty-second year; the warrior who had preserved his strength in spite of fatigues, his freshness of mind in spite of misfortunes, his mild serenity of soul and body in spite of malady, in spite of Mazarin, in spite of La Vallière: Athos had become an old man in a week, from the moment at which he had lost the support of his latter youth. Still handsome, though bent; noble, but sad; gentle, and tottering under his grey hairs, he sought, since his solitude, the glades where the rays of the sun penetrated through the foliage of the walks. He discontinued all the strong exercises he had enjoyed through life, when Raoul was no longer with him.

He did not even desire that all letters that came should be brought to him directly. He knew very well that every distraction which should arrive would be a joy, a hope, which his servants would have paid with their blood to procure him. Sleep had become rare. By intense thinking, Athos forgot himself, for a few hours at most, in a reverie more profound, more obscure than other people would have called a dream. This momentary repose which this forgetfulness afforded the body, fatigued the soul, for Athos lived a double life during these wanderings of his understanding. One night, he dreamt that Raoul was dressing himself in a tent, to go upon an expedition commanded by M. de Beaufort in person. The young man was sad; he clasped his cuirass slowly, and slowly he girded on his sword.

"What is the matter?" asked his father tenderly.

"What afflicts me is the death of Porthos, ever so dear a friend," replied Raoul. "I suffer here of the grief you will feel at home."

And the vision disappeared with the slumber of Athos. At daybreak one of his servants entered his master's apartment, and gave him a letter which came from Spain.

"The writing of Aramis," thought the Comte; and he read.

"Porthos is dead!" cried he, after the first lines. "Oh! Raoul, Raoul!

thanks! thou keepest thy promise; thou warnest me!"

And Athos, seized with a mortal sweat, fainted in his bed, without any other cause than his weakness.

Then commenced for Athos a strange, indefinable state. Free to think, his mind turned towards Raoul, that beloved son. His imagination painted the fields of Africa in the environs of Gigelli, where M. de Beaufort must have landed his army. There were grey rocks, rendered green in certain parts by the waters of the sea, when it lashed the shore in storms and tempests. Beyond, the shore, strewn over with these rocks like tombs, ascended, in form of an amphitheatre, among mastick-trees and cacti, a sort of small town, full of smoke, confused noises and terrified movements.

Night then came over the scene; a night dark upon the earth, brilliant in the firmament. The large, blazing stars which sparkled in the African sky shone without lighting anything even around them.

A mild and pale moon arose behind the declivities of the coast, and streaking at first the undulating ripples of the sea, which appeared to have calmed after the roarings it had sent forth during the vision of Athos — the moon, say we, shed its diamonds and opals upon the briers and bushes of the hills. The grey rocks, like so many silent and attentive phantoms, appeared to raise their verdant heads to examine likewise the field of battle by the light of the moon, and Athos perceived that the field was now strewed over with fallen bodies.

Then, while his eye was wandering over the plain, turning on all sides, he saw a white form appear behind the resinous myrtles. This figure was clothed in the costume of an officer: it held in its hand a broken sword: it advanced slowly towards Athos, who, stopping short and fixing his eyes upon it, neither spoke nor moved, but wished to open his arms, because, in this silent and pale officer, he had just recognised Raoul.

At length he gained the crest of the hill, and saw, thrown out in black, upon the horizon, whitened by the moon, the elongated aerial form of Raoul. Athos stretched out his hand to get closer to his beloved son upon the plateau, and the latter also stretched out his; but suddenly, as if the young man had been drawn away in spite of himself, still retreating, he left the earth, and Athos saw the clear blue sky shine between the feet of his child and the ground of the hill. Raoul rose insensibly into the void, still smiling, still calling with a gesture: — he departed towards heaven. Athos uttered a cry of terrified tenderness. He looked below again. He saw a camp destroyed and all those white bodies of the royal army, like so many motionless atoms. And then, when raising his head, he saw still, still, his son beckoning him to ascend with him.

CHAPTER LX

THE ANGEL OF DEATH

Athos was at this part of his marvellous vision, when the charm was suddenly broken by a great noise rising from the outward gates of the house. A horse was heard galloping over the hard gravel of the great alley, and the sound of most noisy and animated conversations ascended to the chamber in which the Comte was dreaming. Athos did not stir from the place he occupied; he scarcely turned his head towards the door to ascertain the sooner what these noises could be. A heavy step ascended the stairs; the horse which had recently galloped, departed slowly towards the stables. Great hesitation appeared in the steps, which by degrees approached the chamber of Athos. A door then was opened, and Athos, turning a little towards the part of the room the noise came from, cried in a weak voice:

"It is a courier from Africa, is it not?"

"No, Monsieur le Comte," replied a voice which made the father of Raoul start upright in his bed.

"Grimaud!" murmured he. And the sweat began to pour down his cheeks. "Raoul is dead, is he not?"

Behind Grimaud, the other servants listened breathlessly with their eyes fixed upon the bed of their sick master. They heard the terrible question, and an awful silence ensued.

"Yes," replied the old man, heaving up the monosyllable from his chest with a hoarse, broken sigh.

Then arose voices of lamentation, which groaned without measure, and filled with regrets and prayers the chamber where the agonised father sought with his eyes for the portrait of his son. This was for Athos like the transition which led to his dream. Without uttering a cry, without shedding a tear, patient, mild, resigned as a martyr, he raised his eyes towards heaven, in order to there see again, rising above the mountain of Gigelli, the beloved shade which was leaving him at the moment of Grimaud's arrival. Without doubt, while looking towards the heavens, when resuming his marvellous dream, he repassed by the same road by which the vision, at once so terrible and so sweet, had led him before, for, after having gently closed his eyes, he reopened them and began to smile: he had just seen Raoul, who had smiled upon him. With his hands joined upon his breast, his face turned towards the window, bathed by the fresh air of night, which brought to his pillow the aroma of the flowers and the woods, Athos entered, never again to come out of it, into the contemplation of that paradise which the living never see. God willed, no doubt, to open to this elect the treasures of eternal beatitude, at the hour when other men tremble with the idea of being severely received by the Lord, and cling to this life they know, in the dread of the other life of which they get a glimpse by the dismal, murky torches of death. Athos was guided by the pure and serene soul of his son, which aspired to be like the paternal soul. Everything for this just man was melody and perfume in the rough road which souls take to return to the celestial country. After an hour of this ecstasy, Athos softly raised his hands, as white as wax; the smile did not quit his lips, and he murmured low, so low as scarcely to be audible, these three words addressed to God or to Raoul:

"HERE I AM!"

And his hands fell down slowly, as if he himself had laid them on the bed.

Grimaud, by anxiously listening, perceived that the Comte no longer breathed. Fear seized him; he rose completely up, and, at the very moment, heard some one coming up the stairs. A noise of spurs knocking against a sword — a warlike sound, familiar to his ears — stopped him as he was going towards the bed of Athos. A voice still more sonorous than brass or steel resounded within three paces of him.

"Athos! Athos! my friend!" cried this voice, agitated even to tears.

"Monsieur le Chevalier d'Artagnan!" faltered out Grimaud.

"Where is he? Where is he?" continued the musketeer.

Grimaud seized his arm in his bony fingers, and pointed to the bed, upon the sheets of which the livid tint of the dead already showed.

A choked respiration, the opposite to a sharp cry, swelled the throat of d'Artagnan. He advanced on tip-toe, trembling, frightened at the noise his feet made upon the floor, and his heart rent by a nameless agony. He placed his ear to the breast of Athos, his face to the Comte's mouth. Neither noise, nor breath! D'Artagnan drew back.

All at once, the bitter flood which mounted from minute to minute invaded his heart, and swelled his breast almost to bursting. Incapable of mastering his emotion, he arose, and tearing himself violently from the chamber where he had just found dead him to whom he came to report the news of the death of Porthos, he uttered sobs so heart-rending that the servants who seemed only to wait for an explosion of grief, answered to it by their lugubrious clamours, and the dogs of the late Comte by their lamentable howlings. Grimaud was the only one who did not lift up his voice. Even in the paroxysm of his grief he would not have dared to profane the dead, or for the first time disturb the slumber of his master. Athos had accustomed him never to speak.

At daybreak, d'Artagnan, who had wandered about the lower hall, biting his fingers to stifle his sighs — d'Artagnan went up once more; and watching the moment when Grimaud turned his head towards him, he made him a sign to come to him, which the faithful servant obeyed without making more noise than a shadow. D'Artagnan went down again, followed by Grimaud; and when he had gained the vestibule, taking the old man's hands, "Grimaud," said he, "I have seen how the father died; now let me know how the son died."

Grimaud drew from his breast a large letter, upon the envelope of which was traced the address of Athos. He recognised the writing of M. de Beaufort, broke the seal and began to read, walking about in the first blue rays of day, in the dark alley of old limes, marked by the still visible footsteps of the Comte who had just died.

The Duc de Beaufort wrote to Athos. The letter destined for the living only reached the dead. God had changed the address.

"MY DEAR COMTE," wrote the Prince in his large, bad schoolboy's hand,—"a great misfortune has struck us amidst a great triumph. The King loses one of the bravest of soldiers. I lose a friend. You lose M. de Bragelonne. He has died gloriously, and so gloriously that I have not the strength to weep as I could wish. Receive my sad compliments, my dear Comte. Heaven distributes trials according to the greatness of our hearts. This is an immense one, but not above your courage. Your good friend,

"LE DUC DE BEAUFORT."

The letter contained a relation written by one of the Prince's secretaries. It was the most touching recital, and the most true, of that dismal episode which unravelled two existencies. D'Artagnan, accustomed to battle emotions, and with a heart armed against tenderness, could not help starting on reading the name of Raoul, the name of that beloved boy who had become, as his father had, a shade.

Then followed the details of the expedition, and of the victory obtained over the Arabs. D'Artagnan stopped at the account of the death of poor Raoul. "Oh!" murmured he, "Unhappy boy!"

And turning his eyes towards the chamber of the château in which Athos slept in eternal sleep. "They have kept their words to each other," said he, in a low voice; "now I believe them to be happy; they must be re-united." And he returned through the parterre with slow and melancholy steps. All the village—all the neighbourhood—were filled with grieving neighbours relating to each other the double catastrophe, and making preparations for the funeral.

CHAPTER LXI

THE LAST CANTO OF THE POEM

On the morrow, all the nobility of the provinces, of the environs, and wherever messengers had carried the news, were seen to arrive.

D'Artagnan was struck at seeing two open coffins in the hall. In reply to the mute invitation of Grimaud, he approached, and saw in one of them Athos, still handsome in death, and, in the other, Raoul with his eyes closed, his cheeks pearly as those of the Pallas of Virgil, with a smile on his violet lips. He shuddered at seeing the father and son, those two departed souls, represented on earth by two silent, melancholy bodies, incapable of touching each other, however close they might be.

"Raoul here!" murmured he. "Oh! Grimaud, why did you not tell me this?"

Grimaud shook his head and made no reply; but taking d'Artagnan by the hand, he led him to the coffin, and showed him, under the thin winding-sheet, the black wounds by which life had escaped. The captain turned away his eyes, and, judging it useless to question Grimaud, who would not answer, he recollected that M. de Beaufort's secretary had written more than he, d'Artagnan, had had the courage to read.

Taking up the recital of the affair which had cost Raoul his life, he found these words, which terminated the last paragraph of the letter:

"Monsieur le Duc has ordered that the body of Monsieur le Vicomte should be embalmed, after the manner practised by the Arabs when they wish their bodies to be carried to their native land; and Monsieur le Duc has appointed relays, so that a confidential servant who brought up the young man, might take back his remains to M. le Comte de la Fère."

At length arrived the moment when the cold remains of these two gentlemen were to be returned to the earth. There was such an affluence of military and other people that up to the place of sepulchre, which was a chapel in the plain, the road from the city was filled with horsemen and pedestrians in mourning habits. Athos had chosen for his resting-place the little enclosure of a chapel erected by himself near the boundary of his estates. He had had the stones, cut in 1550, brought from an old Gothic manor-house in Berry, which had sheltered his early youth. The chapel, thus re-edified, thus transported, was pleasant beneath its wood of poplars and sycamores.

It was to this place the two coffins were brought, attended by a silent and respectful crowd. The office of the dead being celebrated, the last adieux paid to the noble departed, the assembly dispersed, talking, along the roads, of the virtues and mild death of the father, of the hopes the son had given, and of his melancholy end upon the coast of Africa.

By little and little, all noises were extinguished, like the lamps illumining the humble nave. The minister bowed for a last time to the altar and the still fresh graves, then, followed by his assistant, who rang a hoarse bell, he slowly took the road back to the presbytery. D'Artagnan, left alone, perceived that night was coming on. He had forgotten the hour, while thinking of the dead. He arose from the oaken bench on which he was seated in the chapel, and wished, as the priest had done, to go and bid a last adieu to the double grave which contained his two lost friends.

A woman was praying, kneeling on the moist earth. D'Artagnan stopped at the door of the chapel, to avoid disturbing this woman, and also to endeavour to see who was the pious friend who performed this sacred duty with so much zeal and perseverance. The unknown concealed her face in her hands, which were white as alabaster. From the noble simplicity of her costume, she must be a woman of distinction. Outside the enclosure were several horses mounted by servants, and a travelling carriage waiting for this lady. D'Artagnan in vain sought to make out what caused her delay. She continued praying, she frequently passed her handkerchief over her face, by which d'Artagnan perceived she was weeping. He saw her strike her breast with the pitiless compunction of a Christian woman. He heard her several times proffer, as if from a wounded heart: "Pardon! pardon!" And as she appeared to abandon herself entirely to her grief, as she threw herself down, almost fainting, amidst complaints and prayers, d'Artagnan, touched by his love for his so much regretted friends, made a few steps towards the grave, in order to interrupt the melancholy coloquy of the penitent with the dead. But as soon as his step sounded on the gravel the unknown raised her head, revealing to d'Artagnan a face inundated with tears, but a well-known face. It was Mademoiselle de la Vallière! "Monsieur d'Artagnan!" murmured she.

"You!" replied the captain, in a stern voice—"you here!—oh! madame, I should better have liked to see you decked with flowers in the mansion of the Comte de la Fère. You would have wept less—they too—I too!"

"Monsieur!" she said, sobbing.

"For it is you," added this pitiless friend of the dead,—"it is you have laid these two men in the grave."

"Oh! spare me!"

"God forbid, madame, that I should offend a woman, or that I should make her weep in vain; but I must say that the place of the murderer is not upon the grave of her victims." She wished to reply.

"What I now tell you," added he coldly, "I told the King."

She clasped her hands. "I know," said she, "I have caused the death of the Vicomte de Bragelonne."

"Ah! you know it?"

"The news arrived at court yesterday. I have travelled during the night forty leagues to come and ask pardon of the Comte, whom I supposed to be still living, and to supplicate God, upon the tomb of Raoul, that He would send me all the misfortunes I have merited, except a single one. Now, monsieur, I know that the death of the son has killed the father; I have two crimes to reproach myself with; I have two punishments to look for from God."

"I will repeat to you, Mademoiselle," said d'Artagnan, "what M. de Bragelonne said of you at Antibes, when he already meditated death: 'If pride and coquetry have misled her, I pardon her while despising her. If love has produced her error, I pardon her, swearing that no one could have loved her as I have done.'"

"You know," interrupted Louise, "that for my love I was about to sacrifice myself; you know whether I suffered when you met me lost, dying, abandoned. Well! never have I suffered so much as now; because then I hoped, I desired—now I have nothing to wish for; because this death drags away all my joy into the tomb; because I can no longer dare to love without remorse, and I feel, that he whom I love —oh! that is the law—will repay me with the tortures I have made others undergo."

D'Artagnan made no reply; he was too well convinced she was not mistaken.

"Pardon me, the last time, my affianced Raoul!" said she. "I have broken our chain; we are both destined to die of grief. It is thou who departest the first; fear nothing, I shall follow thee. See, only, that I have not been base, and that I have come to bid thee this last adieu. The Lord is my witness, Raoul, that if with my life I could have redeemed thine, I would have given that life without hesitation. I could not give my love. Once more, pardon!"

She gathered a branch and stuck it into the ground; then, wiping the tears from her eyes, she bowed to d'Artagnan, and disappeared.

The captain watched the departure of the horses, horsemen, and carriage, then crossing his arms upon his swelling chest, "When will it be my turn to depart?" said he, in an agitated voice. "What is there left for man after youth, after love, after glory, after friendship, after strength, after riches? That rock, under which sleeps Porthos, who possessed all I have named; this moss, under which repose Athos and Raoul, who possessed still much more!"

He hesitated a moment, with a dull eye; then, drawing himself up: "Forward! still forward!" said he. "When it shall be time, God will tell me, as he has told the others."

He touched the earth, moistened with the evening dew, with the ends of his fingers, signed himself as if he had been at the fount of a church, and retook alone—ever alone—the road to Paris.

EPILOGUE

Four years after the scene we have just described, two horsemen, well mounted, traversed Blois early in the morning, for the purpose of arranging a birding party which the King intended to make in that uneven plain which the Loire divides in two, and which borders on the one side on Meung, on the other on Amboise. These were the captain of the King's harriers and the governor of the falcons, personages greatly respected in the time of Louis XIII, but rather neglected by his successor. These two horsemen, having reconnoitred the ground, were returning, their observations made, when they perceived some little groups of soldiers here and there whom the sergeants were placing at distances at the openings of the enclosures. These were the King's musketeers. Behind them came, upon a good horse, the captain, known by his richly embroidered uniform. His hair was grey, his beard was becoming so. He appeared a little bent, although sitting and handling his horse gracefully. He was looking about him watchfully.

"M. d'Artagnan does not get any older," said the captain of the harriers to his colleague the falconer; "with ten years more than either of us, he has the seat of a young man on horseback."

"That is true," replied the falconer. "I don't see any change in him for the last twenty years."

But this officer was mistaken; d'Artagnan in the last four years had lived twelve years. Age imprinted its pitiless claws at each angle of his eyes; his brow was bald; his hands, formerly brown and nervous, were getting white as if the blood began to chill there.

D'Artagnan accosted the officers with the shade of affability which distinguishes superior men, and received in return for his courtesy two most respectful bows.

"Ah! what a lucky chance to see you here, Monsieur d'Artagnan!" cried the falconer.

"It is rather I who should say that, messieurs," replied the captain, "for nowadays the King makes more frequent use of his musketeers than of his falcons."

"Ah! it is not as it was in the good old times," sighed the falconer. "Do you remember, Monsieur d'Artagnan, when the late King flew the pie in the vineyards beyond Beaugence? Ah! you were not captain of the musketeers at that time, Monsieur d'Artagnan."

"And you were nothing but under-corporal of the tiercelets," replied d'Artagnan, laughing. "Never mind that; it was a good time, seeing that it was always a good time when we are young. Good day, monsieur the captain of the harriers."

"You do me honour, Monsieur le Comte," said the latter. D'Artagnan made no reply. The title of Comte had not struck him; d'Artagnan had been a Comte for four years.

They could already catch glimpses of the huntsmen at the issues of the wood, the feathers of the outriders passing like shooting-stars across the clearings, and the white horses cutting with their luminous apparitions the dark thickets of the copses.

"But," resumed d'Artagnan, "will the sport be long? Pray give us a good swift bird, for I am very tired. Is it a heron or a swan?"

"Both, Monsieur d'Artagnan," said the falconer; "but you need not be alarmed; the King is not much of a sportsman; he does not sport on his own account; he only wishes to give amusement to the ladies."

"Shall we see the King early?" asked d'Artagnan of the falconer.

"At seven o'clock, monsieur, I shall fly the birds."

"Who comes with the King? How is madame? How is the Queen?"

"Better, monsieur."

"Has she been ill, then?"

"Monsieur, since the last chagrin she had, Her Majesty has been unwell."

"What chagrin? You need not fancy your news is old. I am but just returned."

"It appears that the Queen, a little neglected since the death of her mother-in-law, complained to the King, who replied to her,—'Do I not sleep with you every night, madame? What more do you want?'"

"Ah!" said d'Artagnan,—"poor woman! She must heartily hate Mademoiselle de la Vallière."

"Oh, no! not Mademoiselle de la Vallière," replied the falconer.

"Who then——?" The horn interrupted this conversation. It summoned the dogs and the hawks. The falconer and his companion set off immediately, leaving d'Artagnan alone in the midst of the suspended sentence. The King appeared at a distance, surrounded by ladies and horsemen. D'Artagnan, with an eye a little weakened, distinguished behind the group three carriages. The first was intended for the Queen; it was empty. D'Artagnan, who did not see Mademoiselle de la Vallère by the King's side, on looking about for her, saw her in the second carriage. She was alone with two of her women, who seemed as dull as their mistress. On the left hand of the King, upon a high-spirited horse, restrained by a bold and skilful hand, shone a lady of the most dazzling beauty. The King smiled upon her, and she smiled upon the King. Loud laughter followed every word she spoke.

"I must know that woman," thought the musketeer; "who can she be?" And he stooped towards his friend the falconer, to whom he addressed the question he had put to himself. The falconer was about to reply, when the King, perceiving d'Artagnan, "Ah, Comte!" said he, "you are returned, then! why have I not seen you?"

"Sire," replied the Captain; "because your Majesty was asleep when I arrived; and not awake when I resumed my duties this morning."

"Still the same!" said Louis in a loud voice, denoting satisfaction. "Take some rest, Comte; I command you to do so. You will dine with me to-day."

The King passed a few steps in advance, and d'Artagnan found himself in the midst of a fresh group, among whom shone Colbert.

"Good day, Monsieur d'Artagnan," said the minister, with affable politeness; "have you had a pleasant journey?"

"Yes, monsieur," said d'Artagnan, bowing to the neck of his horse.

"I heard the King invite you to his table for this evening," continued the minister; "you will meet an old friend there."

"An old friend of mine?" asked d'Artagnan, plunging painfully into the dark waves of the past, which had swallowed up for him so many friendships and so many hatreds.

"M. le Duc d'Alméda, who is arrived this morning from Spain."

"The Duc d'Alméda?" said d'Artagnan, reflecting in vain.

"I!" said an old man, white as snow, sitting bent in his carriage, which he caused to be thrown open to make room for the musketeer.

"Aramis!" cried d'Artagnan, struck with perfect stupor. And he left, inert as it was, the thin arm of the old nobleman hanging round his neck.

Colbert, after having observed them in silence for a minute, put his horse forward, and left the two old friends together.

"And so," said the musketeer, taking the arm of Aramis, "you, the exile, the rebel, are again in France!"

"Ah! and I shall dine with you at the King's table," said Aramis, smiling. "Yes; will you not ask yourself what is the use of fidelity in this world? Stop! let us allow poor La Vallière's carriage to pass. Look, how uneasy she is! How her eye, dimmed with tears, follows the King, who is riding on horseback yonder!"

"With whom?"

"With Mademoiselle de Tonnay-Charente, now become Madame de Montespan," replied Aramis.

"She is jealous; is she then deserted?"

"Not quite yet, but it will not be long."

They chatted together, while following the sport, and Aramis's coachman drove them so cleverly that they got up at the moment when the falcon, attacking the bird, beat him down, and fell upon him. The King alighted, Madame de Montespan followed his example. They were in front of an isolated chapel, concealed by large trees, already despoiled of their leaves by the first winds of autumn. Behind this chapel was an enclosure, closed by a latticed gate. The falcon had beat down his prey in the enclosure belonging to this little chapel, and the King was desirous of going in to take the first feather, according to custom. The *cortège* formed a circle round the building and the hedges, too small to receive so many. D'Artagnan held back Aramis by the arm, as he was about, like the rest, to alight from his carriage, and in a hoarse, broken voice, "Do you know, Aramis," said he, "whither chance has conducted us?"

"No," replied the Duke.

"Here repose people I have known," said d'Artagnan, much agitated.

Aramis without divining anything, and with a trembling step, penetrated into the chapel by a little door which d'Artagnan opened for him. "Where are they buried?" said he.

"There, in the enclosure. There is a cross, you see, under that little cypress. The little cypress is planted over their tomb; don't go to it; the King is going that way; the heron has fallen just there."

Aramis stopped and concealed himself in the shade. They then saw, without being seen, the pale face of La Vallière, who, neglected in her carriage, had at first looked on, with a melancholy heart, from the door, and then, carried away by jealousy, she had advanced into the chapel, whence, leaning against a pillar, she contemplated in the enclosure the King smiling and making signs to Madame de Montespan to approach, as there was nothing to be afraid of. Madame de Montespan complied; she took the hand the King held out to her, and he, plucking out the first feather from the heron, which the falconer had strangled, placed it in the hat of his beautiful companion. She, smiling in her turn, kissed the hand tenderly which made her this present. The King blushed with pleasure; he looked at Madame de Montespan with all the fire of love.

"What will you give me in exchange?" said he.

She broke off a little branch of cypress and offered it to the King, who looked intoxicated with hope.

"Humph!" said Aramis to d'Artagnan; "the present is but a sad one, for that cypress shades a tomb."

"Yes, and the tomb is that of Raoul de Bragelonne," said d'Artagnan aloud; "of Raoul, who sleeps under that cross with his father."

A groan resounded behind them. They saw a woman fall fainting to the ground. Mademoiselle de la Vallière had seen all, and heard all.

"Poor woman!" muttered d'Artagnan, as he helped the attendants to carry back to her carriage her who from that time was to suffer.

That evening d'Artagnan was seated at the King's table, near M. Colbert and M. le Duc d'Alméda. The King was very gay. He laid a thousand little attentions to the Queen, a thousand kindnesses to Madame, seated at his left hand, and very sad. It might have been supposed to be that calm time when the King used to watch the eyes of his mother for the avowal or disavowal of what he had just done.

Of mistresses there was no question at this dinner. The King addressed Aramis two or three times, calling him M. l'Ambassadeur, which increased the surprise already felt by d'Artagnan at seeing his friend the rebel so marvellously well received at court.

The King began to chat with his sister. It was very plain from the embarrassed appearance of Monsieur, how much of the conversation of the King and Madame annoyed him. The eyes of Madame were almost red; was she going to complain? Was she going to commit a little scandal in open court? The King took her on one side, and in a tone so tender that it must have reminded the Princess of the time when she was loved for herself, —

"Sister," said he, "why do I see tears in those beautiful eyes?"

"Why — sire —" said she.

"Monsieur is jealous, is he not, sister?"

She looked towards Monsieur, an infallible sign that they were talking about him.

"Yes," said she.

"Listen to me," said the King; "if your friends compromise you, it is not Monsieur's fault."

He spoke these words with so much kindness, that Madame, encouraged, she, who had had so many griefs for so long a time, was near bursting, so full was her heart.

"Come, come, dear little sister," said the King, "tell me your griefs; by the word of a brother, I pity them; by the word of a King, I will terminate them."

She raised her fine eyes, and in a melancholy tone, —

"It is not my friends who compromise me," said she; "they are either absent or concealed; they have been brought into disgrace with your Majesty; they, so devoted, so good, so loyal!"

"You say this on account of Guiche, whom I have exiled, at the desire of Monsieur?"

"And who, since that unjust exile, has endeavoured to get himself killed every day!"

"Unjust, do you say, sister?"

"So unjust, that if I had not had the respect mixed with friendship that I have always entertained for your Majesty —"

"Well?"

"Well! I would have asked my brother Charles, upon whom I can always —"

The King started. "What then?"

"I would have asked him to have represented to you that Monsieur and his favourite, M. le Chevalier de Lorraine, ought not with impunity to constitute themselves the executioners of my honour and my happiness."

"The Chevalier de Lorraine," said the King; "that dismal face?"

"Is my mortal enemy. Whilst this man lives in my household, where Monsieur retains him and delegates his powers to him, I shall be the most miserable woman in this kingdom."

"So," said the King slowly, "you call your brother of England a better friend than I am?"

"Actions speak for themselves, sire."

"And you would prefer going to ask assistance there."

"To my own country!" said she, with pride; "yes, sire."

"You are the grandchild of Henry IV as well as myself, my friend. Cousin and brother-in-law, does not that amount pretty well to the title of brother-germain?"

"Then," said Henrietta, "act!"

"Let us form an alliance."

"Begin."

"I have, you say, unjustly exiled Guiche."

"Oh! yes," said she, blushing.

"Guiche shall return."

"So far, well."

"And now you say that I am wrong in having in your household the Chevalier de Lorraine, who gives Monsieur ill-advice respecting you."

"Remember well what I tell you, sire; the Chevalier de Lorraine some day —— Observe, if ever I come to an ill end, I beforehand accuse the Chevalier de Lorraine; he has a soul capable of any crime."

"The Chevalier de Lorraine shall no longer annoy you — I promise you that."

"Then that will be a true preliminary of alliance, sire — I sign; but since you have done your part, tell me what shall be mine."

"Instead of embroiling me with your brother Charles, you must make him my more intimate friend than ever."

"To the effect that I must go to London, my dear brother."

"I fancy you already on your road, my dear little sister, and consoled for all your griefs."

"I will go, on two conditions. The first is, that I shall know what I am negotiating about."

"This is it. The Dutch, you know, insult me daily in their gazettes, and by their republican attitude. I don't like republics."

"That may easily be conceived, sire."

"I see with pain that these kings of the sea — they call themselves so — keep trade from France in the Indies, and that their vessels will soon occupy all the sports of Europe. Such a power is too near me, sister. Your second condition for going, if you please, sister?"

"The consent of Monsieur, my husband."

"You shall have it."

"Then consider me gone, my brother."

On hearing these words, Louis XIV turned round towards the corner of the room in which d'Artagnan, Colbert and Aramis stood, and made an affirmative sign to his minister. Colbert then broke the conversation at the point it happened to be at, and said to Aramis, —

"Monsieur l'Ambassadeur, shall we talk about business?"

D'Artagnan immediately withdrew, from politeness.

"Monsieur," said Colbert to Aramis, "this is the moment for us to come to an understanding. I have made your peace with the King, and I owed that clearly to a man of your merit; but as you have often expressed friendship for me, an opportunity presents itself for giving me a proof of it. You are, besides, more a Frenchman than a Spaniard. Shall we have, answer me frankly, the neutrality of Spain, if we undertake anything against the United Provinces?"

"Monsieur," replied Aramis, "the interest of Spain is very clear. To embroil Europe with the United Provinces, against which subsists the ancient malice of their conquered liberty, is our policy, but the King of France is allied with the United Provinces. You are not ignorant, besides, that it would be a maritime war, and that France is not in a state to make such a one with advantage."

Colbert, turning round at this moment, saw d'Artagnan. He called him, at the same time saying in a low voice to Aramis, "We may talk with M. d'Artagnan, I suppose?"

"Oh! certainly," replied the ambassador.

"We were saying, M. d'Alméda and I," said Colbert, "that war with the United Provinces would be a maritime war."

"That's evident enough," replied the musketeer.

"That is why I told Monsieur l'Ambassadeur," said Colbert, "that Spain promising its neutrality, England helping us——"

"If England assists you," said Aramis, "I engage for the neutrality of Spain."

"I take you at your word," hastened Colbert to reply with blunt good humour. "And talking of Spain, you have not the *Golden Fleece*, Monsieur d'Alméda. I heard the King say the other day that he should like to see you wear the Grand Cordon of St. Michael."

Aramis bowed. "Oh!" thought d'Artagnan, "and Porthos is no longer here! What ells of ribbon would there be for him in these decorations! Good Porthos!"

"Monsieur d'Artagnan," resumed Colbert, "between us two, you will have, I would wager, an inclination to lead your musketeeers into Holland. Can you swim?" And he laughed like a man in a very good humour.

"Like an eel," replied d'Artagnan.

"Ah! but there are some rough passages of canals and marshes yonder, and the best swimmers are sometimes drowned there."

"It is my profession to die for His Majesty," said the musketeer. "Only, as it is seldom that in war much water is met with without a little fire, I declare to you beforehand that I will do my best to choose fire. I am getting old; water freezes me—fire warms, Monsieur Colbert."

And d'Artagnan looked so handsome in juvenile vigour and pride as he pronounced these words, that Colbert, in his turn, could not help admiring him. D'Artagnan perceived the effect he had produced. He remembered that the best tradesman is he who fixes a high price upon his goods when they are valuable. He prepared then his price in advance.

"So, then," said Colbert, "we go into Holland?"

"Yes," replied d'Artagnan; "only——"

"Only?" said M. Colbert.

"Only," repeated d'Artagnan, "there is in everything the question of interest and the question of self-love. It is a very fine title, that of captain of the musketeers; but observe this: we have now the King's guards and the military household of the King. A captain of musketeers ought either to command all that, and then he would absorb a hundred thousand livres a year for expenses of representation and table——"

"Well! but do you suppose, by chance, that the King would haggle with you?" said Colbert.

"Eh! monsieur, you have not understood me," replied d'Artagnan, sure of having carried the question of interest; "I was telling you that I, an old captain, formerly chief of the King's guard, having precedence of the marshals of France—I saw myself one day in the trenches with two other equals, the captain of the guards and the colonel commanding the Swiss. Now, at no price will I suffer that. I have old habits; I will stand to them."

Colbert felt this blow, but he was prepared for it.

"I have been thinking of what you said just now," replied he.

"About what, monsieur?"

"We were speaking of canals and marshes in which people are drowned."

"Well?"

"Well! if they are drowned, it is for want of a boat, a plank, or a stick."

"Of a stick, however short it may be," said d'Artagnan.

"Exactly," said Colbert. "And, therefore, I never heard of an instance of a marshal of France being drowned."

D'Artagnan became pale with joy, and in a not very firm voice: "People would be very proud of me in my country," said he, "if I were a marshal of France; but a man must have commanded an expedition in chief to obtain the baton."

"Monsieur!" said Colbert, "here is in this pocket-book, which you will study, a plan of a campaign you will have to lead a body of troops to carry out in the next spring."

D'Artagnan took the book tremblingly, and his fingers meeting with those of Colbert, the minister pressed the hand of the musketeer loyally.

"Monsieur," said he, "we had both a revenge to take, one over the other. I have begun; it is now your turn."

"I will do you justice, monsieur," replied d'Artagnan, "and implore you to tell the King that the first opportunity that shall offer, he may depend upon a victory, or seeing me dead."

"Then I will have the fleur-de-lis for your marshal's baton prepared immediately," said Colbert.

On the morrow of this day, Aramis, who was setting out for Madrid, to negotiate the neutrality of Spain, came to embrace d'Artagnan at his hotel.

"Let us love each other for four," said d'Artagnan, "we are now but two."

"And you will, perhaps, never see me again, dear d'Artagnan," said Aramis;—"if you knew how I have loved you! I am old, I am extinguished, I am dead."

"My friend," said d'Artagnan, "you will live longer than I shall: diplomacy commands you to live; but for my part, honour condemns me to die."

"Bah! such men as we are, Monsieur le Marshal," said Aramis, "only die satiated with joy or glory."

"Ah!" replied d'Artagnan, with a melancholy smile, "I assure you, Monsieur le Duc, I feel very little appetite for either."

They once more embraced, and, two hours after, they were separated.

Contrary to what always happens, whether in politics or morals, each kept his promise, and did honour to his engagements.

The King recalled M. de Guiche, and banished M. le Chevalier de Lorraine; so that Monsieur became ill in consequence. Madame set out for London, where she applied herself so earnestly to her brother, Charles II, that the alliance between England and France was signed, and the English vessels, ballasted by a few millions of French gold, made a terrible campaign against the fleets of the United Provinces. Colbert had promised the King vessels, munitions, and victories. He kept his word, as is well known. At length, Aramis, upon whose promises there was least dependence to be placed, wrote Colbert the following letter, on the subject of the negotiations which he had undertaken at Madrid:

"MONSIEUR COLBERT, — I have the honour to expedite to you the R. P. d'Oliva, general *ad interim* of the Society of Jesus, my provisional successor. The reverend father will explain to you, Monsieur Colbert, that I preserve to myself the direction of all the affairs of the Order which concern France and Spain; but that I am not willing to retain the title of general, which would throw too much light upon the march of the negotiations with which His Catholic Majesty wishes to entrust me. I shall resume that title by the command of His Majesty, when the labours I have undertaken in concert with you, for the great glory of God and his Church, shall be brought to a good end. The R. P. d'Oliva will inform you likewise, monsieur, of the consent which His Catholic Majesty gives to the signature of a treaty which assures the neutrality of Spain, in the event of a war between France and the United Provinces. The consent will be valid, even if England, instead of being active, should satisfy herself with remaining neutral. As to Portugal, of which you and I have spoken, monsieur, I can assure you it will contribute with all its resources to assist the most Christian King in his war. I beg you, Monsieur Colbert, to preserve to me your friendship, as also to believe in my profound attachment, and to lay my respect at the feet of His Most Christian Majesty.

(Signed) LE DUC D'ALMÉDA."

Aramis had then performed more than he had promised; it remained to be known how the King, M. Colbert, and d'Artagnan would be faithful to each other. In the spring, as Colbert had predicted, the land army entered on its campaign. It preceded, in magnificent order, the court of Louis XIV, who, setting out on horseback, surrounded by carriages filled with ladies and courtiers, conducted the *élite* of his kingdom to this sanguinary fête. The officers of the army, it is true, had no other music but the artillery of the Dutch forts; but it was enough for a great number, who found in this war honours, advancement, fortune, or death.

M. d'Artagnan set out commanding a body of twelve thousand men, cavalry and infantry, with which he was ordered to take the different places which form the knots of that strategic network which is called La Frise. Never was an army conducted more gallantly to an expedition. The officers knew that their leader, prudent and skilful as he was brave, would not sacrifice a single man, nor yield an inch of ground without necessity. He had the old habits of war, to live upon the country, keep his soldiers singing and the enemy weeping. The captain of the King's musketeers placed his coquetry in showing that he knew his business. Never were opportunities better chosen, *coups de main* better supported, errors of the besieged taken better advantage of.

The army commanded by d'Artagnan took twelve small places within a month. He was engaged in besieging the thirteenth, which had held out five days. D'Artagnan caused the trenches to be opened without appearing to suppose that these people would ever allow themselves to be taken. The pioneers and labourers were, in the army of this man, a body full of emulation, ideas, and zeal, because he treated them like soldiers, knew how to render their work glorious, and never allowed them to be killed if he could prevent it. It should have been seen then, with what eagerness the marshy glebes of Holland were turned over. Those turf-heaps, those mounds of potter's clay melted at the word of the soldiers like butter in the vast frying-pans of the Friesland housewives.

M. d'Artagnan despatched a courier to the King to give him an account of the last successes, which redoubled the good humour of His Majesty and his inclination to amuse the ladies. These victories of M. d'Artagnan gave so much majesty to the Prince, that Madame de Montespan no longer called him anything but Louis the Invincible. So that Mademoiselle de la Vallière, who only called the King Louis the Victorious, lost much of His Majesty's favour. Besides, her eyes were frequently red, and for an Invincible nothing is more disagreeable than a mistress who weeps while everything is smiling around her. The star of Mademoiselle de la Vallière was being drowned in the horizon in clouds and tears. But the gaiety of Madame de Montespan redoubled with the successes of the King, and consoled him for every other unpleasant circumstance. It was to d'Artagnan the King owed this; and His Majesty was anxious to acknowledge these services; he wrote to M. Colbert:

"Monsieur Colbert, we have a promise to fulfil with M. d'Artagnan, who so well keeps his. This is to inform you that the time is come for performing it. All provisions for this purpose you shall be furnished with in due time, — LOUIS."

In consequence of this, Colbert, who detained the envoy of d'Artagnan, placed in the hands of that messenger a letter from himself for d'Artagnan, and a small coffer of ebony inlaid with gold, which was not very voluminous in appearance, but which, without doubt, was very heavy, as a guard of five men was given to the messenger, to assist him in carrying it. These people arrived before the place which d'Artagnan was besieging, towards daybreak and presented themselves at the lodgings of the general. They were told that M. d'Artagnan, annoyed by a sortie which the governor, an artful man, had made the evening before, and in which the works had been destroyed, seventy-seven men killed, and the reparation of the breaches commenced, had just gone, with half a score companies of grenadiers, to reconstruct the works.

M. Colbert's envoy had orders to go and seek M. d'Artagnan wherever he might be, or at whatever hour of the day or night. He directed his course, therefore, towards the trenches, followed by his escort, all on horseback. They perceived M. d'Artagnan in the open plain with his gold-laced hat, his long cane, and his large gilded cuffs. He was biting his white moustache, and wiping off, with his left hand, the dust which the passing balls threw up from the ground they ploughed near him. They also saw, amidst this terrible fire, which filled the air with its hissing whistle, officers handling the shovel, soldiers rolling barrows, and vast fascines, rising by being either carried or dragged by from ten to twenty men, cover the front of the trench, re-opened to the centre by this extraordinary effort of the general animating his soldiers. In three hours, all had been reinstated. D'Artagnan began to speak more mildly; and he became quite calm, when the captain of the pioneers approached him, hat in hand, to tell him that the trench was again lodgeable. This man had scarcely finished speaking when a ball took off one of his legs, and he fell into the arms of d'Artagnan. The latter lifted up his soldier, and quietly, with soothing words, carried him into the trench, amidst the enthusiastic applause of the two regiments. From that time, it was no longer ardour: it was delirium; two companies stole away up the advanced posts, which they destroyed instantly.

When their comrades, restrained with great difficulty by d'Artagnan, saw them lodged upon the bastions, they rushed forward likewise; and soon a furious assault was made upon the counterscarp, upon which depended the safety of the place. D'Artagnan perceived there was only one means left of stopping his army, and that was to lodge it in the place. He directed all his force to two breaches, which the besieged were busy in repairing. The shock was terrible; eighteen companies took part in it, and d'Artagnan went with the rest, within half cannon-shot of the place, to support the attack by *échelons*. The cries of the Dutch, who were being poniarded upon their guns by d'Artagnan's grenadiers, were distinctly audible. The struggle grew fiercer with the despair of the governor, who disputed his position foot by foot. D'Artagnan, to put an end to the affair, and silence the fire, which was unceasing, sent a fresh column, which penetrated like a wimble through the posts that remained solid; and he soon perceived upon the ramparts, through the fire, the terrified flight of the besieged, pursued by the besiegers.

It was at this moment, the general, breathing freely and full of joy, heard a voice behind him, saying, "Monsieur, if you please, from M. Colbert."

He broke the seal of a letter which contained these words:

"Monsieur d'Artagnan,—The King commands me to inform you that he has nominated you Marshal of France, as a reward of your good services, and the honour you do to his arms. The King is highly pleased, monsieur, with the captures you have made; he commands you, in particular, to finish the siege you have commenced, with good fortune to you and success for him."

D'Artagnan was standing with a heated countenance and a sparkling eye. He looked up to watch the progress of his troops upon the walls, still enveloped in red and black volumes of smoke. "I have finished," replied he to the messenger; "the city will have surrendered in a quarter of an hour." He then resumed his reading:

"The accompanying box, Monsieur d'Artagnan, is my own present. You will not be sorry to see that, whilst you warriors are drawing the sword to defend the King, I am animating the pacific arts to ornament the recompenses worthy of you. I commend myself to your friendship, Monsieur le Marshal, and beg you to believe in all mine.—Colbert."

D'Artagnan, intoxicated with joy, made a sign to the messenger, who approached, with his box in his hands. But at the moment the marshal was going to look at it, a loud explosion resounded from the ramparts, and called his attention towards the city. "It is strange," said d'Artagnan, "that I don't see the King's flag upon the walls, or hear the drums beat." He launched three hundred fresh men, under a high-spirited officer, and ordered another breach to be beaten. Then, being more tranquil, he turned towards the box which Colbert's envoy held out to him. It was his treasure, he had won it.

D'Artagnan was holding out his hand to open the box, when a ball from the city crushed the box in the arms of the officer, struck d'Artagnan full in the chest, and knocked him down upon a sloping heap of earth, whilst the fleur-de-lised baton, escaping from the broken sides of the box, came rolling under the powerless hand of the marshal. D'Artagnan endeavoured to raise himself up. It was thought he had been knocked down without being wounded. A terrible cry broke from the group of his terrified officers; the marshal was covered with blood: the paleness of death ascended slowly to his noble countenance. Leaning upon the arms which were held out on all sides to receive him, he was able once more to turn his eyes towards the place, and to distinguish the white flag at the crest of the principal bastion; his ears, already deaf to the sounds of life, caught feebly the rolling of the drum which announced the victory. Then, clasping in his nerveless hand the baton ornamented with its fleur-de-lis, he cast down upon it his eyes, which had no longer the power of looking upwards towards heaven, and fell back, murmuring those strange words, which appeared to the soldiers cabalistic words,—words which had formerly represented so many things upon earth, and which none but the dying man longer comprehended.

"Athos—Porthos, farewell till we meet again! Aramis, adieu for ever!"

Of the four valiant men whose history we have related, there now no longer remained but one single body; God had resumed the souls.